TROLL

BRADY PHOENIX

To Scott and Sara,

Thank you for being the friends I needed during the toughest of times. I cherish our laughs throughout our struggles.

Chapter 1

March 2015

Ten miles outside Felton's small town, the fog from the night sky spread through the countryside and into the Wisconsin air. Dewdrops gathered on the blooming plants surrounding the abandoned parked cars, further rusting the winter-worn automobiles like a graveyard of deteriorating metal. The remaining snow clusters melted off the vehicles' chipped hoods, enlarging the clay-like mud puddles around the flat tires.

Among the half-naked pine trees, the screams of young adults reverberated. They stumbled out of the narrow entrance, trying to maintain their footing on the wet ground and battling the effects of their drinks. A girl stumbled onto her knees as a minuscule chunk of bile exited her peach-glossed lips. Dozens of teenagers gathered around a small bonfire, dancing to Florida Georgia Line's "Cruise," playing from speakers attached to a vibrating smartphone.

With giggles, the three girls, all dolled up, drank their fruity concoction from red solo cups. Porcelain-white hues glowed when they smiled at each other. The individual in the middle grabbed her phone to take a picture. Another fixed her hair's long, red curls as she cradled some strands over her purple sweater. Flicking her straight strands of brunette behind her, the third woman licked her teeth to remove the red lipstick from them. The blonde extended her arm as her clenched fist gripped her phone, pursing their glossy lips to take a picture. Commemorating their recorded escapade, the trio embraced one another tightly, forging a treasured recollection at yet another senior gathering.

"That looks good!" the redhead chimed in, giddy, taking another swig of her drink.

"So good!" replied the blonde. "I'm going to change the filter before I post it to my eLookBook account."

"Make sure we look perfect!" the brunette giggled. "I don't like pictures that make me look like a booger!"

The blonde concurred, nodding. "I know. I've been talking to this guy from Philthrop High in Dawnton. We haven't met yet, but he likes what he sees so far!"

"Well then, don't mess this up, Veronica!" said the redhead.

Veronica's shoulder-length hair swooped behind her head to better her vision. She slid her fingers across the glass screen to change the light exposure, making their once darkened skin glow in the dim firelight.

"I can't believe you are seeing a Panther, Veronica," said the brunette, fiddling with the tips of her hair as she inspected the strands for split ends. "There are plenty of guys in this school. Ones that Maxine hasn't fooled around with."

Despite her friend's comical evaluation, Veronica paid no attention as her joke left the redhead speechless.

"At least I'm not shallow like you, Destiny!" Maxine said back, guzzling another sip of her drink, eyes rolling.

The music's rhythm shifted as the next song began, capturing the girls' focus. Veronica posted a picture of her closest friends, her fingers creating the final taps on the screen. Displaying her editing masterpiece, she proudly turned the phone to her pals. Maxine and Destiny marveled at how the skin blur minimized their blemishes, prompting them to snuggle together for a heartfelt hug. The fragrance from three floral body sprays produced an unpleasant odor that tickled their nostrils.

"Aw, I wish Ellie could've made it with us!" Destiny said, whining as the trio separated.

"I know!" Maxine said, agreeing with her lip curled. "I can't believe she ditched us again!"

"Forget her!" Veronica pouted. "She never cared about us."

"I still don't get why she just cut us off. We didn't even do anything," said Destiny.

"She's so lame," said Maxine.

While making their way to the rest of the crowd, the three girls rolled their eyes. Their teenage peers made out as the girls wrapped themselves snug in their flannel blankets. Their masculine counterparts' soft yet forceful arms cradled around their buzzed demeanor. Tongues danced around the insides of each other's teeth; their exchange of liquor-flavored saliva trickled bits of drool onto each other's laps. Five boys raced to chug their beers; the mud moistened further from the leftovers running off their peach-fuzz-covered chins. A different pair of couples participated in a game where they bounced a ping-pong ball onto a folding table, attempting to make it land in cups containing light, watery alcohol. One couple was winning as their side had eight to the other side's three, with the guy sinking in another shot.

"I am the king!"

Boasting, the bald football player proudly displayed his chiseled muscles, his purple and orange letterman's jacket open to reveal his tight-fitting t-shirt. Metal buttons slapped the top of his stomach as he huffed a victorious howl.

With a sense of defeat, the other couple tilted their cups to take a gulp from one of the remaining cups. Their eyes peered at each other, knowing they were too drunk to recover from their overwhelming loss. The intoxicated jocks celebrated with a bump of their chests against each other, trying to avoid any collision with their faces. Destiny and Maxine bit their lower lips, hypnotized by the testosterone that flooded their competitive nature and oozed out of their personas. Another gulp of their drink warmed them and allowed the hormones to take over their judgment.

"You are so good at this game, Bryce," Maxine said, her eyes scoping up and down to check out his athletic physique. "You sure know how to shoot!"

Bryce instantly recognized Maxine's nonchalant flirtation; his head tilted and his mouth salivated. Knowing that his competitive nature would swoon another young girl, he exhaled a remarkable sigh, causing his dimples to become deeper from the shadows of the fire.

"I think we can call this game done," Bryce said, chuckling as the losing couple gagged upon the gigantic gulp that caused one of their opponents to sprint into the woods. Vomit sprinkled out from her puffy cheeks like a squeezed water bottle. "Let's go, Tanner."

Tanner ran his hand through his shaggy blonde hair. The mixture of his perspiring scalp mixed with the moisture of the night air as his fingertips untangled the dampened locks of greasy strands. With his black and white sneakers squishing over the muddy terrain, he approached Bryce, who was engaged in talking to Maxine, with Destiny twirling a lock of her hair. Her heart fluttered at the slow and confident strut Tanner had. Tanner's eyes scoped every bit of her straight but slightly curvy silhouette that flickered in and out of the dancing bonfire flame. Destiny reached out her arm to assist his guidance towards a nearby open bench. Their palms warmed each other from their enticing interest.

Destiny's bones trembled as her sobriety slowly spread throughout her body. Her legs shivered as an icy breeze tickled her thin black leggings. Her teeth began to chatter like a wind-up joke prop. Tanner removed his letterman's jacket and handed it over to her to gain points in chivalry. A gleaming smile sparkled with each metal button becoming clasped up her torso. Click by click, the jacket fastened itself shut, warming her chest before she noticed the middle button was missing.

"What happened here? Cigarette burn?"

Tanner huffed, his fingertips grazing the felt surface around the hole.

"You know I don't smoke. This jacket is almost four years old since I lettered in football freshman year. It was going to start falling apart sometime since I wear it so damn much."

Destiny laughed as she resumed buttoning the rest of the jacket. Before joining Veronica, they navigated through the minuscule patch of mud, their fingers scrolling through their smartphones. Veronica's focus was so tight on her screen; the small light illuminated the pupils of her eyes, her lips pursed with disdain.

"What are you doing, Veronica?" Destiny asked, catching her breath, noticing Veronica's eyebrows more angular in the flame's light. "You do know that there's a party happening, right?"

Veronica's eyes remained focused on the phone, double tapping her thumb and typing on her keyboard like tap-dancing shoes on a hardwood floor.

"I'm just going through my feeds," she said with a faint chuckle, ignoring their presence. "I'm reading the comments on our photo. So many likes!"

"Really?"

"Yes, and any person who thinks otherwise, I'm taking care of!"

"What do you mean, 'taking care of'?" Tanner asked, his eyebrow suddenly cocked.

"They don't like my pictures; I won't like theirs," Veronica said, snarky.

The two paused, trying to figure out Veronica's rationale. Her smile grew closer to her ears. Firelight flickered to cast menacing shadows along her well-groomed eyebrows.

"I just go into their pictures and give a little honest opinion!"

"You know, they can see who is posting the comments," said Destiny, dumbstruck.

"I don't care."

"You should care," Tanner said, concerned. "At least you can create a fake profile to say what you want."

"Wait, what do you mean?" Destiny asked, confused.

Tanner pulled out his phone to open the eLookBook app on his screen. His proud glow drew attention to his profile and football pictures from the school yearbook. Underneath his eggplant purple and blaze orange jersey, his physique bulked up from his protective pads. The white bottoms knelt on the pruned patch of grass he posed upon. He used grease to part the strands of his shaggy hair away from his forehead, with ends curling away from his face. He scrolled down his profile to show his posts containing videos of cats falling into bathtubs of water and other photos that brought a smile to his face. More pictures of him and his football buddies were underneath that, with goofy faces made for fun. The candids were joyous with his friends having a good time at various events throughout the school year. From chanting for the volleyball team to win to parents' night on the field.

"See?" he asked.

Veronica's head rose as he gathered her attention.

Tanner then turned the screen back to his face, tapping the buttons to log out and quickly back in. Within a few moments, he pivoted the phone back to the girls, exhibiting an image of an unclothed, fit torso to showcase the countless hours spent working out in the gym. Washboard eight-pack abs and V-shaped obliques met with a low-rising pair of indigo jeans that stooped low against his bare, well-groomed lack of body hair. The two girls' eyes widened at the image, admiring the defined crevasses of each muscle.

"Hot!" Veronica said, slurring before taking another chug of her beverage.

"Very nice," Destiny agreed as she looked at Tanner's body next to hers, studying the muscles in front of her. "But I've seen you without your shirt on at football practice. That doesn't look like you."

"So, you pay attention?" Tanner said, impressed by Destiny's memory from studying his body. A sparkle in his eyes pierced into hers, biting his lip to control a rising urge.

"That's not the point," Destiny said, pointing back at Tanner's phone. "I'm just saying this profile doesn't have your pic."

Like a needle popping a child's balloon, his lust dwindled. She wasn't easy prey for him to pursue further.

"Who cares if it's not me?"

Tanner scrolled down his profile to show the name "Tim Durst" from Shenbrook, Ohio, before basking in the number of followers on his list, which was over a thousand. Subsequently, he carried on showcasing the posts on his wall, exposing an article about an assaulted woman in the headline, along with an image of a person weeping while being comforted by two police officers. Destiny looked at the comment above the article that read his statement.

"I'm sure she asked for it!"

Disgusted, Destiny looked back to Tanner with her jaw dropped. The phone slid down her palm as her extremities became loosened, frozen in shock.

"What the hell is this?"

"It's my profile," he answered, his smirk cocky. "I can do whatever I want."

She continued to scroll down to the next image he commented on, containing a teenage boy with his face made up of a perfect polish. His skin was so flawless with airbrush quality. By applying a dark brown shadow, the teenager achieved perfectly contoured cheekbones and meticulously penciled his brows as they arched over a gorgeous, well-blended red, smokey eye. Underneath the image, read another hateful comment.

"Wipe that shit off! Fag!"

Scrolling to the last image of a well-defined sculpture containing a fairy sitting pensively on a boulder. Hovering above her round and detailed breasts, the chiffon overlay of the was defined, draping over her clavicles. Her face looked up towards the sky in desperation, as though she was longing for freedom to find the love of her life.

"Kill yourself!"

The air was instantly sucked out of her lungs. While experiencing the crackle of the glass screen shifting, shock intensified within her body as her fist firmly held onto Tanner's phone.

"Why would you do something like this?" she asked him, huffing in disbelief.

"I don't want to ruin my reputation," he answered, trying to hold back a tiny giggle. "I've got a scholarship I can't lose."

"Then why don't you just keep the comments to yourself?"

"Where's the fun in that?" he said, now bursting into laughter.

"Fun?" she asked, her eyes narrowing as she slowly shook her head.

"Yes, fun. Why can't I say whatever I want? Everyone else does!"

Destiny took in a deep breath, frustrated. Her lips clenched tight while she puffed a deep exhale out of her nose.

"Because nobody else should do this! These are real people with feelings!"

She stood up from the bench, feeling her feet again sink in the mud. Startled by Destiny's reaction, Tanner exhaled in disbelief.

"Just chill out," he said, annoyed. "You don't even know these people. I don't see why it's such a big deal for you to defend them."

"Exactly," said Destiny, slowly unbuttoning his letterman's jacket. "You don't even know these people either! But here you are, going onto their page where they express themselves, and you just say whatever you want, no matter how hurtful it is. Then, you live your life knowing that you did nothing wrong because you hide behind a fake account, and no one points a single finger in your direction. What if the person you told to kill themselves actually did?"

Tanner sat there, frozen in shock. The remaining crowd of teenagers became silent from the interrupting intensity that expelled out of Destiny's lips. Veronica started to scoot away from her, trying to disassociate herself to avoid linking her reputation to Destiny. She took the last sips of her drink before reaching over to grab Tanner's full cup.

"You are nothing more than a fucking coward!" Destiny said, pelting his jacket towards the ground, slapping the back and sleeves into the thick mud.

Destiny's footing skidded over the terrain of the wet ground as though she were skating on ice. Her silhouette disappeared into the opening of the wooded surroundings to be greeted by the land of rusty automobiles. Tanner's anger intensified from his jacket being tarnished, flicking off chunks to try and prevent staining. As the crowd of people looked at him with confusion, his face became flushed with embarrassment. He reached for his jacket to brush off whatever mud he could get off his clothing. Huffing, he donned himself back with the outerwear, noticing Veronica with the brim of the cup perched inside the small opening of her mouth. Her body jiggled as her giggling became more enticing. Tanner's testosterone was looking for something more, regardless of how the night had gone. He shook off his jitters and scooted closer to Veronica as the crowd's attention resumed their original conversations.

"Some freaky friend you got there," he said facetiously.

"She's not my friend," she said, dismissive, taking another sip from his cup.

"I thought you had all been friends since middle school."

"You know how this game goes," she huffed coldly. "If they hold you back, then it's time to let them go."

Tanner grinned in agreement. Her confidence made his stomach churn in knots. Something about her dominance made his heart beat faster, his palms became sweatier. None of the others in the class were that forward in their gameplay in their politics.

"I don't see the problem with your profile," she said. "I just don't see why you can't just use your profile to say what you want instead of having to create another one."

"I have my reasons," he said, lips pursed.

"Ooooh. So mysterious," Veronica said, scooting closer to him. Their hips touched each other; the warmth of their bodies radiated from their piqued interest. "I find that to be quite sexy."

"Really?" he said, his tone rising with appeal. "What about the senior from Dawnton?"

"What about him?"

"I thought you were seeing him. I thought you found *him* sexy?"

"What he doesn't know won't hurt him," she mumbled, her face creeping closer to his. "Besides, what if I find somebody else more attractive that could make me forget about him?"

Tanner shed a smirk; his attraction toward Veronica magnetic. Her breath warmed his face, mixing the beer aroma of his breath with the fruity liquor-like flavor of hers. With a slow, steady motion, her hand crept onto the upper part of his thigh and began to rub up and down the outer part of his leg. His dry hand reached over to the backside of her head, caressing the blonde hair behind her ears while he guided her head closer to his. Their chapped lips rubbed over one another like moistened sandpaper as pecks upgraded by the slip of the tips of their tongues. Their bodies became one as they kept caressing closer to each other, jolting Veronica's stomach. She pulled her head back as her gut twitched, hurling a gust of air from behind her throat. Her heaving alerted her, halting her attraction before backing off and scooting toward the other end of the bench. Distracted, Tanner became startled by the sudden change in demeanor; his eyes opened to see the distance between the two. The cooling air clapped over the once-heated spots on his leg that were once attended to by her caressing hand.

"Is everything okay?" he asked, laughing at Veronica as the color of her face whitened.

"Yes, I—" she said, a gag of her throat caught her off guard. "I'll be right back. Too much to drink."

"Do you need help?" he offered, holding back a laugh as he placed his free hand inside his pocket.

"No, thank you. I don't like it when people watch me throw up."

"Okay. Will you see me when you're done?" Tanner asked, grinning. "I liked what we had going here."

She smiled before her hand hovered over her heaving lips.

"Destiny is my ride home, and we should leave soon," she said, walking away, closer to the cluster of bushes in the shaded pool from hovering trees. "How about you swing by after the party?"

He laughed again, his body heating once more.

"I'll have Bryce take me home and walk over to your place."

Filled with a sense of fulfillment as his evening plans unfolded successfully, Tanner observed Veronica's silhouette disappear into the shadows of the trees, consumed by the intense desire that coursed through his veins.

"Sounds like a plan."

The darkness concealed over her visibility, disappearing into the unknown. The sound of the radio died down. Vomit crept closer to the exit of her mouth before she was far away from the group, entering pure silence.

VERONICA CONTINUED to stumble from her over-intoxication; her feet received a reprieve from the transition of unsteady mud to a more stabilized patch of brown needle brush. Moving erratically in all directions, she struggled to locate the suitable spot to hide herself as vomit started spewing from the gaps in her teeth. With a lurch, she positioned herself behind a gigantic tree and proceeded to let out a heap of green and pink puke onto the brush that surrounded the base of the chipped bark. The dominating flavor of bile flooding her taste buds had devastated her formerly fruity breath. She fought the panting breaths to re-gather herself after emptying the contents of her stomach. Trees doubled in quantity, spinning like she was getting off a spinning roller coaster. The world leveled out, accompanied by the crackling of sticks, followed by a louder one as though someone had stepped on it.

"Is somebody there?" she slurred, squinting her eyes to keep her focus at the base of the tree that was becoming foggy.

Nothing.

Her stomach lurched again, handicapping her perceptions of her surroundings. Hunching over, she spewed another generous wad of saliva. Breathing as calmly as possible, she massaged her hand over her stomach to calm it down. The fog grew around her body, making her feet barely visible. Closer to Veronica crept the silhouette of a statue over the puddle of fluid. She looked up to follow the shadow disappearing from the small opening that glowed in the moonlight, glistening over a small body of water.

"All right, guys, cut it out!" said Veronica, wiping the small chunks of vomit off her lips with her sweater.

She strolled toward the beginning of the woods. A gust of wind slapped her face, with another tickling her legs, sending chills down her body. Her hair smacked her eyes, causing temporary blindness until she used her fake eyelashes to comb it back into place. Step by step, the opening became more prominent and more visible. Chilled, nighttime spring air tightened her lungs as she cradled her arms around her chest to retain warmth.

Greeting her was a soft moonlight winking a bit of reflection of the brown, swampy water that congregated around a tiny plot. On top of a swaying mound of dewy grass, a tree perched. Bare leaves danced by the force of the night breeze, with decayed bits landing at the tops of her damp shoelaces. She kicked them away from her, causing them to fly one last time before the weight of the water kept them sturdy next to small chunks of melted ice.

Another gust crept into the crook of the back of her bare neck, rattling her body. This wind was fresh, with more warmth and intensity than the others that snuck closer to her. She took in the last bit of the scenery with fresh air, sobering herself up before heading back. Veronica turned around, and the shadow met her again, raising its arm to grab her. Collapsing helplessly onto her knees, desperation gasped from her lungs. A gloved hand clutched her hair. The painful sting of her roots caused her to black out in a frantic panic.

"STOP!"

THE REMAINDER OF THE guests separated as the fire died down to a dull flicker of a lone flame. Pairs of teenagers stumbled out of the wooded area to head towards their parked cars, away from the cluster of abandoned vehicles and their dissected parts that crowded close to the open patch of land. The buzzed male counterparts securely escorted the girls towards the opposite end, where they used the remotes on their keychains to deactivate the alarm systems that protected their doors. Headlights flickered with a tiny honk in unison with the chuckling of the jubilant conversation that continued to conclude the evening's festivities. Bryce and Tanner, who ended the pack of students, strutted towards Bryce's black Mazda, skating over the softened surface of the moistened ground.

"Some party, huh?" Bryce asked as his joy lowered with every slippery step.

"Yeah," Tanner said faintly, his hand hovering by his sides to assist his balance. "It was good."

"Too bad I couldn't go home with Maxine," Bryce said with defeat, jumping on top of the rusty hood of one of the abandoned cars.

"Why didn't you?"

"Destiny was giving her and Veronica a ride home."

"Ah."

Bryce allowed the mud from the bottom of his shoes to guide him off the hood. The transition of the slide allowed him to keep his hands in his pockets to contribute to his attempt at a chilled demeanor.

"We made plans for tomorrow night," he reassured, walking next to Tanner once again. "She has to go to church with her dad, and then when he goes to do Sunday service, she will do some servicing of her own!"

The two chuckled, followed by a high five to praise Bryce's plan. "Nice!"

"What about you and Veronica?" Bryce asked as they watched the first group of cars trudge out of the parking zone. "I noticed you were starting to get some."

"I was until she threw up," Tanner answered with a giggling huff.

Chunks of mud dashed away from the tires as the cars accelerated to avoid getting stuck. One swerved to the left, and then the right, which caused members of the football team in the back seat to howl with enjoyment.

"You should've gone with her to seal the deal!"

"I wanted to!" said Tanner, frustrated, kicking an empty beer can. "But she wouldn't let me go with her!"

"Looks like you lost another piece!" Bryce said, his hands thrown hopelessly into the air.

"I'm going to meet up with her later tonight after she sobers up."

"Are you, now?" Bryce said, his tone raised higher with intrigue.

His eyebrow perched closer to the start of his buzzed hairline. There was warmth in their pale skin that was illuminated from the glowing moonlight. Even the slight chilly breeze couldn't compete with the warmth of his body.

"Well, she doesn't have to go to church tomorrow," said Tanner, putting some more swagger into his strut. "But I'm sure we will be awake until service begins, so maybe we can stop by and say hi to Destiny."

"All-nighter, Nice!"

"Hell yeah! That's how I roll!"

The two high-fived once again; the clap of their palms echoed into the darkness, followed by dogs barking like they were prepping for a football game. They cheered on the last of the cars as they left the parking area, leaving theirs as the last vehicle to leave the party. A tiny sore developed along their temples because of the invigorating effect of the gusty air, caused by the stench of exhaust fumes and gasoline.

"Some people need to take it easy on their cars!" Bryce said, gasping for fresh air as his hand ushered the cloud away from his face.

"Let's just go," Tanner said, coughing into his muddy sleeve. "I've got work to do!"

Bryce unlocked his car; the aroma of gasoline more robust as they neared their respective doors. Allowing gravity to slide themselves down the leather interior, they took their seats. Shutting their doors in unison, they reached over their shoulders to buckle their seatbelts, with Tanner patting all over the back of his shoulder, concerned that he couldn't find the bit of metal right away.

"Where is my seatbelt buckle?" he asked.

"I've been meaning to get it fixed," Bryce replied without a care. "A girl I used to date slashed that seatbelt, and the buckle has been missing."

"Well, we're only fifteen minutes from town. I think we'll manage if you don't drive like hell."

"You can trust me. I'm barely buzzed."

Once they had found their place in the vehicle, they observed Bryce searching his jeans pocket extensively for his keychain. Chimes jingled in their ears from the keys banging together.

The remaining bit of light extinguished, like a cloud covering the moon. Darkness became prominent as the last bit of life from the fire had been extinguished. A haze clouded their vision, making the windshield appear grimy. Tanner twisted his head, only to discover the drag of a black cloth that drifted behind the car.

"Do you see that?" Tanner asked, frantic.

"See what?" Bryce said, fumbling through his keys for the starter, ignoring Tanner's anxiety.

"That!" Tanner yelled, pointing behind them.

A hooded cloak stood thirty feet from the automobile. Fabric hovered in the ever-growing fog that continued to overtake the premises and creep around the vehicle's wheels. Bryce, startled, jammed his key into the ignition. The engine rattled to the pace of Tanner's panicking heartbeat. Tanner desperately continued to pat his muddy hand on Bryce's shoulder, agitating him further as he kept slapping it down.

"Hurry up!"

"I'm trying! Shut up!"

The engine rattled one last time while Tanner caught another glimpse of the shadow moving further away from the teenagers. Tanner's adrenaline settled down with each step as the figure moved away from them. He relaxed his head on the headrest as the car started with a revving engine followed by an abrupt *click*.

BOOM!

Flames erupted from the engine and traveled toward the inside of the car through the vents. The sleeves of their jackets lit up with the growing blaze that continued to overtake their metal surroundings. With each attempt to open the door and escape, their screams raised an octave, pelting the agony of their inner organs boiling. Smoke blackened more and more with each passing second. Each wheeze became heavier with each panicked pound at the window that weakened with each failed attempt. The fire continued to burn through their clothing and scorch away at their flesh. Hair cinched, diminishing closer to their scalps like a burning candle wick. Skin slowly melted away while they each let out one final breath to dedicate to their last cry for help. Their consciousness submitted to the blazing force, ending their life in the metal coffin. Flickers of the hooded figure's reflection drifted away from the sightline of Tanner's rear-view mirror, disappearing into the mix of blackening smoke conjoining with the nighttime fog.

Chapter 2

Two months later

The students at Felton High School struggled with the afternoon slump. Ms. Woods's history class was full of students who battled the monotonous exhaustion of another midweek lecture. Teenage girls formed a cluster, chewing bubble gum to combat the boredom, indulging in their fantasy-filled dreams of impressing their next boyfriend. Students concealed their heads with the tightly strung hoods of their black sweatshirts to partake in their afternoon snooze session. Drowsy eyelids struggled against drifting daydreams as a black and white video showed a protest march on a small TV at the front of the class. With the elegance of a figure skater, Ms. Woods glided her marker across the whiteboard to get ready to conclude the lesson. The desks, broken-down and wobbly, accumulated drool as students rested their chins on their arms, revealing chiseled notes.

Resting in the middle of the class was a young woman who was one of the few highly focused students. On the upper bridge of her freckled nose were her thick, black glasses. Her hazel eyes were at risk of being poked by the sharp edges of her choppy, brown bangs as she stared at the television screen that showcased passionate activism. With her fingers clenched, she diligently wrote many notes on her plain white notebook paper using a mechanical pencil. Despite the scribbles dominating the top heading, the paper was packed with protest facts. Her forehead perspired, and the periwinkle sweatshirt absorbed it like a sponge. The bothersome snoring of her athletic neighbors interrupted her focus as she attempted to write. The credits rolled and brought an end to the documentary, but the sudden return of the bright fluorescent lights blinded the children.

"All right, class," said Ms. Woods, her hands clapping together to gather attention. "Nap time is over!"

The tired adolescents shook off their sleepiness, moving their heads to dispel their dormant mood. A girl grasped her chest and tried to swallow the gum she was choking on; her friends chuckled at the struggle.

"I see that you are all focused on this lesson!" Ms. Woods continued, her eyebrows raised.

The room echoed with moans and groans, harmonizing with the sound of deep breaths from yawning.

"I know that graduation is only a few weeks away. Couldn't get out of high school fast enough when I was your age."

The class chuckled, unconvinced by her effort to understand. No teacher could empathize with their struggle with getting to graduation, even if they were closer in age than the others.

"Hey now," she huffed with light-hearted humor. "I've only been out of high school for a little over half a decade! I'm not as ancient as you all think."

The students stared at the clock in silence, waiting for the hands to reach three o'clock and the class to end. They grabbed their belongings, getting set for a sprint to escape. The motivation to dash out of the classroom and start enjoying their evening became strong.

"I need you to push through your complacency and finish your senior year strong!" she said as she shuffled a stack of papers and placed them inside one of her books, topping it off with a binder to sandwich them into place. "Your final papers are due in a little over a week. Based on some of your previous essays on World War II, you will need to kick it into high gear."

With heads bowed and notebooks closed, the class let out a collective sigh of defeat. Last-minute homework cast a burdensome cloud, dampening their eagerness to engage in their spring plans.

"And some of you still need to turn in your last essay. Right, Wesley?"

The back row caught the glare of Ms. Woods's eyes. A thin yet well-dressed young man sat with his arms crossed over his chest tight. His faded blonde hair accentuated his olive skin and rolling blue eyes.

"I told you, I lost it," Wesley hissed as he huddled deeper into his letterman's jacket.

"Let me guess, your dog ate it?" Ms. Woods asked with sarcasm. "I've heard all the excuses. Some of them were said by my classmates. I don't care what happened to it. I would like it turned in by the end of the week!"

"But I have track practice! I have to prepare for the big meet."

"If you put as much effort into your homework as you do with running, you'd be in great shape."

As the class whispered gossipy chuckles, Wesley's embarrassment grew but he stayed silent. Knuckles crunched from the peril of his clenched fist. His lower lip disappeared into his mouth from the grit of his teeth.

"Either turn in the paper by Thursday, or you're going to cheer for your teammates from the bleachers. That is final, got it?"

"Got it," he muttered, annoyed.

Just as Ms. Woods was asserting her authority, the bell chimed and interrupted her. From the speaker box, a female voice with a raspy tone came forth.

"And now, it's time for the afternoon announcements before another school day comes to a close," the voice said unenthusiastically.

A low murmur broke the enveloping silence in the classroom. The students at the opposite end of the room were eager to leave, unable to hear the other students' comments about Ms. Woods's attempt at relating to them.

"Don't forget to show your support for the Felton High Falcons during our pep rally this Thursday afternoon in the gymnasium. Bring your spirit and wear our colors with pride to show your support."

Among a group of classmates, Wesley's confidence shone bright. It was hard to catch sight of his growing smile as his chin rose high. Wesley's imposing stature commanded attention as the one they would be cheering for.

"And don't forget to join us for the graduation ceremony for our seniors who have left us too soon. Let us not forget that some are unfortunate in finishing their high school careers, and we shall remain united in paying tribute to them. Join us at the football field this evening for a vigil honoring Bryce Martin and Tanner Stohl, as we remember Veronica Huffman. Your support is as appreciated as it was during the families' time of need in preparation for the funerals and search parties."

With the completion of the remaining announcements, a girl in the back corner emitted a hiss of disgust. While the announcements were being made, the greasy, black-haired girl turned around and rolled her eyes, capturing the class's attention. The pleats of her red tartan skirt gracefully fluttered over her knees. The grooves of the fabric caught small hairs covering her black turtleneck sweater. She shrugged her shoulders with an utter lack of concern, embodying apathy.

As the announcements ended, the sound of feet tapping and papers shuffling grew louder, leading to a rush of children running toward the door.

"Don't forget to work on your final essays!" Ms. Woods said, hoping they would hear her.

Students swarmed the door in a rush. Bodies in the cluster pushed each other, clearing the room like water draining through a passage.

"Ms. Benson, may I have a word with you?" Ms. Woods asked as she walked fast toward the growing crowd of exiting pupils.

The students, in a controlled manner, left the classroom because of her presence. Pausing her steps, the girl in the periwinkle sweater waited for her peers to vanish. She became more isolated, causing her knees to buckle and prompting her to meander back to a seat at the center of the classroom. Navigating the uneven desks, her eyes locked onto the poster of presidents, positioned next to the American flag hanging by the speaker system. Settling into her lukewarm chair, she adjusted her scarlet skinny jeans, allowing the whiskering wrinkles on her thighs to breathe. Ms. Woods's slow pace compelled the girl to adjust her glasses for undivided attention.

"Yes, Ms. Woods?" the meek young woman said, her thumbs twiddling at the center of her desk.

Ms. Woods sifted through another pile of organized papers on her desk. The contrast between the white and her bright red fingernail polish was striking.

"Wendy, I wanted to talk to you about your essay on World War II."

Withdrawing her hand from the shuffling papers, she extracted a lone packet and spruced the remaining ones beside her faux daisy pot on the organized desk. The tiny ceramic figurines of woodland animals congregated around the pencil cup at the corner, with the fox and owl facing each other in conversation.

"Okay?" Wendy said, followed by a thick gulp.

With the fluttering of her eyes, her bangs bounced around her forehead, resembling butterfly wings. Beads of sweat made their way through the ribbed cuffs of her sweater from her palms. The white marble-tiled floor echoed with the annoying sound of her black and white sneakers, like a dripping faucet.

"Relax, Wendy," Ms. Woods said, sitting on the desk before her.

Pleats on her black skirt swooped over her black tights as she crossed her legs. She grabbed one of the canary figurines, stabilizing it in her other palm as though she were Snow White. Wendy attempted to exhale a relaxing sigh, blowing out only half a shaky breath of faint trust in the teacher's request.

"I read through your essay, and I thought it was very well written," the teacher praised, her smile beaming with pride. "Your citation is spot on with several well-thought facts that flowed effortlessly with clarity."

Like a dog being presented with a treat, Wendy's head perked up in anticipation. Out of her pink-chapped lips emerged her ivory teeth. A choked breath of relief escaped through her nose, quivering.

"You have a future with writing, research, or even teaching! Have you considered your future after graduation? "

"I'm taking the year off," Wendy answered, her shoulders more relaxed.

"Really? Why would somebody as smart and talented as you want to do that?"

Wendy paused with apprehension at Ms. Woods's flattery. Lost in reflection, she nibbled on her lip.

"Look, I was just like you when I was your age. I wasn't at the top of the popularity chain. I've experienced my share of jerks; people like Wesley and others. Those people will end up stuck in their own little fantasies in this small town because they can't step outside of themselves and work hard. I would hate to see you end up like them."

"Don't worry, I won't," Wendy reassured her, moving a bit of her hair behind her shoulder. "I just want to figure out what I want to do with my life before committing to many loans."

"I know that all too well! Just wanted to see where your head was at since I care about all your successes. I just cheer a little louder for the ones who apply themselves."

With a chuckle, Ms. Woods descended from the edge of the desk with ease. Wendy's smirk grew, solidifying her superior's effect.

"I-I think I should head out," said Wendy, slowly rising from her chair and pacing toward the exit.

"Okay, well, I meant what I said," Ms. Woods said warmly before placing Wendy's paper back with the others. "If you need any advice, you know you can talk to me about anything, okay?"

Wendy pressed forward into the crowded hallway, making her way toward the exit along with the rushing students. In a gesture of appreciation toward Ms. Woods's kindness, she nodded slightly and turned the cold, sticky doorknob to leave.

IN SEARCH OF PEACE amidst the ongoing high school drama, Wendy opted for a leisurely walk on the wooded bike trail. Once more, she was steering clear of the couples and their soap opera-like fights and avoiding the "he said, she said" drama. It's become routine to witness athletes taunting and sabotaging the progress of less fortunate students with an innocent bystander being thrusted against a locker. Despite the town's growth, teachers continue to give preferential treatment to specific students, especially those with influential last names, since there was one that witnessed the entire tussle but kept their head down to play oblivious. This was what irritated Wendy the most, but she had to remain under the radar and not create enemies.

The trees that were once bare now adorned themselves with vibrant leaves, hiding the careful labor of mother birds gathering debris for nesting. Colorful blossoms emerged from the ground, reaching toward the sky. The refreshing aroma of pine greeted Wendy's nostrils, prompting her to pause and enjoy the calm escape from her day at school. Every deep breath made her nerves go away. They would drift behind her like the butterflies that chased each other on the grassy ditch.

"Gotcha!" a boy screeched as his hand grabbed Wendy's shoulder behind her.

Trembling with sudden fear, Wendy gasped in astonishment. Textbooks and notebooks littered the asphalt trail, dispersing into the surrounding grassy areas. When she turned around, she noticed Zachariah, her classmate, chuckling with delight at his successful scare. With each joyful laugh, his robust physique heaved.

"What did you do that for, Zachariah?" Wendy said, annoyed as she hunched toward the pebbly terrain to pick up her scattered papers.

"I just wanted to say 'hi,' that's all," Zachariah said sarcastically.

He squatted toward Wendy's level to reach for her homework. With each extension of his arm, the leather sleeves on his letterman's jacket crinkled like thick paper.

"A simple 'hello' would do the trick!" she hissed, crawling to trek into the grass to beat an abrupt gust of wind that pushed one sheet.

"Chill out. I was just trying to be nice."

She couldn't contain her frustration and let out a deep sigh. Sandy pebbles flaked back onto the ground when she wiped her palms on her pants. Another breath brought her back, containing the rush of thoughts like a caged animal.

"What can I do for you?" Wendy asked as she perched herself back on her feet, the blood rushing back down to her tingling ankles to combat her unsteadiness.

"I just wanted to see how you were doing, that's all," Zachariah confessed, gathering the last few papers on the opposite side of the trail.

"You need help with your homework again, don't you?"

"I could always use a study buddy. You just happen to be better than the rest."

In an effort to be humble, Wendy smirked while accepting his warm flattery.

"Couldn't you enlist in one of the smart-alecs like Wesley?"

Zachariah shrugged his shoulders. Sunlight made his playful grin sparkle.

"He has to write his second paper. He'll be too busy."

Zachariah let out a cynical laugh at his own humor as he brought himself back onto his feet. Wendy stood frozen, apprehensive, as she observed his linebacker-like physique.

"Besides, I miss hanging out with you."

He returned her notes to her possession. His reach was full of sincerity. Wendy collected her papers from Zachariah, stumbling over her words as he spoke sweetly. Quicker heartbeats and fluttering sensations filled her stomach.

"A-aren't you going to be late for track practice?" she asked, trying her hardest to change the subject.

"They can wait," he said, ignoring the faint screech of the whistle as his eyes gazed into hers. "I wanted to see you, like we used to in middle school."

Wendy felt the earnestness pouring out of his mouth. There was ease in him with the casual smile that was beaming from him. The sunlight brightened the bits of freckles on his cheeks and made his bushy eyebrows shine. Battling to maintain control over her emotions, she pressed her teeth against the inside of her mouth as memories of junior high rushed back.

"I have to go," Wendy said, walking with haste from Zachariah.

She caught a tiny glint of his head, bowing down toward the pavement. The more Wendy moved away from him, the deeper his sigh became. There was a bit of satisfaction that made her feel complete with the conversation. Leaving him hanging like a dog chasing a treat on a string was entertaining for her, but there was always the part of her that admired the moments of kindness he would display when it was just the two of them.

"Zachariah."

With a slow movement, he turned around. His frown spread across his face like a heavy burden, getting tighter as he forced a smile that was only a slight curve from the straight line.

"It was great to see you."

The warmth in Zachariah's mouth counteracted his cold and hopeless feelings, bringing him equilibrium. On his way back to the school, he leisurely strolled, placing his hands in his jean pockets and admiring the sky. There were two clouds that hovered next to each other, but never touched. He related to the distance between the polymorphic figures, trying to find positivity in any encounter he tries with her.

Wendy felt a boost of energy in her step, making her feet feel lighter. The sun's rays awakened her face, replenishing her with a vital dose of Vitamin D. Her hair danced in the wind as she stepped into the peaceful pine clearing, allowing the symphony of birds to chirp away the day's stress.

Chapter 3

Wendy absorbed the final breath of fresh air from nature before leaving the forest trail and heading back to Felton's small community. The main street buzzed with cars full of teenagers, eager to pass the time. Silent remnants of decaying fall leaves swooped in the gutters, filling the cracked roads. Teenagers indulged in the delicious treats of maple long johns and sprinkled cake doughnuts from the nearby bakery, finding comfort as the brown frosting coated their delicate fingers. Middle schoolers scoured for empty soda cans to affix to the front of their bike tires, mimicking the experience of riding down a steep hill nearby as if they were on a motorcycle. The aluminum forcefully smashed onto the metal bike frames while the burning rubber tires glided past the sparsely populated small businesses.

Prior to going to the Felton Public Library, Wendy greeted the mail carriers at the post office and crossed the narrow street. One of her preferred havens to escape to was the old-fashioned stone building. This structure's historic nature lacked preservation compared to the town's contemporary appearance. The allure of antiquity compelled her to dedicate as much time as she could to showcase the town's continued interest in traditional research, instead of relying on the internet from the comfort of home. She was passionate about preserving Felton's history and would do anything to ensure its integrity since nobody else would.

The sound of her tapping toes echoed as she ascended the crumbling cement staircase to the premises' highest point. The final glass door was in a state of disrepair, with cracks resembling spiderwebs from acts of vandalism. By employing her fingertips, she tugged on the rusty handle and entered, promptly coming across the musty fragrance of numerous dusty pages tucked away inside captivating book covers. The charming smell of paper filled her with the hope that one of the remaining patrons would find the book enticing enough to borrow and read. The stacks of withered hardcover publications shed pages that dangled like an explorer holding on for dear life on a cliff. In the circular lobby, six elderly ladies chatted and crocheted with thick yarn, adding to their collection, while children scattered pop-up books on the maroon carpet. Chunks of thickened cardboard were chipped away from the literary contraptions that once contained surprising additions to stories, which sparked the imagination of young, innocent minds. She ran her hand over the piles of old magazines, gathering layers of untouched dust on their covers.

"Wendy, is that you?" said an old, raspy male voice.

Onto the hip of her jeans, Wendy brushed the heap of dust. While pacing toward the checkout desk, she experienced a tickling sensation in her sinuses as particles floated up her nasal cavity, along with the sound of a man coughing in his seat.

"Oh, hey, Jeff," Wendy said as her nose sniffled away the allergens.

"I was hoping to see you today," said Jeff, his hand continuing to click frenetically onto his ivory mouse as it glided over the green camouflage pad that was fading.

"I'm sorry. I've been working hard on my schoolwork. I'm all over the place to try to get things done."

"It's okay. I just look forward to seeing my regulars, no matter how few there are."

Concealed by his thick, black spectacles, his hunter-green eyes peered out from beneath his raised, bushy, grey eyebrows. Sunlight seeped through and glinted off the shiny, diamond earring that dangled from his sagging ear lobe. His clean, black turtleneck sweater caught the light, revealing the shadows and wrinkles that life had etched onto his face.

"I wanted to see if you would be interested in helping out at the benefit next weekend for the homeless that the library is sponsoring," Jeff asked, his charcoal mustache dancing above his lip. "I told you about it a few weeks ago and could use your help."

"I'm sorry, I can't make it," she said regretfully. "I've got our family vacation after graduation. My brother will be back from college tonight, and we'll all be together for the first time in months."

"It's okay. I thought I'd ask."

"Don't worry," she said, resting her hand on the desk closer to his. "I still support your work with how much you've done for us."

Jeff's crow's feet became more defined by his gracious smile.

"I have to get to work on this paper, though," she said, snapping her attention back to reality as the textbooks became heavy. "Sorry, again."

"I dusted off your regular spot. It should be nice and clean for you to work!"

"Thank you. Now, if only there was a way to get the dust off the rest of the building."

"That's so much work," he said as he sank back into his chair. "Nobody wants to volunteer their time. And I can't do it myself. All the wear and tear on my body from my younger years has caught up to me. That's why I enjoy sitting at this desk in silence and out of pain."

"We can arrange a fundraiser or something to change that."

"Perhaps," he whispered, a wink creating a twinkle. "You better get to your homework."

Wendy nodded in recognition, embracing her collection of books and papers protectively. She passed the cranky older woman, sidestepping a rolling ball of aqua-blue yarn that cascaded down her delicate, frail leg. The neglected computers, with their outdated hardware, emitted a loud scream as their hard drives overheated. Numerous wads of chewed gum in various colors hung from broken desks, resembling cave stalactites. Under the broken chairs, they protected an excessive amount of crumpled-up notebook papers and crinkled food wrappers, which were used to stabilize their uneven legs.

Toward the rear of the building, there was a single desk positioned next to the cleanest and most noticeable window, surrounded by rows of worn wooden bookshelves that weren't overcrowded. Not a single stack was nearby, unlike the other precarious ones that lingered throughout. Longing for a break from their busy routine, a couple rested on the grass and took pleasure in the clouds above. In an effort to escape their busy routine, they found solace lying on the grass and gazing at the clouds. The chair cushion molded to her every contour, perfectly supporting Wendy's back. In a collage-like arrangement, she spread out her stack of old history books after opening them.

The monotonous paragraphs with their black and white pages made her eyes droop from their hypnotic repetition of similar facts. Graduation drew near and her mental discipline waned as she empathized with her bored peers, who lacked the motivation to finish strong. Her head sliding down from its previous position resulted in the easing of the cramping in her wrists. The pages became cold against her face and were as gentle as a pillow against her ear as she dozed off.

THE STUDENTS AT FELTON Middle School were looking forward to their recess period. Batches of children emerged from the entrances, running carefully to avoid getting sick from their meal, as *they approached the enormous metal playground that stood ready for use on a peaceful, cloudy afternoon. The cracked blacktop of the basketball court reverberated with the sound of balls being dribbled by athletic sixth-grade boys who were eager to impress others. A few girls chatted and practiced their makeup skills on the nearby bench, attempting to draw their eyebrows naturally as shown in tutorials. Many came with their piles of playing cards, readying themselves for an intense battle and the subsequent exchanges of their decks of rare creatures. Three well-dressed people placed their backpacks on the grass, laying out their textbooks, completing their homework with care to secure top grades in the class.*

Beneath the tallest structure in the center of the playground, away from the active children, they discovered a hidden nook. A boy and girl, seated together, focused on their assignments. The digits of their calculators were bombarded by buttons hurled from their fingertips.

"I'm glad we have time to finish our homework," the boy said, relieved as he zipped up his pea-green hooded sweatshirt. "I could use your help with these math problems, Wendy!"

"I'm happy to help, Zachariah," Wendy said as she unzipped her red-plaid backpack, the zipper tracks shimmering in the light. "You should do these yourself, though. You won't learn anything if other people do the work for you."

"I do the work myself!" he said earnestly, opening his blue binder to scope his notes. "I just don't understand some of the harder stuff."

Wendy chuckled while she leaned over to inspect his work. Deciphering his handwriting proved to be a challenge due to the messy scribbles and eraser smudges.

"This isn't that difficult. It's advanced long division."

"Well, know that I'll owe you one if you ever need help."

"At this rate, that'll be when we are bags of bones!" she said sarcastically as she rubbed the eraser over his incorrect answers.

"I mean it. I really do appreciate your help."

"I told you I was happy to help," she said, before huffing out a generous breath to launch the coat of shavings from the sheet.

"And our friendship."

Zach's blue eyes glistened from the cracks of revealing daylight creeping from the structure's opening. The gleaming braces enhanced his gracious smile; the warmth emanating from his heart as it pulsated. Holding onto her focus, she blushed and tucked her shoulder-length hair behind her ears.

"I like you, too," she whispered, the shadows darkening her blushed cheeks.

Zachariah responded to her proximity by taking off his hoodie and using it as a makeshift blanket to cover her shoulders. Inside the pocket was a chain holding a little charm. Wendy glowed at the sight of the corgi charm that dangled from her fingers.

"When I moved here in fourth grade, nobody wanted to be my friend," he said, rubbing his hand gently on her bicep. "Until I met you, I felt alone."

A grin spread across her face. Her heart raced faster than her stomach churned. Recognition sent shivers down her spine, and gratitude filled her soul. The memories of their time together brought warmth to her.

"You didn't look at me differently, being chubby with bad teeth. You saw me as me."

"I know what it's like to be left out," Wendy said, removing her small circular glasses to clear the fog on her lenses from her heavy breath. "I knew you needed a friend just as bad as I did. I'm glad we're together."

Wendy's interest became even more evident as she leaned in closer. Zachariah noticed his cheeks becoming moist from her heavy breath. Sailing downwards, her hair grazed her lips as they gradually formed a pout. His nerves, filled with tremors, gave him a sense of lightness in his head. He wanted to delve deeper into his growing emotions and experiment with the long-awaited first kiss. The edges of their mouths made contact, but another classmate startled them. With a mischievous giggle, the boy dressed in black poked his head through the openings, finding amusement in the pair's innocence.

"Hey guys!" the boy hissed, jolting Wendy and Zachariah apart. "Look at these two losers!"

The sudden disappearance of his head startled the two in the crawlspace, causing them to quickly gather their belongings and leave. As they entered the playground, their classmates stopped their lunchtime activities and turned their attention to the awkward situation. The girls' braids fell apart when the distraction no longer added rubber bands to complete their style.

A gust of wind blew notebook papers, making Zachariah tremble. Unattended basketballs filled the court and pages tumbled around. Wendy's body froze as laughter and judgment reverberated in her brain.

"Well, if it isn't the two lovebirds," the said boy, pointing toward the two with an obnoxious chuckle.

"Shut up, Ian!" Zachariah hissed; the bones in his knuckles crackled from the intense clenching of his fist.

"What are you going to do about it? What are you and your girlfriend going to do? She's such a weirdo."

"Back off, Ian!" Wendy said, hunching into Zachariah's hoodie, her head slowly retreating like a turtle.

"Dahm, you can do better than her," Ian insulted. "You may not be the best looking in our class, but there is no need for two trolls to be together."

Filled with rage, Zachariah stormed toward Ian with the intensity of a furious bull facing a provoking matador. The air flowed past his face with aerodynamic precision as Ian hesitated and flinched, resulting in an increase in his charging speed. With a swift motion, his shoulder collided with Ian's lanky gut, resulting in a forceful release of air from his lungs. The sight of shocked expressions grabbed Zachariah's attention as someone bravely confronted the tormentor. Ian's head collided with the blacktop pavement, causing his jaw to slam shut. Fragments of chipped teeth marred his forehead. The continuous assault of Zachariah's fists on his face and stomach interrupted his agony, resembling a rapid-fire of bullets. The chorus of cheers from her classmates made her jaw drop and her palms sweat, like spectators at a hockey game. She pushed her classmates aside, swiftly evading the swarm as they closed in on the furious young man. Zachariah entertained them by yielding to his anger as she tried to mediate his emotions.

"Zachariah, stop!" she said, screaming as she shoved aside one of the kids.

"FIGHT! FIGHT! FIGHT!" the students chanted.

An open book slipped from their fingers, causing loose notebook papers to rain down on them. While moving closer to the person she trusted most, Wendy's pleadings were drowned out by chants.

"FIGHT! FIGHT! FIGHT!"

Wendy tore the seam of Zachariah's t-shirt, leaving his shoulder stained with dark red blood. Despite this, the bully's face remained unrecognizable due to the mixture of blood, saliva, and tears sputtering. In a swift motion, she launched herself onto the furious boy, clutching his shoulders and neck like a panicked cat climbing a shaky tree trunk.

"FIGHT! FIGHT! FIGHT!"

"Please, STOP!"

Wendy's unbalanced weight disrupted Zachariah's hunched stance, causing him to tumble backward onto the pavement and leaving her nerves unsettled. As his chest stopped its frantic wheezing, his pulse slowly returned to its regular rhythm. Blood flowed from his blistering fists, enveloping his arms like elegant silk gloves. The combination of Wendy's tears and his perspiration soaked his t-shirt.

Ian's two minions scurried to grab the sobbing victim of Zachariah's wrath, cradling him upon their shoulders to drag his half-conscious body to the nurse's office. Zachariah struggled to stand up straight, attempting to recall the events that led to his sudden outburst.

The bell signaled the end of their recess period. Students started to disperse from the crowd surrounding the sturdy boy, experiencing a sense of relief that the bully had been taken down. Despite the blood staining his long-sleeved shirt, one linked his arm around him.

"Nice tackle you got there!" said one of the boys, intrigued. "I don't think we've hung out before. I'm Wesley. Have you thought about joining the football team?"

Wendy was abandoned when they disappeared into the school door. Her hands shook as she gathered her glasses that they had carelessly been thrown away. Shards of broken glass mirrored the white in the sky. Her close companion has left her in the dust. He focused on the opportunity and never looked back. Strands of her hair brushed against her flushed cheeks as a powerful gust of wind carried away the tears escaping from her eyes filled with sorrow.

VIBRATIONS NUDGED WENDY'S chin. The faded memory corrupted her dream. Tears soaked the words on the dirty textbook, leaving moistened fibers on her cheek. As her vision returned, the fog lifted, and she saw her cell phone buzzing with a notification near the corner of her desk. Her sweater sleeve became soaked as she rubbed herself clean. With a swift motion of her thumb, she opened a message from Penny.

"I'm outside the library. Come out!"

Chapter 4

Wendy's sneakers swept away dried leaves as she transitioned from the green lawns to the sidewalks. Clinging to their floppy shoelaces, the stems dug into the stringy fibers. The rainbow hues peeking through Penny's tennis shoes enlivened the earthy monochromatic particles, as if a storm had concluded and left behind a vibrant and colorful aftermath. Lawnmowers and leaf blowers hummed like bees, competing with the chorus of chirping birds feeding their young. As the books slid down Wendy's hands, the drifting pollen clung to her sweaty fingers like slimy snail entrails.

"I've been waiting for you since after class," Penny complained, adjusting the tie-dye strap to her pastel purple backpack. "Where were you?"

"I just needed time to myself," Wendy said, hiking the books back into a firmer grasp.

"Well, let me know next time. I saw a couple of girl fights. Even Wesley was trying to pawn off another assignment to someone else!"

With the help of her free hand, Wendy chuckled and brushed her bangs to the side, uncovering her bushy eyebrows.

"He just got called out for another missing assignment," Wendy said, her eyes widening with sarcastic shock. "Ms. Woods threatened him with redoing the assignment or getting benched at the meet. She took no prisoners!"

Penny's blonde Jojo Siwa side ponytail spun like a helicopter as she giggled.

"When will that meathead ever learn?" Penny said, rolling her eyes at Wesley's desperate refusal to complete work.

They made their way to a different suburban block by crossing the street. Breaking their conversation, the neighborhood mailman greeted them. Two mothers in their thirties took a break from their outdoor exercise, parking their strollers and catching their breath while catching up. The retelling of *The Bachelor* episode from last night was passionate; the debate on who should've been eliminated became fierce. On the worn-out blacktop street, a duo of young boys dribbled their semi-inflated basketball. To reach their humble homes, the neighboring cars swerved to avoid the players.

"Did you want to hang out after the vigil tonight?" Penny asked. "You are going, aren't you?"

"I dunno," she answered reluctantly, stepping onto the curb of the next street. "I didn't care for any of them."

"But we should pay our respects. You didn't go to their funeral either."

"Yeah, but have they respected either one of us?"

"Not really," Penny agreed, her hands readjusting her backpack straps over her shoulders once again. "But wouldn't it feel better to take the high road instead of stooping to their level?"

Wendy hesitated. Clutching her books tightly to herself, she pressed the hardcover surface against her bosoms.

"Think about it," Penny said, stopping in front of a white picket fence and caressing the entrance door latch. "I'd hate for you to have regrets about something like this."

"I'll think about it," Wendy promised; her tone sunk silent, causing Penny to shed a slight grin of approval.

"Penny!" a mature voice cried out, more cheerful than Penny's.

"Consider it, okay?" Penny asked once again.

"All right! I'll go!" Wendy hissed; the sharpness in her tone dug like daggers from her annoyance.

"PENNY!"

"I'm coming, Mom!" Penny said.

Penny directed her attention to the woman standing on the wooden porch stairs. Every impatient tap of her foot made the hem of her flared, bell-bottom jeans swing. Taking off a red, white, and blue scrunchy freed the messy bun on her frosty blonde head.

"I'm sorry, Mrs. Hershey," Wendy said, smiling at Penny's mother with only her two front teeth. "By the way, I'm sorry I didn't get a moment to view your blog this week."

"Oh, no worries, Wendy!" Mrs. Hershey chuckled facetiously, limping her wrist to shush away her non-viewership. "It will be there next week. But don't get too far behind, or you'll never catch up on 'Hershey's House'!"

Wendy's smooth-talking failed to impress Penny, evident from her eye-rolling. As her lips drew near, they became tense and pinched together.

"You know how much I hate it when she does this shit," Penny whispered at Wendy like a snake while she swatted at a bee flying near her face.

Wendy emitted a suppressed giggle and had the look of someone who had just released a faint burp. The sound of screeching tires filled the air as they narrowly missed hitting a bouncing ball on the road. People blared their horns and screamed profanities at the children, overwhelming their ears.

"I need all of my fans to see me before 'Hershey's House' becomes popular!" the mother said, her weight shifting from one leg to the other in excitement.

"Can't you name it something else, Mom?" Penny whined, unimpressed. "Like 'Caroline's Corner' or 'Caroline's Crafts?'"

"No, sweetie," she said, declining with pride. "I've already established the name and my brand."

"But everybody at school makes fun of me because I'm associated with your stupid blog."

"Honey, they would associate you with my talents regardless," she said coldly. "And besides, if you weren't marching around looking like Lisa Frank's vomit with all that color, maybe people wouldn't pick on you."

"There is nothing wrong with my outfit! You bought this for me!"

Wendy carefully moved backwards, distancing herself from the conflict involving her best friend and stubborn mother. Her shoulders tightened, moving up toward her earlobes. She scuffled over an anthill in the sidewalk's crack, her shoes brushing against the dirt ground.

"I gotta go," Wendy said meekly. "Bye, Mrs. Hershey!"

"Bye!" the two responded in unison; their eyes remained focused on one another.

Penny approached her house as the picket fence door slammed shut. The sound of her friend's rainbow shoes hitting the sidewalk was like a giant stomping on innocent bystanders in a fairy tale village. Each step away from their home caused the sharp yells of the two to fade slowly.

Wendy reminisced about the day that left her with a sense of being depleted and it seemed never-ending. Throughout the next three blocks, she pondered her racing mind, battling conflicting thoughts about her future after high school. Avoiding the shark-like bullies who patrolled the hallways, searching for targets to alleviate their own suffering, was a draining challenge. Facing daily hateful comments that could linger in her thoughts and shape future insecurities was something she wished to avoid during her transition into adulthood. As graduation approached, she had a sense of achievement in her skill to go unnoticed by her peers.

The sudden chill of the air wrapped around her body. The sky's once-bright colors shifted to a mix of purple, orange, and blue, creating a nighttime atmosphere on the horizon. As the minutes passed, the stars got ready for their night shift as the sun finished its day.

With a click that resonated, she locked the door behind her as she entered her forest-green house. Feeling relieved, she dropped the stack of books near the coat rack, noticing the tension leaving her biceps and settling into her stiff shoulder blades. With a rhythmic clapping sound, her sneakers made contact with the polished hardwood floors as she made her way into the kitchen and swung open the door of her shiny chrome refrigerator to retrieve a can of soda. The chilly aluminum caused her sweaty palms to cool. By employing her chipped, black polished fingernail, she opened the beverage by tucking it under the tab. Bubbles of fizz from the cola tickled her teeth before trickling down her throat.

She found solace on the gray marble countertop, releasing sighs of relief. The candid photos of her family were adorned with fridge magnets collected from various tourist attractions. In the picture, her older sister could be seen with a big smile, hugging her younger sibling from behind when they were ten and eleven; the top of the marshmallow turned black as it oozed off the poking stick at their treasured campsite. At his graduation the year before, her brother's arm cradled his proud sister. His squinting eyes, which were barely protected by his bushy, long hair, were blinded by the intense brightness of the sun; Wendy's pasty-white cheek twitched when the tassel of his cap tickled her, right before the flash went off. Ever since her brother grew up and left home, fluttering butterflies filled her stomach, symbolizing her yearning for a connection with him. Amidst the chaos of school, his support for her was a soothing oasis.

She longed for his presence.

IT WAS A SUNDAY AFTERNOON. A couple hundred chairs were arranged in rows, adorning the football field. Blue jays gathered in flocks and landed gracefully on the stable goalposts. Baby-pink redbud petals trickled into the crowd of royal purple satin graduation gowns, while neighboring trees swayed in the light, cooling breezes. Glimmers of bright orange tassels adorned the square caps, providing shade from the sun. The hypnotic speech from the short, meek valedictorian left the bored seniors dozing away.

"As we move onto the next chapters of our lives," the young lady said, monotone like a feminine Ben Stein. "Either it is with college, work, families, or anything else you choose to do with your lives. Remember that we're all a family here. A family of unique, smart, and talented individuals who each bring their own skills to our life experiences. We may not have gotten along, and some of you may not appreciate each other. But we cannot deny that only we have the experiences that one can relate to."

Among the seniors, a third chuckled and silently passed judgment on the girl's eloquent and well-thought-out speech. Wendy concealed her frustrations by biting her lip as her proud parents and sister listened, rolling her eyes in disgust at their immaturity. The loud screech of the rusty hydraulics brought the crowd's attention as they squirmed on the heated metal benches.

"Congratulations, class of 2014. Now go out there and make our teachers, families, and peers proud!"

Amidst the concluding ceremony, the crowd applauded, no longer overshadowed by the valedictorian's speech.

"Thank you, Miss Beckett," said the older gentleman, patting his dampened toupee.

"Thank you for everything, Principal Stuart," replied the young lady, her metal braces reflecting the sunlight from her proud smile.

"*Now, class, go out there and do some good for the world,*" Principal Stuart declared with relief. "*And more importantly, do some good for yourselves.*"

The spectators got on their feet, cheering and clapping. One hundred caps were strewn across the grass as a tribute to the freedom and opportunity that had blossomed during their time in high school. As their children took their first steps toward independence, parents wiped away tears that were mixed with pride and relief that their parenting duties have lessened. Wendy navigated around clusters of mothers bombarding their children with an abundance of wet kisses and fathers grappling with the zoom feature on their cameras. After a long search, she found her brother in the company of a younger blonde-haired classmate, locked in a tight embrace. Her grasp was as tight as a boa constrictor, showing no intention of loosening.

"Hey, Veronica, do you mind if I have a moment with my brother?" she asked, irritated with her clinginess as she dabbed the sweat on her forehead.

"You will have your turn when I'm done with Malakai!" Veronica hissed, shielding herself around Wendy's brother as though he were about to be attacked.

"It's graduation, and we are his family."

"Wendy, we'll have our turn with him after his girlfriend," her father interjected, trying to keep peace as another person's shoulders nudged into him.

Wendy rushed past her family, treating them like a swinging door in an old-fashioned saloon. With no clouds to lessen its intensity, the sunlight blinded her while cicadas buzzed in her ear.

"You know she cheats on him all the time," she whispered to herself as she disappeared back into the crowd.

The sweat-soaked bangs on Wendy's face pricked against the top of her orbital socket, a hair's breadth away from poking her eye. Passing by Veronica's devoted henchwomen, she observed Destiny, Maxine, and

Ellie grooming their hair prior to snapping selfies with a bunch of testosterone-charged jocks who engaged in chest-bumping while taking photos. High-tech cameras captured candid moments, giving proud parents prints to showcase on their mantles.

Wendy settled into the foldable chair, noting the heat it gave off, as she surveyed Veronica's every artificial mannerism. She observed the overly enthusiastic hugging directed at her parents and sister, offering support by wrapping her arm around her mother. The brown eyes around him glowed with warmth as he reached his moment of achievement, then locked with hers. Observing Wendy's disappointing slouch, sinking shoulders, and the sadness in her eyes, her brother realized she was being overshadowed by someone who had recently become a part of the family.

The family split up to catch up with Veronica, as Malakai's proximity to his sister caused her to become less engaged in their socializing. His cheeks wore a distinct smirk, unlike any he had shown while with Veronica or the rest of their family. It was a testament to the special relationship that existed between a brother and sister. Wendy looked back on their childhood filled with imaginative castle play and remembered how they dealt with social challenges during their awkward teenage years, with puberty bringing acne, voice changes bringing self-consciousness, and hormonal fluctuations contributing to confusion.

"Hey, sis," Malakai said, embracing his deserted sister as he sat in the empty chair beside her.

"Hey," Wendy responded, raspy from her sadness.

"You didn't think I'd forget about you, did ya?"

"Of course not," she said, sniffly. "I just don't see what you all see in her."

"What do you mean?"

"She's so awful," she said, crossing her arms over her chest, ignoring the damp sweat pockets under her arms. "You don't even know what she does when you guys aren't around. Why are you all so hypnotized by her?"

"I see what she does. I'm going to break it off with her before I go to college at the end of summer.

"Why don't you break it off with her sooner?"

She lightened her voice as another group of underclassmen scurried past her. The next generation of popularity was something that made her nervous. As one's reign of social power faded, another one would take a different form.

"Well, why not have a little more fun before I go?" he said, winking at her.

"Gross!"

They found it amusing and chuckled. He mocked the English teacher snarling at them as she caught wind of their humor. Feelings of relief coursed through the educator's veins as she was finally able to release her restraint on the students that made her job more difficult.

"Well, it doesn't matter, I guess," she said sarcastically, noticing a twinkle of sunlight in his eyes. "If it's not you with her for the fun, it will be somebody else since she's flirted with a fourth of my class."

"Well, in her defense, she's given me more confidence in myself. I don't know if I could say or do what I wanted without her help."

"Being rude?"

"No. She helped me find some new friends on the eLookBook app. I've met up with a few of them, and without her, I would be starting my freshman year feeling alone and left out."

"Whatever," she said, sluffing off his unacceptable rationale. "If she created a fake and scripted version of what she wants you to be, then the friendship isn't real."

"Please don't fight with me on this," he pleaded. *"You can choose how you want to start your life, and I won't judge you for it, and I ask the same from you."*

Witnessing the change in his character, Wendy had a mixture of disappointment and surprise, as it was not in line with the person she had known since childhood. She experienced a strong urge to refrain from further disrupting his moment, considering the impression he left on her. He was right, though; it was not suitable to undermine the hard work and achievements he had shown over the last four years during graduation.

"You're right," she said, biting the inner part of her lip to conceal the frustration before shedding her pearly-white teeth. The taste of salt lingered on her tongue because of the sweat on her chin.

"Now, let's join everybody else before we look too out of place."

"Sure."

"Just know that you are always my little sister, and I love you more than anything."

"I love you too," she said, her dimples now creased on the apples of her sun-kissed cheeks.

"I will always have your back and be there for you, too."

"Me too."

"And nothing will happen if I have that die you gave me from casino night at the community center."

Wendy grinned, remembering the day she found this red, opaque die that was found in the corner. It was buried under a bunch of popcorn and trash. For some reason, she found the need to enjoy the beauty in it and hung onto it for good luck. Ever since then, her and Malakai continued to win throughout the night. They continued to think of it as a good luck charm and agreed to share it, turning it into a keychain with him needing it during his transition into adulthood.

As the two siblings approached their family, they observed Veronica gathering with her posse of girls. Before posting their final product on their eLookBook profile, they traded phones to compare pictures and make any necessary touch-ups. Destiny's lengthy hair cascaded down her back, trembling with every giggle from their lungs.

"Wendy, are you ready for pictures?"

The siblings formed a tight group, hunching close. Their older sister interposed herself, fastening her black Chanel blazer and tidying her white button-down ruffled blouse to conceal any signs of moisture. While she concentrated on capturing the flawless picture, she couldn't shake off the fear of being ridiculed by her colleagues at work.

"Jennifer, can I have one picture with Malakai and me?" Wendy asked innocently.

"Sure."

Jennifer smiled at the visible, unbreakable bond that couldn't go unnoticed if they even tried. Blocking the sun's reflection, she gave their parents a moment of respite from the blazing heat. They hugged each other, tilting their heads and flashing a proud and joyful smile, preparing to pose for a close-up photo for their father.

"Okay, say cheese!"

WENDY SENSED THE INDISTINGUISHABLE feeling of warmth that had illuminated his graduation day. The memory was always the source of motivation to make it through another day, surviving the last days of high school. Her nerves, which had controlled her and made her withdraw, settled. Despite her sense of alienation, she had to stay within the protected zone, far from bullies, teachers, and boys.

The can of cola touched her lips as she tilted it for another drink. A man leaped from around the corner, shattering her calm. In a sudden motion, her fist clenched, and the crushed aluminum pierced her palm. Cold brown liquid erupted, drenching her face and chest. The fizz made her eyes tickle and blinded her while she attempted to remove the leftovers from her after-school snack. All that was visible to her was the hazy figure of a tall, skinny man; their shaggy, long brown hair fell onto their shoulders.

"Surprise, sis!"

Chapter 5

Wendy wiped the cola off her freckled skin, removing the sticky syrup. The blurry vision she experienced was exacerbated by the fluorescent lighting in the dining room and kitchen. Shaping the brown hair took longer, as the ends curled away from the forehead. With his thin face, the guest had a nose that jutted out, creating a three-dimensional effect.

"Malakai?" she asked, wringing out the hem of her shirt, fluid droplets raining onto the tiled floor.

"In the flesh!" he responded with glee, extending his arachnid-like arms for a hug. The bottom of his shirt rose closer to his chest as curls of similarly colored belly hair crept out.

"What the hell!" she giggled, happiness overtaking her startled state.

"Did you miss me?"

"Of course, I missed you. It's just that this isn't a horror movie. There's no need for the jump scares."

"Well, what fun would that be?" he said, rolling his eyes like a cartoon.

They pulled close, intertwining in a loving hug that lasted for a significant amount of time. His soft hood offered comfort as her clenched fists absorbed his warm body heat. Her brother's love enveloped her like a security blanket, freeing her from the fears and anxieties that had fueled her daily life. She was now more open and vulnerable; with her protective and rational brother by her side, there was no need for her to worry—her fears would vanish like storm clouds before a brave and comforting sun.

"No, really, what are you doing back? Summer semester is about to start."

Wendy's eyebrow perched closer to her hairline, concealing itself into her bushy bangs.

"I'm back for the vigil," he said as he placed his hands into the pouch of his sweatshirt. His shoulders sank closer to the floor. "I wanted to pay my respects since I couldn't make it to the funeral."

Veronica. How can I forget? Wendy thought to herself with disdain.

"I know you didn't like her, but we must pay our respects to those in trouble."

Do we, though?

"I know," she said in agreement, her voice scratchy. "I just don't know if she would do the same for me if the shoe was on the other foot."

We all know she wouldn't.

"Well, that is between her and her conscience," he insisted, knowing that Wendy was right. "If that's what she chooses, she has to live with it."

"Among countless heartless choices."

"Yeah."

"Sometimes taking the high road is a better route than the easy route," he preached, rubbing his hand over her forearm before pinching her bicep. "Stooping to Veronica's level will not make you any better of a person than she's been."

"Why do you have to always be right?" she said sarcastically, chuckling at her brother's encouragement.

"Because I'm your older brother. I'm always right!"

Wendy's nose had his pointer finger resting on its tip. The urge to scratch caused her to press her face into the ribbed neckline of her shirt.

"Shut up!"

Laughter filled the air as the two siblings embraced love and understanding. Their level of sincerity was beyond measure. This was what Wendy missed last year. Loneliness during the nights craved this positivity. Even if they agreed to disagree, there was always a sense of understanding that they were each entitled to their own opinion, and it was a safe space to express it to each other.

"Did you want to go together? Mom and Dad must still be on their business trip until next week."

"Sure," she said, nodding, guiding her hair behind her ears. "I need to shower first."

"Yeah, you better! You stink!"

"Screw you!" She laughed. "I gotta get this soda off of me. I'm all sticky now!"

"Please spare me with your personal problems," he said, shoving her away from him.

Wendy's mouth moved like a nutcracker, with skin creases forming on her chin as she teased her brother and playfully punched Malakai's arm before leaving the kitchen. In a leisurely manner, she traversed the living room before climbing the stairs to her bedroom, marveling at every family photograph that captured moments throughout the years. Her heart fluttered as she looked at the memories preserved in black-trimmed frames, portraying the happiness and innocence of Malakai and herself. There were Christmas candids in front of the shedding, overly decorated pine tree with needles scattered along the floor. Then, there was a ridiculous Halloween shot with her dressing in a handed-down princess gown passed down from their older sister while he paraded in his disheveled pirate costume, looking into the lens of the camera to show off the pride in their faces as their orange, jack-o'-lantern buckets overflowed with assortments of sweets.

Making her way across the hallway's distorted floorboards, a sliver punctured Wendy's black sock as she headed toward the bathroom as she reached for her cell phone. Noticing the absence of notifications on her eLookBook app, she smiled and tapped her thumbs on the illuminated screen. She opened her messages and texted Penny, adding a smiley face emoji.

"I'll see you at the vigil."

IN A REPETITIVE MOTION, Wendy vigorously moved her head toward the floor, as if she were jamming out to a heavy metal band from the 1980s. Her split ends, damp with moisture, delicately swept across the oak floor, resembling the strokes of a horsehair brush. She dressed in a crimson sweatshirt over a crispy baby blue button-down shirt, carefully arranging the tangled strands before tucking it in. Thankful for her brother's encouragement, she observed her reflection in the mirror, determined to finish her senior year as strongly as she had started it. Yet, she detested spending her valuable time grieving for individuals who wouldn't give her the time of day for a bit of sympathetic attention.

While descending the staircase, she observed Malakai hadn't switched out his indigo-blue jeans and was now wearing an untucked periwinkle-blue pinstriped button-down shirt along with his beloved light-wash denim jacket. It was surprising for him to see his sister looking more put together than the disheveled image he had in his mind. With a smirk, he gazed at her natural beauty, the corners of his lips moving toward his ear.

"You look good," Malakai said, placing a hand inside his jeans pocket.

"You're supposed to say that. I'm your sister," she said, chuckling bashfully.

"No. I *get* to say that because you're my sister."

In a playful manner, she rolled her eyes to dismiss his sarcasm. Compliments were rare for her, leaving her unsure how to manage her feelings upon receiving them.

"Are you ready to go?"

Nodding, she skipped the remaining steps and jumped straight to the main level. The act of tying her shoes resulted in the formation of bunny ears on the top. As she reached for the door, she flicked away a small piece of lint from her thigh.

Before getting into Malakai's 2006 black Altima, they locked the front door of their house. The car's exterior bore the scars of speckled scratches and rusted wheel wells, evidence of surviving many winters. With a cry of screeches and creaks, the door pleaded for a generous spray of WD-40 on its tortured hinges as she opened it. Stains from spilled soda and food embellished the fabric of the passenger seat.

"Don't you think it's time to upgrade?" she asked facetiously as she strung the seatbelt over her shoulder.

"She still has some life left!"

"So, Mom and Dad stopped making payments?"

"Yeah. They pulled the plug after that F in psychology last semester. I have to retake it this summer."

"Don't you see that life is more important than just going to frat parties and football games all the time?"

"It's about the total experience," he said, his hands making a little circle to justify himself before he turned the key in the ignition. "College is more than just getting grades. It's about preparing you for the real world."

Backing out of the driveway, the car came close to hitting their neighbor's overflowing green garbage dumpster.

"Getting good grades prepares you for the real world. You need a career, don't you?"

Malakai expressed his displeasure with his sister's reasoning as the car crept through the empty downtown area.

"I know you haven't had the best of luck in the friend department but give yourself the chance to open up to people. There are more people on your side than you think," he said, peering over to her in between each car he passed.

"Like Veronica and her posse?"

"Not them," he said quickly, chuckling.

She didn't laugh with him.

"I know you told me to take the high road, which I'm doing. My life has become a living hell because of those girls, and you have no idea."

Malakai stayed quiet, concentrating on avoiding the other cars as they recklessly swerved across the yellow dashed line. The presence of poorly parked vehicles made navigation more difficult as they encroached on the driving space.

"Do you hear me?" she asked, her tone more pointed to make him realize her perspective.

"I do," he said, Adam's apple bouncing to the lower part of his neck as he let out a generous gulp.

"Do you, though? Growing up has been easier for you. You've always had some group of friends to hang around with."

Her heartbroken face flickered in and out of the darkness, illuminated by streetlights. Tears formed at the bottom of her eye, reflecting small bits of red.

"Yeah," he agreed. "But I was still a shy kid."

"But you had others to feel shy in front of. I'm not the Barbie doll type, and we don't come from money or a last name, so it's harder for someone like me to have a group to cling to."

"It's not about the quantity. It's about quality," he said, making a sharp turn into the next street.

"Why the need for a social life in college?"

"It's difficult to explain. You'll understand when you go next year."

"I'm not going next year."

"What?" he asked, startled as the car halted at the end of a block. "I thought college was everything for you?"

"It is," she said softly, shamefully. "I just don't want to rush into something I don't know if I want."

"I thought academia was your life?"

"It is. I just don't want to waste my time and money on something I might regret."

"Well, don't regret not seizing the moment and enjoying your freedom," he said, winking at her with pride.

"I'll try, and I'll try to be more open to friendship."

"Atta girl!" he cheered with enthusiasm. "If it doesn't work out, Penny and Andrea will be there for you."

Wendy hesitated, sensing a sudden awkwardness disrupt the flow of the conversation.

"Andrea and I aren't friends anymore," she said, her head bowing closer to the dashboard.

"What? Last year you two were so close. What happened?"

"It's complicated."

In the high school parking lot, the car drove among many parked automobiles. Between two faded yellow lines, the engine fell into a slumber, causing the headlights to vanish into darkness. Malakai absorbed his sister's confession and the sadness it evoked, causing an uncomfortable silence to fill the interior of the vehicle.

"Complicated?" he asked, confused by his sister's update. "What do you mean, complicated?"

"We'll talk about it later," she said, her glazed expression dismissing him. "We're here. It's high-road time."

Chapter 6

Following the two siblings' exit from their vehicle, the citizens fell in line behind them, giving them the role like a parade's grand marshal. The closer they got to the football field, the more their classmates' heads drooped. As people held candles, sadness intensified and the nighttime air filled with flickering fireflies. Each grieving guest began to sniffle and snort as tears flowed from their sorrowful eyes.

Positioned on an elevated bandstand, a single podium stood while three framed portraits of high school students who couldn't graduate adorned the area. Tea candles illuminated the belongings of the departed—stuffed animals and football equipment. The heartfelt gifts and mementos served as a bittersweet reminder of their loved one's absence.

The overwhelming amount of sadness surrounding her overcame Wendy. Opting for the high road appeared incredibly challenging. The risk of standing out in rebellion amongst a depressed crowd, like a castaway on a deserted island searching for rescue, was not worth taking. The peoples' grieving was just as intense as it was two months ago, and it made her uneasy. They made their way to the highest part of a bleacher; the grating sound of the rusted screech assaulted her ears, akin to nails on a chalkboard. The remaining crowd arrived to become part of the melancholic assembly. Principal Stuart walked up to the podium and tapped the microphone to test it before clearing his throat to start his dedication.

"Good evening, students, families, and citizens."

A hush fell over the crowd as the faint rumblings of conversation ceased. A couple of sniffles interrupted the stillness. The soft harmony of an Enya song from the speakers was quiet, attempting to bring peace amongst the heartbreak.

"I'm going to keep this short so we can pay our respects," he continued, adjusting his shaggy gray toupee. "We're all here to mourn the loss of two of our best and brightest students."

Brightest? Yeah, right! Wendy thought, holding in a tiny chuckle.

"Some of you knew Bryce Martin and Tanner Stohl as a good friend. Others may know of them as fierce competitors on our football team. I'm sure all of you have had exchanges with their friendly conversations as you passed in the hall on your way to your classes."

The premises echoed with cries as the principal paused to clear his throat.

"We also have the unfortunate disappearance of Veronica Huffman. A strong and dedicated member of the student body who has made many grand contributions to the betterment of our school. An outstanding leader who has helped reallocate our school funds for upgrades to our new basketball court, our track surrounding us tonight, and updated athletic uniforms that show who we are in the eyes of our competitors. Furthermore, she earned a reputation for being loved by her peers and for her selfless dedication to her classmates, always prioritizing them."

"You've got to be shitting me!" roared a lone female voice that resonated sharply over the declaration.

Finally, someone agrees with me!

"Wh-who said that?!" Principal Stuart asked, angered by the abrupt vulgarity.

The same age as Wendy, a teenage girl stood without hesitation. She had jet black hair that was tightly pulled back, giving the appearance of a horse's mane trailing behind her charcoal sweater and maxi skirt.

The onlookers were appalled, as someone had the audacity to oppose the exaggeration of their three classmates' identities. Gusts of angered huffing grew that she contradicted the speech that made her classmates appear more innocent than even a respectful obituary could highlight for someone else.

"Who is it?" Malakai asked, squinting his eyes to focus on the source of the voice through the crowd of stunned individuals.

"Andrea," she whispered to herself.

"Ms. Crispin, please keep your comments to yourself. We are here to pay our respects," Principal Stuart commanded; his hand grasped the base of the microphone to hold back his urge to bark back.

"Like how you all did for my sister when she died?" Andrea hissed, her voice cracked with sadness.

"I-I don't think that has anything to do with what's important here."

"Because she wasn't important to y'all? It's funny that she passed away, and nobody at this school gave a shit. No one threw a memorial for her, and nobody cared that she was gone!"

"Ms. Crispin, I—"

"And spare us the speech about how kind those three jackasses were to everyone else! They were rude as fuck to most of us. Or is it because they have last names, and their contribution to the school benefited what mattered, by cutting funding to the arts and library for a few cosmetic enhancements?"

"THAT'S ENOUGH!" he screamed, causing a god-like thump of an echo with his authoritative voice carrying fiercely throughout the field.

"Screw this!" Andrea yelled as a nearby teacher escorted her away from the crowd. "I guess being popular gets you a funeral people care about!"

"Get her out of here, please!" Principal Stuart pleaded to the staff, shaky that the crowd rattled amongst each other like a cyclone of mixed emotions.

Into the dim-lit parking lot, Andrea's silhouette faded away. As her ponytail whooshed back and forth, her rant subsided into silence. Wendy's jaw remained wide open in shock and entertainment, inviting mosquitoes to join her. Regardless of its inappropriateness, she was grateful that someone had the audacity to speak up. Andrea had valid reasons for saying what she did; they were far from being the nicest in the class. Every day, they made at least one of their peers' lives unbearable. While they could have been someone's relative, it was important to bring their hidden darkness to light and expose the school's embellished story, fostered by oblivious staff members.

Principal Stuart's voice trembled through the speakers as he desperately tried to hold the crowd's attention, who were waiting for him to defend the honor of the children. Mutters from the kids discussed the validity of their statement, only to be fought back with defenses to justify the actions of the departed.

"I-I apologize for that outburst," he resumed, coughing into the sleeve of his blazer. "As upsetting as Ms. Crispin's statements may have made some of us, we must remember that grieving can take many forms."

Apathetic hisses echoed from the bleachers, evoking the image of venomous snakes. The groups eagerly waited to leave so they could confront the student.

"Come on, now. Ms. Crispin has lost somebody close to her, too, and we can't invalidate her frustrations. This is part of her healing, no matter how harsh her tact may have been toward others. But let's remember that this night is about paying our respects to Bryce, Tanner, and Veronica. Let's focus our energy on their peace and solace and hope Veronica will return home safely."

The crowd broke up, with the majority making their way to the bandstand to give gifts of memories and respect to the three. A small percentage of the group left with outrage, spewing mutters of angry responses to Andrea's rant. Football players, eager for revenge, let slip threats of harm from their breaths. Witnessing loved ones confronted with others' perceptions was a painful moment for some.

"Well, that was quite a show, wasn't it?" Wendy asked her brother, stunned.

"You can say that again!" Malakai agreed, confused with mixed anger and sadness.

"Did you want to go to the bandstand?"

"I don't know," he answered, skeptical as he brushed his hair back.

"Are you okay?" she asked, concerned with his hands fidgeting with one another.

"I will be. Maybe you should go with Penny. I need to catch up with some people."

Chapter 7

Like fish beneath the icy surface of a lake, the audience dispersed around the bandstand; their glazed expressions waiting for a spark of sunlight to warm their frozen disposition. Acquaintances embraced in hugs, merging their comfort and emotions into a hopeful, uplifting harmony. They tried to hide the devastating loss of the people who had influenced their lives, regardless of how they perceived it or how Andrea's declaration hurt their preconceived notions.

Veronica's mother cried out in hope and desperation as Wendy made her way through, yearning for her daughter's safe return. The middle-school-aged brothers consoled each other with guilt, realizing the trouble they had caused their older sister over the years; if only they had more time together to bond and not annoy each other. Their heads bowed, tears flowed as they listened to their mother's wailing, wishing they could take back all of their sister's frustrating headaches in exchange for her safety. Wendy made a brief gesture with her wrist to wave at the kind librarian. His sagging lobe held onto his earring, while a lone diamond shimmered in her eye.

"Hi, Jeff."

She resumed passing by the cluster of supportive faculty members as their math teacher, Mr. Turlington, conversed with Ms. Woods, whose eye contact focused on a compassionate approach for their students. A mysterious glint caught Wendy's attention when she noticed Mr. Turlington's peculiar fascination with Veronica's girlfriends perusing their eLookbook updates. He lost focus on his teaching plans when he laughed with another student across the space as though he knew exactly what made her giggle.

"Are you okay, Wendy?" Ms. Woods asked as she gave up on him, her hand reaching to Wendy's arm to comfort her.

"Yes," she responded meekly, with an accompanying nod.

"Okay. It's good to see you out there supporting your classmates tonight."

"Thank you," she replied quietly. "I'll see you tomorrow."

As the shy student moved away from the teachers, Mr. Turlington's eyebrow raised in a devious manner as he scanned her from head to toe. Even with her back turned, she could feel his stare piercing her. With all the noise and presence from the crowd, she felt like she was drowning. The rainbow sequins on Penny's athletic jacket reflected the football field lights, catching Wendy's eye and giving her a sense of safety. The uncomfortable stares of her classmates made her shrink and interrupted the deep conversations she was trying to join. As her awareness increased, her priority changed to assimilating into the background.

"Hey!" Penny shouted.

She attempted to regain Wendy's attention by signaling her over, reminiscent of a crossing guard. Mrs. Hershey shamelessly talked about her vlog, attempting to promote it to anyone nearby, causing Penny to distance herself from her.

"And I hope you tune into my next post, where I show you guys how I make my famous chicken noodle casserole. It's a family recipe you have to try!" Caroline boasted as she caressed her hand over her stomach.

Senior Hershey's eggplant-colored lips became licked, forming a smile of bleached white teeth to sell her show. She tried to ignore the citizens with their glazed eyelids drooping with uninterested boredom. Her persistence was always something that could be admired; she would knock on any door until one would open in order for her show to become a success.

"We can't wait, Caroline," said one woman as she grabbed her husband's bicep; her nudge to gesture to him to wrap up the conversation became more aggressive the further the entertainer became engaged. "Come on, honey. We should pay our respects."

"Oh, yes, don't let me take up your time," Caroline said, taken back from her interruption.

"It was nice to chat with you," the woman said, rushed.

"It was nice to chat with you as well!" Caroline replied, biting her lip as the couples dispersed away from her into the crowd like cockroaches to light.

Wendy experienced a brief moment of instability when the husband's shoulder bumped into hers. The couple grumbled as they dismissed the information dumped on them like a pushy salesman. In a rush, the wife glanced back at the mother, hoping she hadn't joined the crowd. Every five feet she had to double check that Caroline wasn't following them for another pitch.

"Hey."

Wendy was apprehensive when she noticed the adrenaline radiating from Caroline's demeanor, her fists clenched. Only a tiny glint of a tear formed in her eye with the face of another rejection, almost breaking the waterline of her crisp, black liner. Within a second, she blinked, resetting her focus away from the rejection and refreshing herself for a new opportunity.

"Hi, Wendy!" Caroline responded, her pitch raising high as though she were a teapot with boiling water.

"Some speech, huh?" Penny asked with sarcasm, her forehead creased with three small wrinkles from her raised eyebrows.

"Yeah," said Wendy. "She had a good point. Just might need to work on the delivery a bit."

"A bit?" Caroline chimed in, her cheeks beginning to flush. "There is no place for that type of behavior. If that was my kid, I would have a few words with her about that."

"Well, aren't we all glad you aren't her mother?" Penny said quickly, rolling her eyes.

"I beg your pardon?"

"H-hey, Caroline. Isn't that the Van Buemans?" Wendy interjected, frantic to avoid an altercation. "I heard they started tuning in to your show, and they thought it was a hit!"

"What?" Penny's mother asked, her chin perking up like a stimulated dog getting sudden attention. "Well, I need to solidify my following. I'll talk to you guys later!"

"Bye, Mom," Penny said, relieved as she couldn't finish her farewell.

The two friends experienced the rush of air against their skin as they giggled while her mother power walked toward the middle-aged couple. The charging social media rookie's pursuit of advertising caused fear being reflected in their widening eyes. Despite the wife's persistent efforts to convince her husband to accompany her, she sighed in defeat as Caroline made her presence known.

"One more word out of you, and she would've gone all Joan Crawford on your ass!" Wendy said, chuckling incessantly as her hand covered her lips. "You better be careful of that."

"Meh, her bark is worse than her bite," said Penny without a care. "She has been too focused on becoming famous. A tornado could destroy our home, and she wouldn't even notice. She'll let it all go as long as she has the internet connection and the equipment to film her stupid show."

So she is Joan Crawford, Wendy thought.

"Haven't you told her that maybe she is too committed to her channel?"

"Would *you* tell her?" Penny asked, her hands raised in desperation.

"Good point."

No, wire hangers, ever! Wendy thought again. The visual of Caroline chasing Penny around with a hanger made her stomach flutter with warmth.

"She puts about ten percent of her attention to me and my brothers, and the rest is dedicated to her show," she continued, a glint of abandonment reflected from the pupils of her frosty blue eyes. "Luckily, they are old enough to fend for themselves and aren't interested in spending quality time with her."

"Didn't your dad say anything to her about this?"

"He was fine with it until he wasn't," Penny explained, trying to answer her. She was eager to move on as her sneakers rapidly tapped onto the ground with a hasty muffle. "I don't even think she knew he left."

With a hopeless shrug, she tried to conceal her nervous smirk and hold back her words.

"Should we go pay our respects now?" Wendy asked.

She placed her hand on Penny's jacket. The rigid edges of the multi-color sequins crunched against her fingertips while they tucked underneath her fingernails. Bits of elastic thread twisted into the light hairs on her knuckles.

"Sure," she consented. "Enough about me?"

The pair made their way through the cluster of girls. Without Ms. Woods by his side, Mr. Turlington stared at them like a predator. With an intense gaze, he observed as the girls directed their attention toward the memorial at the bandstand. His hands were tucked away in his pants pocket, shielded by his black jacket. He repeatedly clenched and unclenched his fists, fingers inching toward his zipper, leaving uncertainty whether he sought warmth or something more.

"Hey, Mr. Turlington," Penny said, her voice dragging with innocence like she was serenading him with a song. "I think I saw your wife over by the bleachers paying their respects to your students. Your son is such a cutie patootie, by the way! What is he, five now?"

Mr. Turlington was taken aback when his peeping was interrupted by his obligations as a spouse and father. He dashed to the bleachers, where a shy, slender woman and a small boy were located. The child was enveloped in a red and blue checkered fleece blanket, looking like a ghost with long ties trailing behind. He looked back at the two girls; his lowered, bushy eyebrows became more defined. The dominant presence of a curly, chapped lip countered Penny's "Smart-Alec" behavior. With her sequins catching the light, her cocky smirk emitted yellow and blue reflections. Pink dots floated over her eyes and forehead with her arms crossed as she experienced the success of calling out her math teacher's actions.

They kept going until they successfully merged back into their adolescent society, all the while mourning their beloved classmates. The memorial contained dozens of pictures documenting various stages of their three childhoods. Progressing photographs showcased the journey from toothless infants to elementary school-aged children, capturing moments of friendship and childhood adventures. Veronica's tea parties were a source of excitement and innocence, fueled by her vivid childhood imagination and her abundant collection of fluffy stuffed animals. There was an occasion when she tried out makeup, and it resulted in a Picasso-like appearance, with overdrawn, ruby-red lipstick smudged on her lips and cheeks, and flecks of pigment on her buck teeth. Experiencing a nauseating sensation in the pit of her stomach, guilt washed over Wendy as she reconsidered her initial judgments of the three teenagers. Her spiteful resentment decreased as she became aware that humanity, similar to her, possessed a shared history as innocent children with a mixture of joy, happiness, and imagination, along with insecurities, fears, and dreams.

I wish they knew that we were the same.

"I think we should go now; I'm not feeling too well," Wendy said, cradling her stomach.

"Oh, Wendy," said Penny, expressing concern as she noticed the tear forming in her friend's eye. "Should I take my mom's car?"

"No, I think we should walk home tonight," she answered. A slight chill ran up her spine. "I could use the air."

WITH THE EVENTFUL FUNERAL activities starting to bore and the crowd dying down, the citizens and classmates dispersed toward their vehicles to conclude their night. Brightly flashing headlights marked the lines of departing vehicles. The faded lines on the blacktop lot glowed like festive decorations.

Malakai headed toward a cluster of his male friends and their partners, walking behind the bleachers. To ward off the growing nighttime chill, the partners held onto their suitors tightly during the ceremony, finding security in their arms against the brisk air that kissed their exposed legs and chests from their mini dresses. A man in a sewage-green jumpsuit walked by, carrying a big black garbage bag, tossing away crumpled programs and trash from snacks. The janitor's face showed three distinct forehead wrinkles as the wind blew his hair.

"Hi, Gary," Malakai greeted, cradling his arms over his chest. "Good to see you again."

The janitor had yet to respond. His chapped upper lip twisted, revealing his bushy mustache streaked with gray. He bent down to pick up more garbage and threw it into the expanding bag before moving toward the flickering lit tea candles on the emptying bandstand.

"What's up?" said Malakai, chill, to acclimate to the masculine vibes.

Every step closer to them felt like walls that were closing in on him. He gave the guys a nod to acknowledge their presence, only to be met with focused stares. Fog puffed out from their huffing nostrils like a raging bull.

"Long time no see," said Wesley with sarcasm, his hand reaching over to clasp his palm for a bro-shake. "Some show out there, don't you think?"

"That was something," added Zachariah, his back cracking when he reached his arms out for a good stretch. "I have to get going. I'll catch up with you guys tomorrow."

"I'm sorry. I'll be back on the road to get ready for summer semester," Malakai said.

The last cluster of classmates left the service. The whisper of a gust of wind made the photographs on the cork bulletin board flutter and tickled the paper. Tanner's little league team photo glided across the field, resembling a plastic bag in the wind.

"Try to come back for the track meet. Our 4x100 relay team isn't the same without you."

"I'll try."

Zachariah vanished among the congested cars in the parking lot. The honking horns drowned out the soothing symphony of chirping crickets as they impatiently waited to exit onto the main road.

"Why haven't we hung out?" Wesley said as he turned his head back to Malakai. "You would think that after all the shit that Veronica and I have done for you, you could return the favor. You were nothing before us!"

"I'm sorry," Malakai said, his hands tucked inside his jeans pockets for warmth. "School has been tough. I needed to focus on my grades. I failed psychology because of all the times I came back to visit."

"I don't care. We had a deal."

"What? Help give me a personality for friendship?"

"No, we make you into something more than the life you had while you help us by any means necessary. And now it's time to cash out!"

A deep snarl twisted his face, causing his nose to pinch and wrinkle. His eyes burned with a fierce intensity, brimming with passion and determination.

"What do you want, then?" Malakai asked, fearful. "I have to leave in the morning."

"Don't worry, it's something you're going to do for us right now."

"Such as?"

"Getting back at that snot that spoke out about Veronica!" Wesley said, his knuckle cracking from his clenching fist.

"Andrea? What do you want with her?"

"We go to her piece of shit house at the edge of town and leave her a brief message."

"Like a note?"

"No, dumbass! I have the spray paint in my car!" Wesley responded, his tone rising with rage.

"No, I won't do it," Malakai said, his throat clicking from a generous wad of spit being forced down. "I'm not breaking the law for your petty revenge."

With each passing moment, his regret over getting mixed up with Wesley intensified, causing his stomach to growl louder as he left. Disgust heated his cold body as he stood his ground against the aggressive bullying, fueled by his frustration. The burly jocks encircled him, cutting off his escape from the unpleasant conversation. Underneath the bleachers, the cracking of knuckles resonated, sounding like crinkling cardboard being pressed together. Flexed biceps made the leather sleeves on their letterman's jackets appear inflated.

"This wasn't a request," Wesley said, hunching closer to Malakai's face. "You're going to do this for me, or I'll take care of your pathetic excuse of a sister of yours. I can have her life ruined by tomorrow morning."

A tightness gripped Malakai's throat, causing his tongue to dry up at the same time. He feared harming his sister so much that his knees gave way. Her laughter reverberated through his thoughts. No matter the price, he made it his mission to safeguard his sister, driven by love and a sense of urgency.

"Okay," Malakai said, raspy with sadness. "I'll do it."

Chapter 8

By going through multiple blocks and a dark forest shortcut, they reached the empty downtown square. Chipped-black streetlights flickered intermittently in the abandoned blocks. Buildings appeared bigger without sunlight casting upon their structures. Stray cats scavenged for the businesses' leftovers, chomping down at the diner's special spaghetti noodles. A partially eaten apple rolled onto the curb and then dropped into the small stream flowing through the filthy sewer grate. Rusty garbage cans had their cardboard box's flaps knocked off by powerful gusts of wind. Penny's sneakers made a series of defeated punts, their echoes resonating off the chipped brick buildings.

"Are you feeling better?" Penny asked, her high ponytail swung around her cheek like a helicopter propellor as she pelted the can once more.

"Yeah," Wendy groaned while the wind brushed her bangs away from her eyes; dirt particles flew into her eyes, blinding her. "I was just a little overwhelmed by everything."

"Overwhelmed?" Penny asked as the flickering lights bounced off her sequins; flashes of rainbow colors shed before them like a disco ball. "It's just Veronica and her friends."

"It's more than that," Wendy responded, tucking her fists inside her pockets, her shoulders hunched closer to her chest. "It's about Andrea."

"What about her?"

"Andrea and I were close for a long time. Since we were little, we would hang out and do everything together. We helped each other with our homework, and I trusted her with my secrets while she trusted me with hers."

"Like what we have?"

The two stepped out of the downtown boulevard to enter the last few suburban blocks before nearing Penny's house. Plastic siding took over from the brick establishments, causing the streetlights to be absorbed more. The sky was violet with only mere twinkles of stars making their presence known.

"Yes, like what we have," Wendy whispered. "I felt bad for not being there for her when Nora died."

"Oh, yeah. Nora."

"Andrea loved her with all her heart, more than anyone would know. They were the best of friends."

"Well, I noticed that after her rant," Penny said with sarcasm. "She sure has more love than I do for my brothers!"

"And when Nora died, Andrea retreated into a dark hole and shut everybody out."

Penny kicked the lone basketball next to the hoop, bouncing off the white picket fence in her yard. Garbage scattered onto the nearby driveway when the ball hit the corner of a trash can. The dogs across the street were barking in the backyard, defending their home against the scattered bits on the ground.

"I think I should go," Penny said, her fingers fidgeting with the gate latch to escape their spill. "I'll see you tomorrow. Did you want to walk to school together?"

"I have to get there early to work on my paper. I'll see you there."

As the porch lights turned on, Wendy scurried away from the neighbors. In a fit of anger, one of the neighborhood fathers cursed vehemently, like a drunken sailor. His robe trailed behind, unveiling his backside that required underwear.

Upon reaching the next block, Wendy slowed down, moving closer to her home and further away from the disorder. Her perspiring body heat eliminated the icy sensation in her cramped muscles. Amidst the rustling of tree branches that mimicked gently shaken maracas, the hound's bark diminished with every step, going unnoticed. Under the weight of lonesome silence, her breath huffed out like cigarette smoke. The growing paranoia of being by herself intensified, as there was no one around to offer a sense of safety or comfort.

"You look like you need a friend to walk you home," said a feminine voice, eerily low in tone.

Wendy's body twitched, startled like a cat as her fatigued muscles came alive like a jolt of caffeine, returning to the only street sign, concealed by the shaded shadows from the streetlamp across the road. The silhouette of the young woman became almost unidentifiable under the cover of darkness and her dark clothing. The black hair blowing around her cheeks framed her pale, white skin, which glowed.

"Andrea?" Wendy asked, squinting to focus her vision to decipher the similar black lipstick and smokey eyeshadow. "What are you doing here?"

"I needed to cool down after the memorial," Andrea said as she walked closer to her; her tattoo-like penciled-in black eyebrows became more defined with each step.

"Yeah, it was a bit heated back there," Wendy said, her arms crossing over. "How are you doing?"

"I'll be fine," she answered coldly. "It's funny that you care about how I'm doing now, because you haven't even reached out to me since Nora died."

The sensation of a small dagger piercing her stomach overwhelmed Wendy, as her nerves took control. Her attempt at reaching out for care was immediately slapped away from her.

"Look, I'm sorry I haven't been around when you needed me the most."

Wendy brushed her hair behind her ears, taking a minimal gulp of spit as her mouth dried.

"Oh, you're sorry now," she hissed with apathy. "What a great friend you are!"

"I don't know what else I could say or do to make my damages disappear. But I want to make it up to you."

Andrea's stoic demeanor amplified as her internal rage consumed her. Shades of pink colored her cheeks in a flush. Her shadow grew like a ghoul following behind her.

"You'll never feel how I felt. Maybe I'll consider giving you an ounce of my breath if you ever felt like I did."

Andrea vanished into the shadows. Wendy experienced a sense of cold abandonment after being left behind by her former best friend. A single tear rolled down Wendy's frigid, pale face, descending to moisten the pavement. Toward her home, she walked slowly, covering the remaining block and a half. Her senseless vanishing caused guilt to grow toward the friend who deeply cared for her. The disappointing nibble of her top jaw caused a sharp piercing sensation in the bottom of her lip. Her eyes narrowed as tears poured relentlessly from the corners of her eyes. The time had come for her to face her shame head-on, with no possibility of escape. The damage she had caused was impossible to deny any longer.

MS. WOODS REDIRECTED their focus, interrupting Wendy's zombie-like demeanor. On a rainy May afternoon one year ago, the teacher's garden sundress brought hope to her students for their summer dreams. Veronica played with her phone's dim-lit screen while wearing

ripped jeans and chewing bubble gum. Typing away, her fingertips danced on the keyboard, adding another comment to an eLookBook post. Instead of writing the important points of the lecture about the history of All Hallow's Eve, Wesley and Zachariah entertained themselves by scribbling nonsensical stick figure doodles on the top corner of their notebook sheets. A crumpled piece of paper, which she unraveled to read her message, covered Wendy's mid-length jean skirt.

"Sleepover again tonight?"

Wendy's smirk melted away, replaced by a beaming, shimmering smile as she stared at Andrea, suppressing her delight after taking in the colon and right sided parentheses to indicate a smiley face. Her stomach fluttered at the genuine message from her friend. Andrea's lower lip trembled with excitement, moving up and down in a subtle jolt.

"Excuse me," chimed in Ms. Woods as her palm tapped on top of her desk. "Am I interrupting something?"

The sudden interruption of authority startled and woke up the two girls. With a mix of guilt and innocence, their eyebrows lowered toward their eyes, much like a dog caught in an accident on an expensive rug. As they battled fatigue from the lecture, the rest of the class glared at her with indifference.

"Veronica, I'm going to ask you one more time to please put away your phone," Ms. Woods commanded. "Anything with an on/off switch should have it off."

Veronica rolled her eyes, popping a small pink bubble with nothing to say back to her.

"What is so important that you can't share with the rest of the class?"

"None of your business," Veronica hissed, her lip snarled.

"Well, it's interrupting my class. Teaching is important to me, and learning should be important to you," Ms. Woods preached; hands placed on her hips. "So please, try me."

KNOCK! KNOCK! KNOCK!

Principal Stuart strolled into the room. The police officer mirrored his deep sadness as they walked, his frown a clear sign of his depression.

"Sorry to interrupt, Ms. Woods," Principal Stuart said, adjusting the belt on his slacks, his thumb tucking in the baggy remnants of his pastel-yellow dress shirt underneath.

"Not at all," replied Ms. Woods, grabbing a stack of withered textbooks and placing them back onto her bookshelf. "It's perfect timing for one of our students to fess up to what's so important on her phone. Maybe the principal could help."

"Monica, I don't think that now is the time to—"

"No, no! I think it's the perfect time. Go on!"

As she stood up from her chair, Veronica's hair fell over her face while she discovered she was outnumbered by the authority figures who shifted their focus to her. In order to avoid another offense, she quickly swallowed her gum and adjusted her cami to cover up her exposed cleavage. Closing the thin-jersey cardigan over her thin spaghetti straps, she pressed the refresh button on her screen. In a sudden motion, her jaw dropped as she read a breaking story on her eLookBook news feed.

"Oh my god!" Veronica said, gasping with shock. "Some girl from our school died."

As the group of startled adolescents turned on their cell phones, Principal Stuart and the officer took a careful step forward. As the eLookBook app unveiled the article's details, their shocked faces were highlighted by the illuminated screens displaying their disbelief. The expressions on people's faces were almost identical. Tears cascaded onto Andrea's desk as she opened a barrage of text messages and noticed the chaos of ten missed calls, her face overcome with a mixture of shock and distress.

"Call me."

"Call your mom ASAP!"

"Please answer. This is an emergency!"

"Your sister died. I need you home now!"

"Nora?!" Andrea screamed, her voice cracking full of heartbreak.

Andrea's mouth emitted cries of agony as Ms. Woods's hands shielded her dropped jaw. The room became increasingly suffocating as Amber's breaths became panicked bursts, her classmates' glazed expressions adding to her paleness. Wendy became detached and overwhelmed as she watched Ms. Woods and the officer holding Andrea's motionless body, unable to react or process her own feelings. Cries were being muffled by the excessively loud gossiping of her classmates as they compared notes about Nora's passing. Upon exiting the classroom, her best friend stepped into a new reality and encountered a sense of isolation without her beloved sister disconnected from others.

AFTER COLLECTING THE mail, Wendy unlocked her front door. Her sweaty palms let go of a glossy magazine, which slid out slowly. Bright lights filled the dining room, blinding her and washing out her vision. As she leaned on the door frame, she descended toward the shoe rack, collapsing. She found herself experiencing the identical numbness as the year before. Her eyes overflowed with tears of sorrow as she grasped the extent of the pain she had brought upon her friend through neglect. The sensation of being forsaken plagued her, akin to a damp wool blanket, never finding comfort even in the presence of her nearest and dearest during her bleakest moments. With a heavy heart, she tried to understand the lasting consequences of her actions.

Chapter 9

With the departure of the community, the parking lot was free of congestion as the cars unjammed themselves. People became more relaxed as the anxious traffic vanished like a serpent into a cold, wet abyss. Fog thickened around the solitary group of teenagers that gathered near the trunk of a black dented Suzuki. On top of the car, two adult girls embraced each other for warmth in the boys' letterman jackets, growing more impatient as they watched the senior boys come up with a plan. Huddled together like scouts around a campfire, the boys studied a paper map of the town while devising their plan to seek revenge on their outspoken classmate.

"So, here's the paint," Wesley directed, shoving the cardboard box toward Malakai. "I want you to leave her a message she will never forget!"

"Like what?" Malakai asked, defeated.

"I don't know," he hissed back at him. "Get creative!"

The last cars left the parking lot. The once bright headlights that illuminated their gathering were now dimmed, leaving only the moonlight as their guide. No deer were in the field, ready to go venture into the woods. All the birds were slumbering in their nests, preparing themselves for the next day.

"Well, I barely knew her. I need something to go off."

"Just lay into her for being a freak, just like her sister."

"That's not nice to say about someone who died!"

Wesley's companions stared at him with hostility. They encircled him, creating a formidable barrier he couldn't break through. Their dates stared at their men, eyes wide as they looked into the side of them they never saw.

"Who cares?" Wesley defended cockily, picking the box up. "This world is about who matters to others."

"She mattered to someone," he said, rolling his eyes in disgust.

"She didn't matter to me or anyone else in this school for that matter," Wesley said, snotty; Malakai's lanky arms took the shove of the box he thrust.

Malakai found himself overwhelmed by how forcefully Wesley made his demands. Like a terrified cat, his forearms trembled from the weight of the box that were straining his wrists. Just as he started walking towards his vehicle on the other side of the lot, he was taken aback by the moving figure that revealed his older appearance in the streetlights. The man's ebony hair mixed with the cool evening atmosphere as the fog illuminated his tanned skin.

"Get back here. It's Mr. Turlington!" Wesley whispered, commanding Malakai as his waving hand signaled him back to his vehicle. "Why is he still here?"

Malakai froze with trepidation, fearing their cover might be compromised. The teacher's appearance left Wesley and his minions, who were terrified, with the opportunity to break free from their mafia-like hold. Relief washed over Malakai's face as he took a step toward the educator, but Wesley's threat silenced him.

"You are going to do this for me, or I will take care of your pathetic excuse of a sister of yours."

Overcome with fear, Malakai remained motionless, anxious about hurting his sister. Defeat replaced his previous burst of energy, leaving him deflated as he shuffled back toward Wesley. In order to conceal their plan, one of Wesley's followers closed the door just as he hurled the box of spray paint back into his trunk. In perfect synchronization, the boys spun around, their bodies quivering as they attempted to mask their unconvincing smirks. The girls joined the two, jolting off the hood as their heels clapped upon the concrete like Clydesdales. Zipping up his crimson-light jacket, Mr. Turlington approached the teenagers with his hands snug in his pockets.

"What are you all still doing here?" Mr. Turlington asked, concerned as his pace increased towards them.

"N-Nothing, Mr. Turlington," stuttered one of Wesley's henchmen, hunching closer to his master.

"I find that hard to believe. What's going on?"

"We were just catching up with an old friend," Wesley answered, his grin more convincing than everyone else's. "We were just about to leave."

A small gust of wind slapped their faces, causing a shiver down their spines. By the entrance to the high school, a single tree displayed fluttering leaves. A lone piece of bark flaked off the trunk, tumbling onto the lot.

"I think that would be a good idea," he agreed, adjusting his jacket collar closer to his ears. "You should all be a little more careful about staying out too late."

"Yes, sir," they all agreed in unison, jaws jittering.

While about to depart, Mr. Turlington was unexpectedly approached by the two girls. Their beauty surprised him as they trembled from the cold, their formal dresses emphasizing the shaking of their breasts. Legs shivered, allowing their thighs to jiggle. The teacher noticed something brighter when the moonlight bounced off a sequin.

"Do I know you from somewhere?" he asked the dark-red-haired young lady, puzzled as his squinting eyes wrinkled the corner of his eyes.

"From class?" she answered with uncertainty as her inflections rose in her answer.

"I recognize every student I teach and don't remember you."

He examined every contour of her physique. In an attempt to hide, she leaned in closer to the other girl's demure shape. When he saw her exposed neckline, his eyes widened, and she snarled in disgust.

"I don't know then," she said, frustrated. "I remember you, though. Now, can you please stop staring at me? I don't think your wife would appreciate you checking out another woman."

Mr. Turlington huffed out a gust of air from his nose. The clenching of his fist made his jacket's polyester fabric crinkle like paper being crushed. Even without his superiors present, he couldn't get a satisfying encounter with an attractive person to bring him elation.

"Get home, now!"

"Yes, sir," they all responded as they scurried to their vehicles.

The fog rolled in, slowly obscuring Mr. Turlington's body in the lot. Wesley's friends dispersed to their beat-up pickup trucks. Malakai ran toward his car, clumsily trying to find the correct key on his keychain. His key tip dancing around the keyhole resulted in scratches on the black metal.

"Aren't you forgetting something?" Wesley asked, impatient as his hand signaled him back over.

Malakai sighed in defeat as he had to continue with the plan he believed was ruined by their math teacher's orders. With great haste, he made his way back, seized the box from the open trunk, and retreated to his car, hoping to remain undetected. The fog engulfed his feet, causing the tires to disappear as if dry ice were bubbling in water.

"And Benson, don't even think about backing out of this plan. My boys were told where to park to see the deed done."

Maliciously, Wesley slammed his car door and laughed. Left alone and frightened, fear paralyzed Malakai as the provoker disappeared, leaving him with no one to protect or console him during his desperate time. The staggered release of air from his lungs caused his trembling breaths to become visible. He desired to avoid Wesley's plan, but could not find an exit strategy.

At the intersection of the running trail and sidewalk by the north exit, a black silhouette appeared through the dense fog. Similar to a ghoul haunting a barren graveyard brimming with wandering spirits and motionless cadavers, the entity levitated. Malakai's attention was caught by the movement of the cloaked figure as it disappeared into the shadows of the pine trees. The hairs on his arm became rigid; goosebumps appeared on his skin's surface.

He wasted no time in opening the door to his vehicle, placing the paint box on the passenger side before buckling up. Turning the key in the ignition caused a slow transition from cold to warm air coming out of the vents. Slow, drifting gusts of air swept the vibrant green grass, creating a hypnotic effect to try and ease his anxieties.

ON A SWELTERING SUMMER day, two kids were enjoying themselves in a park nearby. The boy pushed the girl with jubilation, causing her to end up on her back on the swing. The wooden plank beneath her propelled her body into the air, aided by a chain rope. With powerful momentum, the girl's black baby doll dress danced, their faces filled with laughter and happiness. Four girls noticed her as she relaxed in the shade while they played with their long hair. Braids tightly woven, they discussed the cootie pandemic while boys play tag nearby in the outfield.

"Higher, Malakai," little Wendy said, elated, full of glee; the wind aerodynamically passed her cheeks. "Higher!"

"I'm trying!" Malakai responded, huffing with each forceful push.

"I want to break my record! I want to jump farther!"

Malakai exerted all his effort, grabbing the back of her dress as she retreated, while the force lifted his feet off the ground to aid in his backward push. Wendy closed her eyes and took a deep breath. Air filled the gaps between her fingers as she released the chains. As she slid off the plank, gravity tugged at her feet, drawing them closer to the jungle gym with its red and yellow paint. As her body flung onto the lush, manicured blades of grass, her knees absorbed the powerful thump. Excitement coursed through Malakai as he joyfully tackled his sister, impressed by her progress at surpassing her previous distance by one foot.

"You did it! You broke your record!"

The nearby railroad tracks brought the steel wheels to a stop, silencing the children's giggles, while the vehicle's exhaust pipe strained as it passed the small town's city lines and ventured onto the dirt road of the countryside. The boisterous boxcars drowned out their innocent happiness and diverted their attention.

"I think we should go home," Malakai proposed, cupping his hands over his ears like earmuffs.

"What?" Wendy asked, unable to hear as she turned her head closer to him for her ear to get closer.

Grabbing her hand, Malakai escorted her out of the park, eager to get back home. With each step away from the park, the sound of the moving train diminished. Their eardrums were granted a small respite when they made it across the street to the next block. Malakai's temples throbbed with pain, echoing like a booming drum. The pounding headache driven by anxiety that caused his throat to close. Beads of sweat dampened the tips of their hair as they became deeply absorbed.

"Malakai, look," Wendy said, pointing to the blue house down the street. "Moving vans!"

"Yeah," he said, mumbling in agony. "It looks like we have new neighbors in town."

"Let's go check it out!"

"I don't know. I'm not feeling too well."

Sunlight reflected off the metal on the gutters, enhancing the sight of the green bushes along the sidewalk. As Malakai tried to keep up, bits of sidewalk crumbled under his sneakers. Ants scurried onto the grass, hoping that the press of a foot wouldn't end their lives.

"Come on. Don't be such a baby."

With a firm grip, Wendy's hand dug her sharp fingernails into Malakai's wrist like a snake's bite. Waves of pain didn't help his headache; it contributed to soreness behind his eyes.

"Just for a minute."

"Okay."

They went to the block's end. The neighborhood lawn mowers overpowered the sound of the train, making it difficult to hear. The invigorating aroma of fresh-cut grass refreshed their nostrils.

They arrived at the front of a house, which was positioned parallel to the red moving van. Muscular men waddled together, carrying heavy furniture. By performing minor adjustments to the leather on their weight belts, they wrestled with the bulging muscles that kept their backs properly aligned. Sweat stains that matched the gradient of light-tan marked their white shirts.

A woman with short black hair appeared through the front door, her hair just barely touching the straps of her salmon tank top. Her frayed jean shorts had fluttering white strings that moved with each step she took onto the lawn. With the help of the condensation, the cups slid along the tray as she placed it on the table.

"I have beverages in case you would like something to drink!" announced the woman, using the moisture to cool down her forehead before helping herself to a glass.

The opaque, yellow drink quenched the woman's parched lips. As Wendy and Malakai examined the moving boxes, her sunglasses slipped down her nose. The removal of the moving men's shirts exposed their glistening, sun-kissed skin; sweat sparkled in the crevasses of their muscles as they longed for a moment of relaxation.

"Hello," greeted the woman before taking another sip.

The pair of children hesitated, unsure if she was focused on them, captivated by her sheer attractiveness. Humidity caused the air to blur behind them while their tongues became dry.

"Would you like a glass of lemonade?" she asked, her small chuckle was inviting.

"S-sure," Wendy said, inching her way closer to her. Her hand felt her brother's grasp tugging, preventing her from moving forward like a dog on a leash.

"We should go," he insisted with apprehension, massaging his temples with his other hand.

"Oh, I do insist," the woman said. "I can even get you a little something for that headache of yours."

"I-I don't have a headache, ma'am," he said, squinting from the blinding reflection of the sunlight that attacked him from the hood of a passing vehicle.

"Oh, nonsense! A mother knows when a child is in despair. Now, come on and sit. Enjoy a glass of lemonade while your head gets better."

The children approached the table. The fragrance of citrus blended with the subtle musk of testosterone and the smoky haze of cigarettes. They didn't know if they should've been enticed or disgusted by the contrasting aromas.

"Thank you, ma'am," Wendy thanked the woman; both hands cradled the cup, allowing the chilled glass to cool down her palms.

"Please, call me Beverly. I'm Beverly Crispin."

"Nice to meet you," Malakai said, relaxing under the awning's shade.

With the glass nearing her lips, Wendy's complexion grew less pale.

"Y-you're a mother?" she asked, licking her lips.

"I have two girls," Beverly answered; the ice cubes in her cup clanged like a wind chime. "I have Andrea playing over there. I think she's having a tea party."

"A tea party?"

Wendy's head became alert after she took another generous sip. The ice cubes in Malakai's glass caught his attention, floating together like buoys. Her lips were moistened from the quenching chill of the drink, making her question if she should take her time with consuming it so she can enjoy the brisk reprieve.

"I'm sure she wouldn't mind having an extra guest."

"Really?"

"You should go join her!"

With a swift movement, Wendy propelled herself off the chair, causing her lemonade to spill onto the grass. She quickly ran to the side of the yard, where six stuffed animals surrounded a small purple table. Andrea's laughter beckoned her to enter the realm of her imagination. Malakai beamed with gratitude and happiness as he observed his little sister's contagious joy. Meanwhile, she acted out pouring tea into the pastel-pink coffee cup as if from an imaginary kettle.

"I'm sure you're not into the whole tea party thing," said Beverly, handing Malakai two tablets of children's aspirin.

"What gave you that thought?" he said with sarcasm.

Their giggling overshadowed the enjoyment of the tea party. The two girls dipped their imaginary cookies into the cup, which was filled with air, before lifting them together for a joint toast. Memories of when he would play pretend with his sister warmed his heart, the picnics they had in their backyard consuming the invisible entrees brought a smile to his face.

"If you want to catch a little shade, my other daughter Nora is over there drawing. You're more than welcome to join her."

Beverly directed her finger toward the tree in the front yard, protected from the glaring sunlight by loose papers scattered across the lawn. The wind breathed life into the frayed bits of notebook paper, making them bounce on the grass. Nora's jeans overalls, splattered with paint, contrasted against the shadowy tree bark.

"We should get going," he dismissed. "Thank you for everything, but our mom will expect us home shortly."

"Oh, don't you worry about that, honey," she said, patting her hand on his shoulder. "I can give you two a ride home once I get my guys to finish unloading my furniture."

Beverly's convincing persuasion trapped Malakai, causing him to grin with apprehension. Witnessing the joy in his sister's eyes as she made a new acquaintance eased his heart. Wendy's smile made him feel safe. There was nothing out of the ordinary with a new neighbor being kind enough to take care of them in the brink of the heat, and the company embraced them with ease. Beverly's kindness made his nerves slowly dissolve like a pill to water, especially with his taste buds craving a second helping of lemonade.

"Go make a friend with Nora. She is a little different and could use one. She isn't all that excited about moving to a new town. Perhaps you can show her it won't be that bad?"

"Okay."

"Thank you. I appreciate it."

Beverly left the table and joined the movers to discuss her strategy for completing the challenging transition. Like a dive bar from the 1980s, the smoke enveloped the air and made her cough. Her vocal cords grunted into a deeper tone, gasping for air with an alto pitch.

Malakai sauntered toward the tree, his sneakers shuffling on the grass. The pounding in his temples subsided as the children's aspirin mixed with the hydrating lemonade. As he approached Nora, he couldn't resist the hypnotic red and white stripes on her t-shirt, surrounded by colorful plastic cups holding countless shades of pencils. A long, black cloak was hanging from a broken tree branch, functioning as a coat hook. As Nora's voice hummed, his stomach twisted with nerves.

"H-Hi," said Malakai, the glass almost erupted from the top of his firm grip.

Nora turned her head gradually to observe him. Clay-colored freckles dotted her dainty-pale skin, resembling orangish-brown sequins on a ghostly-white piece of fabric. For someone who didn't dress traditionally like the other kids, even the outcasts scoped out people for abnormalities in their own reality.

"Hi," she responded quietly, brushing pencil shaving off her sheet.

"I-I'm Malakai."

"Nora."

"Nice to meet you," he said, awkward. "Mind if I join you?"

"Sure," she answered as she grabbed another pencil.

With his knees bent on the grass, Malakai sensed a gentle chill from the shaded blades tickling his legs. He picked up a sheet of paper and scribbled with the essence of artistry. The intricate landscapes of the Bob Ross aesthetic, with deep shading on the underside of trees and glacial snowcaps on distant mountains, left him astonished. Rhythmic waves filled the river bend, mimicking the effect of a pebble dropping onto the surface.

"These are great!" Malakai said, picking up another masterpiece, a shoreline.

"Thank you," she responded, focusing on blending yellow ochre with burnt orange.

"How did you get so good at this?" he asked, intrigued, as he shuffled through more sheets.

"I just draw what I see in my dreams."

"Well, that's neat. You should sell your work someday."

"I'm just a kid!" she said, chuckling faintly. "I can't sell my drawings."

"You can with time. Keep practicing, and some will love and appreciate your work.

Nora grinned; the support from her new acquaintance became warm. Her two front teeth gleamed through her happiness. With a smile, her lips opened, showing the tiny space between them. Sunlight caught the flicker in her forest-green eyes, while her freckles spread toward the edges of her face, accentuating her smile.

"Come on, Malakai," Nora chirped, grabbing a clean sheet of paper and scooting to the edge of the base of the tree to make room. "Let's draw a picture together."

MALAKAI'S CAR SAT NEXT to the park in town, engulfed in the cold and lonely silence. The tree branches swayed as the whistling winds filled the outskirts of town with darkness. With the whistling winds, the baby leaves were uprooted from their new homes and fell to the ground. As the rusty chains clung to the old metal hoops, the wooden plank swung back and forth on the swing set, creating a horrid screech.

Malakai popped open the trunk to get the spray paint. A sharp chill pecked at his neck, causing his baby hairs to stand on end and his skin to break out in goosebumps. The touch of the cold cans made his fingertips numb as he gripped them, awakening his nerves. With caution, he stowed two cans in his pocket, checking the surroundings to avoid revealing his identity. On the opposite side, Wesley's henchmen had parked their truck. Malakai barely made out the two as they took a light nap, their heads tilted back.

A powerful gust of wind surrounded him, causing a whirlwind of leaves. The hems of his jeans clung to his calves, like they had been soaked and were now bonded to his skin because of the swift draft. The tree's decay was enhanced by the addition of a white piece of paper, catching flickering colors from the intermittent streetlight. With curiosity, he made multiple attempts to grab it, reminiscent of a person in an arcade trying to push cash from a windy force. With a pinch of his fingers, he unfolded the crumpled sheet to reveal its mystery. In a blinded state, he moved closer to the streetlamp in order to understand what was inside.

The horizon displayed a stunning illustration of a solitary mountain intricately drawn and merged with deep blues and purples. The sky's intricate etchings seamlessly transitioned into the earthy tones of autumn, ranging from orange and yellow to dark green and brown. With its exquisite wooden shingles and shimmering shale accents, the small cottage was a masterpiece of detail. The image resembled a Thomas Kinkade painting with flawless shading that captured the essence of brushstrokes.

"Nora," Malakai said, gasping with fear.

With a worried glance, he realized that the girl had passed away in the previous year had her work showing up out of the blue. His jaw trembled in fear, grinding against his molars with each bite. Within his immediate field of vision, the swing was the sole source of movement, swaying like the pendulum of a grandfather clock, entrancingly responding to each breeze.

At the boundary between the concrete and gravel, a solitary figure in black stood in the distance. The force of Mother Nature's touch caused the frayed fabric to move in a rhythmic dance. Malakai found himself captivated by the cloak's mystery as it drifted further away into the dark ditch surrounded by tall grass. The cloak because it looked familiar. Driven by curiosity, he sprinted to pursue it, feeling the tension in his knees as his heels hammered down on the road. The cold air weighed heavily on his lungs as he huffed and made his way into the steep ditch.

"Nora!" Malakai yelled again, being muffled by the rustling branches. "Is that you?"

He deftly maneuvered through the thick branches, which caused scratches on his face. His body contorted and maneuvered through the prickly terrain, as if avoiding a laser alarm system that tore through his jeans. Frustration heightened as the cloak disappeared in a patch that became visible. With a surge of nervous reassurance, he picked up his pace, realizing that his long and difficult journey through the undergrowth was nearing its conclusion.

Stepping onto the exposed land, the rocky terrain beneath his soles made him uneasy. Malakai faced the stoic cloak, which glared at him, while the huffing clouds of breath hit the torn hem.

"Nora, I thought you were dead," he said, panting, his hand nursing his chest.

The figure remained silent, glaring at him. He tried to look through the concealed blackness that circled underneath the oversized hood but couldn't see anything, not even the green eyes he remembered.

"People have been worried about you. I'm worried about you, and I'm sorry I haven't been around to be the friend you deserve. I miss you."

A small, growing beam of light illuminated the billowing bottom of the cloak, showcasing the angular wizard sleeves. To Malakai, Nora's arrival seemed like an angelic intervention to prevent him from causing harm. His heart throbbed with intensity as the pounding rhythm reverberated in his ears. With each passing second, the light sharpened, causing him to be blinded as the shadow vanished. The pounding transitioned into a grating horn that blared in his ear. The sudden and powerful collision of a fast and heavy locomotive caused his back to be crushed, leaving no opportunity for him to react or turn around.

Malakai's body burst open when the train struck him. Each passing wheel cut into his severed veins, flinging his arms into the ditch, and mutilating his legs. Blood cascaded onto the brown and green bushes, propelled by the impact of his ruptured stomach and heart like a burst water balloon on the rocks. Soaked denim patches cradled his open wallet, onto which the black spray paint cans tumbled. The only trace of his identity was the blood that pooled around a picture of his graduation, where his little sister lovingly held him with pride, as his fragmented body lay scattered along the tracks.

Chapter 10

At five-thirty, Wendy's alarm clock made an obnoxious buzzing to wake her up. Waves of energy shot through her legs, snapping her out of her dreamy trance. The closer she got to graduation, the stronger her desire for freedom from Felton became, which made her urgency to get out of bed a little harder. Her only desire is to flee from those who hurt her, and provide a new chance for those in need, never abandoning them.

Through the blinds, sunlight appeared, drying her tears that soaked her pillow before she was able to drift off to sleep. Her pillowcase bore the consequences of her negligence toward her friend, with various shades of black splotches representing guilt. She rubbed the crusty debris from her eyes, ready to embrace the new day with fresh eyes. With a sudden burst of energy, she propelled herself out of bed, sensing the strain in her tight hamstrings as the blood rushed back to her lower body. After donning her black hooded sweatshirt and boot cut jeans, she briefly glanced at her reflection in the vanity mirror to see if her hair was too unruly. Bags under her eyes sagged closer to the apples of her cheeks, reflecting sadness on her face. Haunted by Andrea's voice, all she could hear was the sorrowful tremor in her jaw.

"You were never there for me when I needed you!"

"Why would you think about yourself when I gave you all my attention when you needed me?"

"You are so selfish!"

Journeying through the suburban streets, the dewy grass greeted her under the early morning sun. The rooftops were shining like a disco ball with glistening shingles. As she made her way through the downtown square, she joined the store managers in unlocking their doors and preparing for the start of business. To survive until the nighttime dump, the alley cats dispersed to avoid the dump truck that took away their weekly meals. The birds hopped on the sidewalk, following her shadow as she led them to the bush-filled entrance of the bike trail in the woods.

Delicate rays of light filtered through the opening buds, gently warming her skin. Shadows cast from branches adorned the blacktop trail with organic mosaics, as gravel bounced off her sneaker. The birds sang a soothing hymn to refocus Wendy's mind and lift the heavy clouds of distraction.

On a moss-covered tree stump, Zachariah sat perched. Moist bark stained the back of his blue jeans. With an intense gaze, he looked through the jumbled branches that framed the breathtaking view. Beneath a glazed patch of sky, the empty cornfield showcased rows of tilled mounds of dirt. The tall grass hung over the barbed wire fence, like strands of hair.

"Zachariah," Wendy said, surprised. "What are you doing here?"

"I go here all the time to think," he answered, startled by her greeting.

"At six in the morning?"

"I couldn't sleep last night," he said, deflating deeper into his fist; his chest expanded with a deep breath. "I had a lot on my mind."

"Is everything okay?" she asked, stepping off the trail, her shoes sinking into the mud.

"Yeah. I just feel unfulfilled."

"What do you mean?"

"We graduate soon," he said, standing up to usher his hand towards Wendy to guide her towards him. "I just don't feel proud of my accomplishments."

"You're going to graduate, and you had great football and track seasons," she said, confused by his guilt. "What more do you need?"

The two squeezed their behinds together while perched on the stump. Zachariah's body emitted a furnace-like heat that warmed Wendy's cold legs.

"I don't know. It's hard to explain," he said, melancholy. "I have a lot of regrets about how I was."

"Regrets?"

The orange and black wings of the lone monarch butterfly fluttered towards him. He paid no attention to its beauty, pausing on his knee. The black antennas twitched, trying to get his attention.

"I sold out people I cared about for me to be popular."

"Are you talking about what happened to us?"

"Yeah. I miss us and everything that we did."

"I miss us too," she said, patting his back.

"I'm serious, Wendy," he said, his tone lowering with disappointment. "I really care about you, and it was wrong for me to abandon you like I did. I just got caught up feeling wanted, but it wasn't worth it."

They observed the butterfly as it took flight to explore again. With a pinch, Wendy's hand grasped the top of his shoulder, making the leather on his letterman's jacket crunch. Her mouth stayed still as she acknowledged Zachariah's twitch, trying to not show any indication of how she really felt.

"It's okay, dude," Wendy said, cocking a quivering smirk. "I still care about you, too. I think about you every day and what could've been."

Their eyes met, innocent and filled with tears, their pupils trembling with emotion. Opening up to Wendy lightened Zachariah's burden of sorrow and regret. He reached out his hand to her shaky fingers as she held back her feelings of abandonment and isolation. To avoid adding to his shame, she refrained from telling him the truth. Since they were still friends, now wasn't the moment to confront him. Her upper lip pressed against her teeth as she bit down.

"I-I should get going," she interrupted, quickly returning to the trail. "I have some work to do."

"Yeah, I should go, too," he agreed, following her. "I should shower to wake up. Can I walk with you?"

Wendy found herself cornered. It was fair for him to join her on the trail since she didn't own it. Her key priority for the day was to stay focused on her morning strolls and remember the ultimate objective. She could only nod her head to avoid hurting his feelings.

They set off on foot to cover the last mile and reach the parking lot. Huddled together, Zachariah's closeness made Wendy uneasy as they neared the edge. Her ankles wobbled on the uneven, chipped blacktop, on the verge of slipping into the nearby gravel.

"And Wendy. Thank you for always being there for me. I wish people could see your kind and beautiful soul."

Witnessing his genuine warmth, Wendy's smile shifted from artificial to authentic, and her complexion exuded a radiant glow. Whenever he wasn't with his peers, she fought against the return of caring emotions. She leaned in, reaching her arm over his bicep and curling it around the middle of his shoulder blades, gesturing a warm embrace. Zachariah agreed to her expression of thanks by enveloping her shoulders with a similar wrap. Like a thick shield, his taller body protected her.

The two could only revel in the tranquil serendipity of their walk, savoring the refreshing air that energized them like an espresso. The peaceful sound of birds chirping created a harmonious melody for them. Zachariah provided genuine comfort to Wendy by clasping her arm. She nestled against his chest, experiencing the plush yet supportive texture reminiscent of a memory foam mattress. His soft kiss left a wet peck on her forehead. Time seemed to freeze as she eagerly waited for the moment they had anticipated since childhood. With nothing to hold her back, her worries momentarily disappeared, freeing her.

Wendy withdrew, uneasy as her shoulders tensed before leaving his comforting embrace. Memories of neglect caused him to experience remorse and cast a shadow over the joy. Despite her frequent attempts to forgive him for abandoning her, it would always come back. Healing takes time, but this wound required extra time despite the years that have passed.

"W-What are you doing?" she asked, retreating to the other side of the trail as they exited the woods.

"I'm sorry," he said, startled by her reaction. "I just got caught up in the moment."

"In the moment?" she asked, frustrated, a tiny breeze slapped her cheeks. "Saying a few kind phrases that are past due to make up for the years of ignoring me isn't going to just make my pain disappear."

"Pain?" he asked, feeling the sharp heartbreak. "I thought you said it was okay."

"I forgave you for the pain you've caused. That doesn't mean that I trust you the same way again."

"I said I was sorry. I don't know what else I can do."

It's easy for you to say that since you weren't the one hurt.

"That doesn't fix how I feel about you," she said before power-walking away from him, ignoring the sudden strain in her legs. "I have to go. I'll see you in class."

I know he's sorry, but there's something not right about this.

Zachariah walked respectfully, moving slower as he faced the consequences of his actions. Wendy checked on him, seeing Zachariah's face in his hand, tears streaming down. Grasping the strap of her messenger bag, a surge of exhilaration washed over her as her truth slipped away. With confidence, she made her way from the trail to the parking lot, where three police vehicles had their blue and red lights flashing on the side of the brown brick. Officers standing next to the doors questioned principal Stuart and Ms. Woods, their hands on their belts to showcase their handcuffs and gun. Tears streamed down Ms. Woods's face while her handkerchief fluttered like a flag in her hand.

"Wendy!" Ms. Woods yelled, waving it to gather her attention.

Wendy's sense of pride diminished as her gulp became more pronounced, making her hunch her shoulders, dreading the thought of being apprehended. As they stood, the policemen rested their hands on their belts, revealing their holsters containing handcuffs and handguns. Police always made her blood rush, even when she knows she's innocent. There's something about their authority that caused her heart to pound harder.

"Hey," Ms. Woods said cautiously as they joined within the last ten feet. "We need to talk."

"Am I in trouble?" Wendy asked, pinching her forearm as she gawked at the policemen.

"No, you're not in trouble."

"Then what is it? What's going on?"

"It's about your brother."

"W-What happened?" she asked, terrified as her heart sank.

"There was an accident."

"An accident?" she asked, tears building.

Zachariah's shadow cast a cool shade that provided relief from the sunlight when he caught up to her. The lights became brighter and made her unable to see. Yet another gust of wind slapped the leaves above her, carrying a profound sense of sadness.

"What's going on?" Zachariah asked, concerned.

"He's dead."

Wendy was at a loss for words and couldn't respond. Vibrations from the trembling in her hands traveled through her bones. With each passing second, the tears running down her cheeks caused a jabbing chill to spread across her neck. She crumpled to the ground as her knees gave way and her head grew faint. Surprised, Zachariah held her tight while trying to comfort her crying. Before her head landed on his lap, the sharp stubble on his chin brushed against her forehead, allowing her a view of the opposite side of the parking lot. Positioned next to a lamp post, a young woman dressed in black had her long black hair blowing in the wind.

Andrea.

Observing her old friend's grief over losing a sibling they loved deeply, Andrea couldn't help but wear a smirk of empathy, having been in the same situation before. Another gust of wind blew her hair, hiding the sorrowful glaze in her eyes. Wendy understands the experience of losing something she cherished with no control or warning.

Chapter 11

Her legs tingled as blood circulation was reduced, sitting in the empty, white room on a wooden chair. Tears pooled on the worn table as she grieved her brother's departure. While the sheriff made the call to her parents in the adjacent room, questioning the sequence of events before their son's demise, an eerie silence echoed in her ears.

How could this happen?

An officer entered through the door, holding a white Styrofoam cup. Inside, the cola beverage produced a hiss as a brown fizz bubbled over the top like a hurdle.

"How're you doing?" asked the officer, balancing the contents from tipping from the top.

In silence, Wendy sniffled and swallowed her runny mucus. Bloodshot eyes resulted from the countless hours of heartbreak she endured. The closer she got to her locker to switch out her belongings and turn in her assignments, the students' intense stares hindered the ability to be at ease when approaching her and carrying on the conversation. The weight of her emotions transformed an ordinary long day into an overwhelming amount of work.

"Your parents are trying to get back from their business trip in the Netherlands as fast as they can, but they're dealing with some nasty weather. They recommend that you stay with Penny for the night. I took the liberty of calling Mrs. Hershey."

Wendy's heart shattered once more, haunted by her mother's desperate weeping from across the ocean. She could only imagine the turmoil they're experiencing while waiting at the terminal for the storms to settle. They didn't deserve this; she didn't deserve this; nobody deserved this.

"Okay," she responded solemnly.

Wendy watched as the bubbles in the cup floated toward the surface after the officer slid it closer to her. Seeing her reflection was a challenge; the only thing worse than before were the pronounced bags under her eyes, worse than they were this morning.

"Is there anything that would've caused this accident?"

If I knew, I would've told you hours ago!

"I-I don't know."

"He wasn't suicidal or anything?"

How could you ask that? He would never!

"No."

"You don't see any reason why he would allow himself to get decapitated by the ongoing train?"

"No!" she yelled, her throat scratching fiercely.

"I just want to gather all the facts," the officer said, remaining calm.

"I understand." Her tone lowered back to normal, her fingers tapping on the top of the table. "Malakai came home last night, and we had a good time catching up before going to the vigil. He seemed like his normal self."

The officer nodded, understanding and sharing Wendy's grief. Scratching sounds filled the air as he used his pen to document his observations on the small notepad. Disappointed, he sighed heavily as he realized there were no answers to be found for the tragedy.

"Okay, you're free to go. Your parents wanted me to see if you're okay with staying at your friend's tonight. They feel bad about leaving you alone, but they're trying their best to come back. They're not taking all of this too well."

I'm struggling too!

"Sure."

The heaviness of her tensed muscles made it a challenge for her to get up from her chair. Her lack of appetite persisted throughout the day, and now she's experiencing the consequences of running on empty. The walls of the small interrogation room reverberated with the sound of scuffling shoes. Her trembling hand sensed a faint chill as it held the cold doorknob.

"Oh, Ms. Benson?" he said.

What now?

"Yes?"

"You don't happen to know anything about your brother's group of friends he hung out with, do you?"

"No," she answered coldly, raspy. "I don't."

The officer's thick mustache inched toward his nose as he displayed a tight smile. Wendy, consumed by sadness, exited the room before the officer could ask any further questions.

The cacophony of ringing phones and overlapping conversations as the staff delved into the sudden uproar of trouble in the once-quaint town overwhelmed Wendy. Her thoughts scattered as she scanned the room, searching for the nearest way out. Clutching her chest, she longed for silence and a breath of fresh air as her lungs tightened. With a queasy stomach, she sprinted to the closest restroom, seeking a moment of peace.

Wendy's sneakers creaked with each careful step she took toward the row of porcelain sinks, breaking the silence that was needed. Despite the pungent smell of urine and old cleaner, it didn't faze her. She wasted no time and dropped her backpack onto the floor, turning on the faucet and holding her palm underneath. She enjoyed the refreshing chill of the water as she took a couple of sips before splashing some on her clammy face. Her shirt collar soaked as she absorbed the harsh truth of her departed sibling, tears and sweat blending with the cold water.

"*Wendy...*" a sharp whisper spoke.

Disregarding the commotion, she peered into the mirror, studying her profound sadness. Wrinkles formed on her face. Her flushed cheeks grew irritated as the tips of her wet hair touched them, prompting her to secure her locks in a messy bun at the back of her head.

"*Wendy...*" The whisper grew louder as it echoed in the silent room.

Surprised, she spun around and glanced at the pea-green bathroom stalls. The place was empty, with no one in sight. Everything was silent, serene.

"I-Is someone there?" she said, nervous. The room grew smaller from her heightening paranoia.

Crouching down, she scanned the floor in search of shoes in the stalls, hoping to find a person to accuse of the strange greeting. Crinkled toilet paper and dust bunnies adorned the scummy bases of the toilets. Not a human extremity in sight. Her temples throbbed faster, resembling the beat of a tiny drum. Her nervous, long breaths warmed her cold, wet face.

"*Are you still my friend?*" the voice asked eerily, accompanied by a young girl's giggle.

Grasping the strap of her backpack, she ran toward the door, fingers trembling. She groaned in fear and thrust the door open as she ran down the adjacent hallway toward the empty lobby and out the main door.

In an attempt to combat the brisk chill of the night breeze, she crossed her arms tight. The diner lights battled against burning out as they flickered on and off next door. The lively chirping of talkative crickets disrupted the quiet parking lot, leaving her on edge as she struggled to make out the voice emanating from the bathroom. She desperately sought solace under the next streetlight, but the voice's persistent question lingered in her mind.

Are you still my friend?

Her vision blurred as pain shot through the back of her head, accompanied by a growing voice. Approaching headlights blinded her, accompanied by the sound of a honking horn. The engine's loud roar distracted her from her inner turmoil.

"Get in!" a familiar womanly voice hollered at her.

She covered her eyes and attempted to figure out who was in the blue minivan that came to a stop in front of her. Two sets of blonde hair were just visible through the windshield, their brightness gradually increasing. Penny and her mother locked eyes, suppressing their sorrow. Wendy let out a sigh of relief before entering the back seat.

Thank God!

"Hey, Wendy," Penny said, full of sorrow as her friend buckled herself in. "I'm so sorry about Malakai. I can't believe this happened."

Neither can I.

The car picked up speed, moving through each block on its way back home. Parked cars flew past her with their speed; the streetlights came and went. All she could think about was the thought of what her brother was feeling when he was struck by the train. His anguish made her chin quiver.

"Honey, you're more than welcome to stay with us whenever you want," Caroline said, a glint of a teardrop reflected off the rear-view mirror.

"Thanks," Wendy responded quietly, trying to contain her sadness.

"We went ahead and picked up some of your things," Penny said, reaching behind her to place her hand on her friend's knee. "We can have ourselves a slumber party like the good ole' days!"

"Sure," she said, monotone, turning toward the window to distract herself from the passing houses.

Silence enveloped the vehicle, tension mounting and causing Caroline to chew on her lower lip. Tapping on the black leather steering wheel, her fingers made a rhythmic sound. The huffs of impatience became increasingly prominent.

"Perhaps a 'thank you' should be in order?" Penny's mother asked sharply, fishing for acknowledgment.

"Mom!" Penny said, distraught as she noticed Wendy not reacting to her mother's rudeness.

"What?" her mom asked without care, shrugging her shoulders. "The least she could do is thank us for taking her in for the night."

"Her brother just died! Could you be any more insensitive?!"

"Don't you start with me."

Penny sat back in her seat. With each breath, her anger expanded like a balloon, ready to burst into overstretched fragments. A sense of shame started to emerge as she sympathized with her best friend. Clenching her seatbelt, the only sound disrupting the prolonged silence was the crackling of her knuckles, as the car approached the end of its journey up the slight incline of the driveway. Wendy had no more energy left in her to acknowledge their drama. All she wanted to do was sleep.

The car parked in the open garage. It became turned off, just like the daughter of the selfish mother who thought nothing other than herself, even in the tragic moments of life. Moments like this were familiar to Penny. This time, it has gotten out of hand. This time, Mrs. Hershey had gone too far with her desire for attention.

Chapter 12

Penny's slammed door created a rumble that shook the room. The shelves trembled because of the teenager's anger, causing the paint cans to shake. Just as the ladies were about to enter their home, the fluorescent light flickered and blinded them. The worktable lost a basketball, which dribbled aimlessly in the open space.

"Easy there, Penny!" scolded her mother. "I don't want anything to happen to this car."

Penny hissed at her, apathetic to her demand.

"I have an image to maintain, remember?"

Oh, shit. This won't end well.

Wendy took Penny's backpack and duffel bag to the door while Penny bit her lip. Wendy had no desire to be part of their drama. Their frequent squabbles were entertaining, but only when observed from afar. Her attempts to break up their argument often led to a negative outcome for one or all of them. With her time already in shambles, she didn't want anyone to discourage her further.

"Wendy, can you give us a moment?" Penny asked. "I need to have a word with my mom."

One step ahead of you!

Wendy nodded and left, closing the door behind her, leaving the mother and daughter. The roles were reversed as Penny glared at her mother. As her mother crossed her arms, ready to assert dominance, her eyebrows furrowed toward the end of her eye socket. Yet, her mom's presence did not instill fear in her, not this time.

WENDY ASCENDED THE wooden stairs after walking past the immaculate living room. The glow from the modern ash-colored lampshades covered the lightbulbs, making the taupe walls shine, and the beige couch, loveseat, and eggplant accent pillows darker. As she reached the next flight, the wall was adorned with pictures of the family, capturing their genuine moments of joy. Upon reaching the next flight, a collage of candid moments greeted her, capturing her best friend's family in pure joy. The sight of Penny's happiness as her younger siblings buried her at the beach filled her heart with sadness. The image of Penny behind them at their elementary school graduation resembled the one of her and Malakai from the year before.

This was never happening again with her brother.

Loosening her grasp on the banister, she made her way down the hallway, moving past the unoccupied bedrooms of her twin brothers, untouched and anticipating occupancy. The polished porcelain in the white bathroom reflected sparkling light, illuminating the space.

Upon reaching Penny's room, she closed the door, leaving herself alone with the multitude of faces from magazine clippings and posters on the wall. Standing side by side, Serena and Venus Williams appeared in her favorite photograph, an old blown-out advertisement that rested next to the dresser. The white beads contrasted with their all-black tennis outfits, showcasing their muscular bodies and exuding confidence as accomplished athletes who embrace their success as tennis champions. With a fierce gaze, they stared into the camera, a thick, white milk mustache adorning their lips. The reminder of her sibling's love and closeness consumed Wendy with sadness, making everything, even tennis players, a reminder of that bond.

She discarded her tear-and-sweat-soaked t-shirt on the floor as she took it off. Bathed in light, her black bra gleamed while the scent of lavender oils filled her lungs and her muscles eased. She battled to suppress her emotions, overwhelmed by a profound sense of isolation, aside from the sight of Penny's well-worn brown teddy bear nestled among two striking blue pillows. As Wendy changed from her black, tight jeans into gray sweatpants, the last remaining black button eye kept a watchful eye on her.

TAP! TAP! TAP!

What the hell?

The rattling of the window next to the desk caught her off guard. Startled, she swiftly turned around, her messy bun causing strands of hair to fall onto her exposed back. She strained her eyes to make out a purple and orange letterman's jacket amidst the rustling leaves, despite the glare of the light. With her shirt shielding her breasts, she inched nearer to witness the robust form of a young man seated on the thick tree limb, deftly managing his weight as he flashed a smile at the exposed woman.

"Zachariah?" Wendy asked, puzzled.

Fog accumulated on the glass of the window from her heavy breath. With a gradual movement, she opened the window and experienced a shiver down her back as a refreshing breeze caressed her exposed body, causing goosebumps to appear. The Michael Jordan t-shirt was revealed as Zachariah's open jacket fluttered during his balancing act.

"Hey, Wendy," he said, grasping the branch's base with his arm, attempting to appear effortless.

"What're you doing here?" she hissed, flabbergasted.

His eyes scanned her unclothed body before moving on. To control his growing desires, he clung to the branches. A baby twig snapped between his fingers with tiny fragments sprinkling onto the grass.

"I just wanted to check in on you. I was waiting for you at the station, but I saw you get into Mrs. Hershey's car," he answered, redirecting himself back to his intentions. "I'm sorry about your brother. I know how much he meant to you."

Wendy cracked a slight grin. Her mouth curled upwards, inching closer to her ears.

"He was a good friend and a great brother."

"He was," she agreed, raspy, as her throat grew thicker.

"H-How're you holding up?"

"Not too well to be honest," she said, teardrops forming on the bottoms of her eyelids; her lip quivered melancholy waves.

"I bet. I can only imagine how difficult it must be. If I lost one of my younger brothers, I would lose it," he said, his eyes watering with her depression becoming contagious.

"Yeah."

Their longing gazes met. In the moonlight, Zachariah's teeth glistened, revealing their straight and white perfection. Just like Wendy's mood, his warmth and ease had the same contagious effect. For a moment, her troubles became less of a weighted burden. There was a glimmer of hope that she could survive this storm unscathed.

"Well, if you need to talk, I'm always here for you."

The two fell back into silence, and her stomach twisted in knots, much like tied shoelaces. Warmth flooded her body as her heartbeats quickened again.

"Thanks. Maybe when I'm not naked, perhaps," she responded with sarcasm.

Zachariah chuckled, acknowledging her humor as he came close to losing his balance.

"God, I missed our laughs."

"Me too. I'm sorry about what happened earlier."

"Me too."

Yet another longing stare interrupted their conversation. Memories from her childhood flooded back as Wendy nibbled on her lower lip. It was before he left her, not at that exact moment. It was as though they had been transported back to sixth grade with the press of a reset button. The longing for innocent happiness was a feeling she deeply missed.

"I-I think you should go," she said. "If Penny or her mom catches you up here, they'll lose their shit."

"Yeah, you're right," he said, feeling a slight deflation at ending their conversation.

"Have a good night," she said, reaching for the window, bending her elbows to brace herself to shut it.

"Wait, one more thing!"

With the strengthening breeze came a growing chill, causing her smirk to disappear and annoyance to set in.

"I have something for you."

With a clenched fist, Zachariah withdrew his hand from his pocket and extended it toward her. Her palm felt a tickling sensation from the metal chain links as she inspected the nickel charm. With its beady eyes and tongue sticking out, a corgi sat straight, exuding innocence in its tiny form.

"You kept it?" she asked, surprised, clenching the jewelry close to her chest.

"Of course I did," he said with excitement accompanying his smile. "That was such a great day when we got the matching necklaces at the arcade."

"They came from a gumball machine," she corrected him, giggling.

"I don't care where we got it. I've looked at it every day ever since we got them."

The necklace slipped from her sweaty hand, causing her heartbeat to increase once again. The trembling of her fingers resulted in her dropping the shirt onto the floor. Her figure caught Zachariah's attention, causing his eyes to widen.

Dammit!

"I'll go now. Have a good night. I'll be thinking about you."

I'm sure you will!

With a subtle wink, he gripped the branch with both hands. With the finesse of a skilled gymnast, he swung his body to safely land on the ground while falling backward. Before closing the window, Wendy saw Zachariah one last time as he strolled away. She exhaled a gentle breath of air while resting against the window. He didn't need to make any extra effort to make her feel special. She giggled like an ecstatic schoolgirl receiving a note from her crush. The security momentarily pushed aside her sorrowful nerves and became more alert, as if she had consumed a cup of black Colombian coffee. Heading back to the bed, she continued changing into her pajamas, prepared to try and conclude her eventful day on a positive note, pausing for a last glimpse at the corgi. Verklempt, her tears started soaking the pillow as she tried to distract her grief with the memory.

LIKE TINY HAILSTONES, Caroline's pristine white sneakers tapped restlessly on the cement floor. Penny stood with defiance, placing her hands on her hips in response to her mother's insulting remarks. With a heated flush on her face, she unzipped her hoodie and watched as the sequins fell to the floor.

"What the hell was that?" Penny asked, throwing her hands in the air.

"I don't see the problem here," her mother answered blankly, picking up the wandering basketball.

Caroline pressed the button on her remote. The garage door began to shut, and she looked outside, praying that no one witnessed their intensifying confrontation.

"Her brother just died! How can you not see the problem here?!"

"Don't you use that tone with me!" Caroline hissed, her finger pointing fiercely at Penny.

Penny blinked her eyes furiously; her eyelashes bounced up and down.

"I just don't appreciate her lack of gratitude."

"Can't you think for a second that she has other things on her mind than to say, 'thank you'?" Penny asked.

"She's shown no appreciation for anything I've done," Mrs. Hershey continued, hiking the strap of her purse over her shoulder.

The door stopped at its resting place. The cement walls echoed with the heavy breaths of the women. As Caroline placed the ball back on the table, the paint cans started trembling. A wooden dowel rolled off the edge and onto the floor.

"Like what? For not giving a shit about your stupid show? Do you think that anybody who doesn't like your show is an enemy?"

"Watch your language!" Caroline yelled, stomping her foot. "And my show is not stupid. It's my career!"

"Oh, please. That show is the only thing you think about. Dad left us and took Hayden and Harper with him. You got fired from a decent job because you were so distracted with creating content, and now you work part time for a customer service hotline."

"You will sound so foolish when my show becomes a hit," Caroline defended, dismissing Penny's facts.

"And when will that be?" Penny asked, walking closer to the door. "You've already been doing this for five years and only have a small following. You even forgot my birthday two years in a row, so you can keep filming!"

"Don't you criticize my parenting! I'm trying to provide a better life for you," Caroline interjected, the light reflecting off the polish of her manicured nail as it pointed to her daughter.

"A better life for me or for you?"

"This is not fair!"

"No wonder Hayden and Harper chose to live with Dad. I would've left too if I didn't have my life here."

Caroline went silent, sensing the piercing heartbreak from her daughter's confession. Tears formed as she bit her lip. She secured the purse beneath her arm, gripping it tight.

"Come on, let's go downstairs to the studio and talk this out," she proclaimed, desperate to get through to Penny. "I love you so much. I would do anything for you, even if this means cutting back on my show. Please, just give me a chance to be the mother you hoped I would be."

Penny's fury came to a temporary halt as she pondered the authenticity of her mother's compassion. A gentle smirk played on her face as she stared into her mother's piercing blue eyes, searching for the profound connection they had lost.

In the desire to hug her little girl, Caroline stretched out with open arms. Wrapping her arms around Penny, she brought her head down to rest on her shoulder. Penny embraced her mother and ran her hands over her back. The texture of her frosty blonde hair was thick between her fingers. Her mother's sincerity tugged Penny's heartstrings, resulting in guilt over her outburst. Her mother kissed the cheek of her embarrassed child, pecking the top of her glossy lips onto her face.

"I'm sorry, Mom," Penny said.

"Me too," she agreed, letting out a sigh of relief. "Now, let's go downstairs to the studio. This would make a great episode to discuss our relationship as we work on my bracelets."

The sting of her mother's selfishness felt like a dagger in Penny's heart, causing her to withdraw. Filled with repulsion, her stomach writhed like a roller coaster, desperate to eject vomit onto the floor. She wiped away the tear that was forming, causing a small spot to appear between her feet.

"As soon as I graduate, I'm out of here. I don't want to see you ever again."

Penny slammed the door behind her, inviting devastation to creep inside her mother. With each stomp, she made her way up the wooden staircase, causing the family portraits on the wall to tremble as the frames swung like tiny pendulums. With a forceful slam, Penny closed the bathroom door and then collapsed onto the toilet. She broke down, running her fingers through strands of hair. Grief consumed her like a looming storm cloud, reminding her of the loss of someone she had once loved, similar to the dear friend she held close, unlike her mother.

TEARS STREAMED DOWN Caroline's chin, causing the cement floor to grow damp. Her bun looked messy, like a drunk sorority sister, with strands sticking out everywhere. Upon grabbing her tartan Louis Vuitton bag, she proceeded to enter her home. She then made her way to the kitchen, where she stored her wine rack in the closet pantry. With ease, she pulled the cork out of her preferred bottle of Chablis. As she poured the blood-red alcohol into her glass, she fixated on the gradual rise of the liquid. She moved towards the basement door next to the entrance of the dining room while swirling the contents.

With caution, she descended the wooden staircase covered in sand-colored carpet, engrossed in her phone, eagerly awaiting new subscribers on her eLookBook profile. On her notification tabs, she saw that only one "like" appeared, followed by comments on her recent DIY video where she shared her household cleaner tutorial. The comments were critical, offering corrections and recommendations.

Vinegar is better if you want the best natural cleaner.

She snarled, curling her lip and hissing a disapproving comment, then took a big drink. Upon checking her follower list, she observed a decrease of twenty from three hundred.

Frustrated, she tapped the glass on her makeshift marble counter, burying her face in her hands and pulling out more strands of hair from her bun. In her half-finished basement, she created a studio that resembled a modern kitchen. Downstairs, the only items that looked well-maintained were the all-white countertops, black counter space, and a collection of fruits and small appliances. The artificial window displayed a sunny backyard with lush green grass and a radiant yellow sun in a clear sky. As she took another sip from her glass, she reflected on the early days of her show and the strong connection she had with her daughter, recalling the nurturing of her career.

FIVE YEARS AGO, CAROLINE watched her twin boys playing with their father from the clay-colored back deck while sipping from her pastel-pink kitty mug. With a fit build, the man flexed his arm, revealing his bulky biceps, as his black fire department t-shirt hugged his figure, highlighting every contour. His shoulder blades were enormous; the six-pack was ready to be drunk. While waiting for his

turn, Harper adjusted his cap and punched his glove before throwing the baseball to Hayden. Hayden focused on the ball that flew closer to him; the sphere's reflection dilated the pupils of his forest-green eyes.

Joy increased with each toss; happiness radiated from the boys' bond as the coffee continued flowing down Caroline's throat. With a longing in her eyes, she desired the same special bond with her daughter that her husband had with their boys. From the kitchen window, her gaze fell upon the dining room, where Penny and her friend were sitting in an elegant wooden chair.

"Honey," she said, trying to grab her husband's attention. "Are you ready to help me with my next segment?"

Dropping the baseball onto the freshly cut grass, her husband paused his playtime. He rolled his eyes and raised his hands, mirroring the actions of an irritated teenager.

"Can't you see that the boys and I are in the middle of something?" he asked, displeased.

"But you promised, Matthew!" she whined, slamming her mug onto the railing.

"I did, but I missed hanging out with the kids. I've been working extra hours in the department. Plus, the electric bill has gotten much worse, and I've had to take up a job at the hardware store just to pay for it."

She positioned her angular eyebrow closer to her hairline and rested her arms on her sides, giving the impression of a child on the brink of a tantrum. He closed the distance between himself and his wife, joining her at the barrier. Frustration and dismissal became evident in their exchanged expressions.

"Look, I've worked with you on your show after work for the past year. I haven't been with the kids for a long time since they've been in school. I will get to you later."

"You know we have a deadline," she hissed, leaning closer to him. "I must post my content every Wednesday. This can't wait!"

"Seriously?" Matthew asked, disgusted. "I have helped you every morning when the kids go off to school, late at night, during breaks at work, and even skipping dinner as you order takeout for them to eat without us. We need to be there for our kids."

She pursed her lips. Nothing was getting through to her husband; there were no tactics. The raised eyebrow couldn't convince him and withholding herself wouldn't do since she hasn't since she started the show.

"The answer is no," he said.

"You're pathetic."

"And you've changed since I first met you; I don't even know who you are anymore," he said, repulsed. "You are unbelievable! If there is anybody pathetic in this house, it's you."

After storming away from his wife, he went back to get the glove and ball to continue bonding with his boys. Suppressing the tears, Caroline snarled at him. Aware of the impending collapse of her marriage, she felt helpless. By grabbing her kitten mug and marching back inside, she ignored his plea. Penny filled the kitchen with joyful giggles as she had a deep conversation with her friend, while the soft scratching of scribbles added to the ambiance.

"I'm so happy that it's summer!" Penny said, smiling as she switched her indigo pencil to sea-foam.

"Me too," said her friend, placing the utensil on the table. "If I had to deal with Veronica's crap for another day, I would have to punch her."

"She sucks!"

"I don't know what everyone sees in her," the girl resumed, brushing the pencil shavings onto the hardwood floor. "She's cruel to everyone and dumb as crap."

"Her boobs came in early," Penny answered, rolling her eyes. "The minute those puppies came right in, she had to show them off with the most revealing clothes. She even stood taller, arching her back to shove them in everyone's face."

"I could slip from the puddles of drool that fall from these moron's mouths as they oodle over her."

Caroline set her mug on the countertop before reaching for the pot to add more to her beverage. Observing through the window again, she saw her husband's delight as they wrestled for the ball, laughing while it slipped from their hands. The brightness of his pearly-white teeth matched the radiance of his love for his kids. She longed for the moments when he would experience incredible delight, so overjoyed. The person she shared a bed with was unrecognizable.

She brushed them off and focused on Penny, holding her warm cup tenderly. Steam dampened the top of her forehead.

"Sweetie, can I ask you for a favor?"

Caroline flashed an awkward smile as the two girls stopped what they were doing and turned to her. As she nibbled on her lip, a small crevasse appeared around her mouth.

"Could you help me with my show today?" she asked, hands trembling, causing her coffee to ripple close to the rim.

"I'm in the middle of something, Mom," Penny said, dumbstruck, as she signaled to the table with papers and colored pencils and the company of her guest.

"Oh, you two can hang out later. I could really use your help right now."

"I'm sorry, but Nora and I are hanging out."

In her frustration, she exhaled sharply through her nose, causing a small sound that shattered the awkward silence in the room while her hands tightened around the mug. Her complexion turned a warmer shade of pink, resembling a light sun-kiss.

"Fine," she said, short. "Well, then you need to clean all of this shit off the table."

"What?"

"You heard me. This is an antique dining set, and I don't want any scribbles messing up this beautiful piece."

"We are not making a mess!" Penny argued, acknowledging their controlled chaos.

Caroline found amusement in Nora's resignation, watching her head lowering in defeat. Her eyes had no desire to make contact with Caroline's. If it wasn't for Penny's father, she wouldn't even be allowed to hang out at the house at all because Caroline didn't want to associate herself with Nora's awkward personality.

"Look at all of this crap," she said, picking up the finished pieces of Nora's beautiful work. "This is garbage, and you need to do something more with your free time."

"My work is not garbage," Nora said, rising from her chair. "This is my art, and I'm going to make something out of it some day!"

With a lion-like intensity, Caroline locked eyes with Nora, ready to strike. Nora trembled, trying to remain brave. She stared the adult down, fingers fidgeting with her need to stand up for her passions.

"Oh, really," she said, inching closer to Nora; their noses were centimeters away from touching.

Without uttering a word, Nora stood frozen in fear as a loud gulp resonated through the silence.

Caroline set the sketches down, gathering them near Nora's spot at the table. Reaching her arm out, she slowly tilted the mug of coffee. Contents emptied on the sheets of paper, drowning out the bright hues into shades of brown. As the child cringed in despair at her ruined work, Caroline glared at Nora with a sense of satisfaction.

Nora broke out into a rapid stream of tears. As the colors faded into stains, she attempted to salvage her crumbling work. Pieces of paper broke apart into chunks of slushy wads. As she collected the colored pencils, Caroline's nails appeared to elongate into wicked claws, her teeth grinding together as she locked eyes with the heartbroken girl who sobbed over her loss.

"This is not art!" Caroline said coldly.

With force, she threw the handfuls of colored pencils onto the floor, causing taps to reverberate in the room. Without bothering to close the door, Nora ran out of the house, her head in her hands. Penny's shoulders drew closer to her ears in tension, locked in a state of intimidation and disgust. Her nostrils flared as she fought back angry tears. Caroline elegantly moved towards the door, keeping her eyes on Nora as she faded into the distance, satisfied, and then closed it.

"You're going to help me today, understand?"

Stricken with fear, Penny gulped heavily. With no other choice, she nodded in acknowledgment of her mother's demand. A tan waterfall of coffee pooled on the floor, drenching her bare feet that curled to combat the warmth that was becoming too much to handle.

"I'll meet you downstairs." She strutted toward the basement door. "Clean this shit up first. After we're done, you're going to re-polish the table. We must maintain our image, after all. And change into that sequin jumpsuit I bought you. Sparkles bring life into our brand!"

The door closed with force, leaving her daughter alone and filled with fear. With her mother's departure, Penny found relief and allowed herself to cry, releasing the fear she had been holding onto. With a lack of enthusiasm, she walked to the kitchen and took the paper towels and garbage bin. The towels absorbed the coffee puddle as she placed a generous pile of sheets on the table. She guided the soggy disaster into the trash bin, observing Nora's labor fade away as their friendship did.

DOWNING THE REST OF her wine, Caroline attempted to bury the memory of Penny's pain. The floor shifted from fake tiling to bare cement as she made her way to her equipment. By activating two spotlights that were plugged into an electric generator, Caroline bathed the set in a hospital-like fluorescent light before placing her empty glass on a small table. She activated the last circular light to illuminate her face, placing her smartphone on the stand. As she switched on her camera, she quickly returned to her station while the video played. She opened the drawer to find her lucky hot-pink scrunchie. In the midst of the utensil chaos, her accessory remained elusive.

"What the hell?" she whispered, frustrated, slamming the drawer shut with an accompanying sigh. "I always leave it here."

Her hair fell to her shoulders as her remaining bun came undone. She restored her calm and took a deep breath to regain her composure. As she wiped the tears from her face, she smudged her eyeliner, giving her a messier appearance than she typically maintains.

"Good morning, Mama Hershey here!" she said; her enthusiasm was tense and unconvincing. "I hope you're ready for a fun activity! We are going to make matching beaded bracelets for you and your daughters. Nothing is more special than a bond between a mother and their daughter."

She paused; her throat became thicker. The memory of slamming doors reverberated in her thoughts, a constant playback of the times Penny walked away from her, unable to tolerate her actions. Without a solution, her mind stayed blank on how to reconcile with herself and her children.

"We guide them through their lives, discussing life changes and menstruation. We comfort them during their tough moments, either in breakups or figuring out what they want from life. We help them pick their prom dresses and maybe even a wedding dress for their special days."

With another pause, she lowered her head to observe the countertop, realizing that she had completed none of the actions listed in her script. Holding back her emotions, she inhaled some loose mucus.

"Today, we're going to show our love for them!"

To get a large glass punch bowl, she reached beneath the counter. A massive heap of round plastic beads of various sizes and colors filled the interior. After placing the bowl down with care, she retrieved a hefty spool of twine and a pair of black shears.

"This project will be so easy and rewarding. All you'll need is beads, thread, and some scissors. As you create your daughter's bracelet, think back to memories that you could emulate into your bead selection. Decorating them with their favorite color will make it even more special!"

Not knowing Penny's favorite color, she bit her lower lip, saddened. Blue? Purple? She didn't know what her favorite food was or her favorite movie. She knew nothing about her. Before she could continue, the wine glass fell from the table across from her, shattering into pieces.

"Shit!" she whispered, aggravated.

Walking across the studio, the spotlights blinded her. The room became nothing as it drowned out the brightness. The sound of crunching grew louder as her sneakers made contact with the small fragments. With an eye roll, she crouched down to pick up the fragments cautiously. The gradual roll of an object accompanied the sound of glass pieces clinking together in her hand. Struggling to see in the darkness, she noticed nothing unusual except for the pile of totes and boxes by the walls. A crimson-red colored pencil rolled from the other side, pausing as she tapped her feet.

"What the hell?" she asked as she picked it up, dropping the glass shards back onto the tiles.

Once the shards landed on the floor, a group of colored pencils began rolling toward her. Overwhelmed with confusion, her heart raced as she watched the vibrant spectrum of the rainbow shimmer in the remaining light.

THUMP!

Startled by the noise, Caroline turned to the counter and discovered the spool of thread had fallen onto the floor. A black-clad figure stood where she once was, documenting her episode. The oversized hood shrouded their face in darkness. Even the spotlight couldn't illuminate it.

"Penny, is that you?" Caroline asked, shading her hand over her eyes, trying to see who it was.

The figure said nothing, did nothing. Each angry huff caused the cloak to rise and shrink while doing nothing else.

"Okay, enough of this," Caroline hissed, rolling her eyes. "Come and help me clean this up."

The figure didn't listen. It remained at the same spot, caressing its hands over the marble countertop. Its black gloves danced upon the punchbowl's brim like fingers tickling a piano's keys.

"What are you doing?"

The hands lifted the punchbowl. Beads spilled out of the brim, tumbling onto the counter as the edge tilted. A colorful pile of beads cascaded onto the floor, moving closer to her feet. Shocked, her eyebrows drew down towards her eyes as she observed her show being ruined by the plastic assault.

"Now you've pissed me off!" she huffed, pointing furiously at the figure.

She took a step to get closer to scold the uninvited guest. Her shoe's sole became uneven when she stepped on colored pencils, resulting in stumbling. As she struggled to stay steady, her muscles cramped, preventing her from hitting the floor. Her hands flailed like she was trying to prevent herself from slipping on an icy sidewalk as the mix of pencils and beads made each step worse. As she stumbled, her neck jerked back like she had slipped on a banana peel, causing her to crash onto the broken glass. As the glass pierced her back, she emitted a groaning shriek. Gasping for air, she extracted the largest crescent-shaped fragment from her lower back, grimacing at the sharp three-inch-deep ache. The sweat mingled with the accumulating blood on the tiles. The spotlights dimmed as the cloaked figure watched her struggle.

"W-hy?" she asked, terrified, coughing a wad of light-pink saliva.

The figure revealed the black shears, clasped in its hand as it was removed from behind its back. The figure's closer approach caused Caroline's eyes to widen, and she frantically crawled backward, shards piercing her hands and fingertips once again. Like ripping off a Band-Aid, the figure lodged the shears right above her navel. In agony, she cried out and collapsed to the floor, overwhelmed by sharp pain. A growing splotch of blood on her long white and black sleeve shirt made its way towards her chest. She was helpless, her gaze fixed on the spotlight that expanded with every labored breath. Blood seeped from the edges of her mouth, she struggled to breathe as it filled her windpipe.

With a shove from the figure, the bulb grew brighter and moved closer to her head. Glass shattered onto her forehead, cutting into her skull. Emitting a loud groan, the electrical shocks surged through her bones, causing incessant agony. As her muscles tightened, she clenched her teeth, crushing her molars together. Her lifeless body slumped onto the puddle of blood, glass, pencils, and beads. Her head, blackened and scorched, released smoke that carried the revolting aroma of overcooked rotten meat. The figure walked away from the host, stopping by the perched phone, ending the recording, ending her life, and canceling her show.

Chapter 13

As the sun ascended above the horizon, it roused the two girls in Penny's queen-sized bed. As Wendy stretched her arms and legs, her muscles trembled like shockwaves pulsating through her tendons. With an enormous yawn from her diaphragm, her jaw descended toward her chest. In her sluggish state, Penny moved her pillow to get some extra time to snooze, not wanting to confront another day under her mother's care.

Wendy's knuckle brushed against the glass of water, teetering it on the edge as she snatched her phone from the bedside table. Unlocking her home screen was as simple as typing in her six-digit passcode. Wendy turned off her alarms to avoid being startled by the annoying reminders, especially after seeing the heartbreaking picture of her and Malakai at Christmas as her wallpaper. Checking her eLookBook to pass the time, she scrolled through her newsfeed of grievances from the community of her followers' posts.

He was so loved.

To satisfy her sudden parching thirst, she drank from the glass. After spending fifteen minutes reading touching posts from her classmates paying tribute to her deceased brother, she came across a post that seemed different from the rest.

"A year ago today, I lost my sister. Nora was full of life and ambition and chased after dreams. She didn't get enough praise for her talents, sharing the beauty of her experiences while finding light in the darkness surrounding her. With all the losses that our town has experienced over the past few days, I find it saddening that nobody batted an eye at Nora's death as much as they have for others. She never caused trouble

or offended anybody. And yet, our community forgave those who caused trouble and considered them innocent and better than those who never stood out by choosing to be more of a normal person. Don't get me wrong, I feel bad for the lives that were lost and for the fact that their lives were taken from them too soon. People close to them won't get to see them thrive as human beings. But Nora was also someone's daughter, sister, friend, and mentor. I wish people could see how beautiful of a person she was, just like the others. Rest easy, sis. I miss you so much, and you are loved."

The photo below the post shows Andrea hugging Nora from behind in an old Polaroid. The image had a gritty quality and depicted them exploring a small meadow with a solitary tree on a patch of land resembling an island. They smiled with love, and their missing baby teeth gaps gleamed with pride. The post received only twelve likes and people left apologetic comments. One post caught attention amidst all the sympathetic messages.

"Way to disrespect the dead! Nora wasn't in any sports or contributing to the community. She kept to herself and only worked on her stupid art projects! Good riddance!" Read one comment.

"She wasn't even that good!" Read another.

Disgusted, Wendy looked at the profile that posted the comment. A grayed-out bubbly figure showed the absence of a profile picture. All that showed was the username "WarriorTree22." When she accessed the profile, she discovered no details about the unknown perpetrator. No educational background, no hobbies, no pictures, no idea.

Why does it even matter? She's gone and meant something to people, Wendy thought.

Penny woke soon after. Wendy reflected on the post, extending her arms before getting up from the bed. In a tired state, she walked over to her dresser, took her toothbrush, and headed toward the bathroom. Wendy followed her friend after placing her phone on the end table, observing as her friend applied toothpaste to the bristles.

"Morning," Wendy greeted over the slight rush of water from the faucet.

"Morning," she muttered as the toothbrush rubbed against the inside of her cheek.

"Is everything all right?" she asked, taking a whiff of the heavy peppermint. "You have said nothing since last night."

Penny ignored her, spitting a wad of white, foamy saliva into the top of the drain.

"What was it you and your mom talked about?"

"Nothing," she said, running her brush under the water for the second cleaning round.

"It doesn't seem like nothing."

Staring at her friend like she was playing with fire, Penny glared at her with annoyance.

"My mom and I had a fight."

"About what?"

"It was nothing," she dismissed. "Just another one of my mom's stupid antics. She just doesn't get how much she hurts people."

"I know she means well," Wendy defended, apprehensive because she was right, but it wasn't her place to judge. "After all, she is your mom, and she's only doing what's best for you."

Penny rolled her eyes as she flicked the water off her brush and turned off the sink.

"You don't know my mom like I do," she hissed, walking past her back to her room.

"You're right. But she's put a roof over your head, clothes on your back, and food on the table."

"My dad paid for the house, and his child support payments did everything else. If it weren't for my dad being drained of money, we wouldn't be living here. She only cares about her show and her image."

Wendy remained silent, taking in her perspective. By poking into the edge of her gums, the bristles eradicated the plaque from the previous night.

"We never hung out unless it was to benefit her show. She doesn't know what I like or hate, and I can't recall a decent memory where she isn't making it about her. She can burn once I go to college."

While preparing for her shower, Penny didn't give Wendy an opportunity to speak as she headed to her dresser to get her clothing. Lavender garments stacked together, showcasing a variety of shades. Giving her friend space, Wendy ceased conversing further and got ready herself. She knew that Mrs. Hershey was different compared to her own parents, she just didn't know the extreme of Penny being treated as an accessory rather than blood. Wendy became dumbstruck that Penny was good at hiding her feelings, just like her mother.

WENDY WALKED THROUGH the main doorways of the school and noticed her classmates giving her sorrowful and anxious looks as they rummaged through their lockers. Penny dispersed away from her, allowing space for her depression. Whispers of her brother made her feel like her mission of flying under the radar had been foiled. Everybody at her school knew about her. She sank into her shoulders; the girls on the softball team acknowledged her presence with a kneeling bow, paying their respects.

Is that necessary?

With each step towards her locker, her unease intensified, resembling a deep-sea diver descending into an unknown abyss. Penny snarled at Mr. Turlington, who was talking with the girls' track and field team, encouraging them for the last meet tonight, while their curves captivated his attention as they jumped and cheered with excitement. He placed his hands back into his pockets, his clenched fists that moved closer to the inside of his zipper.

Two girls in short jean skirts and pastel tank tops came out of the girl's restroom. As they came closer to Wendy, their hair, both brunette and red, bounced. Two football players in the chemistry lab doorway let out a whistle and flexed their biceps to impress. The attention that interrupted their confident walk caused Destiny and Maxine to roll their eyes and smirk. Wendy discreetly made her way to her locker, using the open door to protect herself from their curiosity.

"Hey, Wendy," the two girls said in unison.

"H-Hi Destiny," she said meekly, unzipping her bag. "Hi, Maxine."

"How're you doing?" Maxine asked, chewing her bubble gum loudly; the smacking of her lips made it hard for Wendy to focus.

"I'm fine," she answered, placing her textbooks into her locker, her biology binder teetering off the ledge of the steel shelf.

"We're so sorry about Malakai," Destiny said, placing her hand on Wendy's shoulder. "It must be horrible to lose a brother like that."

"And so young," Maxine piped in.

"It is," Wendy agreed, exchanging her chemistry for her Advanced Algebra textbook. "I have to go. Thanks for checking on me."

"Wait!" Destiny said, halting her by softly grabbing Wendy's arm.

Wendy cradled her books against her chest, releasing an annoyed exhale through her nose. Streaks of sweat glazed the top of her equipment from her palms. Her fingers trembled to cope with holding back the urge to reject any attempts in confiding.

"We were wondering if you would like to go with us to the graduation party tomorrow night?" Destiny said, her straight-white teeth beaming warm-heartedly.

"I-I don't know," she said, reluctant. "I don't feel like being around people I don't know."

"But this is a party for just us seniors," Maxine said. "It'll be our last hoorah before we go our separate ways."

"With all due respect, you guys never invited me to do anything with you."

"Yeah, you're right," Destiny agreed, looking at Maxine for support. "Ever since Veronica's disappearance, we felt like we were unfair to many people. We want to make it up to you and end the senior year on a high note."

Standing at the end of the hall behind the girls was a young woman, her ripped skinny jeans exposing the skin of her legs as she placed one foot on the locker behind her. Resting upon her tight, V-neck emerald-green shirt was her long, black, blown-out hair. As she stared at the trio, she raised her impeccably groomed eyebrow closer to her hairline while pursing her glossy lips.

"What about Ellie?" Wendy asked, uncomfortable from the peer's glare. "I thought you were close with her?"

Maxine popped a giant pink bubble from her mouth, hissing with angst. Her eyes rolled like a marble. The strap of her purse was wrinkled from her firm grip.

"She doesn't want to be friends with us anymore," Maxine said, moving her lips to gather the remnants of her chewy candy back into her mouth. "Right before the night of Veronica's disappearance, she just distanced herself from us."

"It was like we were the plague or something!" Destiny added.

"Right," Wendy said, checking Ellie out again, observing the resistance she guarded herself with from a boy trying to converse with her. "Well, I'll think about it. How does that sound?"

"Sure," the two acknowledged, both shaking their heads.

"Great. See ya."

Wendy's hair trailed behind her as she strolled between the two girls. Feeling remorse washed over them as their guest disappeared among the students.

"Wendy!" Destiny said abruptly. "We really are sorry."

Wendy's smile tightened, creating wrinkles on her chin as she brushed off the conversation and hurried to class. Their attempt to mend fences brought defeat to Destiny as Wendy faded towards the staircase, watched by both her and Maxine. They couldn't escape isolation after allowing someone to make decisions that harmed their social life. Even though Veronica was no longer present, Destiny and Maxine now had to face the repercussions of their queen bee's behavior.

Their former friend, the one who escaped prior to Veronica's disappearance, witnessed Destiny and Maxine's facade from a different perspective. It seemed as if she had broken free from a cult, observing the rest of the members getting sick from the Kool Aid, and not because it was cherry flavored. With her hair bouncing, Ellie strode behind Wendy, chuckling with pity at the two lonely girls fading away in their invisible existence within their teenage society.

WHEN WENDY AND ELLIE entered the classroom, the rustling chatter of students stopped as they were greeted with nervous stares. They alternated between observing Wendy's sadness and gazing at the wall of math equations on the other side of the room. Wendy held her position with tension, permitting Ellie to walk in front of her. The black-haired beauty turned to her, shining a pleased smile. Although Ellie may have been included in the group, she had evolved her personality into a more relaxed and hospitable one. With a gentle nod, Ellie motioned for the person to join her in the back seat. Wendy joined her and placed her materials on the scratched surface of her desk.

"Hey, Wendy," a squeaky voice said, startling her.

She turned to her classmate, acknowledging the shorter girl. Her thick, black glasses fogged up as she huffed from her asthmatic breath, releasing a musty garlic odor from her teeth covered in braces. The window allowed the sunlight to highlight her glistening acne.

"Hi, Astrid," she whispered. "How're you?"

"Tired," Astrid sighed, her greasy, sandy-blonde hair falling to her freckled cheek. "I've been up late last night working on a paper."

"I thought you work ahead?" Wendy joked. "It's unlike you to be working at the last minute on homework."

"I know!" she agreed, her body sinking back into her chair. "I just wanted to make sure everything was perfect."

"Working hard until the very end of your high school career. You already got into college. Take it easy!"

"I will after I graduate."

The two laughed; Ellie rolled her eyes at their joy and scribbled into her notebook. Her fingers flicked a couple of strands of hair behind her ears.

"So sorry about your brother, by the way," said Astrid with a snort.

"Thanks," she said; the sincerity was more accepted than the others.

"If you want to hang out this summer before I go to the University of Chicago, just let me know."

"I'd like that," Wendy smiled, patting the back of Astrid's stained maroon sweatshirt.

"Cool," she said with escalating enthusiasm, like a dog about to wag its tail. "Oh, and are you going to the track meet tonight? Maybe we can hang together?"

"I don't know," she answered with reluctance. "I think I just want to keep to myself."

"I understand, but I got you if you need a friend."

"Thanks."

As Mr. Turlington walked toward his desk, Wendy nodded in agreement and began preparing for his lesson by opening her notebook. Two desks ahead of Wendy, Andrea stood up from her chair, snarling at Wendy while she made her way to the pencil sharpener. Every crank on the tool got more powerful along with her tilting head.

Engraved onto the surface of the wooden desk, there was a message above Wendy's wrist. Andrea's eyebrows furrowed with disbelief. The blue in her irises became darker as they filled with anger along with the flush of her skin straying away from pale. She couldn't help herself but to throw the pencil at Wendy's head.

"What the hell is that?!" she yelled at Wendy, her fury growing.

"What are you talking about, Andrea?" she asked, rubbing her head to ease the minor pain.

"That!" she said, turning pink. "What you scratched on the desk!"

Wendy's confusion grew as she observed the heart signs with couples' initials and the pencil-drawn equations, designed to aid in cheating during tests. In the top left corner, someone etched a message with aggressive scratches, reminiscent of a primal caveman's writing.

"NORA CRISPIN IS A PIECE OF SCUM!"

"I didn't write that!" Wendy defended, startled.

"Bullshit!" Andrea said, ignoring Wendy's confession. "Couldn't get enough sympathy from the loss of your piece of shit brother, so you put down Nora to make Malakai a better person?"

"What are you talking about?" Wendy said, rising from her chair, insulted.

"All right, let's settle down," said Mr. Turlington, rising from his chair, sighing with defeat to assert his authority.

"Yeah, chill out," Ellie said, defending Wendy. "She didn't do it!"

"She was talking with me!" Astrid piped in, coughing. "She didn't do it!"

"Look at all your friends standing up for you. Be careful, she may just abandon you like the cowardly bitch she is."

Steam rose from the pores of Wendy's head; she felt the rising fury blind her judgment. Inching closer to Andrea, she cracked her clenched knuckles and stood just an inch away, using the proximity to intimidate. They stared intensely at each other, like a scene from a western, waiting for someone to show a sign of weakness. A single tear formed in Andrea's blue eyes as she locked gazes with Wendy's pained expression.

"Your brother deserved to die," Andrea hissed coldly.

Without a second to block the insult, Wendy pounced upon Andrea. Their bodies collided with the wall because of her strong momentum. Wrestling amidst the fallen textbooks, they clung to each other's necks, gripping with their fingernails. Astrid moved with caution away from her seat, trying to steer clear of the aftermath of their assaults as she took a breath from her inhaler. Ellie leaped forward to separate the two, while Mr. Turlington shouted at them. Screams expelled from the three like rabid cats fighting for dominance, screeching into everyone's ears. Wendy resisted as Andrea's warm breath brushed against her sweaty face, struggling against Mr. Turlington's tight grip on her hands.

"That's enough!" the teacher roared like a Bengal tiger, scaring them as their distance grew.

The girls panted, trying to contain their breaths. Their hair appeared frizzy and disheveled, as if someone had electrocuted them. The pink marks caused by slaps and grasps were fading away from their skin. Their teacher's eyes expanded like enormous craters while his nostrils twisted in rage.

"Office, NOW!"

Chapter 14

As the clock struck three-thirty, students assembled in the corridors, relieved to have successfully completed another day. They swerved through groups like Black Friday shoppers. The touch of shoulders and elbows disrupted deep conversations as students shared the latest gossip with their closest allies in the survival game. Teachers were eager to get closer to the summer vacations they had worked so hard for, exhaling another sigh. They were becoming less and less tolerant of students texting or launching spitballs during the lesson.

Astrid's sneakers clapped on the floor; her lungs expelled a rattling breath as she reached for her inhaler. Despite the presence of predatory personalities, her attention stayed fixed on the minuscule pathway, avoiding any potential grief. With her arms crossed over her chest, she felt her textbooks glide against her sweater, creating a space between them and her ribcage. With utmost caution, she arranged her belongings in her locker, mimicking the precision and organization of a bookshelf in a majestic library. With her peers following, anticipating vulnerability to mock, she felt the room shrink around her. The growing shadows made her visibility fade and her shoulders tense.

"Astrid, is it?" asked a voice, tenor in tone.

"Yes, that's me," she answered, turning around with trepidation. "How's it going, Peter?"

"Fine."

The metal braces kept her alert as her tongue dabbed the top of her teeth.

"Can I help you with something?" she asked, hugging her textbook like a shield across her chest.

"I was just seeing how you're doing."

"I already answered. We haven't talked in years. You don't even remember my name."

"Really?" he asked, trying hard to remember. "It's Angie, right?"

"No, Astrid. It's pathetic that you don't remember being in marching band together or algebra class. It's not like we've never worked together."

The number of students decreased, causing the hallway to lighten up. Astrid's accusation caused Peter to huff in frustration. Enlarged and flaring, his nostrils expressed disdain through forceful exhalations.

"Listen, I need a favor from you," he said more directly, locker doors slamming across the hall behind him.

Astrid rolled her eyes, aggravated from being ignored.

"I need you to catch up on my biology worksheets."

"What the hell?" she roared with anger. "I have enough to do!"

"I'm five chapters behind, and Mrs. Oleck is giving me until tomorrow to turn them in."

"Are you kidding me?"

"I'm not," he said. "I can't afford to fail and be back here for summer school. I have theater camp, and this is my year to get the leading role."

"So?"

"It's fucking *Romeo and Juliet*!" he said with passion.

"And?"

"They're going to be filming this, and I could use it for my audition tape to get into Juilliard."

"You know theater majors just turn most of you into professional baristas."

"Listen, I didn't come to you for guidance counseling," he hissed, aggravated. "In fact, I'm not really asking for your help."

"Excuse me?"

"All it takes is one post on eLookBook to ruin the rest of your life."

Astrid's eyes blinked rapidly as they processed the penetrating gaze focused on her. His eyebrows, meticulously waxed at an angle, lifted in an intimidating manner. The slam of another locker door overshadowed a loud, nervous gulp.

"I'm graduating soon," she defended, with a tiny glint of bravery flickering like a tea candle. "I'm out of here once I get my piece of paper. What life are you going to ruin if I disappear?"

"True, but what about your little sister?"

She paused; the books against her chest felt the thrust of her throbbing heart. The increasing sweat on her hands made her grip slip. Her lenses became foggy at the bottom. Her stomach lurched from the possibilities of torment that would be inflicted for her noncompliance.

"I don't think she would appreciate it if her older sister's mistake ruined her high school career."

"You're bluffing!"

"Am I?" he asked, stepping closer to her. "You know who my family is. You're nothing in this town, and my dad can ensure that your reputation is tarnished for the rest of their time here."

Her hands trembled with intimidation, leaving her speechless as her books shook. Fear made her knees tremble and her balance waver. As the hallway cleared, the air grew more stagnant compared to when it was bustling with students.

"Nobody in this town cares about anything you do or say. You know there is nothing you can do. So, be a good girl and do this for me."

He placed a stack of papers onto the top of her books. Light bounced off the top of the staples as the paper's edge grazed her neck. Before he turned away, his teeth, perfectly aligned, twisted into a grimace. Astrid rolled her eyes at his cocky strut, letting out a huge sigh of disbelief that sprayed saliva on his homework. She fiercely kicked the locker door, slamming it shut. The metal banging sound echoed in their ears, jolting and spooking the last few students around her.

Frustrated, she exited through the back door to the football field. While hauling her pastel purple JanSport backpack, her shoulder cramped. As she made herself comfortable, she could feel the sun's heat reflecting off the bleachers and warming her bottom. She took note of the track team, warming up by jogging around the dusty field before their meet. The sense of camaraderie confirmed the inner loneliness she experienced. No one stopped Peter from harassing her for his own gain. There was nobody to protect her loved ones when they were at risk.

She ignored the minivans hauling concessions to prepare for their sales. The crockpots emitted odors of pulled barbecue pork and cumin in the taco meat. She couldn't help but hiss at the atrocity of the grammatical errors in her new project. Seeking to rectify the mediocrity, she forcefully applied her eraser, leading to the peeling off of rubber fibers from her paper.

MR. TURLINGTON PREPARED the refreshments as a small wagon rolled onto the field, filled with watery-yellow Gatorade to replenish his team. The grass muffled the thumping bangs from thrown shot put balls from the throwers to improve their distances.

With each two-mile jog, the runners' breath grew more intense. The sprinters' fast movements kicked up clouds of dirt, thickening the air and creating a veil over the bleachers.

"What do you want?" Wesley asked, reaching his toes.

Beneath the bleachers, Zachariah and Wesley were stretching along the brackets. Their calves began straining as they lunged their feet to an acute angle for a good stretch. Black leg hair stood out on their pale legs that craved sunlight.

"What happened with Malakai?" Zachariah asked, whispering loud as his eyes looked around for any teammates snooping around.

"Hell if I know," Wesley answered, cocky, loosening the muscles on his shoulder blades.

"I think you do."

"Oh, really?" he asked, his fingers combing through the delicate fibers of his peach-fuzzed chin. "What makes you think that?"

"Because I know you two were talking the other night."

"I talked to a lot of people."

"Yeah, but nobody else died."

"Coincidence."

The hurdling crowd walked past them. The synchronized clapping of tennis shoes on the sidewalk masked their nervousness as they exchanged jokes. Giggles erupted that followed a joke of someone getting over their fear of hurdles by getting over them.

"What did you even talk about?" Zachariah asked, checking to see if the coast was clear.

"Just catching up," Wesley said, wiping the bit of sweat off his forehead with his jersey.

"Bullshit."

"It's been a year. We had a lot to catch up on," Wesley said, chuckling, his bony ribs tensed with each laugh.

"What, on the debt he owes you?"

"Perhaps," Wesley answered coldly. "He owes me for all I've done for him."

"For giving him an eLookBook account?" Zachariah asked, snarky. "Anyone can make their own account."

"For giving him a new life. He was nothing but an awkward mess until he met me."

With pride shining in his eyes, Wesley touched his damp hair. His arm reached to the opposite side, using his other to support and stretch his shoulders. A tiny bit of wind made crinkled candy wrappers travel on the dirt like tumbleweeds.

"So?"

"He was sick of being a nobody. No girls wanted to talk to him, and everybody else had nothing in common with him. Nobody plays with Yu-Gi-Oh cards anymore! He didn't want to carry his reputation with him to college."

"And you're the expert at making that happen?" Zachariah asked, his eyebrow raising.

"I mean, look at me!" Wesley boasted with confidence, turning his entire body to show off every inch of himself. "Who doesn't want to be me?"

"I sure don't," Zachariah hissed, raising his arm over his head and bending it behind for a good stretch to his triceps.

"You better watch yourself," Wesley said to Zachariah, his finger inches from his face. "The life I created for you can easily be taken away. Do you want the life you used to have, being the person nobody wanted to be around?"

Zachariah's Adam's apple bounced down the chute of his neck. Sweat droplets formed on his forehead as he observed sprinters doing another 100-meter practice dash, stirring up dust.

"All it takes is one post. One hashtag to break the internet and ruin you. People will never look at you the same way again. Employers will think twice before offering you a job. You will even get no ass again. Is that what you want?"

"No," he answered, hesitant; Wesley's icy blue eyes may be bright, but all Zachariah could see was pure darkness.

"That's a good boy," Wesley said, his finger tickling the tip of Zachariah's chin.

Zachariah's face flushed into patchy hues of pink. His fist's knuckles crackled as they pressed against his palms. The collapse of the infrastructure rod under his weight made the bleachers buckle, accompanied by a desperate screech of rust. The overhead riser sank closer to them by an inch.

"Now, let's get out of here before this piece of crap falls on us. You would think that Veronica would have advocated for the school to update these like she did for our basketball court."

Like a burglar evading laser beams in a high-stakes heist, their bodies deftly moved between the crisscrossed rods. With the aid of discarded cups for support, they moved carefully across the pebbles, creating a crunch under their shoes.

A group of girls giggled while pouring water on themselves, wetting their hair and dampening their shirts. As he studied the reflections on their bodies from the dewy water droplets, Mr. Turlington let the whistle drop from his lips. Zachariah began to jog; his feet scuffled upon the dirt. Weighed down by the burdening force, his lungs were compressed, dragging him closer to the earth. The lap around the track was nothing compared to the extensive mental journey he embarked on, trying to overcome the sickness in his gut caused by the fear of Wesley's threat and the uncertain aftermath of his promise.

BACK INSIDE THE SCHOOL, the girls' restroom cleared out as students released their bladders and bowels after holding it in during their study time. As the toilets settled after rapid flushes, water gushed out of their tanks. After enduring a tumultuous month, a freshman girl wiped away her tears and regained composure following her breakup with her boyfriend.

The door swung open, and two seniors walked inside. Their flip-flops clamored onto the dirty tiled floor. Bubble gum popped in Maxine's mouth, creating an echo that sounded like a bang snap.

"Get out!" Maxine demanded to the youngster; the freshman scurried with cowardice and fumbled with grasping the door handle with her slippery fingers.

"Gee, Maxine. She wasn't hurting anybody," Destiny said with disgust.

"Those freshmen know better than to be sharing their presence with us."

"Whatever," Destiny hissed, rolling her eyes.

"Anyway, what the hell was up with Ellie?"

"I know," Destiny agreed. "She's definitely changed. Ever since she backed out on the party, she's had something up her ass."

They entered stalls next to each other. They wriggled their tight jeans down as they began their business. A cold chill radiated from the metal barrier. Another phone number was etched next to the knob along with a vulgarity associated with an underclassman.

"I don't even know what we did for her to shun us," Destiny said, concerned.

"I think it was something Veronica said that pissed her off," said Maxine.

"Shocker. She never had a filter."

"Maybe she couldn't handle it."

"Well, what about all the good times we had?" Destiny asked, distracted and unable to urinate. "How could she forget all the times we stayed up all night just talking? Veronica wasn't much of a bitch then. There was more of a real side to her when there weren't people to impress."

"Some people are so sensitive. Maybe she's on a never-ending period. I dunno."

Their toilets flushed in unison with Destiny pretending she went. The rush of water splashed within the containments of the metal walls. Moving toward the sink, they wetted their hands and witnessed the gelatin from the dispenser fizz into soapy suds.

"Do you know something about what went down between the two?" Destiny inquired, her palms rubbing together like she was trying to warm them up.

"All I know is that she was a bitch that doesn't deserve us."

"What's left of us," Destiny said somberly.

"What's that supposed to mean?" Maxine asked, running her scrubbed hands underneath the water.

"Well, you and I weren't too close until after Veronica went missing."

"And?"

"What's going to happen to us after we graduate?"

"We'll still hang out this summer," Maxine said, dumbstruck that Destiny didn't see the obvious.

"It's not going to be summer forever," Destiny said softly, picking up the bit of skin on her cuticle.

"I wish it would."

"I don't think you're thinking the way I am."

"Who can think like you? You can never stop thinking!" Maxine said as she flicked her wrists to shake off the drops from her fingertips.

Droplets of water from Maxine's fingers splashed onto the mirror, flowing down the glass and returning to the sink like blood spatter.

"I just don't think you're looking at this seriously."

"Are you calling me dumb or something?" she asked, upset.

Maxine reached over to the paper towel dispenser. With each pull, she yanked out a sheet as if she were tugging on someone's hair. Maxine crumpled the wad of material to the size of a bocce ball.

"No, I'm just saying that we had nothing in common except for Veronica," Destiny said.

"Screw you!" Maxine yelled, squeezing harder.

"Hey, I'm just saying that maybe we should clean the slate and start everything over," Destiny said, flinching from the echo of Maxine's sandal.

"You don't think that what we had was real?"

"No, but what I do think is that we had to watch what we said in front of Veronica."

"How dare you say that about her!"

Maxine pelted the ball onto the floor. The paper bounced across the space before stopping at the corner. She lifted her purse strap onto her shoulder and proceeded towards the door with determination. With great fury, she pulled the door open with force, causing it to slam into the wall.

"Maxine, wait," Destiny said faintly.

"When you're ready to see how much we've put into our friendship, talk to me."

The door shut behind her; the echo of the door pelted audibly along the eggshell-colored walls. Destiny's eyes welled up with tears as she reached into her purse for a tampon. Her car keys jingled along the case of her compact contouring kit.

"*Destiny,*" whispered a voice from behind her, soft and light.

Startled, she spun to the stalls behind her. The bouncing of the fluorescent light above her head caused her to be in darkness intermittently. The air was still, with only the faint sound of water droplets hitting the lime-coated drain.

"Someone there?" Destiny asked as she hunched closer to the floor to check the stall for feet.

Nothing was there. No sign of companionship in the bathroom.

Her breath became heavy; her hands trembled themselves dry.

"Come here. Let's hang out?" asked the voice, its cadence ghoulish.

The lights jumped back into darkness. Destiny's hands patted the floor in search of her purse. Her heart raced as she grasped the leather strap. The unpolished tiles stuck to her palms, leaving a gritty residue of scum on her fingers.

"Why won't you be my friend?"

The light turned on again. Destiny's jaw dropped as she looked at her reflection in the mirror. Behind her was a shadow. Its black silhouette overshadowed the stall doors as it leaned against them. Destiny ran to the door as the shape's scream shook the glass, her long hair flowing behind her before the light went off again. Her hands patted the wall as her blinded vision paralyzed her. As she wept for salvation, tiny cries for help escaped her lungs. The room brightened when she crawled through the passage, guided by a small beam of light. A classmate's arm pushed her back toward the drinking fountain by bumping into her shoulder.

"What the hell?" asked the student, irritated that her journey for relief was foiled by panic.

"There's someone in there," Destiny yelped, hyperventilating. "It's trying to kill me!"

"Bullshit," hissed the girl, ignoring her as she opened the door again.

The light was as bright as it was when Destiny initially entered. The silence made the room ambient with only the trash can laying on the floor with sprinkles of wadded paper towels spread across the floor.

"There's nobody in here."

"I swear, there was someone in here. I'm not crazy!"

The student entered the room, her attention fixated on examining the lower sections of the stalls. Her patience was tested by the lack of people using the toilets. The white tiling revealed no hidden dark shadows.

"Girl, you must be on a mad period," the girl said to Destiny, grunting in discomfort. "Now, can I have some peace and quiet before I piss my pants?"

The door shut behind her. Destiny power-walked to the end of the hall, tears streaming down her face. Her terrifying episode brought shame to her. As she walked past different groups of lockers, the echoes of the mysterious voice became more pronounced.

"Let's hang out!"

With confusion in their eyes, the teachers glared at her as they observed the moisture seeping down her leg. Their noses wrinkled at the musty scent of liquid. In an effort to preserve her flawless appearance, Destiny's nails embedded into her palm as she gripped her purse. While aware of the shadow's darkening presence, she concealed her terror.

"Come on, don't be such a downer!"

Applying force to the doors, her arms struggled against the heaviness, her frightened muscles gradually losing strength. The glass became soaked in urine as she leaned against it while trying to go outside. A chilling breeze traveled up her legs, making her jeans feel icy. Trembling with fear, her teeth chattered as she searched for the origin of the tormenting voice. Nothing was following her but her shame and humiliation.

Chapter 15

Silence engulfed the lobby of the principal's office. Taking a brief break from her administrative duties, the secretary opened her eLookBook page to find content. The sight of an orange tabby cat sinking into the bean bag like a pile of leaves brought a chuckle that left her lips. Deep sniffles distracted her break, with a boy pressing a tissue against his nose. He sat next to the trio of girls and reflected on the altercation that brought him to this point. The victim faced the consequences after another taunting incident led him to defend himself.

Ellie's lips produced a tiny explosion as she blew a pink bubble that grew larger than expected. Andrea's eyes remained fixed on the water cooler across the room, anticipating the next bubble to break the surface.

Wendy's foot tapped upon the rubber-tiled floor, sounding like a metronome. Feelings of sadness and guilt overwhelmed her as she grappled with another day without her brother. She knew that with him around, she could contain her frustrations until she got home and vented to her confidant. No fights would erupt when provoked, and she knew someone had cut her leash. If she had centered her work ethic on the task and filtered her concerns, her focus would have been as straight as an arrow.

That was not the case anymore.

Wendy couldn't help but notice Andrea's distant expression, her eyes locked on the photo of Felton High School, silently fighting back tears. Memories of her sister's laughter tugged at her heartstrings. She missed Nora's utterance being interpreted by pencil and paper and her courage to expand her medium to a broader audience.

A TEENAGE COUPLE COVERED their conjoining faces with an issue of Highlights *magazine. Their tongues intertwined as they waited for a study room to become available, their minds set on a romantic escape. Kids sprinted through the library, clutching hardcover books like wings, pretending to be flying birds. The combination of old papers and toddlers vomiting because of excessive sugar consumption produced an unpleasant odor. A cascade of books crashed onto the floor, producing a resounding thump. Elderly ladies became startled; their needles plucked their fingers and interrupted their embroidery. A sewn branch broke; a piglet's eye bled. So much going on, yet, the teenagers didn't notice it.*

"Hey, would you knock it off!" Mr. Willow said, startling the studious pair of boys cramming at the last minute for their test the next day.

The children ignored the demands of authority; their carelessness, in fact, got worse as they shoved each other into the bookshelves. Their backs were pushed against books, causing the text on the other side to tilt.

"Damn kids."

As he lifted himself off his chair, Mr. Willow's uneven legs revealed the strain caused by his heavy belly. Emitting frustrated grumbles, he hunched over to gather the contents, his spirits dampened by the ongoing neglect of his literary pieces. He experienced heartbreak when he recalled the week before, where someone spilled Mountain Dew on the pages of six books. The fall caused pages to break away from the spine.

Juliet and Rapunzel fell from their towers.

Jack and Jill tumbled to the floor before they continued down their hill.

Utmost respect was given to the atrium in the back. Mothers set aside time from their busy lives to get lost in the thrilling narratives of their romance novels. Fathers skimmed the pages in search of pictorial representation to narrate the story more clearly; the details in the text overwhelmed them. In the back corner sat two girls; their engagement in the material was cohesive as they compared notes.

"Did you manage to write anything on the Spanish Flu of 1918?" asked Wendy, finger-surfing through the text to find the correct facts. "I was writing these other notes and couldn't keep up."

"Nothing too detailed," Andrea responded, tangling her eraser along the ends of her black hair. "I only got the basics."

"I hope we don't get hit hard with that section on the test tomorrow."

"Me too."

They studied the incomprehensible scribbles on their sheets to decode the notes they had written to each other. As she chewed on the eraser, Wendy realized the pencil had a chalky rubber flavor. Her fingers pinched the corners of her sheet, fiddling a small crease next to her punctuation.

Sneakers tapped on the floor, getting louder as a young woman approached the study buddies. Before covering a multitude of open textbooks, earnest steps were taken.

"Sissy, look!" Nora whispered, trying to not disrupt the fellow readers.

Andrea's eyes refocused on the sheet; the saturated blending of blue and green hues became clearer, zoning in on the intricacy. The transition from seafoam to aqua, indigo, and denim created a beautiful ombre effect, while the silver skies added a touch of sparkle. Together, they formed a breathtaking backdrop resembling an aurora borealis, with barren trees atop a hill. With its stringy texture, the tall grass moved delicately in the slight wind, enhancing the tranquility of the scenery.

"Nora, this is great!" Andrea responded, her heart feeling full of inspiration.

"Wow, you are so talented," Wendy agreed, her finger touching the colors that deceived her with visible texture. "But I never had a doubt about that."

Nora's smile grew closer to her ears. Her back straightened in pride as she received the most elation from the flattery she had ever felt. Wrinkles became defined on her forehead from the raise of her eyebrows. Hard work and sleepless nights had yielded results. Video tutorials did more for her than give her a headache. But something was holding her back; there was a sense of trepidation from the flattery, like a barrier filtering the compliments.

"Really? I don't think that I'm that good."

"Oh, don't be so hard on yourself," Wendy said, handing the piece back to her. "There's enough room in this world for all kinds of art."

"Yeah," Andrea agreed. "And besides, it's not bad. This is next level."

"It really is," said Wendy. "Have you thought about selling your work?"

"Actually, I have," said Nora, meek, as she carefully placed the paper on her sketchbook to avoid damage.

"Why don't you?"

"I'm just nervous that people won't like it."

"Nora, don't think like that," said Andrea, raising her eyebrow. "There will always be those that won't appreciate your work."

"Exactly. You're robbing yourself of your passions if you hold yourself back and wait for everybody to be on the same page as you. Life's too short, and you'll be dead if you're waiting for everyone to love your work," said Wendy.

"*Some people just can't see what goes into a final piece. They just take it at face value. Even if there were pieces of shit out there, people will never know the time and money that was sacrificed.*"

"*Yeah, I guess you're right,*" Nora said.

"*I'm proud of you, Nora,*" Andrea said wholeheartedly; her eyes pierced into her sister's. "*Just remember, you have a fan club with our full support.*"

As Nora's teeth reached their maximum brightness, her small gap revealed her tongue pressing against the back of her smile. Her head sank closer to her shoulders with glee. The leash had been loosened; she allowed herself to soak up the compliments and be proud of her work. The excitement illuminated her skin, infusing her mind with vibrant colors to fuel her imagination.

"*Well, I have been doing a little research on how to showcase my work,*" she said more confidently, fighting back a tear.

"*There you go!*" Andrea said, nudging Nora's arm with her fist. "*Start with something small, and then you can expand yourself further when you're ready.*"

"*Exactly. You're in charge of your own destiny.*"

Nora felt empowered by finding her support system. She rushed to her table in the other room to pour her inspiration on another page. Her hip contacted a boy's shoulder, causing him to pause while navigating through the many bookshelves. Tears streamed down the child's face as he protected his elbow, which was stinging from a rug burn. Lungs wheezed; crackles huffed out of Mr. Willow's chest as he leaned on the end of a neighboring shelf. His mustache glistened with specks of sweat.

"*See, what did I tell you?*" he asked the child, ignoring his cry for pity. "*This is what happens when you screw around.*"

Andrea shook her head with laughter before honing her focus back to her sister. The multitude of pencils and her sister's stare combined to create a heartwarming feeling. Burnt-orange hues scratched the surface of a clean sheet; her happiness for Nora's passion fortified her love. Her *respect for reckless abandonment was fierce. This is all that Andrea wanted for her sister: for her to live her life full of pride and full of thriving talent.*

THE THREE SAT IN SILENCE with only the secretary's fingers pelting on the keyboard. Wendy's perception hid behind a veil of shame because of their fight. With her sister's enthusiasm in mind, she overlooked Andrea's depression. Her eyeliner, thickly applied, became wet and threatened to run down her face.

The door to the principal's office opened; Wendy's breath cut short as she faced authority. The act of granting permission for a damaged person to utilize their shared pain as a weapon had resulted in her previously unblemished record becoming tarnished.

"I know that it's been a very troubling time for everyone these past few days," said Principal Stuart, adjusting the lapel of his blazer. "However, fighting doesn't resolve any issues. It never does."

Wendy bowed in shame. Andrea didn't make eye contact with the principal. Ellie refreshed her gum by inserting another piece of Bubblicious into her mouth. The wrapper crinkled between her fingers, being pinched into a tiny ball.

"You're almost done with high school, so why not promise that we can be cordial to each other for your last days? Don't make me hold your diplomas through the summer."

They nodded slightly in agreement; Ellie's eyes rolled to the back of her head.

"Well, Mr. Turlington is busy preparing his team for tonight's meet. I will have you help our custodial staff catch up on some cleaning. How does that sound?"

"Do we have a choice?" Ellie asked, her wad smacking in her teeth.

"Not really," the principal answered. "Maybe that will help you think twice before you resort to fighting."

She hissed a sigh of angst. Andrea shared the same feelings of defeat and desired to escape from school, the town, and her life.

"The janitor is waiting for you in the gymnasium and will direct you from there. I anticipate you will all be at the meet tonight to show your support for the team?"

"Why?" Andrea asked, sniffling a moist breath. "You guys don't show support for the other groups."

"Save it," he said, ignoring her attitude. "We're a family here, and you'll be there to support them, especially after your stunt the other night. Do I make myself clear?"

"But—"

"I don't care what you have to say. I know that losing your sister has jaded your perception of the student body. But I will not allow this behavior to become toxic to our community."

His confirmation of apathy left Andrea shocked, causing her to withdraw into her seat. Her crossed arms formed a protective shield around her heart.

"Besides, this will be part of your detention. And if you choose to not participate, you will have your diploma withheld. And I assume you don't want your senior year to extend into the summer."

"Yes, sir," Andrea said reclusively, cornered.

"Okay, now head off to the gym and get started."

With defeat weighing them down, the three stood up from their chairs, their silence speaking volumes. The janitor stood at the center of the gymnasium, illuminated by the overhead lights. Desperately in need of repairs, the soda machine roared behind them.

"Afternoon, ladies," the janitor grunted as he rearranged the small wad of tobacco in his jaw.

They said nothing; their anxiety about finding out their punishment was eating away at them with their stomachs turning in anticipation. The prospect of removing the copious dried-up gum beneath the old bleachers made their hearts quicken. Ellie retreated to her happy place, hoping there were no toilets to scrub throughout the school; her manicure could not be destroyed.

"Looking forward to having you help me reorganize the boiler room."

They sighed a deep breath of loss and their chins quivered in disgust. History had never shown them to ever be down in the lower level of the school.

"Right this way."

He strutted to the other side of the room, happy to have help with his task. They entered a stairwell met with the polished brick being cold from the lack of insulation. Each step became darker as the gymnasium's light became less accessible. The door emitted a sinister creak as it swung open, giving them access to the corridor. The locker room vents released steam from the previous gym class shower session as they passed by. Stacks of totes grew in quantity the closer they got to their destination.

The greeting of a high-pitched whistle screeched inside their ears; the boiler made its presence known. The stacks of garbage bags and equipment almost touched the ceiling, creating a maze-like mess. Their nostrils wrinkled in revulsion as the foul smell of filth permeated the air.

"Yuck!" Ellie yelled, pinching her nose. "What the hell do you keep down here?"

"Budget cuts have affected my tasks if you couldn't tell," he said, frustrated. "I can only do so much because the funds were allocated to upgrades for the athletic department. Plus, my arthritis can't carry all of this."

"Then why don't you retire and let someone else take care of this?" Ellie snapped back, her hand fanning the stench away from her face.

"What are we going to do with all of this?" Wendy asked, trying to maintain control of the group's respect.

"I need you to help take out the trash."

"This is not what I signed up for!" Ellie hissed.

"You signed up for this the moment your hand slapped Ms. Crispin. And since you have a lot of passion for the trash, I will have you help me with that!"

"Ugh!"

"You two will take all the totes and organize them onto those shelves over there."

"What? I want to do that!"

Ellie curled her toes underneath her feet. The garbage posed a threat to her extremities due to the skin exposure from her flip-flops. Her hand cradled over her stomach trying to settle the growing lurch that desperately wanted to throw up.

"The choice has been made for you. Now, chop chop!"

"Yes, sir," Wendy complied, monotoned.

"Bullshit!" Ellie huffed as she released the scrunchie from around her wrist; the loose curls on the end of her hair poofed as she tightened the elastic around the base of her ponytail.

"No one asked for you to put your two cents into our conversation," Andrea said sarcastically, brushing the hair behind her ears and tucking the strands into two bobby pins.

"Shut up!"

"Hey, now! Let's get to work!" Wendy said, equally frustrated but submitting to their punishment.

Frustrated, Ellie stormed off from the group toward the bags, muttering profanities to endure her suffering. Wendy and Andrea moved to opposite ends of the room. Their lower backs burned off the flex of carrying the weight of the totes. Grime injected under their fingernails as they grasped the indented handles.

The whistling became tolerable from their focus on the premises' cleanliness. While the janitor returned for more bags, Wendy attempted to make eye contact with Andrea amidst Ellie. Reflecting on their friendship, she couldn't help but think about the lack of involvement during Andrea's time of need with every breath of the dusty air. Her behavior made her feel like the trash that she cleaned up.

"I really am sorry for Nora," Wendy said, clearing her throat. "I wish I could've told you sooner."

Andrea left no sign of listening to her. She slammed another tote upon the metal grate of the shelf before wiping her palms against her pants. Her eyes wouldn't even look at her to acknowledge the existence of her sorrow.

"I was a shitty friend for not being there, I know that."

Still nothing.

"Will you say something?"

"Just like how you had nothing to say when Nora died?"

"I'm trying to make things right," Wendy said calmly, trying not to lose her cool.

"Yeah, only because you lost your brother," Andrea hissed.

Wendy choked up with realizing her validity. Another knock on her door and it was still deadbolted. Another attempt to try and make it right had been resisted.

"No. But losing Malakai has helped me feel what you did. I never knew how horrible it was to lose somebody you love."

"Well, I'm glad I could be of service to help with your realization! Now, help me with this tote. It's fucking heavy."

Wendy's knuckles crunched as she held back her desire to defend herself. Though she vowed to take the high road like her brother advised, Andrea's increasing snappiness is tempting her to give up on that strategy. Andrea must take some time and accept her apology to rebuild the foundation. She reached the tote; they both prepared to hoist it off the floor.

"One...two..." said Wendy, grunting.

"Three!"

They grunted as they struggled to haul it to the other side. Their arms burned from the tension of their flexion. Steps were uneven from the container's wobbling, dictating their pace's momentum. The bottom of the box rubbed against the floor as it hovered an inch off the ground.

"What the hell is in there?!" Andrea howled, cringing in pain.

"I dunno!" Wendy said, fighting the cramping aches in her palm.

Their grip slipped from the growing accumulation of sweat that lubricated their palms. Fingertips cramped as the handle fell closer out of their security. Every step closer felt like the longest trek without another couple sets of hands to alleviate the burden.

"I'm slipping!" Andrea cried.

"Almost there!"

Their bodies were thrust back to the floor when the container fell. Sweat on their backs became chilled from the concrete. Exhaustion had left them with short breaths and tired eyelids in need of rest. Their eyes made contact; Wendy chuckled to herself and noticed a slight cock in Andrea's straight face in mutual frustration.

"Ready to finish this?" Andrea asked, motivated.

"Let's just push it."

The two went to one end with their grips tight and their focus sharp.

"One...two...three."

Their kneecaps bounced off the surface as their sneakers slid on the floor. The grunts encouraged one another to exert more effort as the block slowly neared its destination. They parked the container next to the shelves, resembling a car with a dead battery. The lid touched the opposite side, fitting snugly in the brick groove.

"We did it," Wendy said, sighing with relief. "Thank God!"

"Yeah," Andrea said, huffing.

Wendy attempted to brush away the dust and grime from her jeans by patting her hands against her knees. In an attempt to cool down, she wiped away the beads of sweat from her upper lip that were absorbed by the neckline of her shirt.

"Well, wasn't that fun?" she asked Andrea, her labored breath getting closer to normal. "This was worse than when I came to help clean your garage."

She didn't respond. The room got silent; only tiny drops of a leaking pipe contributed to the sound. Roars grew once again, whistling from the water heater.

"What do you say? Truce?"

She turned back, only to see the outlines of the dust that once stenciled the box's former home. The air became crisp with chilled loneliness. Lights began to flicker from dim to nothing. Defeat settled over her as she saw the backside of her friend disappear further out of sight and leave into the hall with steam hovering around her.

Chapter 16

Darkness took over the football field as the community reached closer to total capacity. In the parking lot, drivers competed to find convenient spots for their vehicles. Kids dashed around their families, bundled up for the freezing cold that made their muscles tense. Athletes showed their families they were prepared to win by stretching and jogging around the track.

Wendy zipped up her rust-orange hoodie as she braced herself for the required festivities. The mixture of sweat, grime, and dust in the basement caused Wendy to have sticky arms with bits of cobwebs entangled in her hair. Her shoulder ached as the bag's strap pressed into it, weighing her down with the textbooks. Glistening purple bits of pastel sequins caught her eye as she got closer.

"Hey, Penny," Wendy said, yawning.

"Hey! How did detention go?" Penny asked, curious. "My afternoon was not the same without you, ya badass!"

"Fine," Wendy said, solemn as she tucked her hands inside her pockets. "Uneventful. And I'm not a badass."

"What did they make you do?"

"Organize the basement," Wendy said, hiking up her sleeves to show the waxy scum that clung to her arm hair.

"Oh god! That must've been a mess!" Penny said, repulsed, her fingers mimicking touching the filth.

"It was."

"I swear they needed to take out the trash for some time now. That shit has been creeping up to the corner of the gym."

"Yeah, it was pretty rancid."

"For real, I avoided doing my sit-ups over there during gym glass. I almost threw up every time I reached my knees!"

Children yelped from the shove of another young woman; her lungs pelted out gusts of staggered air that fogged up her glasses. Her locks gleamed from the perspiration that persisted in dampening them.

"Wendy!" said Astrid, taking out her inhaler for a reprieve while the two let her catch up.

A small group of athletes jogged through the group, breaking them up after a trip to the restroom. The sound of shoe spikes crunching and clapping echoed on the concrete as Astrid's stumbling remnants lay scattered amidst the fluttering papers. Chip crumbs poked into her soles, getting more populated closer to the concessions table. With each sizzling flip of the spatula, the shop teacher caused puffs of blinding smoke that made everyone's eyes cringe as the hamburgers and hotdogs cooked on the grill. Charred meat was potent, making their stomachs churn.

"Jeez, Astrid," said Penny as she pinched some pages. "I don't recall us getting assigned *this* much homework."

"Yeah. We are at the end of the year, and they have been showing some mercy on our assignments. Are you taking extra classes?" said Wendy.

"It's not all mine," Astrid said, straightening the sheets closer to her chest.

"Then what is all of this?" asked Penny.

"Oh, you know. A little of this, a little of that."

"No, I don't. What the hell does that mean?"

"I've been helping people out," she answered, adjusting her glasses on the bridge of her nose.

"This is more than helping," Wendy said, observing the detailed penmanship.

"Yeah," Penny agreed. "Why don't you just let those idiots do their own work? They can struggle their way to graduation like the rest of us!"

"It's not that simple," Astrid said with shame, her head burying closer to her stack. "I don't have much of a choice."

"Are they threatening you again?" Wendy asked, concerned; her shoulders sank in disbelief.

Astrid froze; her neck clicked a mean gulp as the bottom of her feet rolled small pieces of gravel. Her thick spectacles accumulated a dense layer of fog. Despite her fear, the set of twins continued to chase circles around the trio, with the oldest one screaming and the youngest one flicking their earlobe.

"Astrid, you don't need to deal with their shit," Penny said, her hand comforting her peer's shoulder.

"It's easy for you to say," she defended, still not relaxed.

"What's that supposed to mean?"

"They will ruin me if I don't."

"So?" Wendy asked. "You're about to graduate. To hell with them."

"Easy for you to say. You don't have any younger siblings."

"I do," Penny said with empathy.

"At least they have good looks and are in sports. Mine look just like me."

"You have a lot going for you," said Penny, her hand patting Astrid's back.

"You're not like the rest of them." Astrid continued. "One post can ruin people like me. They can make up a lie about anything that will creep others out, and people will eat that shit up."

Astrid trembled, horrified by the potential of another wave of ridicule. Juniors stomping on Doritos caused bags to burst open. Pieces of chips scattered across the lot like yellow and orange confetti, exploding on two mothers' sandals.

"Well, that's on them," Penny said, avoiding the consequences.

"You're talking as though everyone has thick skin."

"That's not what I mean."

"You clearly have yet to deal with some of the comments online. People can be such monsters when they hide behind a screen. It's like they forget that there are people on the other side that have feelings."

"Yeah, imagine if you said that crap to their face," Wendy agreed. "Wouldn't be so tough."

"My siblings are not that strong yet. They can't handle the bullying. The thought of handling the hate terrifies me. Wouldn't it be scary for you?"

"Yes, it would," Penny said.

"If there is anything I can do to protect my family from these people, I'll do it," Astrid said, her back straightening like a guard.

"You can't protect them forever," Penny said. "At some point, they have to learn that strength on their own. Or they can just ignore what people say."

"That won't be today. You worry about your siblings, and I'll worry about mine."

Her pace quickened as she jaunted further away from the girls. With determination, she vanished into the crowd, ascending the bleacher stairs. Her gusty breath huffed like the exhaust on a train. Wendy and Penny exchanged bewildered looks as they tried to make sense of their discussion. Astrid may have been right about her reasoning, but she couldn't protect them forever.

WITH THE FIRING OF the starting gun, the crowd erupted in louder cheers, and the sprinters began their fierce dash down the hundred-meter track. In order to boast about their excellent parenting and downplay the child's intense training, the parents screamed at their kids, pushing them to go faster. An arm shoved the eater, resulting in a flying ballpark frank and relish raining down on nearby seats.

When the gun fired once more, the runners sprinted in a straight line toward the finish. Light fabrics of their jerseys drifted behind them with each heaping step. Hair tossed back as if under siege by a flurry of fast-spinning fans. Their breaths escaped in huffs, forming perspiring clouds that intertwined with the pain of pushing themselves beyond their limits.

In the middle of the field, athletes stretched their hamstrings and loosened their shoulders to brace themselves. The shot-put balls thudded as they punched the ground, accompanied by grunts. Families applauded and lingered by the end zone, maintaining their distance from the gated entrance.

"Are you ready for this?" Wesley asked as he braced his arm on Zachariah's chest when they stretched at the endzone.

"I think so," Zachariah said, his breath shaky.

The roaring of the crowd resonated inside his ears. The fervent cries of mothers protesting the loss of their child's race made him uneasy. Camera flashes shimmered like specks of glitter. Orange and purple bits of cloth waved by their fathers with passion, winking at him.

"Don't worry about them. You need to win."

"I'm not worried about them."

"Then what is it?" Wesley asked, his eyebrow-raising.

"It's nothing," Zachariah said, somber.

Penny's standout ensemble made Wendy visible to him, despite the surrounding muted tones. Her shirt's sequins caught the light, resembling a traffic sign and revealing their presence.

"Are you still caught up with Wendy?" he asked, disgusted with his lip curled.

"No."

"Bullshit. I've seen you hanging out with her. I swear, you spend more time with her than us."

"She's my friend."

"You don't need friends. You need fans."

Wesley's cheeks flushed with hues of pink. Placing his hands on his hips emphasized the definition of his collarbones. His toned biceps flexed, resulting in his muscles becoming more defined and twitching at him. Scuffling feet on the track created clouds of dirt that blinded Zachariah.

"She means a lot to me," Zachariah said, his breath huffing in defense.

"What has she done for you? She's nothing."

"Don't talk about her like that!" Zachariah said, his knuckles crackling.

The moderator called for Zachariah's name to signal his turn in the discus space. His fists clenched; the cartilage on his knuckles crunched. The chill of the wind couldn't distract his ears from the heated fury building up inside.

He stood at the center of the circle. The crowd ceased their complaints directed at the parents of the competing teams. Satisfaction filled the hungry diners as the sizzle of ground beef patties broke the silence. The palm of his hand cooled down from the polished metal; his fingers cramped as they clenched the surface. Wendy occupied his every thought, and he couldn't fathom why his friends didn't perceive her the same way. Nobody else in his school could see past the surface of her exterior as she was, unlike Veronica or any of her friends. She had something more to offer this world; something that would last longer than his peers' fading beauty.

The field spun in his sight as he prepared to launch the plate. His leg swept around the other; the steps of his feet were precise to ensure he didn't step out of bounds. His gut released a powerful grunt that erupted from his mouth. The light mimicked a firefly as it ricocheted off the metal surface, gliding like a well-thrown frisbee. Two adults guided the dragging of a white strip on the ground to capture the distance of the discus, which bounced like a skipping rock.

"64.4," said the officiant, followed by the overhead announcement repeating the measurement.

The bleachers boasted with cheer; pom-poms fringed in the air with pride. He achieved a new personal record, filling him with pride and breathing a small sigh of relief. His elation grew even stronger when he saw Wendy, with sequins next to her, acknowledging his feat next to the grills. She held the utmost importance to him, unlike Wesley who only showed concern if it benefited him.

A PAIR OF CHILDREN giggled immaturity when the ketchup squirted like flatulence and sesame seeds scattered on the blacktop. Sodas whispered their carbonation with bubbles jumping onto the back of hands for socialization. Cheers muted the grand sizzle on the grill as it tried to make its presence known to cause the linework on the hotdogs.

"Did you see his throw?" Wendy asked, her pride filling her stomach before the hotdog could.

"Of course, I did. How could you ignore it when they stopped service to check it out," said Penny. "Can you hurry with that burger, please?"

The parent kept their pace the same. She took her time, placing a moist tomato and a delicate lettuce leaf onto the patty. They slapped the buns together tight, causing a splatter of toppings to drop over the ground, only mere inches of staining the top of Penny's sneakers.

"I thought you gave up meat?"

"No, that's what my mom wanted me to do."

"I don't see you eating it during lunch."

"She has her little minions to rat me out if they caught me. To hell with them!"

The parent handed over the burger; juices soaked into the bun. Cheese embraced the patty like cuddling partners, forming an inch and a half of deliciousness. Penny's mouth salivated, ignoring the petty nature of her server. Ravaging into the first bite, she was eager to try meat for the first time in years. Condiments trickled down her face like blood to a cannibal; her eyes rolled with euphoria as she savored the flavor of the food she loved most.

"Screw them!" said Wendy.

"Screw her! They're lucky that I don't kill them myself. But then I would be the one paying the price for their horror," Penny said, mumbling with her mouth full.

"Damn girl, you're getting to be feistier than I've ever seen you!"

"I'm tired of school. I'm hungry. And my mother is driving me nuts. I think I'm about to lose it."

"By the way, have you talked to her?" Wendy asked, curious.

"No," she said, her face expressionless without a care.

"Strange. She usually gets on your case if she doesn't see or hear from you."

"I don't care. Maybe she took my words to heart for once. I can't wait to graduate and get the hell out of there."

"We're almost there," Wendy said, chuckling, tossing a pinch of popcorn into her mouth.

"I know, but some days they're really testing me, I swear."

"I get it."

She took another bite; this time, a generous chunk of lettuce hung from the bottom part of her jaw. The watery crunch of the veggies was moist; the juices of the meal were satisfying. Her fingers pinched a generous amount of ruffled potato chips to add texture to her enjoyment.

"Having fun, are we ladies?" said a voice behind them, finding out it was Ms. Woods upon turning around.

"Hi, Ms. Woods," Wendy said as she let her hotdog rest on its plate, tilting it to prevent the sausage from tumbling out of the bun.

"I'm glad to see you out here supporting our school."

"I didn't have much of a choice," Wendy said sarcastically, her tongue licking off the buttery grease from the corner of her mouth.

"You could've chosen to skip, anyway. Good for you for following the rules," Ms. Woods said, turning the tables around with encouragement.

Penny's eyes rolled; this time, it wasn't from the satisfaction of her food. Her cheeks became as full as a chipmunk's as she devoured the remaining pieces. In order to avoid making things worse, she resorted to stuffing her mouth and refraining from commenting. It was dramatic enough for her, and it was fitting to wait for the dust to settle before causing any more commotion.

"Thank you," Wendy said, giggling at her friend's image.

"I'm also sorry for your loss," the teacher said, her hand grazing Wendy's forearm, pushing the fabric of her sweater closer to her skin. "Malakai was such a good kid. I knew he was going to do great things when he graduated."

"Yes, he did," she said, combating the thickening sensation in her throat.

"Goes to show you that you make every moment count. We never know when our time will be up."

"You're right," Penny agreed solemnly.

Penny and their teacher exchanged tense glances, concerned about making Wendy cry. All Wendy did was grab a fistful of popcorn and shove it into her mouth; the uncooked kernels crunched between her molars.

"I know that this may not be the appropriate time to ask you in your time of grievance, but have you given any more thought to your future? I found a college you might like after your time off."

"No, I haven't," Wendy mumbled, trying to swallow her snack.

"She just lost her brother. I think that's the last thing on her mind," Penny said matter-of-factly.

"I know, and I'm sorry. I just want to see you thrive and only want the best for my students. Especially those who've put in the work."

"Thank you for that. I'll think about it."

"That's all I ask for. I'll leave you to it."

The two students said their goodbyes with a nudge. As she made her way to the bleachers, Ms. Woods turned back one last time to acknowledge her care for them; her lips tight and somber. She passed by Mr. Willow, who exchanged a wave at Wendy; his steps were uneven as he waddled closer to find a seat. His balance was unsteady, clenching his bag of popcorn; pieces scattered to the ground around his feet.

"Why doesn't she just leave you alone with this college crap?" Penny hissed. "She just won't let it go."

"At least she cares. Unlike some of these teachers that only invest in the ones who are already getting a free ride. At least she sees the value in our work," said Wendy.

"True. I'm just saying that she should lighten up a bit."

"I know."

Wendy's hand grasped the bun, now soggy from all the juices that had softened its stability. The hotdog was cold when she took her bite; the condiments were warmer than the meat itself. She didn't care anymore. The stress of the day had caused her stomach to knot up, and she needed to eat something to provide nourishment. After enduring a challenging day, she felt a void that craved something to fill it.

A lonesome shed caught her attention from the corner of her eye, set apart from the rest of the buildings at the learning facility. Only bits of the washed-out navy-blue coloring peeked from the rusted metal siding of the lonesome shed. The shingles atop were shedding; the wooden foundation was exposed. Along the corner stood a person; his hoodie was snug with the hood secured along the top. His pale skin let out a smile, so antagonizing as he glared at her. The gaps between his teeth were visible, with some appearing misshapen because of an unsuccessful confrontation. She gulped a wad of spit, which tasted like dill and mustard, as she became stiff at the person from her past who haunted her. The person who continues to show up when things were going okay, especially during recess when she is connecting with the boy she once crushed on.

Ian.

Chapter 17

Chiming keychains dangled from Destiny's and Maxine's purses when the two reunited after their conversation in the bathroom. Destiny's breath was shaky; her jaw was chattering knowing she had to swallow her pride to get her friend back. She kept scanning her surroundings, her head turning in search of anything unusual; no more antics to distress her since she was a blithering mess on the phone when she apologized to Maxine. She was lacking the confidence she usually radiated.

"What the hell is wrong with you?" Maxine asked, rolling her eyes from Destiny's continuous fumbling with her set.

"N-Nothing," Destiny responded, tentative, grabbing her purse strap tight.

"Bullshit. You've been weird since class."

"I'm on my period," Destiny said, thinking of a relatable excuse.

"You've never been this way before. Quit lying to me!" Maxine said, her flip-flops clapping on the pavement.

Destiny's stomach rattled. Mentioning that a ghoul taunted her in the bathroom would result in nobody believing her. Her lack of trust in Maxine prevented her from sharing her bathroom encounter. She didn't trust anybody.

"Do you remember that girl that died last year?" Destiny asked; her body jolted from a child running behind her.

"No," Maxine said softly.

"That artsy kid. Andrea's sister?"

"Oh, yeah. The weird girl."

"I don't think she died."

"Why would you think that?" Maxine asked, confused, noticing the beads of sweat soaking on her t-shirt under her arms.

"I-I just don't think she did."

"Well, I wouldn't put it past her. Have you ever seen her work? She was so weird, and would've done anything for attention. Even faking her own death."

"That's not fair," Destiny said, checking the parking lot's end, hoping nobody had heard that.

"Then what are you trying to tell me? The girl was such a freak. She had every bit of what came to her."

"Will you be my friend?" a voice whispered into Destiny's ear.

The noise made by the spectators watching the mile-long race was louder than any other small talk. Louder than the coaches, who were hollering in disgust that their runner wasn't winning the race but trying to mask their verbiage to appear encouraging in front of their parents. Destiny's spine trembled; the hair on her arms stood.

"What's wrong?" Maxine asked, her eyebrow raised.

"It's nothing," Destiny said, her eyelids fluttering with panic growing.

She had no food in her stomach. But somehow, she had the urge to reject whatever was in her body. A wad of bile desperately wanted to eject out of her gut. The bottom of her feet became sweaty, slicking on her sandals.

"I need to go to the bathroom," she said, groaning, her hand cradling over her stomach.

"Perfect, I'll go with you. I need to touch up my face. These boys are so hot tonight. I don't know about you, but there's something about those runners that makes me not want to be alone!"

"Okay, let's go."

Destiny picked up her pace as she returned to the school. Maxine rushed to catch up, her shoes slapping onto the pavement behind her. The crowd thinned out after their departure. The chatters transformed into the sound of cricket chirps, celebrating their own community. She yanked the door handle; her shoulders strained as she pulled with every ounce of her strength.

Locked.

"Shit!" Destiny said, upsetting her stomach even more.

"Why don't you just barf right here in the lot?" Maxine recommended. "It's not the first time we gagged in weird places. Remember Trevor Haines's party?"

"I need some privacy."

"People have puked in public. Don't worry about it," Maxine said with impatience.

Positioned at the opposite side of the baseball field, two porta-potties stood, their blue plastic siding merging with the dark sky. Footsteps rustled nearby, startling the two. Their hands clasped together, pulses tapping greatly. Destiny's knees buckled, trying to keep her bladder from releasing fluid. The memory of peeling off her soiled jeans that clung to her leg was horrid.

"Now I have to go," Maxine said.

"Let's go to those porta-potties," Destiny recommended, desperate for anywhere to hide.

"Ew, gross!"

"Have any better ideas?"

The crowd gathered by the restrooms by the track. Lines grew in between each event. Hoping to relieve themselves, the racers became increasingly impatient before the next race began. Mixtures of bodily fluid stunk up the air by the concessions. If Destiny wasn't going to puke from her nerves, it would've been from the repugnance that brewed a wicked stench.

"Let's go."

THE BLEACHERS WERE filled. Penny and Wendy maneuvered around every seated member; their knees buckled with uneven steps, maneuvering to not step on everyone's toes. Ankles wobbled like an amateur surfer facing their first gnarly wave.

"Excuse me," said Wendy, straddling over a gentleman's lap to move past him.

"Sorry," said Penny, acknowledging the flinch of a woman's yelp after stepping on a pinky toe.

They ignored the opposing team's disgruntled fans and obstructed their view of their athlete; a couple of seconds of blockage frustrated supporters that missed something important.

They found Astrid close to the top corner, her face buried in stacks of papers. She lost her focus during the intense final stretch of the three-hundred-meter hurdles. Lead scratched onto the sheets; her jaw was locked with tension.

"Mind if we join you?" Wendy asked.

"Sure," Astrid said, not making eye contact, her gaze sharp onto the equations.

Their backsides became pressed onto the metal seats. Adjusting their posture, they heard their spines crackle as they watched the dasher prepare their blocks for a few practice starts. As more bodies joined to stabilize the heavy load, the metal on the bleachers protested with a whining and creaking sound.

"I still don't know why you're doing their homework," Penny said, snarling in disbelief.

Astrid's thick spectacles magnified her eyes as they rolled backward. Her pupils got bigger to focus deep into the Pythagorean theorem.

"You just don't get it," she mumbled, answering for B.

"What? I care for my family, but there are things they must do on their own."

"True. But they must be old enough to develop that strength to handle it."

Penny let out a huff of frustration, not knowing how to respond that would cause her to offend the girl. Even if she spoke her mind, their beliefs would still clash, but she was determined to stand by her logic.

"In case you haven't realized, our world focuses on the gratification of others. We have social media that we're all attached to. You can say that we don't rely on it, but we do."

"She's right," Wendy said, putting her device in her pocket. "We're all attached to our phones."

"Exactly. And all it takes is for one person to spread hate to assassinate someone's character. No matter if they're true or not."

Penny's lips got tighter, letting off a tiny curl. Kernels of popcorn rained onto her hair from a six-year-old on the top row, shaking their bag with sugar-fueled energy. Bits of salt sprinkled onto her lap when she brushed them off her scalp, loathing at their carelessness.

"I'm not one to assume, but you probably didn't have this happen to you yet," Astrid guessed.

"I've had people pick on me!" Penny said, annoyed.

"Yes, but did they drag you and say rotten things, or was it just simple teasing because of your mom's show?"

"I don't think I've heard or read anything bad about you," said Wendy.

"Whose side are you on?" Penny asked, throwing her hands up, deflecting another snack: licorice. "Imagine being called Hershey squirts or fudge puddles."

"I'm sure it sucks," said Astrid.

"It does!"

"I'm not trying to take away from the crap that you dealt with. I'm just saying that people will say or post things that will cause torment. Even to the point of death threats," Astrid said, tucking her sheets under her to weigh them from a tiny breeze growing.

"It could go that far," said Penny.

Another close call came from the track. The finals for the pole-vaulting competition were down to the wire, with third place being finalized; two tall poles stood straight like flag poles with athletes preparing a practice jaunt down the runway. Nerves took over one of them, and the bar raised past their personal record; confidence has deteriorated to nothing.

"Have you been told to kill yourself yet?" Astrid asked, a tear forming, armor starting to crack.

"No. But that doesn't mean that the other words don't suck," said Penny.

"I'm not saying that. I'm just saying that some people get the worst of the worst. And they don't even deserve that type of treatment."

"Yeah, some people do," Wendy said. "There are assholes out there that reap what they sow."

A hiss came from behind them followed by an antagonizing chuckle. Their ears pierced with disdain. Andrea sat four rows behind them; her arms crossed over her knees for warmth, hands dangling close to her calves. Her hair drooped over her eyes, clumped together from the oils and sweat.

"So, do you think Nora deserved what she got?" she asked, disgusted.

"No, not at all," Wendy defended, approaching with caution, waving her hands in front of her. "What happened to Nora was terrible."

"Spare me your fake sympathy. You didn't care when she died."

"I'm sorry," she said, again soft with defeat. "I just didn't know how to respond. It was such a shock to me."

The gun went off; another race started, followed by a roar of cheers from the surrounding people. Passion belted from their mouths, monstrous; eardrums rattling from the screams, competitive.

"How about being there for your friend? I would've been there for you if it happened to you!"

"Yeah, and you proved that when Malakai died," Penny muttered to herself, Andrea barely catching her statement.

"I'm not here to compete with who was the better friend," Wendy said, remaining calm; she fought the trembles in her fingers. "What I did to you is unforgivable, and I understand why you feel the way you do toward me. I just want things to go back to where they were."

"Well, it's going to take more than some dumbass apology to mend what we had!" Andrea said, rising from her seat.

Her knee nudged into the back of the person before her causing them to fall onto those in front of them like an incline of dominoes. The altercation between teenage girls had already annoyed the other families instead of allowing them to focus on what they came for. They tumbled forward, knocking into the back of Astrid's head. Body jolting, papers falling from her hands. While some were lucky enough to land on her shoes, others weren't so fortunate and fell through the bleachers, scattering onto the ground like a dusting of snow.

"Shit! Now look what you made me do!" Astrid said, horrified as she scrambled to ration whatever she could reach for.

"I'm sorry," Wendy said, dumbstruck. "Let me help you get those."

"No, you've done enough!"

Her feet thundered onto the metal. The foundation shook as she ignored every person she knocked into on her way off the seats. Scribbles became soaked in the moistened puddles of dirt. Lenses fogged from the huff of her breath; she bit her lip to hold back the fear of losing all her hard work and ruining the future of her loved ones.

Chapter 18

The announcer boasted another victory for one of the Felton High racers. Children chased around to play tag, not knowing what the big deal was with sporting events; their parents clapped for the placements of their older siblings. Restroom-bound, teenage girls shed tears as their partners ditched them for the summer, seeking commitment-free connections.

Astrid cradled the surviving papers in her arms along the side of the bleachers. Filled with anxiety, her chest thumped with the fear of losing the work she dedicated herself to in order to protect her loved ones. Worries consumed her as she feared her sister would be unequipped to handle the ridicule he would face for something beyond his control.

Pebbles grounded on the pavement became shuffled by Andrea's defeated step before leaning against the wall. Arms cradled over her chest, so vulnerable to fight away her heartbreak.

"Are you okay?" Astrid asked, flicking a glob of mud off the corner of one of the sheets.

"Yeah," Andrea answered, sniffling, avoiding eye contact with her.

"It doesn't look like it."

Tears drenched the tip of her bangs; her head slumped closer to her shoulders. She paid no attention to the parents who had observed the spectacle as another student ran after someone's ex, who left the conversation when being confronted for cheating.

"I'll be fine," she mumbled.

"I really am sorry about your sister." Astrid's hand patted Andrea's.

"I know you are."

"She was very talented and had such a big heart."

"She really was."

Breaking the solid marble-like line, Andrea displayed an accepting smirk. Astrid became the first person in close to a year to break her. Nothing was successful at making her smile; not prom, not when Paramore performed in the state, nothing.

"I'm guilty of not reaching out to you for support in your time of need, like Wendy."

"We weren't that close. It's different," Andrea said; the pain in her eyes was still real.

"Yes, but if I want to say that I'm friendly and kind, then I need to act like it to everybody."

"True."

The two stared at each other; silence became thick as they allowed a father to drag their son by the ear. The sharp cries of disappointment echoed as his kid withdrew from the race, their chances dashed by a twisted ankle in the final stretch of the eight-hundred-meter run. They were tentative in speaking over the parents' remarks.

"I know this isn't appropriate, but could I ask you for a favor?" Astrid asked, her eyes staring at the father, shoving the kid to the ground by the lot, who ignored their limping.

Andrea didn't respond. Her main concern was preventing her classmates from noticing her anxiety, which is why she focused on hiding her tears. Regardless of how others viewed it, Andrea fought her own inner battle. Witnessing a lack of compassion between a parent and child during a time of need was painful for her.

"Show some grace toward Wendy. She feels horrible for what she did," Astrid said.

Still nothing. Her head nudged to hide behind her hair. The strands became a thin veil.

"She's told me all this year how much she misses you and would've been there for you every step of the way if she had a choice to do it over again."

"Well, we don't get a second chance at everything."

Andrea walked away from Astrid. Her breath huffed sad whimpers like a tormented puppy. She didn't want to hear it, no matter how often she was told. Second chances were not something she supported.

"Andrea, time heals everything. Keep working through each day, and maybe there will be a day where you'll find it within yourself to forgive those who hurt you. It takes more energy out of you to forgive than to let that pain weigh you down."

Through her locks, smudged eyeliner became visible, running down her cheeks and nearing her dimples. She rarely acknowledges others in front of her peers, but this time she nodded. It was atypical for her to embrace constructive criticism rather than deflecting blame and using it to improve. A slight smirk cocked from her lips once again, curving closer to her ears.

A small gust of wind beat against their faces, cooling their warmth. The papers shivered their corners; the crisp edges let out a light crunch. Astrid sensed a chilly sensation at the neckline of her shirt, bringing back the purpose of her outing as she noticed a couple more sheets deep within the underpart of the bleachers. She couldn't lose focus on her family, not now.

THE END OF ONE CLASS meant the start of another one, ready to torment the students before lunch. The sleepy children trudged along the hallway toward their lockers, longing for a snack to fuel them for

the rest of their day of learning. Astrid cradled her books close to her, nurturing them like they were her young. Her glasses fogged, passing by every group, hoping she would remain invisible for survival.

"A squared plus B squared equals C squared," she muttered to herself like a witch's chant.

Reciting algebraic equations helped her ignore the fear-inducing people she dreaded. No football players to tease her about her lifestyle. No popular girls to mock her appearance. That was how she liked it and wanted to keep it that way.

She walked by the biology lab, reminders that she needed to finish notes on the fetal pig dissection for one student, and then the English classroom to complete the book report on Hamlet.

It's the easiest one! she thought.

She could never be free. It always seemed like she had something to do for herself or her siblings. Even with a packed schedule, she made it a priority to assist others with their homework without asking for anything in return. Graduating from school and leaving everything behind next year couldn't come soon enough for her. As much as she would miss those who had been kind to her and not taken advantage of her skills, like Wendy and Penny, she couldn't wait to get out of here. Those were the people that would be the hardest to move on from when entering the next chapter of her life. Some people relieved the pressure she brought upon herself.

The door swung open to the art classroom; a couple of students straggled behind as they dried off their hands after washing off the paint from under their fingernails. Veronica hissed with disgust that she got a drop of neon pink onto her light-wash Abercrombie and Fitch jeans. The color stood out from the pre-existing white specks and the strands of frayed fibers.

The classroom was open, bigger than the others. Canvas tarps draped along the wire strung tightly from wall to wall. The work benches bore stains from previous students, who left their mark on their unkempt stations with every color of the rainbow. A blender roared with a sophomore, transforming their concoction of recycled paper, being pureed with water to create new life.

"Hey, Astrid," a voice echoed from the other side.

Another sophomore was at the far corner of the room, past the teacher, who was taking in all the beauty of creativity. Her brunette hair was matted; her face was oily with specks of acne. On the sleeves of her ruby sweatshirt, there was a layer of dried clay, which caused the cuffs to sprinkle tiny pieces of gray soil onto the cement floor.

"Hi, Nora!"

Her workstation was comparable to a five-year-old with pounds of Play-Doh. The thick block of wood supported the pile of clay, seamlessly blending it into the foundation. Intricate details of mounds created illusions of draped chiffon, even showing glimpses of a belly button and a pair of defined nipples. Limbs poked out of the body, creased with every wrinkle and blemish to perfection. The veins on the wings were tiny, lifelike, like they were pumping blood.

"This is beautiful," said Astrid, astonished by her craft; her fingers hovered over each carved strand of hair.

"Thank you," she said with pride; a slight smirk became cocked.

"What made you do something like this?" Astrid said, looking into the eyes of the masterpiece; irises were carved like the sun's reflection on top of a pool.

"I dunno," Nora said; her shoulders shrugged. "I'm trying something new."

"You've been doing a lot of work lately, haven't you?"

"More than you would ever know! It's surprising that my mom hasn't grounded me for coming home late, and I should have been admitted to the hospital for skipping dinners and missing sleep."

"Woah!"

Astrid looked at the legs of Nora's jeans. Colors of every kind spread out like chicken pox on two oversized pieces of denim. Her JNCO jeans looked like she had been wearing the hand-me-downs of an older sibling twice her size.

"You should take it easy," Astrid said with concern, setting her backpack on the nearby table.

"I am," she said, her throat in desperate need of hydration.

"I mean it. You need to take care of yourself."

"Trust me, I am."

"I believe you," Astrid said solemnly, not believing her. "I just want you around for a long time so that you can make plenty more beautiful pieces. Perhaps I'll buy something when I have the money."

Nora's face glowed; her teeth started to shine. Taking pleasure in her work once more, she recalled every hour she dedicated to her project to achieve her desired outcome. Her stomach churned, not knowing if she had feelings of pride or if she skipped breakfast and lunch. Muddy bits fell from her knuckles as she clenched her fist, elated that she had a customer. More importantly, she had a fan, somebody who would support her art and cheer for her success.

THE RACERS DID A LIGHT jog down the straightaway, practicing their sprints as they handed off their batons to the next, hoping they wouldn't fall to the ground. The anticipated four-by-four hundred-meter relay was about to conclude the festivities for the event. In a race that encompassed the entire team, top performers from distance and sprinting groups collaborate in a mid-distance jaunt. Most importantly, it showcased Wesley's and Zachariah's dedication to the entire school.

Concession stands cleared away; the simmering meat has died as the parents closed the shop. People emptied their bladders, and those who waited finally relieved themselves as the restroom line vanished. Disappointed athletes put their sadness aside to support their teammates from the sidelines, yearning for the same prestige as the top four in this race.

Racers grabbed the top of their feet and pressed it close to their backsides to stretch their quadriceps. The organizers placed blocks along the starting line for one last moment in the spotlight for the evening. Palms were sweaty, antagonizing the runners, hoping the baton would slip out of their grips. They fought against nausea and eagerly desired a substantial meal to satisfy their hunger and prevent exhaustion-induced sickness.

"You ready for this?" Wesley asked, his breath shaky.

"Yeah," Zachariah answered quietly, focused.

Fixing his gaze on the bleachers in the distance, he traced the sparkle of Penny's attire to find the person he had been counting on for undivided attention. The sight of Wendy waving her arm and smiling was all he noticed, but it was enough to inspire him to give his best effort. His stomach became warm to have her watch one of the last meets of the season since she hadn't seen him compete all these years, making his heart race with motivation to make her proud.

"Would you give that girl a rest?" his friend said, snarling, his arms swinging in front of his chest to loosen up.

"What?"

"You know what I'm talking about. That bitch is not right for you."

"Who said anything about wanting her?" Zachariah said, huffing in oblivion. "We're just friends."

"Sure, and I'm a virgin! I see the way you look at her. You like her."

"I look at her like everyone else!"

"Bullshit. Every girl I set you up with, you ignore. When are you going to man up and score?"

"Shut up!" Zachariah said, inching closer to his teammates, their breaths fogging around each other's faces.

With a tap on the microphone, the overhead speakers screeched. The crowd's volume transformed into a dull roar as they whispered and cheered for their teams' points, trying to calculate who was in the lead. The crickets were making noise louder than the humans.

"All right, ladies and gentlemen. It's time for the last event of the evening. The four-by-four hundred-meter relay."

The voice roared like a wrestling announcer. People took the event seriously, showing it the same focus and support as the main pay-per-view event. To the parents, this was their Super Bowl.

A COUPLE OF PAPERS tumbled underneath the bleachers. Footsteps rumbled from above. Astrid leaned forward, careful not to hit her head on the metal. As she diligently worked on each sheet, her breathing became steady, reassured that her efforts were bringing her closer to safety.

The gun went off, and the crowd roared; hinges squeaked from the audience, jumping out of their seats to cheer on their team. Popcorn fell onto her face while seeds scattered across the top of her head, kernels running along her scalp. Soda cans crumpled under her feet, making her ankles struggle to balance.

Two times pi times radius.

The space became smaller with her creeping closer to the front; the incline was sharp with chewed-up gum sticking to her knees and sunflower seed shells embedding into her forearms and elbows.

"C'mon, Tommy!" yelled a mother from above her.

"Smooth transition!" another said.

One-half times base times height.

As the second lap of the race began, the batons exchanged hands and a new team member took over. The running spikes slapped onto the track like trotting horses, and when the baton dropped, the coach's clipboard pelted the fence, causing the chains to rattle with fear.

The cheering became louder, more audible. Astrid's ears were pained by the passionate mothers' screams, as they desperately tried to avoid the shame of losing.

Another paper.

Pi times radius squared.

Slithering forward, she pressed her chest against the rocky surface. Pebbles scooping into the neckline of her top. More tidbits were left behind by the people who sat before her on top, their clumsy hands fumbling.

Pencils.

A dollar bill.

A chain necklace from a gumball machine.

More pencils.

Lots more pencils.

Two times pi times radius times the value of radius plus height.

Her fingertips grew burdened as the weight intensified around her hands. Slowly, they sank into the water, as if the gravel had softened and melted into a pudding-like consistency. The earthly delight of gray matter caked around her arms, causing them to sink.

Clay.

Her muscles twitched, lungs cringing with fear, desperate for a suck of her inhaler. There was no other option for her legs but to sink lower. The weight of the earth pressed down on her, making her clothing heavy, as if she was ensnared.

"Someone please help me!" she screamed, squirming with panic.

Another pass of the baton for the third lap. From the midst of the crowd, Wendy's voice was barely audible as she cheered for Zachariah. Witnessing his fighting spirit, Zachariah could see the joy reflected on Wendy's face. With their son's outstanding speed and dominant lead over the competition, his parents celebrated with joyous leaps. Metal scratched against one another, buckling from the weight that crunched the firm surface.

"Please!"

The light became less visible from underneath; the lone spotlight that carried through the opening has now become blocked by darkness. When Astrid saw the movement, her neck cracked and her shoulders strained as she pulled herself to see the black fabric drifting into her sight.

"Oh, thank you for coming! I need help!" she said, wheezy, calming her panic.

Nothing further than the cheers that continued to go; the person stayed there, staring at her as it took in her fret. Her breath caused her glasses to fog, clearing away the moistened earth on her lenses.

The wind picked up; bits of her hair flew into the corner of her mouth. The paper passed over her knuckles, settling into the ground and finding support in the uneven terrain. This paper differed from what she'd seen. She did not include any math equations or self-written summaries on a specific topic. It was close to being a blank sheet with only scribbled words etched from an unsteady hand. Her eyes squinted, trying to make out the scribbles.

Feeling Fine, Friend.

The transition into the final lap had come upon them. The crowd jumped up onto their feet. Parents stomped to get their child's attention to pressure them to push harder. Astrid's cries for help were overpowered by the resounding thumps of sandals and boots above her. Under the weight of the people, the braces began to bend, causing the seats to lower closer to her.

"Come on, Wesley!" said a part of the audience.

Screams of horror belted from a fraction of the group as the thud of a baton fell to the ground. Cries of despair were horrid, with the school disappointed in their disqualification. Metal snapped; the braces broke, with bits of rust sprinkling onto Astrid's face. Spectators tumbled toward the center of the bleachers; their equilibrium disrupted by the sudden slant. As more and more people piled on, the screams of horror increased until the seat gave in under the weight.

Metal pressed against the top of her neck, compressing into her spine. Broken bits punctured into her ribs, lungs crackling as it penetrated. Her femur broke, then her pelvis, then a pair of ribs. Each passing second was another bit of weight burdening her body. Blood splashed out from behind her teeth, unable to cry for help. Light suddenly became brighter than she could see the hem passing by one last time, catching one last glimpse of the last steps of the race and the final equation with the weight of the metal plus broken bones and burst arteries equaling the end of her life.

Andrea wiped her tears; she dodged the start of her community adjourning the event. She peeked around to look for the principal, trying to show him a sign that she had followed through with her punishment. In the midst of a crowd filled with emotions ranging from excitement over their triumph to disappointment in their child's actions, the authority figure was nowhere to be seen. She gazed at the bent bleachers, but her interest was piqued by the shoes that peeked out from underneath the heap of metal. The minty green curls in her laces stood out from the gray matter.

"Astrid!"

Her scream startled the surrounding people. Every second that went by, another individual realized that there was a person trapped beneath the wreckage. The weight of the competition had become too much for the poor girl, resulting in a panic that shoved Andrea further away from her confidant.

SCREAMS GREW WITH EACH gasp, footsteps thundering onto the pavement. Despite the panics occurring away from the porta-potties, Destiny and Maxine were unaware of the collapsing bleachers. With the goal of staying composed, Destiny fought to restrain her tears. Maxine was focused on her beauty; her eyes gazed into the compact mirror cradled in her palm.

"Are you about done in there?" Maxine asked, outlining her lips with gloss.

Destiny's sadness and fear caused her sinuses to be blocked, and she sniffed to clear the mucus.

Grass rustled around the plastic walls. Legs shuffled across the terrain. The door shook, and darkness revealed from the small cracks allowed from the tiny latch.

"Someone's in here!" Destiny said, shaky.

The door continued to shake; the walls started to tremble. Water splashed from the tilt of the rectangle, trying to balance itself out.

"Stop!" she cried, stretching her arms to the sides for stability.

The screams grew louder from the meet, gathering their attention. What was once something that was easy to ignore has now become a screech that made them cringe. Their eyes grew wide as they understood the message, informing them of the tragic death of a girl crushed by the bleachers. With haste, they wriggled their jeans back up to their waist, another parent crying for help by the concessions with agony. They unlatched the door; a signpost slid in front of her reach. The metal impaled the plastic, with fragments sprinkling onto their toes.

Destiny yelled with terror as another one came through; the rusted edges cut deep into her bicep. Flesh tore apart, blood splashing and turning into streams. The front of her spaghetti strapped top became sprinkled with red, darkening the blue. Her breaths became more rapid, with panic making her head feel lighter.

"Stop it, please!"

Another one jolted from behind her, barely grazing her hip.

And then another one.

And another.

"Somebody, please help me!"

She stepped up the rods, climbing to the top of the box. Her fingernails dug into the vent, clinging for dear life as three more impaled her space from every direction. Tears ran down her face, with droplets landing on her open gash; waves of pain pulsated into her shoulders that strained from the clench of her life.

Stakes swarmed the surroundings, much like laser alarms safeguarding the precious jewels. Destiny found solace as her bottom made contact with the nearby metal, a few inches below.

The door shook again; plastic thumped against the frame. Destiny's breath shook, shortening with each tug.

"Leave us alone!" she cried, her throat choking on tears.

The door stopped; gasps surrounded the parameters. Yelps of desperation yelled for the guest to open the door.

"Ma'am, this is the police," said the officer, focused as the door rocked with each tug. "We're here to help you."

Her body relaxed, letting herself down slowly to make her way out. Gasps of pain choked down her windpipe. The urge to vomit came back to her, with her stomach craving for a heave.

"Thank you!" she said, wincing with her arm bearing her weight to climb down. "Get me out of here, please!"

The door yanked off its hinges. Red and blue reflected from the iron of the crowbar. With disbelief, the officer witnessed Destiny's blood flowing down the poles, resembling rainwater streaming from a roof. The floor was wet with a mixture of blood and waste; the stench from the muck stung his nostrils.

Her muscles strained with each hyperextension of her contorting body, letting itself down the pieces. Each inhumane twist and turn caused her spine to crack, getting her one step closer to safety. Blood coated the officer's hand, giving it the appearance of velvet gloves. As she buckled unsteadily on her knees, the grass provided cushioning for her toes.

"Maxine," she slurred; the lights became blurry from her lightened head. "Somebody help Maxine!"

Another door cracked from the yank of the crowbar. Screams pierced the inside of her ears; her eyes tried to make sense of her neighboring bathroom, combating the spinning earth. The same exact amount of posts has impaled her cubicle. This time, the dozen that Destiny was successful with dodging resulted in over half of them piercing through every part of Maxine's body. Her eyes trickled, tears of pain that mixed with the blood falling out of her mouth. Intestines wrapped around the ridges, with fluids puddling onto the floor. Extremities were perched in contorted directions; her femoral arteries busted, drenching the bottom of her jeans. Skin fractured from her shoulder blade burst through her skin, breaking the spaghetti strap of her tank top.

Destiny choked on her breath from the overwhelming screech piercing her head; her eyes rolled as she gave into the unbearable weight of her muscles. The stars twinkled away from her vision, becoming more clouded, more dark. Everything disappeared, and the people's voices became muffled, as if someone had smothered them in pillows. Disbelief set in as she blacked out from the loss of blood and the end of her friendship.

Chapter 19

The next day at school was awkward; most of the school was quiet. The cheerleaders were not being pursued by any jocks, and they were not wearing their usual polished hair and makeup. The teachers did not actively supervise the kids and seemed uninterested. No one bothered to acknowledge the homework workload that had to be finished by year-end.

It was all weird.

Wendy strolled the halls. She focused on trying to ignore the group of people who muttered bits of gossip about Maxine's loss. Penny was quiet; her clothing lacked a stitch of vibrancy as the tones were muted. Andrea stood at the end of the hall, ignoring the mourning of the one girl who was once her cheerleader.

Everyone was off their game.

"Hey," Wendy said solemnly, her mouth cocked a tight smirk.

"Hey," Andrea said, eyes glossy, trying to hold back her tears.

"How're you holding up?"

"Fine."

Another wave of students passed them. More chatter about losing Maxine; the toll of losing somebody in their class was too much for them to handle. Their mouths echoed with cries of sadness as they grieved the loss of someone special.

"Excuse me!" Andrea yelled, angered. "We didn't just lose Maxine last night. We lost Astrid, too!"

"Yeah, show some respect!" Penny chimed in, fuming from witnessing the lack of consideration.

Their protest went unnoticed, just like Astrid wanted to be. She desired neither attention nor involvement in the midst of the drama. Looked like she got what she wished for.

"Who was she?" muttered one voice.

"Who cares?" said another.

Andrea stood in disbelief.

Astrid's only goal was to make it through high school and move forward in life with no trouble, and to protect her siblings from any impending horrors. Her reluctance to be a pariah haunted her departure.

"I care," said one boy who leaned against his locker.

"Finally, somebody who does," hissed Penny, getting some sense of humanity from her peers.

"She was a good person," said Wendy.

"Yes, she was," said Andrea.

They sensed his genuine sincerity. The news of Maxine's death was painful to hear, but there was also a refreshing sense of ease to hear care for Astrid. It would be fair for the school to show an equal level of sympathy for the other person affected.

"You were with her when she died, right?" asked Peter, curious.

"We were," said Andrea.

"Do you happen to know if she finished this paper she was working on?"

"What are you talking about?"

"She was helping me out with this paper so I can get into drama camp this summer."

Wendy's palms warmed up with heat; the hairs on her forearms became stiff. As she pounced on him, her backpack fell to the marble floor, making a loud clap. Wendy's powerful hand caused the ribbed neckline of his t-shirt to rip apart. The force of his body caused a small dent to appear on the locker. A section of hair dripped onto the floor, moving alongside their scuffle like a tumbleweed.

"You selfish piece of shit!" she screamed.

His throat let out a loud gulp.

"You're the one using her for help," Penny joined with equal aggravation.

"I just needed help with my paper!" he whimpered with fear, his arms flinching over his face.

"You threatened her siblings!" Wendy snapped.

Andrea couldn't believe it as she joined the angry duo. Flushing hues of pink adorned her pasty face. With her undershirt sleeves pushed up toward her elbows, she braced herself to unleash the bottled-up sadness she experienced upon witnessing Astrid's lifelessness.

"You're just like the rest of them!" she said. "Assholes that only care about themselves unless you need something!"

Her fist jabbed into his gut. His classmates stopped and observed the tension as he let out a small exhale of air. His sunbed-tan skin became pale.

The overhead speaker beeped loud in their ears; this would be the ring of the bell to signal the next class to begin. This time, it was different.

"Good morning, students," said the voice, which turned out to be Principal Stuart. "As many of you know, we lost two of our students last night."

There was a momentary pause in the girls' anger as they realized they were both being acknowledged.

"Maxine Ryan was active in our cheerleading squad and has also been an integral part of our student council. We also lost Astrid Jennings, who you've also seen around the school."

"What the fuck?" Andrea screamed; her fist made a slammed dent into the locker.

Evading their grasp, Peter fled from the group, whimpering in cowardice. His shirt sleeve tore apart at the seams and dropped to the ground.

"Due to the recent events, we've decided to give you all the rest of the day to yourselves for reflection. Take this as an opportunity to not look at this as an extended weekend, but more on what we've lost and how much we take for granted. Stay safe, everyone."

"They barely mentioned her!" Penny said, furious. "What's wrong with these people?"

Wendy's heart fluttered horribly. Her stomach churned something wicked, and there wasn't anything in there from her skipping breakfast.

What's wrong with me?

"I need to get out of here," she grumbled, her face flushing out its color.

Running through the crowd of people, she noticed the students celebrating with relief that they were free from another day of classes. The sound of multiple conversations, either about going to the mall or having a movie day, echoed in her ears.

Where was the consideration?

Where was the humanity?

She now knew where Andrea was coming from at the memorial. Nobody batted an eye unless there was some sort of status or benefit. Otherwise, they're just a tiny, minute droplet in the big pond.

"Wendy," called out her teacher from nearby, Ms. Woods.

Who am I becoming?

She ignored her teacher, dodging the clusters of children. Even Mr. Turlington was grunting while discussing his student's performance in the track meet.

"Wendy, please!"

Wendy huffed out a deflating sigh. Despite her frustration, she kept her tears at bay. While Penny and Andrea caught up to Ms. Woods, she looked at them with sympathy as she cradled two textbooks near her chest. Ellie emerged from the corner to witness Wendy's frustration.

"What's wrong?" her teacher asked as she reached her arm out to comfort her, only to be met with a retreating flinch.

"It's nothing," Wendy said, noticing the space closing on her. "I just need to go."

I don't know what I've become.

"Please, talk to me," her teacher pleaded. "I hate to see you like this. Let me help you."

"I-I'm sorry. I need to go."

The air around her felt stuffy, causing her chest to weigh down. Her hands trembled as she tightly gripped her backpack straps. Overwhelmed with anger, her knees gave in and she had to take a seat.

"Wendy!"

The doors opened, and out she ran. The fresh air was leveling her out. Cars in the parking lot started emptying out gradually, with some groups of friends discussing their plans for the day. Another person got out of their truck; the rusty hinges of their door screeched inside her ears.

Ian.

"Not now!" she said as she ran right past him.

It was unclear to her whether he had any interest in talking to her or not. Wherever she went, he was always there in the background, ready to intimidate her.

"What's the matter?" he asked, whiny. "Is someone having a moment?"

Wendy ignored him as she crossed the rest of the lot. The sound of his laughter caused her to let out the first tear she had been trying to hold in. All the overwhelming experiences caused her to become something she was not used to.

"Why don't you run along to your boyfriend? You always do!"

With caution tape surrounding them, the porta-potties were a reminder of the previous night's danger as she walked by. The sounds of Destiny's screams pleading for mercy resonated within her; her weeps were filled with horror.

IT WAS ALL TOO OVERWHELMING for her. Too much drama, too much loss. The wildest part of this entire situation was the uneven distribution of grief among individuals. People showed concern for individuals with names or status but ignored those without. It was like they didn't even know that they ever existed. The teachers who witnessed the victories and hardships of every student also showed a tendency to lose interest in certain students.

Would they be sad if I was gone?

The only thing on her mind was the impact she would've left if she wasn't here tomorrow. Would people mourn over the end of her life like Maxine and Malakai, or treat her death like Astrid, where it's essentially the wind that simply passes by? These thoughts nauseated her. The continued visual reminders of their deaths have affected her appetite. The blood mingled with the damp earth after spewing from Astrid's neck, while Maxine's life ebbed away from the open wounds on her limbs.

All of this is too much.

With the wind whistling in her ears, the faint sound of her sneakers tapping on the blacktop path was barely noticeable. The tall grass swayed, revealing hints of lavender amidst the merging of brown and vibrant kelly-green.

The sun irritated parts of her forehead as it rose to the highest point. Her chest rose and fell slowly as she tried to take in the fresh air. She had always desired an escape, like a bug trapped in a jar with no air. Whenever she moistened her lips, bits of her hair would cling to the corners of her mouth. Sweat built up in her armpits, causing her red sweater to become damp.

The trees waved a friendly greeting as she entered the forest path. Wind fluttered the leaves that moved the branches. Red-bellied woodpeckers pecked on tree trunks and yellow warblers chased each other around.

Wendy's heart was calming down; the palpitations became weaker, less horrid. Memories of Malakai escorting her to and from school made her frail. His actions of picking up a stick and using it as a sword or cane made her miss him intensely. Whenever her anxiety arose, his carefree demeanor was there to take the spotlight. He would know what to do if his sister was struggling through life that didn't involve academia; that's where her expertise would benefit him, since he couldn't keep his brain disciplined to complete his homework or even retain the information about the lessons. In adversity, he would balance her. Even though she thought differently, she would feel understood when things got tough.

I can really use you, Malakai. I miss you so much.

She wasn't ungrateful for the other people in her life. Penny had been there since she moved to their town years ago. When she faced difficulties outside her brother's expertise, they offered support to each other. When Penny's mother prioritized her show development, they turned to each other for guidance through their first periods. When they had boy problems, they also didn't trust their parents;

they were too old to understand what it was like to be a teenager in these times. Social media or texting were not available during their youth; the game had changed. Managing the distinctions between flirting and socializing has been diverse, as has addressing the backlash of a vengeful person seeking retribution against the one who deceived them, trying to cause embarrassment. They didn't know how to handle Zachariah back then or now.

Purple and orange peered through the bare branches of a pine twenty feet ahead of her. Twigs crunched under the weight of his shoes. Her heart raced slower, but better than before. Her encounters with him have become more unpredictable. On certain days, he would show authentic concern for her and her well-being, providing her with a sense of security. Other times, it would be like she didn't know him; he wouldn't acknowledge anything that she opened up to him about or consider her feelings. In the presence of his friends, who micromanaged his encounters like publicists, this was what would usually happen.

She fought her urge to smile at him; she was happy to see him but guarded. Because of this, her expression became pinched, and she became woozy. Zachariah's posture straightened and his eyebrows raised in anticipation as he spotted her.

"Hey, everything all right?" he asked with concern as he noticed the cocked smile she shed.

"Y-yes," she answered, her tongue dry. "I'm okay."

"That's good."

He stopped right in front of her. They locked eyes, their irises mirroring the glimmers of sunlight filtering through the tree's canopy. His two front teeth were more prominent as they beamed with comfort. Wendy recognized that this was his true self, free from the judgment of his friends. This was the same person who had melted her heart when he was at Penny's place a few nights ago. His compassion for her grief was something that brought hope that she would come out of high school alive.

"Well, that's been a shitty past couple of days, huh?" he asked.

"Very," she said, dignified. "Too many losses to process."

"I know. And why these people?"

"I dunno."

"It's just strange that all of this is happening a year after that one girl died."

"That girl has a name!" Wendy said, slapping his arm. "Nora."

"I'm sorry. I didn't mean that," he said, flinching, fearful of another strike.

"Well, it seems like many people don't mean to not show any respect to those that don't matter to them."

Wendy started to walk away; her irritation toward him was relative to the others inside the school. Her ears warmed up, with her blood simmering and ready to boil. Despite his good intentions, she has run out of patience due to today's events.

"I know how much Nora meant to you," he said as he followed behind her, desperate to make it up to her. "I remember how it affected you."

"You didn't know the half of it," she said, still avoiding eye contact with him. "I didn't know her too well."

"But you were close with her sister."

"Yes, I was," she said, her throat drying.

"You two were really close. I felt bad for not being around after I joined the team. I was relieved that you had someone that made you happy like Andrea."

The brush crinkled again. Another letterman jacket emerged from the bushes, causing sparrows to fly away from their perches. Shaggy hair wisped from the sudden gust of the chilly wind.

Wesley.

"Yes, she did!" he said, meandering closer to the two.

Not now!

Zachariah's hands sunk deep into his pockets. His shoulders crept closer to one another. Wendy's breath shook over the sigh that expelled from his nostrils.

"You two have been quite the item," Wesley said, leaning onto the nearby tree.

They said nothing. Their eyes peered into Wesley's hazel eyes.

"People have been talking for years about you two. Are you two a thing?"

"No!" she blurted.

"Oh, then it was her brother you were after."

"Wes, you're taking this too far," Zachariah said, his arm shielding Wendy.

"Am I?"

With synchronized head tilts and icy expressions, they mirrored two cowboys on the verge of a pistol draw. Wesley's mouth tightened and his eyebrows crept closer to his eyes. Two squirrels scurried for shelter, hiding inside the trunk of a tree.

"If I recall, I think you said all those things."

"What things?" Wendy asked, confused, her eyes looking into Zachariah's guilt; remorse settled in with his stalemate.

"You didn't tell her?"

"Tell me what, Zachariah? What is he talking about?"

"Oh, Wendy. Your little friend was the one that would always say that you two were a thing."

"What?"

Zachariah's chin moved downward, bringing his head closer to his collar bones. His chin jutted out from its usual position. Even after bird droppings splattered on his jacket, he didn't acknowledge it; nothing would take his focus away.

"He was the one that said that you and Andrea dated, and that you broke up with her because her weirdo of a sister died."

"That's not true!" Wendy said, spooking the rest of the animals lounging nearby; they scattered like a stampede.

"He's said so much about you since joining the team. That's just the start of it. Like about the time when you puked when you watched the video on puberty back in middle school."

"Is that true?" she asked, tears forming.

Zachariah remained frozen. His uncertainty prevented him from knowing how to react or find the right words to extricate himself. His cheek was wet with a tear, and his lip trembled in sadness at the truth being uncovered.

"Yes," he said, his voice raspy and silent.

Wendy cringed with disdain. She weakly clenched her fists as they pelted his chest. His actions caused her to be excluded from everything for years. He circulated rumors in order to feel more confident and avoid becoming a victim in his crowded school environment.

She grasped the straps of her bag and ran, her shoulder knocking into Wesley's. Her steps grew weaker as she sobbed in heartbreak, causing her balance to become precarious.

How could he do this to me?

"You don't need her," Wesley said, cold. "I told you she's holding you back. She always has and always will."

Zachariah's fists clenched tight; his knuckles cracked with his nostrils flared. Saying those words burdened him with shame, like a heavy rain cloud. His intention was to attribute his actions to his social circle, but that wouldn't eliminate the fact that he shared the information with them. Wendy's behavior toward him when Wesley was present showed that she already knew he had been influenced.

"I was going to tell her," Zachariah muttered.

"And now you don't have to," Wesley said, patting his shoulder. "Now, did you want your freshman year to be shit? I can take away everything I've created for you in the blink of an eye. Remember that."

Zachariah said nothing. His teammate's rationale shackled him to his loyalty. His stomach twisted and turned, desperately wanting to eject its contents. Digging into the torn seam, his fingers pinched the polyester lining of his pockets.

"She'll be fine. Let her run off to her books. We have a party to get ready for."

Chapter 20

As usual, the library was quiet, with its regular group of elderly ladies teaching the seven-year-olds how to crochet, despite their uneven loops. After getting notice of the schools getting out early, they weren't prepared to watch them this early to commit to the promises made to their parents. The thoughtless conduct of the children, carelessly dropping their needles and flinging their yarn balls, added to frustrating the already bitter women. The regret of committing to this class became more apparent as these children were far from the attentive adults they had watched their grandkids grow into.

Wendy's toes brushed against the marble floor, almost snagging on the cracks. A man sitting in the corner diligently wrote notes in his notepad, and a cough was heard from another reader. Positioned by his usual spot, Jeff sat at his desk, his attention fixed on the computer screen as it scrolled down a page. Hairs protruded out from his mustache like cat whiskers.

"Hi, Jeff," Wendy said quietly, still drained from her morning drama.

"Hi Wendy," he said back to her, his chair screeched something wicked into their ears from the rust.

"Having a good day so far?"

"It could be better," he answered, irritated.

"Tell me about it."

"First off, I can't find my earring. That was gifted to me a long time ago by my mother. I feel like I'm disappointing her when I lose it."

"Oh no," she said, looking along the surface of his desk, not knowing where to start amongst the cluster of papers scattered along the stacks of returned books.

"It's strange. I put it in the same place every time I take it off. Right on top of my dresser."

"Well, I'm sure it will turn up somewhere. It's not like it grew feet and walked away."

"I'm sure it will. Are we still planning on putting together that event for the homeless?"

Wendy sighed horribly, as though she were in pain. Given the recent losses, volunteer work was the least of her concerns. She sought a break to unwind and heal.

"I'm sorry. I forgot," she said regretfully. "Perhaps we can plan this another day?"

The librarian's head bowed closer to his desk. His eyes focused on the papers and old card catalog cards, realizing the daunting task of transferring the information onto his computer.

"I really am sorry," she said, heartbroken.

He turned to the computer; his fingers pelted the keyboard as they typed hard on the keys. The buttons emitted a terrible pelting sound, resembling rain hitting a window. His cheeks flushed pink; his eyebrows furrowed closer to his eyes.

Cut me some slack!

She walked away from the desk, taken aback by his passive aggression, especially when it was directed at a child. The loss she experienced caused her to become agitated toward people she would never speak to. Now, her failure to prioritize the things that bring her joy by bringing happiness to others has had a negative impact on both of them. On top of it, all she could think about are the possibilities of what Zachariah has said about her. Memories replayed throughout her high school career of the times that eyes were on her, thinking if it was just her peers being observant or if it was based on something he started.

A stack of books tumbled next to her as she passed by it. Dust choked down her throat. With no patrons around, her coughing resonated through rows of shelves, the sound bouncing back as an echo. Moths fluttered out from the pages of the hardcovers that craved someone to read their passages with each book sprawled open.

Every empty desk gave her flashes of every person who departed from her life. Tanner and Bryce were trying to fight off their boredom by rocking back and forth, their eyes fixed on the ceiling, wishing they could be anywhere but in a place of literacy. Maxine, with her legs crossed on top, planted a wad of bubble gum underneath and yearned for company as she stared at the two. Astrid plunged into an endless pile of papers, their pages fluttering, chewing on a pencil eraser; still a nervous wreck in her next life.

Wendy reached back into her oasis; the room was left the same as the last time. The windows were cleaned, revealing a clear view of the green lawn in high definition, unlike the other windows with a faint sepia tint. Her desk was immaculate, showcasing the books she had neglected for days, their pages marked at the point where she had last worked on her paper. Sitting in the chair was a familiar face; his hair was shaggy as always, with strands sticking up from the scalp that drove Wendy crazy. With each step, his black sneakers rhythmically tapped the carpet like a drummer.

Malakai.

"Hey, sis," he said to her with adoration, his eyes glistening.

"Hey, bro," she whispered, her throat tightening. "What're you doing here?"

"I wanted to see you," he said, smiling.

"I didn't know you could do that. You're dead."

"You don't have to rub it in," he said, chuckling. "I didn't know we could come out and visit, either."

A slight nudge tapped her shoulder. Her attention shifted to the chipped pastel nail polish on her pointer finger, then to the ribbed cuff of a faded Robin egg blue sweatshirt. Even in death, her breath fogged up her glasses, and she remained asthmatic until the very end.

"Hi, Astrid," she said, her guilt for her passing brought heaviness in her chest.

"Hey!" she said, her braces reflecting the sunlight.

"I'm sorry about what happened to you."

"It's not your fault!" she said, dismissing her shame. "I know this sounds grim, but I'm glad I don't have to worry about what other people think of me anymore."

"It would've been better once you graduated."

"I know. But the crap follows you after high school. It's just easier to avoid."

The angry screams startled both Wendy and the spirits, caused by one grandmother yelling. One child split open the stitches, ruining their blanket. Profanities became more colorful with each howl.

"I don't think so," Wendy said, watching the child run away from the elder's gimp.

"Easier for you to say. You're not me. You're so pretty and can land anybody as a friend."

"People can change. Life does get better."

"I don't want to fight with you," she said dismissively. "I'm dead and won't be coming back. We can agree to disagree, even in death. I just wanted to tell you I'll think of you and your kindness."

"We all are thinking of you," Malakai said, his shoulders shrank with discomfort. "We're worried about your safety."

"I don't blame you," Wendy said, a tear forming along the bottom of her eye. "People are dropping like flies."

The room became silent, with air filled by a faint screech, which grew rigid. A few taps brushed against the walls, sending a shiver down her back. Wheels screeched from a cart hauling stacks of books, waiting to return to their resting place.

"Do you know who's been doing all of this?"

"We do," Malakai said, his tone shaky with nerves.

"Then tell me," she said, eager to put it all behind her.

Astrid and Malakai exchanged wide-eyed glances. Astrid's thick spectacles enlarged her pupils; the veins darkened like a specimen in a petri dish.

"It's Nora," he answered with fear, even after the train obliterated him.

"Nora?" Wendy said, startled. "But she's dead."

Silence grew again. Their reluctance to explain further became more of a reality.

"There is an evil that roams around this town," Astrid explained, her finger raising matter-of-factly. "And it has been conjuring up something wicked."

"What do you mean?"

"They called for Nora. Her spirit has been terrorizing the town and punishing those who've inflicted pain."

Wendy's jaw lowered a bit. Despite being terrorized in the bathroom at the police station the night Malakai died, she was certain she wasn't losing her mind. The familiar voice of Andrea's little sister was what she thought, but was cast to the side without belief. Rumors of when Destiny was being followed by a mysterious presence were starting to make sense, no matter how much urine trickled down her jeans for justice.

"Be careful out there," Malakai said with care. "I don't want to see you too soon. I want you to have a long and happy life."

"Wait. I need your help. Tell me more."

Her eyes blinked when she opened them; they were gone. It was as if they had never existed. The books Astrid once dug into had disappeared from the desk. All the gum under the tables was dry as can be; Maxine's piece was nowhere to be found.

Wendy's level of paranoia has risen, particularly because of Astrid and Malakai's warning. She doesn't know what to take from her conversation; an old friend's dead sister is roaming the town and killing off people for a reason that isn't clear. There must be something beyond this.

Why would she be back from the dead? And why go after these people?

Another tap came from behind her shoulder. Her heart stopped as she lost her breath. The fear that maybe the spirit was after her left her stomach in knots. Upon turning her gaze, she spotted someone familiar standing before the empty desks and unoccupied shelves. Jet-black hair floated around the face from the static. Sunlight illuminated her porcelain and pale skin, highlighting the black lipstick and eyeliner. Despite her vacant expression, a glimmer of concern could be seen in her eyes.

Andrea.

Chapter 21

"What are you doing here?" Wendy asked, her hand resting over her chest to calm herself down.

"It's the library. Everyone's welcome here," Andrea said, derisive.

A group of children weaved around the desks in a figure-eight formation. The chairs were on the brink of falling when a shoulder nudged her back, causing all four chairs to wobble. They grazed the man who had collapsed next to a bookshelf. Between two thick books, his head found a snug perch on the shelf. His breath reeked of Budweiser; his armpits oozed a stench of body odor and rotting fish guts that were caked onto the hem of his shirt.

"Really? What are you doing here?" Wendy asked again. "You never go to the library. Not for a long time."

"Yes, I do."

"Nobody goes here."

"I can see that," Andrea said, her arms showcasing every nook and cranny that craved attention.

"That's why I like to come here. I don't have to see anybody else."

"Couldn't you just go home?" Andrea asked, sardonic. "You don't have to see anybody there either. I mean, this place is such a disaster. How can you even relax here?"

"I just need a place away from everything. A place where I don't have my parents nagging me or classmates projecting their drama."

"Sounds nice," Andrea said, her eyebrow raised in agreement.

"It is. I enjoy getting away from it all."

"That's why I go here, too."

"You hide out here?"

Andrea's arm vanished into the dark recesses of the towering shelves. The overhead lighting barely illuminated the dull shine of a withered desk; a wink of silky cobwebs glistened in the flicker. Stacks of books with paper fragments separated from their spines. A pile of empty soda cans gathered in the corner, desperately seeking a trash receptacle to accommodate them.

"I'm surprised you don't see me here because I see you."

"I'm sorry," Wendy said, dumbstruck.

"It's not like I wanted to hang out with you," Andrea said, dismissive.

"I understand."

"It's my place to get away from these assholes."

Wendy nodded her head, understanding where she was coming from. Although they didn't have much in common now, they agreed on that one thing. Wendy was aware of Andrea's goal to blend in, but even remaining silent in the hallways proved to be too difficult.

"It's where I connect with Nora," Andrea continued, and a small tear formed. "This was one of her favorite places when the school kicked her out of the art room."

"I remember."

"I remember her carrying stacks of books." Her hand caressed a nearby shelf, ignoring the dust coated on its surface. "She studied every bit of art history and mediums."

"She really was passionate about her art."

Andrea discovered the textbooks that held information on Nora's beloved subject. Every medium of art was within the books she buried her head in, even more than Astrid. Andrea's nails sank into the pages, seeking the folded edges where her sister had tucked a bookmark, reminiscing the feeling of her sister's presence.

"She really was. She was so talented."

THE DAISY SCOUTS FROM the area brought a red wagon loaded with boxes of delectable cookies to a table nearby. They evaded the swarm of mothers hurrying to snatch a copy of Oprah Winfrey's autobiography, eager to immerse themselves in her life story. Printers were loud and hot as preteens printed hundreds of fanfiction pages to store in their three-ringed binders. Kids emptied their candy bags onto the shiny desks, disregarding the slight ache caused by the small cavity forming on their teeth.

Rows of shelves echoed the slap of a stack of textbooks onto the empty desk. Ignoring the number of books in her pile, the underclass girl smirked, excited to fill her brain with knowledge. She took away the uppermost layer of Renaissance paintings, revealing postcard-sized images of the Mona Lisa *and* The Last Supper, *in order to introduce her to the inspiration.*

"Easy there," fifteen-year-old Andrea said to her sister, holding her back as she almost bumped into her stack. "I think you have enough."

"I'm sorry," Nora said, her breath huffing with glee. "I just want to get some ideas down."

"Ideas for what?"

"I want to sell my work," she said, her eyes getting wider with anticipation. "I need some inspiration."

Andrea's eyes wandered around the pages as she opened another textbook. The swirls in Van Gough's Starry Night *reminded her of a drawing her sister made as a child. Although it didn't match up to the original, her practice showed promise in creating a beautiful, original work.*

"If you just pull from what's in your heart, you'll be inspired enough."

"Are you now coming at me with some cheesy Hallmark shit?" Nora asked with sarcasm, her eyebrows raising repetitively.

Andrea's laughter carried over the elderly ladies' class on scrapbooking. Their lack of focus led to imprecise cutting, resulting in eye-rolling. The edges lost their clean lines and became asymmetrical because of a slight curve.

"No, I just want you to express yourself."

"Just like what you do with your music?"

Nora marked the spot in her memory by pinching the corner of the sheet as she turned the page. The pages transformed into stacks of triangles, offering many points of reference to bring her back.

"Sure. It's just that I don't plan on doing something with my music. I just write it to express how I feel on the inside."

"Your insides must be pretty dark," Nora said, facetious.

"They're not that bad," Andrea said, snickering. "I'm just feeling some type of way at the moment."

"This doesn't have anything to do with that boy you've been seeing?"

Andrea glanced at the librarian's desk, observing a boy with messy black hair slamming a hardcover book. Startled by the echo, the ladies let out a small scream that scared the daisy scouts. She disregarded the cringe on the children's faces as their parents woke up and allowed them to play without supervision. Behind a collection of books, his pale skin illuminated the dark corner. The scar above his eye had a shadow cast on it by his pale skin.

Ian.

"No," Andrea said, heartless, her arms cradling closer to her chest. "It's not about him."

"Really? Because I saw how happy you were when he texted you last week."

"This isn't about me. This is about you and your art!" she whisper-shouted.

She ushered her sister toward the desks. Amidst a sea of mustard-colored beanbags, a pair of middle schoolers found solace in their slumber, drowning out the world with music pouring into their ears through headphones. Light blared from the lone monitor on a vacant desk. Andrea moved the mouse to wake it from its inactive snooze. Her fingers tapped the keyboard after she pulled up the web browser.

"What are you doing?" Nora asked, curious as she meandered closer to her.

"I'm trying to help you with something," Andrea said, her eyes fixated on the growth of letters populating in the text box.

eLookBook.

"Oh, come on, Andrea. You know I don't believe in that shit."

Andrea chuckled while setting up a profile with the mouse. Information was being added to complete the content for it. The reality of her sister conforming became more real. Conforming wasn't something she sought out and finding her sister one step with being closer to everyone else nauseated her.

"You'll need to get with modern times if you want to sell your work."

A sigh of defeat expelled from Nora's chest. As her fingers dangled by her side, blood surged to her nails. The screen was bright, blaring into her irises.

"This is a good way to get your work out there. Everybody can see what you're doing and follow along your journey."

Nora moved the chair closer to the desk, her feet scuffling along the carpet. The weight of defeat was heavy on her newly formed presence. She'd seen how irritated Andrea got when she checked her profile. How easy it was to become immersed in the drama of the posts was something she doesn't want to be a part of.

"What if I just sell at some art shows or something?"

"You can do that, but do you see any art shows happening near us any time soon?"

"No."

"Then you have to start somehow," Andrea encouraged. "Give it a try, and I'm sure you'll like it. I even created a profile, so all you need to do is add what you'd like and request friends."

"You know, you can be a real pain in the ass."

"That's called being your sister," she said with a wink, accentuating a twinkle.

With an excess of books, the cart groaned, and the wheels screeched in protest. Dewy drops of sweat on the librarian's forehead caught the light, creating a glistening effect. Desperate for calm, his asthmatic breath huffed out wheezes.

"Hey, girls," the librarian said, his arms resting on the handle that exposed a dampened patch of fabric under his armpit on his button-down shirt. "I heard that you're looking for something to do."

"Not necessarily," Nora said, her shoulders tensing up.

"I was going to say that if you're looking for something, I could always use some help with arranging events here. My schedule gets so busy, and I can't keep up with planning things I want to happen with the boys from the diner."

"That's a great idea," Nora said, apprehensive. "I'll let you know if I have some free time. There's a lot happening right now."

The librarian's lip curled; the freckles on his cheeks disappeared into the blush shade that grew. With a firm grip, his moistened hand made the iron handle squeak. The sound of his loafers clomping on the carpet echoed through the room as he struggled to maintain balance with each step.

"Thanks anyway."

The musty stench of his body odor seeped out of his shirt's neckline, causing Andrea's nose to wrinkle. Nora's eyes fixed on the screen as her fingers clicked on the mouse, struggling to keep up with the rapidly loading images.

"You're a natural at this."

"It's not like I don't know what this website is."

"I don't know what you do with your life!" Andrea said, nudging Nora's shoulder.

"Apparently, you just find ways to put your fingerprint on things."

"That's not it at all. It's just—"

"I'm kidding. God, you worry too much about me."

Their teeth glimmered with a smile so radiant. Their stomachs fluttered with warmth from their security. Sisterhood is a bond that pulsed alongside their hearts. Their mother has been there to support them with a roof over their heads, but the trust in their unconditional love was paramount above any others. Support and trust was something that transcended material possessions.

"I just sent you a friend request!"

DUST CLOUDS SETTLED on Wendy and Andrea's heads, creating a contrast between white roots and their darker hair. In the absence of the elders, the building grew quiet, except for the librarian's slow movements and the mournful sound of a rusty wheel. Asthmatic breaths crept around the space, echoing off the walls.

"I really am sorry for Nora," Wendy said, touching the abstract expressionism textbook.

"I know you are," Andrea said, her arms cradling over her chest.

A smirk came from the corner of Andrea's mouth. All the loss they had endured during the week caused her to abandon her cold facade. Her guard being down, she couldn't shut out the remorse and promises for change any longer.

"I come here often to connect with Nora. Away from all the noise in school or at home," said Andrea, a tear glistening along the underpart of her eye.

Wendy nodded in acknowledgment. Nora held a special place in Andrea's heart, and she was aware of it. Andrea's absence became more noticeable when her sister passed away and she vanished from everyone's attention. She felt the same way when Malakai died, but didn't want to make things awkward. The level of interest in investing in her peers' problems decreased, although not as much as before.

Andrea has the courage to vanish, which sets her apart from Wendy. Although her approach may be subject to criticism, she defended herself and championed Nora's cause. The advocacy for her sister was something that everyone knew about. Her passion for Nora's success was a top priority.

A slight vibration nudged Wendy's pocket. She ignored it by remaining engaged in conversation with Andrea. She received a notification, which cut short her conversation with Andrea. A blinding, white light emitting from her phone dazzled Wendy. Her finger unlocked the home screen. A small red number one hovered in the corner of her eLookBook app's icon. Thoughts crossed Wendy's mind about ignoring it because she didn't have much interest in prioritizing social media over her mending connection.

A small buffer stalled the application's loading from the muffled Wi-Fi connection. The main page displayed pictures of a select few friends she followed, mainly selfies of Mrs. Hershey promoting her show, along with candids of her using casserole dishes from her oven or creating something flashy with rhinestones and an enormous bow. Yet, the top of the page featured something distinct. This was a post on her wall. A message from someone that she never would've seen the day this would happen.

Nora Crispin.

Wendy's heart stopped. Apart from the friend request, she received no messages from her, not even when she was alive. Her limited activity on the platform made her unsure if they were friends. Regardless of her screen time, the message only contained two words.

Miss you.

"Is this some kind of joke?" Andrea hissed, her voice choking up.

Wendy was rendered speechless, immobilized by the thought of how Andrea would feel if she received the message. Trembling hands surpassed buzzing phones in vibration.

"Did you do this?" Andrea asked Wendy, her face becoming red.

She pulled up her phone to show off her screen. Nora's message caught her attention as her fingers found it. A teardrop caused the font to magnify, revealing the exact words.

Miss you, sis.

"What, me?" Wendy asked, shocked. "No!"

"Bullshit!"

"I got the same message! Why would I do this to myself?"

The lights in the building flickered, with the building suddenly cleared out. Frustration grew from the librarian's desk. From the depths of his diaphragm, he unleashed a string of profanities so vulgar that they could make a child wince in fear. Wendy's throat closed in. Andrea's pupils got bigger.

A shadow grew from within the shelves, creeping closer to Andrea's desk. Giggles became faint in their ears, reminding them of Nora's childhood joy. Art textbooks fell to the floor, opening the pages of the inspiration that once flooded the departed, fluttering like an expanding accordion.

"Let's do a painting," the voice said softly, enticing Andrea as she made her way closer to it.

"We should get out of here," Wendy said, her voice raspy with fear.

"I want to know who is fucking with us," Andrea said, annoyed as she stomped her foot. "What kind of sicko would record my sister's voice and use it to scare us?"

"Someone I don't want to mess with," said Wendy, her taunted memory in the bathroom returning to her.

Wendy lost her grip on Andrea's forearm as her hand slipped away. Andrea led the way toward the shelves, causing her knees to tremble with no other option but to follow.

"Come on," the voice continued. "This will be perfect, just like the ones we saw in the books."

"Nora? Is that you?" Andrea asked the voice as she followed in and out of the shelves.

Whenever Andrea caught up on one side, the shadow snuck to the other side again. Andrea moved like Mrs. Pacman, pursuing a ghost after devouring a power-up fruit.

"Andrea, let's go!" Wendy whispered loud, apprehensive.

"I need to know if it's her!" Andrea hissed with impatience. "Tell me who you are!"

The lights turned off, taking a break from their frantic flickers. The room slowly diminished, surrounded by darkness, as the dusty windows filtered in the dim daylight from the cloud-covered sun, which was descending with each passing minute.

"We have the perfect paint to make this happen."

"What are you talking about?" Andrea asked, her fists crackling from the crunch of her knuckles. "What paint?"

At the end of the last bookcase, the shadow ceased. Andrea and Wendy's shoulders lifted and dropped, panting from exhaustion. Palpitations filled their bodies as their hearts beat rapidly in the growing silence.

"It's my favorite color."

"Purple? Purple was always your favorite color."

"No, silly! I have a new favorite color."

Andrea's face became vacant, blank with confusion. Her sister's favorite color, among all the colors in her collection, was purple, even though she admired them all.

Trapped between two shelves of American history textbooks, the shadow confronted the girls. They both recognized the familiar face. Strands of greasy brunette locks draped in front of her chalk-white complexion like she got out of water. Gashes burrowed along her cheeks and forehead, forming scabs, while her lips turned a bruised shade of bluish eggplant. It was Nora, all right, but it was not the one that they remembered. This Nora looked like she went to hell and back, not even talking about high school. This Nora appeared more dead than she ever looked when Andrea found her one year ago.

"BLOOD RED!" Nora's voice groaned; her voice dropped deeper, more demonic.

Books flung from the shelves, pelting the girls in the shoulders. Screams of terror filled the air as pages whirled around them like a tornado from the falling stacks of old books. Carts twirled in place by the computers, spinning like figure skaters.

Wendy and Andrea ran into the central aisle. Nora's face darkened and her mouth dropped to her chest, leaving everyone in shock. Echoing roars filled the space, resulting in monitors exploding and sparks raining down on their shoes. Holding on to each other tightly, they trembled as electric charges escaped from the shattering screens.

"Let's paint a picture, sis!" Nora yelled with a sarcastic laugh. "All the different shades of blood will make my masterpiece!"

Another stack of books fell from the shelves. A burst of white peanuts filled the air like thick snow as the two bean bag chairs exploded. Book series were launched from the shelves with pages becoming destroyed.

Diary of a Wimpy Kid fled.

Goosebumps shivered.

Captain Underpants soiled their drawers.

"We need to get out of here!" Wendy said, her lungs coughing out a tiny wad of Styrofoam.

"But how?" Andrea asked, her eyes wide with fright.

Wendy looked down toward her desk. The fiend destroyed everything except for that one place. The reflection of the clean window winked at her with the sole idea that she could think of throughout the chaos.

"We'll have to break out."

Andrea nodded her head to acknowledge Wendy's plan. Racing past the desks, the shelves fell one by one in a domino effect. The sound of wood and metal clashing filled their ears as the furniture tumbled together. Papers softly rustle against one another like whispers.

Another gust battered their faces, making their hair blind their sight. Andrea grabbed the chair closest to Wendy's desk. Sweat made her palms slippery, and tears aided her grip. Another scream made their stomachs churn.

BANG!

The chair hit the glass. It didn't leave any sign of damage. The serene outdoors was taunting the girls inside, teasing them with serenity.

BANG!

Still nothing. Wendy felt helpless and screamed, realizing that neither her idea nor Andrea's brawn could provide an escape.

"Come on, sis! Let's make magic. This is what you wanted!"

Heat fumed from Andrea's ears. A horrible gritting sensation overwhelmed Andrea as her tears dried up and her teeth clenched. Once again, someone grabbed the seat. Struggling, she strained her shoulder and panted as she attempted to hit the window one more time.

"You're not my sister!" she screamed at the top of her lungs, her throat rattled from the scratch of her intensity.

The corner of the leg hit the window. A tiny web of cracked glass grew into something more significant, more profound. Each shattered piece fell to the floor as another gust of wind kissed them. Upon letting go of the chair, Andrea strained her biceps, but she found solace in witnessing the tranquility of the undisturbed lawn.

"Let's go!"

The bottom of Andrea's shoe crunched on the shattered glass remnants. Her eyes blinked to combat her desire to panic. Yet, this was not the same discrepancy they had just encountered. The sight of the library in disarray left Wendy dumbfounded, causing Andrea to turn back to her. Their hair resembled a gigantic nest, frizzled as if they had been electrocuted.

No more gusts.

No more exploding furniture.

No more Nora.

The place was completely demolished, as if a tornado had torn it apart. Stacks of books had now become piles of rubble. Dust intertwined with the bits of white powder let off by the broken ceiling tiles that have plummeted below. Puddles formed from the sprinkler system, creating mush out of the labored work of the writers with pages becoming nothing more.

"Where did she go?" Andrea asked, confused, her heart rate settling down as her safety became more promising.

"I don't know," said Wendy, wiping sweat away from her face. "One minute she was there, and the next she was gone."

They walked out of the lounge and back into the main space. Light fixtures dangled with the desperation of a fresh fluorescent rod to bring light back. The place where Wendy and Andrea had enlisted for peace had become a deserted mess. One that they could never go back to.

"Are you okay?" Wendy asked Andrea, her chin stopped trembling.

"Yes," Andrea responded, looking through the mess for signs of presence. "Are you?"

They reached each other for a hug. Something they haven't exchanged for over a year. The comfort of their embrace brought a sense of security, causing their bodies to relax. With their arms wrapped around their chests like a weighted blanket, a source of solace to soothe their anxiety. This was the moment Wendy had yearned for ever since she regretted being a neglectful friend. It was during this time that Andrea required emotional support and let her defenses down.

Wendy's eyes widened as she looked back at the space. Amidst the rubble, something appeared out of place, now serving as a decoration for the room. A man stood at the end of the toppled bookshelves. The top of the shelf had embedded its rigid edges deep into his stomach. Red splotches were spread over the wall, like a gunshot wound. A bit of light reflected from the bald spot on the head that collapsed towards the ground, in between the furniture that had split his body in half. Intestines spread over the floor in a pool of blood that soaked up in the pages of the books he guarded for many years.

Jeff Willow.

Chapter 22

Red and blue lights bounced along the buildings. Fire trucks screeched a horrid siren that pierced into everyone's ears. Wendy's gaze remained fixed on the coroner as they transported a black body bag on a stretcher, impervious to any distractions. Death was a universal reality, but it occurring in front of you was a whole new level of intensity. The experience of watching someone cross over from life to the unknown was not the same as seeing the aftermath of their corpse. She would never forget the image of Jeff's tongue, light pink and stained with blood, protruding from his mouth, while his eyes pleaded for release from the torment of the life draining from him. Her memory was now forever tainted by the image of his exposed insides, something she could never erase.

Why did he have to go?

Jeff was like a family member to Wendy. While some perceived him as an average citizen, she admired his loyalty to the community. He provided support for Wendy when she needed someone to talk to, even when he had other projects to focus on. Despite his lack of interest and tendency to avoid eye contact, he remained a non-judgmental sounding board.

"So, you're telling me that a dead person did all of this?" the officer asked, his gaze fastened on his notepad.

"Yes," Andrea said, her tone shaky. "It was my sister."

"Who?"

"Nora Crispin," she answered, displeased. "She died last year."

The officer raised his eyebrows, but confusion still filled his eyes. "Oh yeah, her."

Wendy wiped a tear from her cheek as she witnessed the ambulance doors shut the final visual of her departed friend. Launching herself off the hood of the police car, her eyes rolled at the officer's tone.

"Don't remember her because she wasn't a big name in this town?" Wendy asked, irritable.

Andrea's eyelids fluttered in disbelief. The officer struggled to come up with a valid excuse for his obliviousness as her jaw dropped and her lips slowly parted. No words were able to leave his lips.

"Nothing? All you have to say is nothing?" Wendy continued, umbraged. "I'm assuming she was just nothing to you."

"That's not it at all," the officer defended, his forehead sweaty. "I know you've been through a lot in the past couple of days, but I will ask you to—"

"Are we done with questions?" Wendy said, her eyes piercing into his. "Or are we going to find other ways to justify how we only care about certain people more than others?"

"Yes, we're done. It's just—"

"Great! Let's go, Andrea!"

Wendy refused to listen to anyone who didn't show care for the people she cherished. She clenched her teeth, battling her anger and empathizing with Andrea's grief after losing her sister. People like Nora and Astrid deserved the same respect as Maxine or Veronica.

Not anymore.

Penny turned the corner to meet them at the end of the block. Her sequins sparkled with the lights; the top of her messy bun bounced like a ball. The disheveled nature of her friend made her jaw drop in disbelief.

"Hey!" she said, her breath gusty. "Wait for me!"

Wendy didn't stop for her. She stomped her feet on the sidewalk, resembling a disappointed child denied their desired candy at the store. Andrea exchanged a glance filled with sadness to acknowledge her plea.

"Are you two all right?"

"We just got the shit scared out of us, and another person has died. What do you think?" Wendy said, her hands raising hopelessly; it was the only way she knew how to overcome her cluster of emotions.

"What even happened?"

"You wouldn't believe us if we told you," Andrea said.

"I'm your friend, Wendy. I would believe you."

Andrea's eyebrow cocked high. Her lips pursed together, wrinkling like a drying-out piece of fruit. Her cheeks were covered in caked dust that appeared even darker in the building's shadow.

"I'm your friend too, Andrea," Penny said, sighing with attempted empathy.

They came to a stop at the end of the block to let the emergency vehicles return to their respective spots. The rush of their speed sent their hair flying past their face. Wendy used deep breathing to stay connected with her support system and avoid isolating herself. She needed her army to balance her teetering emotions.

"It was Nora," she said, her eyes watering with fear.

"Nora? As in your sister Nora?"

"Yes," Andrea confirmed softly.

"How can that be? She's dead."

Wendy crossed the street. The loose pebbles caused her shoes to make a scratching sound, which frightened a nearby cat that was digging into a box of leftovers. The metal rattled when a black kitten fell into the bin.

"I told you she wouldn't believe us," Wendy hissed, disappointed.

"I believe you!" Penny defended meekly. "I just don't understand how Andrea's dead sister could come back and terrorize you."

"My sister would never be this horrible. I wish we knew, too."

"And to innocent people," Wendy said as she turned to take one last glimpse of the library as it disappeared from her sight.

"That monster is not my sister," she said with uncertainty, pained by the possibility that it actually could.

"From what I know of her, she wouldn't hurt a fly," Penny added.

"And why now?" asked Wendy.

So many questions flooded their minds. Why would somebody as invisible as Nora Crispin go out and take their lives away from these people? What did they do to deserve this horrible treatment?

As they entered the dark suburban streets, the three of them stayed quiet. The growing congregations of bugs swarmed around the warm bulb of the flickering street lamps, catching their eyes. They clasped their arms against their chests, shielding themselves from the potential dangers lurking in their own streets. The question of whether they were next on Nora's list haunted them, along with the worry of who else would fall victim to her deadly intentions.

A HALF A DOZEN BLOCKS later, the three made it to a familiar house. This time, the trees were wilting, their branches on the verge of snapping under the weight of a baby bird. Feathering from the ground, brown strands of grass pleaded for nourishment. Wood slivers on the siding were poking out, like shedding cat hair.

Andrea's home.

"Good, god, Andrea," Penny said as she noticed the two bushes in front of the door now barren like tumbleweeds. "Your place could use a bit of TLC."

Wendy stayed silent. She didn't want to say anything to agree with Penny. Andrea's frustration would be justified because she didn't make time to visit. But in all actuality, the place was exponentially different from how she remembered it, even a year ago when she came over last. Everything was well kept, down to the fine details of grass cut at a specific measurement.

Not this time.

The door swung open; hinges screeched with resistance from the rust. Wendy's eyes widened. Mold-filled stains covered the bottom of the boxes, which were stacked from floor to ceiling. Shades of cranberry and grape stained the yellowish-brown carpet. Trash encircled the garbage can, creating a fortress-like barrier.

Penny's lip curled with disgust. While she may have disliked her mother's meticulousness in maintaining the house, she was thankful her mother never left it in disrepair like this. Wendy held her breath to avoid smelling cat pee, questioning whether Andrea had a cat or if an uninvited guest had infiltrated their home amidst their sorrow.

"Well, well, well," said a voice, raspy as dishes clattered on the counter. "Look who decided to show up."

A woman walked into the dining room to make her presence known. The greasy auburn hair, twisted into a half-finished ponytail, had gray strands fluttering away. With each exhale of her cigarette, a small cloud of smoke dispersed into the air. Her cheeks became sunken and sharp enough to inflict harm, no longer the roundness Wendy remembered.

Andrea's mom.

"So, you finally decided to care about us after not hearing from you for a year," she hissed as her black bra strap peeked out from the stretched-out neckline of her heather-gray t-shirt, which she hadn't washed in weeks and had multiple stains on it.

"I-I'm sorry, Ms. Crispin," Wendy said, tentative to say the wrong thing. "I have nothing to say that will excuse what I did or make you feel better for what I've done."

A quiet chuckle grew as she took another drag of her cigarette. Returning to the kitchen, she grabbed a bottle of cheap wine and flung the cap toward Wendy's feet after unscrewing it.

"We took you in," she slurred. "We treated you as one of our own."

Her hand gripped the top of the bottle tight, tilting it upward to take a generous gulp.

"I-I know," Wendy said with shame.

"Andrea cared so much about you. Nora adored you."

A stream of purple trickled down her chin, dropping into the carpet's fibers.

"She knows, Mom," Andrea said, nervous as she tried to move the conversation along.

"Don't take her side!" she said with disgust; her finger pointed toward her daughter but missing her sightline. "You said your share of stuff about how horrible of a person she was. Don't get all soft on me now!"

"I'm not!" Andrea grunted back.

"And Wendy recognizes everything she's done," Penny stepped in.

"I have," Wendy confirmed. "I know how bad of a person I was for not being there for you and Andrea during your time of need. I will never get that time back, nor will I ever earn your trust. All I can do is apologize and hope you'll accept that."

Another chuckle grew from Ms. Crispin, slowly forming into a witch's cackle. Sheets of newspaper crunched under her feet as she approached her recliner. Her body went limp as she fell onto the grease stains on her faux suede cushions. More drops dripped down the wine bottle, landing on her grimy sweatpants.

"The fires of hell will have to freeze for me to forgive you for what you've done."

"I understand," Wendy said solemnly.

Penny's head bowed with disappointment, witnessing her sorrow for her best friend as she watched her glazed expression face her consequences. The pain she inflicted is only something she could witness the ramifications of. Every jab toward Wendy made her heart strain.

"Come on, let's go," Andrea said, ushering the two with her arm towards the stairs.

"That's right, go ahead and forgive them. You're so weak. I might as well have lost both of my children a year ago."

"Are you going to let her talk to you like that?" Penny whispered, allowing the stairs to creak over her so Ms. Crispin didn't hear.

"She says this all the time," Andrea said without a care. "You get numb to it when she tells you this over and over again over everything."

The transition from filth to a more normal environment shocked Wendy and Penny. Not a speck of dust was traceable in the hallway; the wooden floors sparkled. Dish soap was fragrant on the walls from an evident fresh scrub. No stacks of papers or signs of neglect existed on the second floor.

"Why isn't the downstairs this clean?" Penny asked, flabbergasted as her finger swiped the wall for dust.

"She's too drunk. She can't make it up the stairs."

"Oh."

"Since I'm the only one who goes up here, I might as well make this more comfortable."

The door to her room opened, and every bit of pop-punk memorabilia was scattered on the walls. From Fall Out Boy to Good Charlotte, every band had a great representation of the real estate of her room.

Wendy remembered all the good times she had with Andrea, from the sleepovers to even going to a Green Day concert. The sadness caused by her heartbreak and the void left by her dear friend burdened Andrea's heart. Pictures of the two had Wendy's face crossed out with a thick X made her stomach churn.

"So many wonderful memories here," Wendy said as her hand touched Haley Williams's fiery hair on her *Riot!* poster, trying to see the happiness of their past.

"I guess we had some good times," Andrea agreed as she reminisced about every group's picture and the moments they jammed out to it.

"Until I fucked it up."

"Yeah, you did."

Penny sank onto Andrea's bed, not knowing how to contribute to the conversation. Observing the sadness in their eyes, she felt convinced that they were on the verge of a significant breakthrough in their friendship hiatus.

"Just so you know, if I had the chance to do this again, I would be there."

"I know you would. You said it a million times."

Andrea's eyes filled with tears, and as they spilled over, her eyeliner began to run, leaving a dark stain on her cheek. Wendy may have said it to her a bunch of times, but this was the moment when she actually listened.

"Seeing her face in the library brought back so many memories of her."

"I'm sure it did," Wendy said. "Nora was a good person."

"She was," Andrea said, her voice choking up. "The more I think about how good of a person she was, the more it reminds me of how bad of a sister I became."

"You can't blame yourself for what happened," said Penny. "It was not your fault."

"Actually, it was."

Chapter 23

One Year Ago

Another day had passed at school. Nora let out a sigh of relief after the bell rang. With urgency, her classmates rushed into the hallway, grabbing their books to take home for yet another evening of arduous homework. As teachers eagerly anticipated their summer vacations, they packed up their belongings.

Away from the children.

Principal Stuart dabbed his forehead, sweaty from intervening in yet another argument between a couple consumed by their typical paranoia of flirting with others. Despite quitting a month ago, he fought the urge to light up a cigarette, his fist clenched tight. Nothing could take away the trembling that made his anxiety even worse.

Nora ran to her locker; the screeching metal concluded another day of monotony. With her bag of paint tubes, she extended her hand towards a canvas. Resting below her textbook and three art history books borrowed from the library, the paint brushes found their place at the bottom of her backpack.

"Hey, Nora," Andrea greeted as she walked around the corner with Wendy following closely behind, her face buried in a textbook.

"Hey," said Nora, her smile beaming.

"Wendy and I were heading to the pizza place to grab a slice and play video games. Wanna join?"

"That sounds like fun. But I have a painting to finish and then I'll be staying with a friend," Nora said with restraint. "I'm almost done with this one. I'm about to sell it on my eLookBook page!"

Andrea fixated her gaze on the canvas that depicted cascades of lavender and tangerine swirling into cloud formations. The withering maze's hedges were empty, with only a few brown leaves hanging on for dear life. Nora's heart swelled with pride as she witnessed the silhouettes of two women holding hands, bravely exploring the labyrinth.

"This looks great!" Andrea said, admiring the brushstroke patterns of the branches that reached out to them for attention.

"Thank you," Nora said, her heart fluttering from the compliment. "I've worked on this painting for close to forty hours."

"Forty hours?" Wendy asked, shocked, putting the book to her side to admire the dedication.

"Yeah. It took me way too long to get the angles of the bodies to be perfect."

"I bet," said Wendy.

"I can't wait to post this. So many people were excited to see the finished product."

"Really?" asked Andrea.

Another group of girls left the nearby bathroom. They spread out the gloss they had just applied by puckering their lips. Their purses jingled with dangling keychains as they walked down the emptying corridor.

"Yeah! Some were happy to hear about your paintings. One of them was happy to feel represented."

"That's cool!"

"And other painters were excited to see my work, too. I've followed them ever since you got me on this app. That community has been nothing but supportive of each other's creativity."

"I'm glad you found people you feel you belong to."

"Me too. It gives me something to look forward to at the end of another day in this hellhole!"

Principal Stuart's door slammed from the end of the hall. A barely audible box clap reached their ears as he scowled at the nosy onlookers eyeing his borrowed cigarette box from his secretary.

"I should get going," Nora said, sensing the glaring tension from Mr. Turlington as he locked his door and scoped out for the girls on his team running toward the locker room.

"Okay, see ya!"

Nora walked out the front door. Fresh air detoxified the thoughts in her brain that held her back. Each slow breath helped her clear away thoughts of her imposter syndrome. While boys showcased their trucks, the chirping of birds provided a soothing escape from the noise of engines and tires. Nothing was going to hold her back. The love she received from her family and friends fueled her determination to make her proud. She couldn't wait to get home and finish this painting.

MIST DRIZZLED ONTO her face as she strolled past the sprinkler system. The small droplets of water motivated her to get ready to complete her artistic journey. Kids were playing in the field beyond their backyard, using the well-maintained lawn as a soccer field and the bushes as goalposts. Mulch lined the pathway and tiny tulips bloomed, adding a pop of color to the surrounding greenery.

"Hi honey," said her mother, placing the Agatha Christie book on her lap as she rested in the lawn chair.

"Hi, Mom," said Nora, the sun blinding her.

"How was school?"

"Same old, same old."

"Awe," her mother said with minimal sympathy. "Cheer up. Soon, those other kids will like you."

"Fat chance," she said under her breath.

Across the street, a door screeched open. A couple in their middle years got ready for an afternoon of tending to their yard. The husband dragged the lawn mower from their shed while the wife wore gloves to yank the stubborn weeds.

"Hello there, neighbor," Ms. Crispin said, her smile tight.

"Hi," they both answered casually.

"Lovely day we're having, huh?"

"Yes, it is!"

"Honey, say hi to our neighbors," Nora's mother said, quiet, so they didn't hear her attempt at congeniality.

Nora's arm rose slowly, turning her wave like a tin man lubricating the rusty hinges of its elbow. Her eyes rolled to the back of her head as she faked it.

"Have a good day," Ms. Crispin said before resuming with her daughter.

"You don't even know those people. Why are you chumming up to them?"

"You will not understand until you have a life of your own. And besides, it never takes too much energy to be kind to everyone."

With a slight tilt of her hand, she made the ice cubes in the glass cup chime and dance. Her club soda and vodka mixed with the grenadine at the bottom of her glass.

"I guess you're right," Nora said, passive aggressive.

"Now, is this another one of your pieces that you're working on?" Ms. Crispin asked, only showing a bit of intrigue with a raised brow.

"Yes, it is," Nora said, beaming with pride.

Nora gripped the canvas, resisting the gentle breeze trying to snatch it away. She was protective of her work, similar to a parent shielding their child. This was her life, and nothing was going to destroy it.

"Oh, don't worry about showing it to me. I'm not one for the arts."

"I know."

"I'm just happy that you're doing something that you want to do."

Nora's stomach churned a little, and her heart beat faster. Sunlight brightened the yard, casting a ray of heat onto her face. It was one of the few times that the sun was on her face for more than a couple of minutes.

"Thanks, Mom."

Nora recognized that her mother would never be supportive of her daughters' creative passions. Permission to express herself creatively and the knowledge of their love was all she needed. It was better for her that they would trust in her vision than to not like it on top of not choosing to find out more about it.

"Just remember what I tell you."

"Make sure you're safe and look out for yourself," Nora said in a monotone, repeating her advice for the hundredth time.

"Exactly. Don't end up broke and unable to care for yourself with this stuff."

"I won't, Mom. I'm only sixteen."

"Yes, but you're out of the house once you graduate. I just want you to prepare yourself instead of waiting for life to bitch slap you across your face."

"I should get to work. I'm going to post this one here shortly."

"Good for you!" her mother said, smiling. "Don't forget to credit your mother for all the support."

The wink she shed made Nora a little uneasy. She wasn't fond of being instructed on who should receive credit for their hard work. The decision and proper recognition were in her hands. Plus, it was implied that the family was credited; that was all she had.

"See you later."

She took off her shoes onto the pristinely clean carpet. Not a single speck of dirt had made its way onto the floor. She trudged up the stairs to her room, next to Andrea's. Every abstract interpretation of medieval characters covered her walls, influencing her admiration. Her proudest one was of a fairy with wings splotched with every color of the rainbow and detailed line-work in the veins that brought art déco qualities. Below was a bundle of little daisies wilting from the lack of fresh water to replenish it; her neglect of everything was prevalent.

She threw her backpack onto her bed and dug towards the bottom to find her paintbrushes. Bristles tickled the tips of her fingers, digging into the underpart of her fingernails. She followed her customary ritual of giving her brushes a little pep talk, expressing gratitude for their assistance before prepping them for the next project.

"Thank you," she muttered to the objects. "We're a team!"

Using a cup of water, she dipped the hairs into it to moisten them. Next, she grabbed tubes of paint and squeezed them onto a Styrofoam plate, mixing the colors needed to achieve the perfect shade for her artwork. Orange and hazel twirled into one another, creating a swirl of earthly delight.

"This will be the piece that will start it all," she said, swiping a dab of mulberry onto her work. "I just know it."

A WEEK WENT BY, AND Nora's day-to-day pattern was nothing different. Wake up, eat, pray that she could survive another day at school, and muster enough energy to make her ideas come to life. All while sacrificing time for socializing with her small group of friends or even her family. At times, she would feel guilty for neglecting to check in with Andrea; they hadn't watched any *Once Upon a Time* in months and hadn't had a slice of pizza together for longer than that.

Her chest hadn't stopped beating faster than usual since she posted the picture of her painting to her eLookBook. By staying awake and hoping that the right person would discover her work, she lost hours and neglected her dreams. Time flew by slowly, hoping that the validation from the community she yearned for appreciation would accept her labors.

She knew this would be an impossible success story, but that didn't mean she couldn't dream it. Especially when she endured the nasty encounters with Veronica and her posse. There wasn't a day that went by when Veronica would give Nora the side eye, scoping out for any enthusiasm to break like a needle to a balloon. What didn't help was people chuckling. Maxine and Destiny would giggle at every dig that Veronica made, with Ellie occasionally enjoying it if the joke was funny. From her appearance to her demeanor, this was second nature that made her cringe.

She eagerly checked her phone for any updates on her app. Wendy and Penny liked the post, bringing a smile to her face when they admired the colors of the sky. Others commented with a heart emoji that were from the art community. Those also made her feel fulfilled.

In her math class, Mr. Turlington pulled out a pop quiz that took her the entire period to finish. Statistics. Unlike her classmates, she was never the type to be glued to her phone during school, unable to go a few minutes without it. Plus, Mr. Turlington had a knack for confiscating phones when they were caught in use; he always believed that using phones was an excuse to be stupid, along with calculators. He would seize the opportunity to inspect someone's figure under the pretense of taking their phone.

As the bell chimed, they made their way out of the class, their feet heavy with defeat, fully aware that they had performed poorly on a test that didn't even include the material they had learned. Nora entered the hallway, noticing extra eyes on her. Heads turned the minute she walked in front of her, as though she had a spotlight highlighting her presence. Suppressed giggles hid behind hands, refraining from using screens to draw attention to her.

"What is it?" she asked one group, not caring that they'd never spoken.

Every giggle sent a twitch of anxiety into her stomach. She checked her phone once she got to her locker, setting her books by her feet. The eLookBook icon on her screen showed a red dot in the upper left corner with the number thirteen next to it. Thirteen notifications popped up in an hour, giving her page the traffic she needed for her art to thrive.

A tiny smile grew as she waited for the app to load her home screen. Pulling the notifications up, her dimples crept closer to her ears, anticipating some likes that could take her notoriety to the next level. Comments flooded her page, all for the new painting she put up for sale.

What the hell is this crap?

Gross!

Ugly!

Her smile collapsed into sadness. Her lips moved closer to her chin. She closed her eyes, hoping that deep breaths would ease the dull headache. Reminders were muttered to herself that it's all part of the process and that there will always be people who won't like her work. Each comment made it harder for her to believe it, especially when it was transcending the work itself.

But when would it end?

Hoping for a glimmer of positivity, she peered at her screen, desperate to find at least one redeeming comment among the sea of negativity. She noticed the last one at the bottom was one she was looking forward to hearing from. Members of the art community who had anticipated seeing this work was what she needed; they would have the experience and compassion to understand the dedication to one's work. This one notified that they shared her image, perking her hope that the painting would go viral.

I followed this person, hoping there would be another artist like me. Someone who is creative, takes her vision into many motifs, and spreads their message, whatever it is. I have to say that I'm very disappointed with this. Inconsistent brushstrokes, off color combinations. This is only the start of the problems, and I can't waste any more energy listing them. I appreciate her support in my work, but sometimes, art lovers shouldn't be artists. Pure trash.

"What the fuck?" she said to herself, carrying over another group of laughter.

Her eyes blinked faster, almost blinding herself. The lockers narrowed in on her like a tunnel, closing the room around her. More people looked at her; the phone vibrated, and more notifications were growing by the minute.

She ran towards the exit, passing by Ms. Woods. Her hand reached out to usher her into the classroom; her requests to calm down the children and cease their comments had little effect. Wendy and Penny were at the opposite side, engaging in arguments with any student who attempted to spread gossip about their opinions of the artist, to protect their reputation from being damaged. They all shouted her name, hoping she would hear them, but she couldn't. The intensity of the hatred became overwhelming, engulfing her like a room filling with water, making the air scarce as it approached the ceiling.

Her legs were cramping up, running to the door to go outside. Principal Stuart stared at her sadness with tears falling at her feet, frozen with the reactions of the entire student body. The door became heavy, and Nora could not push it open. Once outside, the air reached her face, but she found it difficult to inhale and relieve her panic. Her phone vibrated, but more rapidly. This time, it was a phone call with the screen blackened and one word on the top.

Mom.

She swiped her finger to take the call. Her breath quivered as she tried to calm herself down, trying to allow the fresh air to relax her.

"Hello?" Nora said, her voice shaky.

"Hi, hun," her mother said, her greeting lacking sincerity than it usually does. "We need to talk."

"Can it wait?" Nora said as her other hand cradled her stomach as though a fetus was kicking her.

"No, it can't wait," her mom hissed, her tone sharp. "I've had people around town telling me about this painting you posted."

"Really?" she said, choking on tears. "W-what have they been saying?"

"Lots of things. They said that your painting was offensive and inappropriate."

She had been weakened by another opinion that could've been dismissed. Her intention wasn't to be offensive, inappropriate, or disgusting, and certainly not trashy. Word spread fast with a narrative that was created about her character, without an opportunity to defend herself. It was as though she were made out to be the villainous knight in the village and the people attacked her with swords while she had no armor to protect her in addition to a sword and shield.

"Inappropriate? It's just two women holding hands on a walk."

"I don't care. I told you I don't have much of an interest in your art stuff."

"Then what's the problem?"

"A couple of people saw what you put in the post when you showed it. You credited every friend of yours and your sister. But you didn't credit me."

"Jesus, Mom! You know that everything I do is because of your support. Why do you need me to give you an honorable mention?"

"Don't talk to me like that!"

"I'm sorry, Mom," Nora said, her voice weakening. "I'm not having the best day today."

"Oh, here you are playing the victim while you don't even credit me for your hard work!"

Nora's stomach lurched as though they were knotting half a dozen times. The bottom of her esophagus contended with heaving motions, as it wanted to expel whatever was present. Coughs of panicked breaths cause sore ribs to crack.

"I've done so much for you, and this is how you repay me?"

"That's not it at all."

"Then what is it? Do you think I'm a bad mother?"

"No! Why can't you just be proud of me? You know how hard I've worked on this."

"I'm proud of you, but I'm very disappointed," she said dismissively.

"Y-you can't be both," Nora said, hiccupping a gulp of saliva that forced down her throat.

The phone went silent. Nora checked her screen to see if her mom had hung up, but she was still there. Only her breath made its presence, huffing louder like balloons were being inflated.

"I don't want to see you for a while. I have to go out and clean up the mess you made."

Two beeps rang in her ear, telling Nora she ended the call.

The flow of tears down her cheeks was interrupted as she squinted her eyes tight. Her feet became heavy, almost as though the cement she stood on was still wet. Across the parking lot stood someone. Her black hair blew in the wind as the space became pure silence around her.

Andrea.

Relieved, she ran over to her sister. Her chest became heavy, and her breaths were getting more labored, more painful. Numbness crept up her knuckles, causing tingling in her fingertips.

"Sis!" Nora said, sniffling.

"Don't sis me!" Andrea spat, her lip curled.

"What?"

"What the hell is all of this I'm seeing on this app?"

"I know," she said, sobbing. "They're so mean. Why would they say something like that?"

"And what you've done to Mom."

"You know I wouldn't disrespect Mom. Everything I do is because I know that the two of you support and love me. You know that!"

Nora's shoulders sank. Her increasing depression caused her body to become tense. Her ankles were weakening, teetering her uneven body weight.

"Don't give me that. People keep saying things. I'm also hearing that you didn't credit her on purpose. I'm so hurt that you would do this. I thought we meant something to you!"

"You do! Why are you believing these people."

"And you painted two girls."

"Yes. They were sisters guiding each other through the unknown. You saw it last week."

"I didn't think that this is what it was going to become! And now everyone at school thinks that you're some kind of lesbian."

"What?" Nora said, her knees buckling.

The student body congregated outside, watching their confrontation from afar. Phones captured images and videos of their disagreement with laughter roaring quietly. Lights flashed along the corner of her eyes. The back of her eyes became full of pressure with a headache growing to the top of her head.

"Did you even weigh out the consequences of doing this?"

"Y-you told me I should pursue this more."

"I wasn't talking about making something that will give people the wrong idea."

Shades of gray darkened the surrounding sky. As the wind blew, Nora's neck recoiled, and the air turned chillier, causing shivers to run down her spine. Sweat on her scalp trickled closer to the tips of her hair from the drops of rain that became heavy.

"I thought you loved what I did."

"I do. Just not this or anything like this."

Nora's teeth chattered, shaking like a vintage clock with the hammer striking the twin bells. Goosebumps became sharp on her exposed skin from the wind that got colder. Her tongue was dry, rough like sandpaper as it pressed along the back of her teeth.

"I'm going to Wendy's tonight. You're on your own for dinner. We can talk about this when I have some space."

"Andrea! Don't do this to me!" Nora cried out in desperation before a slap of thunder cut her off. "I need you!"

Andrea left her sister in the cold as she walked past and returned inside. She didn't even acknowledge the primal scream that expelled from her sister's mouth. Andrea quickly dismissed her sister's cry for unwavering love, despite the effort she put into her passions, because of misunderstanding.

The rain didn't light up as Nora continued to walk home; in fact, it got worse. Nora couldn't help but read the comments that continued growing on her eLookBook app. Comments from other artists started becoming personal jabs instead of constructive critiques. Someone made a comment where they admitted to giving a thumbs down because Nora previously praised the commentor's painting's execution, but not its appeal to her; a revenge post.

This was not the type of experience she'd hoped for. Despite the extensive research and efforts to find her artistic voice and understand marketing, it appeared to be insufficient. The voices of support were no longer a part of her experience. The comments revealed them, and her fixation on negativity eclipsed the ones that should've mattered. It was too late; it had gone past the point of no return.

She felt like a failure.

Her shoes splashed on the carpet, leaving muddy tracks behind as she ascended the stairs. Her ankles almost gave in with each step up the stairs. With the door slamming behind her, she cried, using up the last of her tears and moisture.

Another wave of vibrations got her attention, once again coming from the eLookBook app. Upon opening it, she discovered a dozen comments, each from a different person, all repeating the exact phrase. The two words formed a tower of revulsion, piling on each other and creating a sense of horror.

Kill yourself.

A relentless voice inside her head amplified her temples' agony, manifesting as a migraine that reinforced her feelings of failure. Her stomach contracted, this time with a sensation of something scratching out to the point where she thought the lining was being destroyed. The tightness on the left side of her ribcage intensified, with sharp pains resembling bullets piercing her lungs and then her heart. As the surrounding space grew smaller and her vision became hazy, she found herself unable to continue moving. The paintings she loved dearly were the only things she could see as the ceiling floated away from her, drifting away into a blinding white light that took her away from the torment and away from the pain.

Chapter 24

The hardwood floors became damp from Andrea's tears. Walls echoed weeping cries of regret. The bags under her eyes suffered from the stress of the day that her sister endured. The memory of her betrayal had haunted her every day. Nothing could be done to take away what Andrea said to Nora; she'd never know if her sister forgave her.

"This is my fault," she said, her chin quivering.

"No, it's not," Wendy said, reaching around her shoulder.

Wendy's hand felt Andrea's heartbeat thumping crazily. The once formidable exterior transformed into something unsettling and filled with remorse. Andrea shed her defensive armor, exposing her vulnerabilities and insecurities.

"I could've been supportive no matter what," Andrea continued, her head resting on Wendy's shoulder, tired of the shame that weighed her down. "All I did was believe what other people said about her, and I became disappointed in her. I'm haunted by how she cried when I accused her of shaming the family."

"Yes, but people have their own opinions."

"And some just don't understand where they're coming from," Penny said as she sat beside them on the bed.

"But I should've tried to understand. I don't know why I assumed the worst. She wouldn't have done that to me."

"You don't know what was going on in her mind that day. She could've been stressed and overwhelmed," Penny added.

Andrea sniffled, wiping her hand under her nose to compose herself. Since Nora's passing, she had been battling the feeling of disappointment towards her sister, knowing that deep down her intentions aren't what everyone else was telling her. She hadn't discussed openly with anyone her feelings about her leaving this life. She only cared about protecting herself from being hurt and, most importantly, protecting herself from her mother's blame.

"I don't even know what happened. All that the medical examiner's office said was that her heart failed."

"She died of a broken heart," Wendy said to herself.

"And that's why I blamed myself for this," Andrea continued. "If she had one person in her corner who would care no matter what, it may have ended differently."

"I know," Wendy agreed. "But we can't change the past."

"Focus on the future," Penny said as she exited the bed. "If we can survive this massacre."

"Yes, we need to focus on that!" said Wendy, her eyes staring directly into Andreas to keep her focused. "Why would Nora come back from the dead? She's not the kind to inflict pain."

"And why is she going after these people?" Penny asked.

Their eyes wandered for a couple of minutes. It was difficult to justify this because their only desire was for the suffering and sorrow to cease. The thoughts of Astrid and Jeff, along with everyone else, begged for justice in their minds. The emptiness in their eyes piqued the girls' curiosity.

"Do you know exactly how much stress she was under that day?" Penny inquired, curious.

"S-she told me she hasn't slept well or eaten much since she started posting that painting she was going to sell," Andrea said, trying to recall as much as she could.

Wendy's eyebrow perched as she got herself out of bed. An idea sent chills down her arms, forming goosebumps. Each memory of Nora's frail disposition made sense of it all. Nora would lean on the lockers during her last encounters with her. There was no swagger involved, only a hand nursing her stomach that was fighting hunger pains. Her hair was even thinning out with strands that stuck to her shirt more than normal.

"What if you weren't the only one giving her hell that day? The whole school was laughing at her before you got to her."

"What are you getting at?" Andrea asked.

"I think we need to look at her account."

"Okay," Andrea said, tentative. "I don't know her passwords or anything."

"Maybe she has it in her room?" Penny asked.

"Yeah, can we go there?"

Andrea's breath became unsteady as she huffed it out in a long exhale. Fiddling with skin flakes near her fingernails, her fingers shook.

"W-we can go there," she said, nervous. "I haven't been in there since she died. None of us have."

"I understand."

"It's just too painful."

"You don't have to go with us if you don't want to," said Penny, her hand rubbing her back to comfort her. "We'll understand."

"N-no. I want to go. We need to stop this."

"Are you sure?" Wendy asked.

"Yes," Andrea answered as she pulled her hair back into a ponytail. "That's not my sister. But I know this has something to do with her."

Wendy and Penny nodded in agreement. Leading the group, Andrea took them through the hallway, passing by the bathroom and closets, before reaching the other side. The passage became smaller and darker. Each cobweb glistened; the neglect of care was apparent. Their shadows cast onto the wood, turning the passage black. Andrea's breath quivered.

"You okay?" Wendy asked, her hand tapping on Andrea's shoulder.

"I'll be fine."

She took another three breaths, moistening the door's surface. The doorknob trembled from her shaky grasp. Andrea pushed open the door, fighting through her torment like ripping off a Band-Aid. Emotions inundated her mind as sadness, pain, and blame intertwined, looking at the center of the space where she found her sister dead on the floor. Every painting she had completed was hung on the walls as she remembered them before; the tops of the canvases were coated in a thick layer of dust.

"Where should we start looking?" Penny asked, her hand brushing away a strand of web.

"For anything that could stand out as something Nora would use as a password," said Wendy as she walked over to her desk.

Andrea pulled up her phone and logged off her eLookBook account. Her fingers tapped on her screen to type in the screen name she helped her create. The identity that started all of this. The persona who everybody came to hate.

Nora_Nirvana.

Andrea tried to type in the passwords of words that she remembered were a few of her favorite things to see if it worked. The possibilities were endless but there wasn't one thing that stood out that would make her hobbies more definitive.

Pepperoni.

EvilQueen.

Grimm.

None of them worked. She went on and tried some of the art references she recalled admiring.

Monet.

Van Gough.

Renaissance.

She let out a sigh of frustration. Perhaps she wasn't as close with her sister as she thought. Wendy noticed the lone painting that Nora posted sitting flat on the surface. Wendy blew a bit of air to clear off the filth. Cobwebs wrapped around the paintbrushes like the start of cotton candy. A pencil rolled off, leaving a clean spot resembling a tan line.

"What are we looking for, exactly?" Andrea said, as she sat on her sister's bed. Her eyes peered around every spot of the room, reliving every lost memory she locked away. "I don't know anymore."

"I found a yearbook," Penny said as she pulled it from the bottom of a stack of books.

The stack teetered from the quick pull. As the orange hardcover faded, the purple color grew sharper and more noticeable. She and Wendy looked through the pages; their lips grinned more with each turn of the page as they relived the memories of the candids taken from their year. The one image of the two of them was enough to satisfy them in the cluster of the same ten people being photographed for all the others.

"Nothing out of place," said Wendy, focused on the lineup of the sophomore pictures arranged alphabetically.

"Damn," said Andrea.

They turned the last page to the white cover matter. Different handwriting styles arranged blue and red scribbles. Wendy remembered her signature, and Penny remembered hers.

"Are we really the only ones that signed her yearbook?" Penny asked, saddened by the reality.

"I guess so."

"What about this one?" Wendy asked, her fingers pointing to one more in black in the corner. A tiny sketch of flower petals started and finished the message, followed by a few sentences written in chicken scratches.

Thanks for the best year of my life. I will always be your little owl. 9/22 will be a day I'll never forget.

"Who wrote this?" asked Wendy.

"Whose her owl?" asked Penny, equally confused.

They tossed the book over to Andrea. She scrutinized the page, searching for recognizable handwriting, but found nothing. The small number of notes wasn't enough to find the writer.

"I have no idea," Andrea said, dumbstruck.

"Try using owl as the password," Penny said.

She typed the word. Her eyebrows lowered in disappointment. "Nothing."

"Does 922 mean anything?" Wendy asked.

"Put that in there too!"

Andrea tried again, her face vacant with hopelessness. Andrea couldn't find anything that fulfilled the necessary criteria to log into her account. It was becoming an impossible task.

The screen buffered, which differed from what popped up with invalid passwords. What appeared was a main page, her sister's main page.

They got in.

Andrea's eyes lit up with the help of the glow coming from the screen. With a smile, she conveyed their success to the other two, who joined her on the bed with a sigh of relief.

Surfing through her page was like touring a war zone. Each click carried a heavy weight as he solemnly navigated through her profile and messages. Every message read brought a tear of sadness to her eye. Tears of pain.

Ugly.

Horrible.

Trash.

"I don't understand why people can be so cruel. It boggles my mind reading these every time," said Andrea with disappointment.

Words of hate blew up the pictures her sister had on her profile, beyond the one that started it all. Comments demolished even the old ones that featured different images and not just her art. Remarks referencing her body image as a pig or a hippo were common. References to the Milky Way were directed toward her acne and blemishes.

"What a bunch of assholes!" Penny said with disgust.

Wendy shook her head, acknowledging equal disappointment.

Then, Andrea picked up the picture, the one that was sitting on her desk. The painting that started it all. The black silhouettes of the women faded away. Dust bled onto the canvas, causing the leaves to become muddier. Orange and lavender that were once vibrant have become more muted, more matte.

The three of their lips tightened into an uncomfortable smile. By uncovering the source of the hate, they realized the comments would keep pouring in.

The first few comments were from people they recollected.

Themselves.

"I appreciated your kindness toward her," Andrea said warmly while she placed the painting back down with care.

"She was very talented," Wendy said. "I thought that her painting was lovely."

The apples of Andrea's cheeks blossomed, rounding out. Her eyes squinted another tear.

Continuing to scroll down the screen, the slew of comments got worse the further it went. Some comments were constructive, but others were downright insulting.

"Everybody's a freakin' critic," Penny said hopelessly. "Why do these artists treat others like they're above them? It's all valid!"

Andrea continued to make her way to the bottom of the comments. The sentences shifted from being complex to becoming more direct and impactful statements.

Kill yourself.

"Why would people say that?" Wendy asked, disgusted. "They don't even know her."

Penny's eyes widened. She reached over and snagged the phone out of Andrea's grasp. Her palms slicked the screen with her sweat.

"Some of them," Penny said, distraught.

"Do you know someone?" Andrea asked.

She turned the screen to them after she zoomed in on the familiar name of someone close to her. The image of a blonde-haired woman happy in her kitchen with her scrunchie secured on her wrist. Steam wisped from the surface of the apple pie, curling into playful shapes.

Hershey_Kisses22.

"That's my mom's profile," she said, her face lighting up with fear.

"How do you know that?" asked Andrea.

"She creates many fake profiles to direct traffic her way."

"What?" said Wendy, her eyebrow raising.

"She only told me that once as an idea to have them boost her likes to change the algorithm. She also said she would comment to bring attention away from them."

"Aren't those comments a little extreme?" asked Wendy, her eyebrow raised.

"I guess I didn't think she would go through with it. Not like this."

They continued to scroll down the comments and found some familiar ones.

BookGuardian was Jeff Willow.

QueenV was Veronica.

PrettyToTheMax was Maxine.

"So what? Is someone killing off these people who said these comments?" asked Andrea. "Yes, they're pieces of shit for saying these horrible words. I don't even think that anybody deserved to die."

"Well, someone thinks differently than these people," said Penny.

Wendy was stunned, her mind visualizing these people's satisfaction when they typed the comments. How could some individuals be so quick to utter such words? Although they may have displayed kindness in person, their true nature appeared to lack compassion when shielded by a screen.

"Punks," said Andrea, cursing at their identity.

Wendy looked back at the screen, noticing another screen name. One that brought a tear to her eye in disbelief. This one hit her hard; it was someone that she thought wouldn't have a mean bone in their body.

CardCaptor49 was Malakai.

"Him too?" Wendy sighed in defeat.

"So, it's official. The killer is after trolls," said Andrea, observing their pictures.

Wendy cringed. The thought of her brother being a troll was something she wasn't prepared to have become a reality. She knew of Malakai and Nora getting along, especially when they first met years ago. He even praised her artwork; he wouldn't shut up about it. She couldn't fathom the possibility of him being a bully.

"Do you think they got my mom?" Penny asked, her fingers fidgeting.

"When was the last time you saw her?" asked Andrea.

"When we picked you up at the station a couple of nights ago. I chewed her out for being selfish, and that's the last I saw of her. I tried texting her since yesterday. The basement door was locked, which she only does when she's not using it so nobody can mess up her set."

She found herself breathless, taken aback by her mother's unusual behavior of not being around or reaching out for days. Nora probably got to her; not probably, definitely.

"What are we going to do now?" Andrea said, overwhelmed, as she set the phone down. "The police don't believe us that this thing posing as my sister was terrifying us. I don't think they will believe us if we tell them this."

"And, no offense, but the town didn't really care too much that Nora was gone. So, I don't think they'll do too much about this."

Andrea nodded her head, understanding the harsh rationale.

"Well, whatever it is, we need to find out who else is being targeted and warn them."

Their eyes scavenged for names that would be familiar to them. Slowly, they needed clarification, since nothing stood out and nobody else would be in danger. But they knew that someone else was in danger. Why else would Nora say she wanted to paint with their blood if it was done? There was more work to be done on her masterpiece, and it can't end with Jeff.

Then another name popped up. Wendy gasped when she saw whose it was.

ShotPutWiz, Zachariah.

"We need to warn him," Wendy said, rushing to the door.

She picked up her phone and frantically pressed on her screen until she got to his name. With every ring, her stomach churned, causing her to feel queasy upon reaching his voicemail.

"Call me back," she said in a panic.

She tried to call again. This time, it went straight to voicemail. Despite her efforts, she couldn't reach him.

"Damn!"

They ran out the door and went downstairs, skipping steps on their way. Penny's hip knocked into a stack of boxes, sending a cat scurrying away like a cockroach to light. Andrea ran to the table and dug through the pile of unopened mail to grab her mother's car keys.

"Where do you think you're going?" her mother hissed, slurring, waking up from her stupor.

"Out!" Andrea said, as she opened the door.

"Of course you are!" she said, her eyes rolling. "All you do is leave. You left me. You left your sister. Who's next?"

"That's not fair," Wendy interjected, her heart racing.

"It's okay," Andrea reassured. "She does this every day. I'm used to it. Let's go."

"That's right. Run away like you always do. I might as well have lost two daughters last year."

The door slammed behind the girls. A small tear fell from Andrea and Wendy's faces, one for pain and one for sorrow. The engine made a muted roar, disrupting the vehicle's snooze. Silence filled the air as everyone struggled for words. Perspective had been something that everybody needed for others to understand their grief.

"So, where do you think Zachariah would be? It's getting dark," asked Andrea as she turned the corner.

"Wasn't there a party tonight at the Byrnes property?" said Penny.

"Looks like we have a party to crash before Nora does."

MS. CRISPIN MUMBLED remarks of pain to herself. All she has been talking about is how much Nora let her down by not crediting her and Andrea for not supporting her when she snapped into her paranoia about how everyone took Nora's work. The foundation rattled with the gust of wind kissing the house. Chiffon danced from the open window, fluttering the shades of yellow stained by cigarette smoke.

The last drop of wine trickled down the side of her chin, claiming another bit of carpet as the cranberry bled into the yellow. Her fingers flicked her lighter, allowing the flame to kiss the tip of her cigarette with a cloud of smoke engulfing the living room like a veil.

Ms. Crispin teetered towards the kitchen, knocking down stacks of newspapers. Her ankle crackled as she slipped on a bit of liquid on the kitchen floor. Yanking the door to the fridge, her balance teetered while she tried to replenish her drink.

She removed the cap of her next bottle, which was only half-full from the previous night. Chill kissed the tip of her lips as she tilted the bottle back; fluid plummeted down her throat and filled her stomach. She squeezed her eyes together, grimacing at the horrible aftertaste, a sensation she hadn't encountered before, one that caused a sharp sting.

Rumbles grew from the pit of her stomach. The urge of something tearing into the lining of her esophagus turned into an acidic burn. Her head became light; the world around her slowed down with beads of sweat turning from cold to hot, then back to cold again. The back of her throat became thicker, resisting her urge to gag. Her eyes glanced at the counter. Among the empty bottles of wine sat a bigger white jug. Its label was blue and white, like the action sequence in a comic book.

Bleach.

Her gait became unstable, collapsing onto the counter. Bottles shattered like a toppling pyramid of champagne glasses. The bottom of her feet crunched into the ever-growing puddle of broken pieces.

Blood rushed through the multiple gashes that spewed out like a leaking waterbed. Her knees buckled, bones shaky, as she collapsed to the floor.

Blood flooded from her back, caused by the growing number of cuts. Fluorescent lights blended into her vision as the ceiling grew further away from her reach. Choking on blood, the last bit of air tried to escape from her swelling windpipe. Standing next to the fridge, a shadow grew in the shape of a cloak. The last bit of life left her as the shadow watched her suffer, not willing to help, just like the daughter who departed with no one to care for her anguish in her final time of need.

Chapter 25

Violet hues emerged as the sun set and the tangerine clouds faded away. In the evening breeze, the leaves fluttered and made a delicate crinkle, reminiscent of paper. Engines revved one last howl with students parking into the open plot behind the lone house in the country, ignoring the bare bit of land that once was destroyed by the blaze of a car explosion months ago. Fueled by dried branches, the bonfire's flames grew higher, providing warmth for the adolescents as they cradled their cups.

With enthusiasm, Wesley placed his arm around Zachariah, hoping to boost his sagging shoulders. The boy gazed at the imprints in the soil, resembling footprints in solidified cement.

"What the hell is wrong with you?" Wesley asked with little care.

"Nothing," Zachariah said quietly, stepping over a patch of taller grass to avoid the bird ox clinging to his jeans.

Depression made his lungs heavy, and the brisk air worsened it. He didn't feel like spending time with anyone tonight, especially those who weren't sincere.

"Cheer up; we have the night to enjoy."

He said nothing. His nose sniffled a bit of his loosened mucus. Inches away from his face, he managed to dodge the pine needles hanging from a tree branch. He wished for the branches to hit him, though; it would distract him from the pain that grew inside.

"Forget about Wendy. She's no good for you."

Zach's head perked up; his eyebrow raised.

"I was going to tell her," Zachariah said, his nostrils flared.

"Well, then you should thank me for helping you. I did the dirty work, as usual."

"It's not for you to tell!" he grumbled, the crackling of his knuckles blended with the dried, burning wood.

"Chill out," Wesley said, his eyes rolling.

He left Zachariah to join another group. One that was more energetic and eager to celebrate the night. A lone stump was at the other end of the fire pit. A gust of smoke blew into his face, causing his eyes to be blinded as he found his new seat. The back pockets of his jeans got wet from lingering wood moisture. The fiery embers screamed with orange and yellow hues, diverting his focus.

Thoughts raced through his mind. Wendy's pain and disappointment filled him with sadness, along with the worries about Wesley blackmailing him if he didn't comply with his persistent threats. Concerned about harming his reputation, he prayed that his hard work to establish a presence would not go to waste. Despite his moral compass pointing one way, his fears and hesitations compelled him to go in the complete opposite direction; it was all too much to process.

Another person joined him, grabbing a lawn chair. Her glazed face was barely visible beneath her black hair. Trauma filled her eyes as she gazed at the coals, yearning for an escape from her stained life. Loneliness flooded her mind as tears streamed down her cheek and her chin trembled.

Destiny.

She cradled her legs tight like a cannonball, tending to the bandaged wounds from the previous night. Preoccupied with grief, she ignored her classmates, who came to offer sympathy one by one. Pain remains despite care.

"You okay?" Zachariah asked.

She buried her face behind her knees and said nothing.

"I know you've heard enough of the fake apologies for what happened. I feel bad for what you've been through, and can't say the same thing about everyone else."

She turned to look at him. Her eyes glistened with more forming tears. Lack of sleep caused dark circles to be illuminated by the fire. The shadows cast on her sunken cheeks reflect her absence of appetite. The stress had caused one strand of hair to turn silver, reflecting in the light.

"You do?" she asked.

"Yes."

She released a long breath. Her shoulders eased, enabling her to rest the side of her head on her knees like a pillow, avoiding eye contact with others.

"I'm scared, Zachariah," she whispered, saddened. "I don't have any friends, and I keep hearing her screaming. I just want it all to stop."

"Maybe you should go home? This just happened, and you need time to heal."

"I don't want to be in my house. I don't feel safe there. The floorboards have screeched more than ever. My windows keep getting tapped by something, and I don't even have any trees that would do that."

"Really?"

"I think something is out there. Something is messing with me."

With a quick glance, Destiny surveyed the various groups. The classmates were enjoying themselves, tipping back their red solo cups filled with inexpensive mixtures. A competitive game of beer pong kicked off with ping-pong balls bouncing on the white foldable table. Everything seemed fine, but she couldn't shake the feeling that something was wrong.

"Well, I won't let anything happen to you," he said, reaching his hand over her back. "I promise."

Her grin expanded, and a sense of solace washed over her, providing a cozy embrace. She stood up and approached Zachariah, her exposed belly button just inches away from his face. Invitingly, she reached out her hand for him to take and join her.

"We can't let this night bum us out. We're here to party, right?"

The flickering light revealed Zachariah's teeth peeking through his lips. Rising from the log, his chest collided with hers. With each passing moment, her breath grew warmer and stronger against the back of his neck, soothing him. As his body succumbed to temptation, his eyes were fixated on the mesmerizing forest green sparkle in hers.

"Will you protect me tonight?" she said, smirking.

He stumbled to think of a quick answer. Thoughts of Wendy came back into his memory. He was filled with anxiety at the thought of disappointing her again. Despite not wanting to be there, he finds solace in the fact that he's not alone at the party.

"I-I will," he said, stepping back tentatively. "H-how about we get a drink?"

"Sure," she said, soft, more normal.

He walked to the other side of the fire and grabbed himself a cup. The plastic echoed the drop of ice cubes, filling them close to the top. Peach schnapps blended into the chill like water before allowing the bleed of grenadine to spread its color. Splashing the orange and pineapple juice on top, the drink became a tie-dye of tropical beauty.

Wesley had his arms wrapped around two junior girls. The excessive laughter and light caresses on his chest hinted at a fantastic night in store. His gaze was fixated on her bare legs, their denim shorts barely concealing their upper thighs.

Zachariah gave the drinks a good swirl; the floating ice cubes became hypnotic, capturing the faint light with each rotation like a dull disco ball. Destiny huddled in front of the fire as she waited for him; her face lit up the closer he got. Gratitude filled Destiny as she smiled at her bartender and reached for her cup. The two touched their cups together for a toast; liquid splashed on the top of his hand.

"What should we toast to?" he asked, the raise of his eyebrow defined in the shadows.

"To take back the night," she said, carefree after giving it a good minute to think about it.

"Yes, let's take back the night!"

His dimples were highlighted by the moonlight filtering through the trees. As they locked eyes, they both took big sips of the beverage, relishing the fruity paradise that filled their stomachs.

From the darkness, another one emerged behind them. Her black sweatshirt was hard to make sense of who it was. Removing the hood, she guided her black strands of hair behind her ears.

"Mind if I join?" asked Ellie, eyes glowing as they focused deep on Destiny.

"Sure," said Zachariah, ushering her towards them.

"O-of course you can," said Destiny with apprehension, her hand squeezing her cup.

"Actually, can you give us a minute, Zach?"

Destiny's eyes got bigger, her heart thumped.

"Sure. Looks like Wesley wants me to show them something."

He returned to the other group, maneuvering through the growing crowd of guests, as nearly forty people joined in on the activities. They stared at him with heightened judgment. What had he done? More importantly, what had Wesley done?

"Hey Wes," said Zachariah, holding back the urge for his head to sink towards his shoulders.

"We were just talking about you!" he said, his eyes twinkling menacingly.

"And?"

"I was just talking about how much you've forgotten about that Wendy girl," he said as he walked over to invite him to the participants.

Zach's lips parted, exhaling bursts of anger he attempted to control. Another conversation he wanted no part in. Another façade to put on to please Wesley.

"I haven't," he whispered, his teeth gritting.

"Yes, you have," Wesley said more directly. "In fact, you said that you were so over her, you wanted to screw with her locker."

"No, I didn't," Zachariah said, taken aback.

"Yes. You did."

Wesley's lips pursed. With his arms crossed, his drink dripped onto his hand and soaked into his jacket's ribbed cuff. The two next to him withdrew into their beverages, attempting to conceal their unease with gulps.

"I guess I did," said Zachariah, his shoulders sinking, giving in to the pressure.

"Atta boy! He even planned on doing it tonight!"

"I did?"

"Yes, you did," Wesley continued, his hand pinching Zachariah's forearm. "And I'm going with you to make sure we can get in and fuck shit up."

"Really?"

"Yes, gotta make sure nothing is left behind. Ready to go?"

The crowd of boys cheered him on like fraternity brothers. Their drinks banged together with the huddle for a toast. Zachariah's drink fell to the ground when a few track team members patted his back. Ice cubes tumbled next to their feet like dice with melted indents on the top, looking like snake eyes.

"And if you back out, I will make sure that you and that pathetic girl's life will be a living hell," he whispered into Zachariah's ear. "Do you understand?"

"What did she do to you?" Zachariah asked, muttering as the group chugged their drinks.

"That's just the cycle of life. People like us need to keep people like her below us."

TWO GIRLS LEFT THE fire. Immediate silence became awkward and tense. Each step intensified the frigid chill. Their spines tingled like a vibrating cell phone.

"So, what's up, Ellie?" Destiny asked, nervous, her arms cradling around her chest for warmth.

"Not a whole lot," Ellie answered without emotion. "I just wanted to check in with you. After all, you are my friend."

Destiny huffed a faint chuckle. She couldn't believe the audacity of her statement.

"Yes, you are," she muttered, her lips pursing tight.

"I mean it. I know I haven't been there for you lately. I've just been going through some shit of my own."

"I understand," Destiny said faintly, holding back her frustrations of Ellie's abandonment.

"Let's be honest, I didn't like how Veronica changed you."

Tree branches cracked. Wind howled with the fire becoming so tiny in their sight.

"What's that supposed to mean?" Destiny asked, concerned.

"You have to admit that Veronica was toxic as all hell," Ellie explained.

"Yes, but she's still our friend!" she defended.

Echoes of car doors slamming bounced in the open air. Owls groaned, a friendly hoot that greeted them into the solitude.

"Yes, a friend that was turning you all into bitches!"

Destiny's nostrils flared. The world turned gray as her vision blurred. Heat warmed her up from the rush of blood, steaming her like a growing fire.

"Don't you remember what she did to Nora?"

"Yes, I do, and I feel like crap for it," Destiny hissed defensively. "That doesn't make us bad people."

"It does when you're the one sharing the post and telling her to kill herself," said Ellie, nudging Destiny's shoulder with a light shove.

"We didn't mean that!"

"It meant something to her!"

"Veronica said it wouldn't hurt her."

"Well, she's dead. And Veronica went missing. She created this mess, and we're paying for it. You're paying for it."

Destiny's breath became short. Maxine's screams became audible in her head. Her memory of the metal penetrating the plastic walls felt like nails on a chalkboard.

"Destiny," a soft voice whispered from the trees.

Fog grew around their feet. Pure gray wiped away all traces of the rest of the group. Confused and worried, only the two of them remained in the unknown.

"What the hell is happening?" Destiny asked, waving her hands in front of her to try to see them.

"I dunno," said Ellie, her eyes wandering for a sign of existence.

Their hearts pounded in fear, unable to find anyone close by. Nobody came to their rescue, not even Zachariah. Nobody hollering to check for their attendance, definitely not Wesley.

"We need to go back," Ellie said, reaching to grab Destiny's arm.

"Where? I can't see them!"

"Let's hang out!" the voice whispered again.

Her voice transitioned from a childish soprano to a tone that became more recognizable. A voice they listened to every day. The voice of a long-lost acquaintance.

"Veronica?"

Chapter 26

Destiny and Ellie searched for each other. The trees' bases were bumped into by them, and more continued to multiply. Nothing became familiar to them; nothing was like their usual partying spot. The murky emptiness thrust into an unfamiliar realm.

"How could there be so many more trees?" Ellie asked, confused by the stub of a branch poking her side with each turn.

Wind whistled inside their ears. The air resonated with eerie chants, as Maxine, Bryce, and Tanner's voices yearned to be heard. From all directions, gusts of wind made shirt hems fly up and whip around.

"Destiny," said a voice playfully.

"Who's there?" she asked, her hands trembling.

"Destiny!" Ellie cried, but the tree branches muffled her voice, crackling like breaking bones.

The voice whispered again. Goosebumps covered Destiny's arms, becoming more visible as they moved towards her neck. The chill whipped against her face, causing her body to freeze in response.

Her silhouette cast a haunting presence as it glided in the moonlit glow, like a ghost. Destiny's breath became shorter, shakier. Hoping for a mutual effort, she extended her arm towards Ellie. As she fought the temptation to let her muscles unwind, stress weighed heavily on her. Yet she required guidance to navigate this.

She needed her friend.

Ellie's hope for a connection vanished, just like her visibility. Despite the silver wisps floating around, Ellie felt hidden in darkness. The urge to vomit overwhelmed her as her stomach sought relief.

The space around Destiny spun. With each repetition, the childish whispers grew sharper in her mind, resonating like echoes in a cave. The shadow swarmed behind her again. The whip of black fabric hit her legs, making the air rush towards her like a wave.

"Come find me."

This voice differed from the others. This voice was more recognizable than the previous one she heard. With a tone that desired attention, the voice sounded more mature and sassy.

Veronica.

UPON PARKING THEIR vehicle, Wendy, Andrea, and Penny noticed they were dangerously close to a dilapidated station wagon on the verge of tumbling into the ditch. The dew of the night slapped the top of their sneakers, moistening their toes. Andrea hugged herself tight, trying to warm up despite her short sleeves.

"Who throws a party in shit like this?" Andrea asked; the thin fibers of her t-shirt shielded a slight gust of wind like a window screen.

"Consider ourselves lucky, then," said Wendy, her eyes searching for people through the sea of cars.

Moonlight bounced off the cars' hoods. The dark vehicles fooled them as the night sky created tree-like silhouettes that resembled human forms.

"Over there!" Penny said, her finger pointing toward the branches that flickered bits of orange.

Running through the wet grass caused their ankles to ache. Chunks of mud from their shoes stuck to the hems of their jeans. Their lungs were burdened with regret as they realized they never took gym class seriously, not even for a second.

"We're close," said Penny, her ponytail flailing around like a helicopter propeller.

Enthusiastic teens, who let out roaring cheers of "oh" and "ah" guided the girls, allowing them to witness the ping-pong ball hitting the cup's edges before plunging into the water. The bonfire made it easier to see in the trees, improving their sight.

"Oh, look who showed up," said one of the track team members, surprised.

His teammates stopped drinking and turned their attention to the trio, who were panting and had sweat-soaked hair. Wendy took a minute to recover from her sprint by placing her hands on her legs and leaning over. Watching the track team last night was enjoyable for her, but she had no intention of joining them at the table. The abundance of people staring at them made Wendy's throat constricted. With all eyes on her, filled with judgment, she faced the one fear she never wanted to encounter, causing her muscles to tighten.

"Piss off," hissed Penny.

"Keep drinking," said Andrea, dismissing them as she tightened her ponytail again, corralling the loose strands. "Nothing to see here."

The remaining students went back to what they were doing. Their cups tilted, occasionally catching glimpses of curious eyes. The stack of wood collapsed, leaving charred bits to sprinkle onto the grass like glitter.

The surrounding trees thickened, leaving gaps that appeared as dark, wooded abysses. Despite the vastness of land, their certainty persisted. The possibilities were endless; any spot Wendy discovered in the distance could have a half-dozen spots where someone could be.

"Okay, let's find him."

DESTINY FELT A POWERFUL push from the wind, as if it were a bully. Thorns growing on tree branches smacked her face, causing cuts on her cheeks. The leaves caught strands of hair and yanked out bits from her scalp.

"Ow," Destiny screeched, her hand nursing the growth of blood on her right side. "Ellie, where are you?"

Ellie was nowhere to be found. She didn't make a sound, completely unresponsive amidst the loud wind. As she left the forest, tears flowed down her cheek, aggravating the growing cuts on her face.

"Why haven't you found me? I thought we were friends."

Veronica's whining was nothing new to Destiny. Whenever she wasn't acting tough, she sought attention from others. The memory of tripping Astrid in the lunchroom for Veronica freshman year, leading to a messy mishap with green bean casserole and a squashed chocolate milk carton, still lingered. The memory of trashing Mr. Turlington's office while he was occupied with one of his girls and pinning the blame on someone else caused her heart to ache, but there was another memory that was even more painful.

The creative underclassman who proudly shared her art with the public. It was fine to put up with Veronica's initial disgust until she gave her a task.

"Share it."

Destiny shared the post under the threat of losing her rank. If she didn't share the post with everyone in school, Wesley would ruin her, so she had no choice but to comply. People were encouraged to indulge in their mutual disgust and promote their disdain for the artwork depicting two women walking through a maze.

"You failed me!"

The shadow ran behind her again. Her eyes grew tired and achy from ceaselessly scanning for help, darting back and forth in search of help. With great force, her jaw chattered, causing the bottom molars to crack. The wind pushed her again, making her lose her balance and move to a different spot.

"Stop!" Destiny yelled with desperation, followed by a loud scream that she hoped would signal for help.

But it didn't even echo.

The mist faded away, scarcely veiling a miniature pond hosting a decaying tree on a tiny island. As the brush slid off her sticky knees, it made a crunch under her feet. To ensure she was okay, she touched her face, dirt caked under her fingernails.

"Why are you doing this?" she said, whimpering.

The cloak's train floated behind her like a tornado flag while the shadow glided. This time, she could follow where it was going. She had neither the force of the wind muffling the sound nor the fog concealing her vision.

It stopped right behind her.

Her eyes fixated on the darkness within its hood. The glow of red flickered in its eyes. Filled with fear, Destiny took a step back. The sound of the brush shifted, turning into the familiar noise from her school days. Although they didn't use it much, they still recognized it among others. Crisp crunching made her steps unsteady.

Paper.

The sheets, white as snow in the fog, mirrored the blankness of her thoughts. In a slow manner, the blank pages showcased content through black letters and colored squares depicting faces. Although some were difficult to discern, she identified Malakai, followed by Tanner and Bryce. Among the three boys, there was one she recognized well.

Her own.

As she picked up the page with her face on it, the shadow once again fixated its gaze on her. The contents disclosed a phrase that she knew well.

Kill yourself.

"I didn't write this!" she hissed, disheartened.

The glowing eyes appeared again, making her heart beat faster.

"I didn't! I just shared it, I swear."

With a bowed head, the shadow felt shame as it glanced at the comments. Their chest rose and fell faster, filled with pain, with each page they read. The gloves' fibers elongated as they clenched their fists.

"I'm sorry. I really am."

It looked at her again. Their hands relaxed at their side. Their gaze focused beyond Destiny, looking behind her.

Turning to face the shadow, Destiny bit her lip, curious to see what it was looking at. Confusion crossed her face, causing her eyebrows to furrow. Her knees trembled; the muscles of her thighs jiggled like jello. Her breath grew shallow as she gasped in the darkness.

Another shadow.

A sweeping motion of the arm was made by the second shadow in front of her. Moonlight reflected from the polish of the metal that swung onto the surface of Destiny's neck.

Destiny trembled; her throat choked on gulps of blood. Lungs gasped for air as they started to close. Her toes felt a tingling sensation, similar to the static of a television. Her paralyzed vocal cords prevented her from being able to call for help. Unable to connect the panic in her body to the thoughts of fear, she became overwhelmed. The darkness of the night sky deepened with each passing second as she struggled to nurse the gash, the fading pressure causing the cartilage to crunch. Weakness overtook her body, her final drop of blood dripping onto the pages of animosity, her last ounce of energy dissipating into the pool of her own creation, bringing about her demise.

TAKING A MOMENT TO breathe, the trio sat by the fire. Running circles around the unfamiliar became tiring. Nobody was within sight around the outskirts; they needed a break to conjure another plan. Somebody was out there; they knew it.

Wendy's muscles became heavy as she watched the dancing flames. The harmonious blend of yellow and red brought envy to her desire for unity. She didn't let the occasional gawks from their classmates become a major problem.

"I didn't know they were talking to each other," said one classmate before gulping their drink. "I thought they hated each other.

"Who knows?" said another casually. "Ever since Veronica went missing, it's like the group turned their backs on each other."

Wendy's interest piqued as she recognized the individual they were speaking of. Her legs burned from the soothing heat, yet relaxed after exercising as she hurried over to them.

"Destiny was here?" Wendy asked, curious.

"Yeah," said her classmate. "Her and Ellie."

"Do you know where they are?" Wendy asked, her breath becoming heavy with fear.

"Why would you want to know? It's not like you'll ever become one of them."

"I don't give a shit about that!" Wendy said, shaking her arm for answers. "Please tell me where they went."

"They went that way," the classmate said, irritated, walking away to grab herself another drink.

Absolute darkness emptied and consumed the farthest section of the woods, punctuated by small openings caused by the fire's flickering expansion. Looking back, she realized that Penny and Andrea didn't follow behind her like she expected them to. Prepared to go beyond her previous limits, she ran into seclusion as the darkness swallowed her.

The fog danced around her feet, dissipating as she walked. With each step she took, she experienced the fading of noise and the replacement with absolute silence. Hoping to catch any clue about the other two, she listened intently.

"Ellie! Destiny!"

Wisps of vapor escaped her mouth like tiny clouds. From the distance among the trees, the dog's howl grew faint. Her spine tingled as she heard the distant crunch of needles. As she sprinted relentlessly to locate them, the air became brisk and made her cheeks go numb, scanning every fallen trunk for a potential spot to sit and seek shelter.

"Ellie! Destiny!"

She took a moment to catch her breath. Leaning against a nearby tree, she used her hand to support her weight. As the seconds went by, her hopelessness grew, realizing she had lost them too. She felt a strong pounding in her chest, making her lightheaded.

With fingernails piercing into her shoulders, a hand grabbed her from behind. Wendy's yelp echoed throughout the entire forest. Preparing to throw a defensive punch, arms extended upward.

"Relax, it's me!"

Her eyes strained to adapt to the darkness, catching only the moon's glow reflecting on the sleek black hair peeking out from her sweatshirt.

"Ellie!" Wendy said, relieved, cradling her chest. "Where the hell did you go? And where is Destiny?"

"I have no freaking idea!" she said, her eyes widening with fear. "One minute I was with her, and the next we got separated."

"What?" Wendy asked, confused.

"There was a heavy fog that broke us apart, with trees that felt like they were attacking me."

Wendy was dumbstruck. Despite the abundance of trees, the spacing between them was generous, and their branches were far beyond their reach.

"Didn't you see the fog?"

"No, I didn't," Wendy said. "Everything looked normal from the fire."

Ellie surveyed the entire forest, spotting the last traces of thick fog in the distance that resembled gray cotton. This cloud appeared somewhat comparable to the abyss she endured.

"There! Destiny has to be there!"

Ellie ditched Wendy, who rolled her eyes because she had to chase after her. Their muscles ached from running too much in tight jeans, feeling burdened by the unnecessary weight.

The tree coverage decreased, allowing the moonlight to illuminate the surroundings. Shades of green and gray filled the air as the leaves fluttered. The mist dissipated, thinning like cigarette smoke, exposing a small pile encased in paper sheets. A glowing hand emerged from the darkness, seeking salvation.

"Destiny!" they both said.

The rush of their tears blinded them as they ran towards her. Deep red spots completely stained the paper. A mix of tears, sweat, and blood saturated her hair, adhering to her face while her eyes looked empty and her mouth fought for air.

They collapsed next to her, muttering apologies. Their knees became cold from the brush. Wendy looked at each piece of paper, barely making out the phrases she remembered seeing in Nora's bedroom. Each one continued to penetrate Wendy's soul more deeply than the last.

Kill yourself.

"I'm sorry I wasn't there!" Ellie cried, her fist punching the ground.

Wendy observed Ellie's remorse. Although their connection was based on someone else's hatred, the friendship was genuine. With each tear, she hoped Destiny would've recognized Veronica's behavior and gathered the strength to depart.

But she couldn't.

When Penny emerged from the darkness, Andrea came out behind her, with her rhinestones winking. Their faces blushed from the cold. As they looked upon Destiny's dead body, their eyes swelled with sadness, shaking their heads in regret for not arriving in time.

"We have to go," Penny said, her breath staggering.

"Now," added Andrea.

"Did you find Zachariah?" Wendy asked, scared as she looked around the premises for anybody else.

"No, but we know where he went."

Chapter 27

Among the many empty spots, the car swerved into the parking lot, almost colliding with the light post. The wind carried candy wrappers, swirling like tumbleweeds. A gentle breeze created a circular motion with grass shavings, resembling a small tornado. Zachariah's fingers wrapped around his sleeves, the fabric protecting his forearms from becoming constricted from his tight grip. He tried his best to not let his shortening breath choke him and show vulnerability.

"Ready for this?" Wesley asked, undoing his seatbelt.

"Yes," Zachariah said solemnly.

His eyes stared out the windshield. The perimeter of the lot was alive with fluttering trees and trembling new leaves. As the specks of sandy dirt meandered like a stream, the black pavement remained devoid of any activity.

Leaving a subtle echo against the brick walls of the school, the doors closed with a hushed sound. Feet tapped on the asphalt, crossing the worn-out parking lines. As they walked to the back side of the building, shadows engulfed them and they passed by the demolished porta potties, which were covered in yellow tape like mummies.

Zachariah's breath trembled; he looked over at Wesley, whose gaze was focused on the door. He had a clear-cut focus, determined to get them indoors. The teen had a lot to share with his friend and couldn't keep it inside any longer.

"Why did you decide to come with me?" Zachariah asked, curious.

"I wanted to see this one through to the end," he explained. "Malakai failed me, and I don't want another favor to not happen."

Show some respect. He's dead, for fuck's sake!

"He didn't fail you," Zachariah said, his fist clenched tight.

"And neither will you."

They reached the door. A twisted arrangement of chains surrounded the pull handle.

Oh damn! Looks like the school failed you.

Zachariah's chest emitted a tiny laugh, but Wesley remained unfazed. With intense concentration, he directed his eyes toward the lock, as if he was trying to use telekinesis to secure it. His hand fiddled around in his pocket. His finger looped into the ring and the keys chimed.

"You didn't think I didn't have a way to break in, did ya?" Wesley said with a cocky snarl.

Zachariah resisted the temptation to bite his lips, tucking them inside his mouth. As Wesley pressed down each key in his loop, Zachariah's face became more and more tense. The scratches inside the keyhole pierced his ears.

Clank!

Their chain fell down, and the links formed a pile on the ground. Dimples appeared within centimeters of Wesley's ears as his grin became more noticeable. By letting his weight do the work, he opened the door.

The hallway became a dark cave. Only the windows of the open classrooms allowed the moonlight to illuminate the marble floors. No paper was crumpled into balls and left on the floor. The walls reverberated with the sound of their feet tapping, causing Zachariah to clear his throat.

It's so different at night. There's actually some peace here.

"Need to stop at my locker first," said Wesley, turning the corner to the next hall.

A tiny light came from one door. Alleviated pressure hissed from a bottle of glass with tiny bubbling fizzes.

"Oh, shit!" Wesley whispered, grabbing Zachariah's sleeve.

Eyes locked on the ground ahead, they cautiously moved around the other corner. Stepping into the hallway was Mr. Turlington. As he made his way to the bathroom across from his office, he set down his beer bottle, resulting in glass clattering as it hit the floor.

"We should get out of here," Zachariah said, hoping Wesley would listen.

"Yeah, let's go. Abort mission."

Walking back to the exit, their arches felt strained from the gentle steps. Wesley's face flushed into a deep red. Despite his efforts, his plans for sabotage were once again foiled, leaving him defeated and sighing in frustration.

They went around the next corner, going past the gymnasium. A musty stench made its way into their noses. The absence of the janitor meant no polished floors. The drinking fountain emitted a faint humming sound as air circulated from the vent.

Turning the next corner, their hearts stopped. Thick strands swept around the liquid, spreading it across the floor. A hunching gray jumpsuit in the shape of a crescent eclipsed the window's light.

The janitor.

"Damn," said Wesley.

They retraced their steps to the gym, climbing the stairs next to the office. The corridor was desolate, darkness prevailing over the lower level. In the center of the area, a solitary garbage can stood, its large shadow surprising them.

"Where should we go now?" Zachariah asked, looking both ways. "We're trapped."

With caution, they made their way down the hallway, listening for any additional footfalls to evade detection. Stickers covered the lockers, giving them the appearance of car bumpers. Signs featuring clip art, which were printed and affixed next to the vents, depicted the school's support for every extracurricular activity.

Without the presence of other students, the filth on one locker became more noticeable to them than ever. Zachariah's skin crawled at the sight of the hateful scratches and comments.

Dead bitch.

Goodnight Nora.

Get out of here!

"Have you noticed any of this before?" Zachariah asked, saddened. "This wasn't here before, was it?"

"Who cares?"

"Cut the crap! No one else is around."

Wesley's eyebrow rose, his head cocking to the side.

"Why do you have to be horrible to her?" Zachariah asked, his patience worn thin. "She's dead, and there's no one around to impress. Cut the shit and show some respect."

"She's nothing."

Zachariah's forehead glistened as the light reflected off the beads of sweat. He pressed his lips together, forming wrinkles.

"Enough!"

His fist pelted on the top of her locker, denting the surface. With a shiver of rattles, the door shook open, its metallic tremors increasing in volume.

"Shhh! Are you crazy?" Wesley said, cringing.

Zachariah froze, and his mouth remained open. Tears wet his eyes, and more began to accumulate. Wesley's throat made a croak, causing him to choke and struggle for air.

The blood cascaded down the locker, creating a miniature waterfall on the floor. Deep red shades now saturate a gingham tie, as navy transitions into dampness and a massive gash appears on its stomach. In the dark, his eye whites were prominent, alongside his twisted ankle up to his face. He had a pale, lifeless look with his mouth wide open, gasping for breath.

Principal Stuart.

DOWN THE STREET FROM the high school, the girls parked the car. The breeze sent chills down their spines. Penny wrapped her arm around Ellie to help her straighten up. Gusts of wind pushed them back as they focused on getting inside. It seemed like some mysterious power was keeping them from going to the school.

"It wasn't this windy ten minutes ago!" said Penny, shivering.

"And look, there is nothing else moving," said Ellie, her jaw clenching.

The tree branches were still, and the leaves remained motionless. The fast food wrappers and litter remained intact on the curb. Specks of sand obstructed their hair, pushing it away from their faces.

Both trembling with nerves, Wendy and Andrea shared a glance. The recollection of the turbulent disturbance at the library hours ago was painful. The surface of their skin became dotted with tiny bumps, with goosebumps showing off with pride.

"We need to find them!" said Wendy, remaining calm.

Thoughts of the damage Zachariah made behind Wendy's back brought consideration to let him get what he deserves in the hands of the vengeful spirit. Regardless of her history with him, nobody should get that type of treatment where pain and suffering should be inflicted. As much as it pained her, the part of her that kept her strong told her to show grace and forgive those that hurt her and others.

Upon reaching the parking lot, the sensation of water greeted them, slapping against their faces. Raindrops as cold as needles whipped onto their cheeks, even though there was not a single rain cloud above them. The thin threads of their shirts became soaked, adhering closely to their skin.

They passed the lone car. The underside had a dark appearance, with slashed tires that looked like black puddles swarming around the base. Faint light revealed silver pencil-like scratches etched all over the black hood. A multitude of letters now hide the once polished exterior. Taking a moment, Andrea shielded her eyes and tried to connect the five letters, spelling out a word that was repeated throughout.

Troll.

With their shoes splashing into growing puddles, they sprinted toward the front entrance. The socks turned squishy and started sloshing around. Tree branches rolled toward them, resembling life-sized tumbleweeds. Just inches away from scratching her stomach, Ellie evaded the attack. Like sweat on monkey bars, Wendy's grip on the door handle slipped away.

It wouldn't budge.

"What brings you ladies here?" said a voice behind them.

The prepubescent shrill caught their attention, causing their hearts to stop. The barely noticeable silhouette of a figure appeared as they turned around. Wendy's view of him became clear only when he approached them with his uneven strut.

Ian.

Their hearts raced and their muscles shivered. The chill from the water made their hands tremble as they held on to one another. Stepping back, their feet splashed into a growing puddle while they tried to get further from him.

"What are you doing here?" Andrea asked, with water trickling down her chin.

"You know why I'm here," he said, his smirk lit up from a sudden flash of lightning that struck the pavement fifty feet away.

"Uh, no! That's why we're asking you!" hissed Penny. Her soaked hood became heavy, with the opening drooping over her forehead.

"I wanted to get you all alone," he explained, walking closer to them. "I wanted to talk with Wendy."

His denim jeans reflected light due to the heavy rain. The translucence of his skin made the shadows on his clenched fist appear more pronounced, emphasized by his lowered eyebrows.

Closer to one another, the girls cradled each other. With every step, fear intensified and their arms trembled from the cold weather. Wendy gripped Andrea's arm tight, straining her eyes to get a clear view of them.

"Don't be the hero," Penny said, spitting slightly.

"Leave us alone, Ian!" Wendy screamed, pushing her back. "We've done nothing to you!"

Ian's shadow loomed over them. His menacing laughter reverberated from the brick walls, growing louder and more profound than ever before. A horrid screech assaulted their eardrums, as the thunder's tempo intensified, drowning out their panic.

A bolt of lightning hit the middle of the lot, close to the car. The power of nature hit them like a whip's crack. Flames erupted from the tree's main branch, causing leaves to burst into growing fire before falling down.

Cringing in terror, the four retreated and huddled together, unable to hide their fear.

His intimidating presence made time drag on as they waited. Wendy became eager when she looked up to locate his position, hoping for a swift and painless experience. But something was different. The rain stopped falling. Contrary to expectations, the parking lot wasn't shimmering with wet stones. Tree remains undamaged, no puddles in sight. With the wind screaming silently, the night sky returned to its clear state. The damp fabric of their clothes was the only proof of the storm. Furthermore, there was another thing missing.

Ian.

AFTER TAKING A MINUTE to gather themselves, they attempted to enter the school through all of its many entrances. Wendy's blood boiled with every unsuccessful attempt. The locks resisted, creating thumping sounds that echoed in their ears. Each footfall on the asphalt echoed in the quietness, gradually blending with moans.

"Help them!" moaned Astrid.

"They need you!" cried out Mrs. Hershey. *"Do it for me!"*

A tear fell down Penny's face. Facing the reality that her mother had fallen victim to the force, her chin trembled as she reluctantly uttered her last words.

"Do it for us!" Malakai said, his voice screeched inside Wendy's ear.

Her blood was pumping, with her fingers trembling.

With a final pull of the handle, the last door moved. When Ellie entered, their flip-flops slapped against the ground. Andrea's shoulder winced from the force of the door closing.

Darkness swarmed the top of the wall into the ceiling like a train tunnel. A small emergency light reflected from the floor. Constantly on alert, they kept their eyes moving, afraid of encountering anything beyond what they had already seen. Ellie's trembling breath caused Penny's neck to become damp.

Papers rustled like fall leaves in the wind, sliding across the floor, causing their hearts to stop in startlement. Once they passed through the main lobby, they climbed the stairs, careful to steer clear of the light pouring out from Mr. Turlington's room. Dampened bangs stuck to foreheads; sweaty palms gripped the metal railing.

Upon reaching the top, they saw the closed doors of the English classroom, study room, and one of the history rooms. The surface of a lone locker gleamed with the moonlight as its door remained propped open. Snot and tears mingled as Andrea grappled with the heartbreak of seeing Nora's locker still adorned with hurtful words, a cruel reminder of her untimely passing.

Along the bottom was a puddle of blood that rested under a limp arm. The group associated the plaid blazer with the school's authority figure. A person who Andrea hoped would ensure justice for those who did her sister wrong, but instead, he just watched it all happen and turned his back on the turmoil.

Their chests heaved as the sound of pounding metal reverberated. Another beat of the locker, like a slow ticking clock, occurred every five seconds.

BANG!

Knees trembled; their brains scrambled to come up with an idea of where to hide. The noise was increasing in volume and becoming more noticeable.

BANG!

Wendy's throat became dry. She had a hard time swallowing. Her eyelids fluttered with panic.

BANG!

They ran into the open door closest to them. Dust filled the air, making it stuffy and leaving a lingering stale taste in their mouths. Nostalgic memories were associated with the library where Wendy and Andrea spent countless hours. The lack of funding for a librarian left the public building, like the school, neglected and with an empty desk.

Wendy and Andrea sought shelter beneath one table, while Penny and Ellie hid under a different one. The weight pressed into their palms, causing their biceps to shake. As the kneecaps touched the crumb-filled carpet, they heard a crunching sound. The dusted glass on the window brought taps of fingers with nails scratching the surface, making it louder.

The banging stopped, and the air became silent. Time stood still; the veins along their necks pulsated like strobe lights.

"Is anyone here?" a voice whispered, not mature.

Uncertain, the group of four exchanged looks, unsure of their desire to reply.

"Someone help us," a different one added.

Relief flooded over Wendy, knowing who it was. Despite the unsteady gait, she focused on the rush of blood returning to her legs. In the room, two jackets in orange and purple were barely noticeable. The burly silhouette became validated.

"I'm so glad to find you," Wendy said, relieved as she reached her arms to brace herself to wrap them around Zachariah.

The rest of the group emerged from their hiding spots. With curiosity, they observed the window, wondering what was causing the tapping sound. Andrea's body became immobile, indicating that there were no objects in proximity to tap on the window. No trees. No animals.

"What the hell is going on?" Wesley asked, his voice shaky.

His eyes, wide and filled with tears, shimmered like a glossy swamp. This side of him remained unseen by everyone else, including Ellie, when she was with Veronica. His vulnerability, which became more pronounced because of his fear, was surprisingly easier to handle than his usual arrogant and dominant behavior.

"You're in danger," Andrea said in panic.

Wesley took in her warning and valued her words with a loud gulp.

"You both are," said Penny.

"W-why?" Zachariah asked, his pounding heart caused his body to stiffen.

"Let's get out of here, and then we can talk about it," said Wendy, more directly as she grabbed his arm.

Her nails dug into the knitted fibers of his ribbed cuff. The tips of her fingers felt the beat of his growing pulse.

Ignoring their principal's dead body, they assembled in the hall. The moonlight at the far end faded, moving closer to complete darkness. Ellie screeched a tiny yelp, pointing her finger to the light; her jaw dropped in terror, starting the apprehension that everyone else followed shortly after that.

The figure.

"Run!" Wendy yelled.

The thunderous footsteps were like hail pounding against a roof. Ellie fought, recoiling from her feet and gripping her flip-flops tight as if they were eagle claws. Penny winced when her foot stumbled on the edge of a step, causing a tiny tweak in her ankle. The surprising kindness of Wesley holding her back allowed her to not slow down.

Passing through the lounge, the silence became horrible. They noticed the room shrinking in their peripheral vision. The hallway closed on them; the door became too far to reach, with their panic messing with their perception.

"We're almost there!" Andrea said, her breath huffy.

They all flooded around the door. Perspiration caused their bodies to become warm. With a collective effort, everyone pushed against the metal surface, covered in slick sweat, to force it open. Panic hindered each attempt, causing the bones to tense further. Observing through the small window, Wendy noticed an absence on the ground.

The chain.

The moonlight glimmered on the dangling piece, casting a reflection. Zachariah thrusted his shoulder into the door like a battering ram. The angry grunts escalated to a level of supernatural fury that anyone had never witnessed. Wesley crumbled to the ground, using his hands to brush away the tears that had gathered. Penny and Ellie stared longingly out the window, yearning for a brief respite from school, from everything. Wendy trembled, facing the realization that she didn't want to meet. Crippling hopelessness engulfed her, filled with doom.

They were locked inside.

Chapter 28

"L ocked?" Ellie screeched, her hands trembling with panic.

They gradually reduced their efforts to break down the door, one by one. Penny was devoid of any feelings. Andrea's eyes drifted, and Wesley shrank into the corner, crying.

"What are we going to do now?" asked Zachariah, catching his breath.

"I wanna go home!" Wesley whined.

His body recused into a fetal position. Wesley's choice to display vulnerability and deviate from his usual arrogance was endearing, but his excessive fear had now become irritating.

"Chill out, Wes!" Zachariah said, his nose wrinkled in disgust. "You act like you haven't seen a dead body before!"

Andrea moved her phone closer to her side to capture a quick video and be part of the conversation. While they shared the same doom, she yearned for her chance to vindicate her sister and expose the cowardice hidden behind their facade of confidence. Everyone would know the real Wesley, unlike her sister who had a fabricated narrative.

"They're after you too," Andrea said, grinning at her content.

"What do you mean?" Zachariah asked, his eyebrow rising.

"What you did to Nora," Wendy said, fearful for him. "They're out to get you."

"For what? Saying a little comment!" Wesley hissed, more like himself.

"It was more than a little comment!" Andrea said, grabbing the top of his shirt. His feet rose off the floor. "You killed her! You all did!"

Penny broke up the growing confrontation. With a sudden jerk, she managed to escape Andrea's hold and push the bully away. Wesley braced himself for an incoming punch, flinching in anticipation.

"Can we talk about this later?" she asked, her fear keeping her focused. "We need to get out of here. We do have someone after us, remember?"

They all looked down the hallway. Not a single shadow in sight. Paying no attention to their silence, they rushed to the opposite end and back to the lobby.

Vending machines roared and cast a dim light on a bag of Cheetos. The dark chocolate in the bottom row had a deeper shade. Toilet water streamed into the toilet bowls from the open bathroom doors. The wooden courtroom floor gleamed with a reflection of the luminous red light from the gymnasium scoreboard, emitting a loud screeching buzz that carried into the hallway. The group dodged basketballs as tennis and softballs came flying toward them.

"What the hell?" Zachariah said, his gut cringing from a softball crashing into it.

"It's here!" Andrea said, swatting away a badminton birdie like a swarm of flies.

The machine shot out soda bottles, barely avoiding them as cola sprayed around in a liquid explosion. They ran down the hall. The inside of their ears felt the sting of hundreds of locker doors slamming, like fluttering window shutters.

Their vision blurred due to the rush of sensory overload. Blinding them, the overhead light flickered as if it were a dying bulb. With the silhouette fading and reemerging in different directions, it was difficult to ascertain the shadow's whereabouts. Books clipped everyone's extremities. Andrea's balance teetered with one slapping her thigh. Pencil tips prodded Penny's sleeve, one even piercing her hand.

"Fuck!" she winced, pulling it out with a speck of blood splattering next to her shoes.

Ellie spun in every direction, horrified with panic. Her hair flipped and almost tickled the front of her throat, as if it were inside her mouth. The school bell kept sounding without pause, creating a deafening noise, as aggravating as a fire alarm but failing to overpower Wesley's piercing scream.

"Stop!" Wesley yelped with desperation.

The hallway became quiet. Lights blacked out back to where it began. Papers covered the entire floor like scattered tiles. Overwhelmed with relief, they savored the calm and stillness.

Penny's hand trembled, taking in the pain that grew. Zachariah grabbed her arm and ushered her toward the principal's office. Ellie and Wesley sought protection behind him, trembling in fear.

Andrea's disheveled hair revealed her eyes, which sported a small grin for caution. Their shoes slid across paper-covered pencils. With a firm grip on each other's hands, they skated toward the open office door, illuminated by a bright light.

The classroom was free of any supplies since they tumbled through the hallway. Not a single sheet of paper was on the floor; no pencils were eager to trip anybody up like a boobie trap. *Tick, tick, tick*, went the clock echoing in the room. The moon's reflection shimmered on the desktops, adorned with paper flakes from a torn notebook.

A foul odor reeked inside the space. Empty beer bottles clanked from Andrea's hip, nudging the teacher's desk. The darkness muted the thicker sheets, which were coated in colored ink. The glowing porcelain sparked Wendy's curiosity, leading her to grab the small stack for a closer look. The closer the images got to her, the more it became clear.

One image was of ten girls. Their matching orange tank tops and short shorts were meshy, with a strip of purple fabric. The two on the end braced the end of a pole as the length moved outside the range, like an acute angle. One in the middle stabilized two metal shots put balls in her hands, cradling them over her chest.

Another image was the track team again. This one was in action, with the group huddling around each other to brace the exhausted runner who had dropped her baton after finishing the race. Their expressions of joy were something to keep in one's memory, with the victory causing the team to celebrate.

The next ones differed from the ones prior. Girls are the same as before. Their expressions were the same, exuding joy with camaraderie. However, this picture included less clothing than the track team had from their already skimpy uniforms. Lace was intricate with the definition of the camera enhancing different colors on their breasts, along with matching briefs and thongs. The fog from the shower made the cement floors slick, as hot water pelted down and condensing drops formed on their lockers.

"Andrea, look at this!" Wendy said, her lip curled in disgust.

Another one was the same underneath. This one had more girls with fewer bras on. Curves stood out under the dim lighting of the locker room.

"What a pervert," Andrea said with her eyes wide.

Mr. Turlington's desk held these images, which validated their accusations about his obsessions since all they witnessed was his gawking expressions being far from subtle. The small wallet-sized frame on his desk held a picture of his family, while the track team's image in the yearbook was much larger. They underestimated the extent it would reach.

Not to the extent of spying on them.

Not to the extent of capturing their picture.

An echo of a door boasted inside their ears, cringing at the slam. A dark corner held the silhouette of a human shape. In the darkness, their muscular bodies became more pronounced as their chests rose and fell rapidly. His knuckles crackled like mylar. Their brow bones became more accentuated, and his eyes appeared like two hollow cavities.

"M-Mister Turlington?" Wendy asked, trembling.

His white teeth glowed from his curling lip. His breath huffed with anger.

"I never liked you two," he growled, his speech slurred.

"I never liked you either," Andrea whispered, unbothered.

"Shhh!"

"Why couldn't they have gotten you? Nobody will miss you two!"

His denim stretched as he readied himself for an attacking lunge. With a swift motion, the teacher's palm made contact with Andrea's face, causing her head to hit the wall, only mere inches below the chalkboard tray.

"Nobody must know!" he muttered a growl, looking around at his collection scattered around the room.

The pit of Wendy's stomach hurled from the thrust of his knee; Her ponytail cushioned the hard blow of her head on the tiled floor. Her neck grew taut as his cold hand clutched it, mimicking the grip of a snake. Tears welled up in her eyes from the pain. Growls churned in her stomach from her nerves, paralyzing her to react; even her fingers weren't strong enough to cut past the surface of his dry hand.

His lips pursed with beads of sweat trickling down his forehead. The pupils of his eyes mirrored Wendy's sense of despair. Her saliva splattered onto his face, unable to be swallowed because of the blockage in her windpipe.

The room was becoming darker, darker than it already was. The clock underwent a transformation, changing from a white, barely legible object to a black blur. The white chalk marks on the board mixed with the color of a billiard table.

She found herself powerless, as her hands grew weaker and failed to put up a fight against his grip. With each powerful muscle pressing against her, he rendered her legs immobile, trapping her beneath him.

Glass sprinkled on her face, and bottles of beer shattered upon the back of the teacher's head. Blood dripped onto Wendy's cheek like a light drizzle from a tap. His eyes rolled backwards, resulting in a decrease in weight and strength. Grunting in a horrible manner, Andrea hammered each empty drink onto his scalp. With a burst of energy, Wendy's forearms shook as she tried to force him off her.

Even with ten bottles reduced to fragments, he remained resilient. Emitting a groan akin to that of a brainless zombie, he remained intent on achieving his objective. Wendy and Andrea were determined to protect themselves and the other girls from him taking advantage. Wendy pressed her hands together, trying hard to secure a firm hold on the bottle. Her fury motivated her to get her revenge. A pattern of wrinkles appeared on his forehead as the eleventh bottle hit.

His eyes crossed.

His nose suffered the force of the twelfth bottle, with the bridge breaking and the tip crushed closer to his cheek like a flattened tomato. More blood poured from his nose, forming a dark red pool around his knees. His lack of traction on the tips of his toes caused him to lose balance. As his fingertips lost their grip, the weakened blow from his biceps allowed the bottle to shatter against the back of his head. The whiskey propelled him onto the floor, where the impact of the tile drained the last of his energy, calming his pent-up rage and causing his consciousness to fade.

Chapter 29

Zachariah burst into the hallway, the sound of shattered glass reverberating through the corridor. Seeking traction on the paper fragments, he wobbles because of the worn-down soles of his shoes. Wesley pursued closely, longing for security within the shelter of his teammate's shielding presence. Zachariah's eyes rolled like marbles, disgusted that he feared this person's tactics; only his words were threatening, not his actions.

The girl's shoes sank into the growing pool of blood, crushing the glass beneath them. Red covered the four legs of a desk that was close by. The door swung into Mr. Turlington's foot; the nudge wasn't enough to bring the man back into consciousness. Witnessing the abundance of glittering fragments and the aftermath flowing out of their teacher's head dent, Wesley's eyes widened in shock.

"Mr. Turlington?" Zachariah asked, his shock paralyzed him.

"Are you okay?" Wesley asked, showing care as he reached for the bruising on Wendy's neck.

"We will be," Wendy said, slapping his hand away, her breath calming down. "I just don't know what he had to do with Nora. I don't even think he has an eLookBook account."

Andrea, who wiped the blood from her lip, voiced the same worry.

At the top of their teacher's desk, Zachariah's eyes looked over with curiosity. Disgusted, each picture caught him by surprise. His wire basket of packets lay neglected as he focused on peeping at photographs, leaving no math test worked on.

"We should go," Zachariah said, disgusted.

Bits of shards sliced into their sneakers while blood splattered under their feet. Pencils leapt toward the lockers, sweeping supplies out of their way like autumn leaves on a sidewalk. The blood on the wet paper made it challenging to kick off their shoes without staining the material.

"I've misjudged you two," Wesley said, tentative from Wendy and Andrea's empowerment.

"What the hell is that supposed to mean?" Andrea asked, confused by some of her rage still boiling in her blood.

"I-I'm sorry for being so bad to the two of you."

"I don't want your half-assed apology," Andrea dismissed.

"I think the person you should apologize to is Nora," said Wendy, dodging his desperate attempt at sincerity.

"And it's a little late for that! You created this mess. You're the reason she's dead."

"I know, and I will make it up to her."

"And how are you going to do that?" Andrea asked, unconvinced.

"I'll fess up. I'll tell everyone that I did it."

Even Zachariah's expressions displayed disgust. The taste of bitterness lingered in his mouth from his cowardice.

"You have no idea how many lives you ruined with this bullshit act you put on," said Wendy.

"Yeah," Zachariah agreed. "You ruined what Wendy and I had."

"Hold on, there!" Wendy said, backing away from him. "He didn't hold a gun up to you and force you to shut me out."

Head bowed, Zachariah displayed his shame. No matter when it happened, he could not receive forgiveness for how he treated her.

"He's right, though," Wesley said nervously. "I couldn't stand you, and we needed him to focus on our team. He had such a crush on you, he couldn't throw good enough."

Wendy's cheeks flushed with some blush. Her stomach lurched as she battled the impulse to observe his actions. Although aware of his coercion to disregard and undervalue her, Wesley's confession validated her feelings.

Another door shut, echoing in the corridor. Their hearts stopped with their hands trembling. Wendy's fingers wrapped around Zachariah's thick knuckles. Wendy's reliance on Zachariah for security brought him pleasure as his eyebrows lowered.

Another shadow became more considerable in the light from the windows. Terrified, the students backed away, thinking it was the end. To make matters worse, when they looked back at the classroom, they observed another thing had been misplaced. Light danced on the surface of the bloody puddle and the broken glass fragments. The liquid stream ceased at the empty spot, illuminated by blood, emphasizing the absent presence of a crime scene's chalk outline. The source of the blood has disappeared.

AS TIME WENT ON, PENNY and Ellie were checking their phones. Still, not a signal to save them from calling for help. The file cabinets lay sprawled open and someone had torn apart the files. Scattered papers covered every inch of the carpet.

"Where do we even start?" Ellie asked, her eyes observing every bit of the disheveled space.

Canvas fibers torn, staff portraits shredded as though it came from a beast's claw. The yearbook spines formed a triangle as they stood upright with their covers on the floor. In front of them, the air was icy and their breath created a visible mist.

"You start over there, and I'll look here," Penny said, her fingers scrambling inside each of the secretary's drawers, the underside of her fingernails poking from the tips of sharpened pencils.

Ellie tapped on the top of the computer's mouse, hoping to wake the snoozing monitor. Empty like the souls of the damned, the screen remained black as the night sky.

"Fuck this!" Ellie said in panic after a good minute of attempts. "Let's just break a window and get the hell out of here!"

She didn't seek validation for her idea. Her stomach felt tight as she lifted the computer off the desk. Cords yanked from behind the monitor. As she neared the wall, her arms shook while she waddled.

Penny approached her with reluctance, unsure of any alternative to seek salvation. Her fingers suffered from being pinched as she crammed them into the machine's crevasse, swinging the equipment slowly while whispering a count to three.

The monitor and window exploded, scattering shards of glass onto the grass which reflected the moonlight. Fog covered the lawn, amplifying the angry moans of Mother Nature.

Ellie's breath trembled as she struggled to regain her strength. Both of them smirked and giggled to recognize their achievement.

"Let's get the others," said Penny, wiping the tiny beads of perspiration from her forehead.

Ellie wasted no time and made her way to the door after nodding in acknowledgment. Her heart stopped, creating paralysis as she froze. Ellie's eyes widened in response, and she could only hear the clock's ticking growing louder and slower.

The door remained out of reach as a shadowy figure blocked their way forward. With each breath quickening, the shadowy figure revealed its angry expression through asthmatic huffing.

Her hand grabbed Penny's ribbed cuff, which was damp. Penny's ponytail slapped Ellie's face as she turned back. As her eyebrows lifted even higher, her fear matched Ellie's, and her stomach churned. The stuffed owl sat on the edge of the counter nearby. Its eyes were black with a stare so solemn.

Pieces rattled from behind them. The grass quivered as the powerful gust of wind blew by. Bits of glass clattered and shook like silverware as they lifted off the ground, hovering in the air like hail poised to drop. Their feet held firm as a gentle force pulled them forward, their grip ensuring they stayed united.

With a cringe, Ellie watched as a fragment of glass whizzed by, barely grazing the back of her arm. Another piece of Penny's sweatshirt flew past her as the back separated. Ellie's shirt hem got destroyed when her hood became detached.

Drawing closer, the two hunched as the remaining glass surged toward them, like an avalanche of snow. Their throats grew scratchy from screaming at such high pitches, capable of shattering any unbroken pieces left.

Ellie's ripped jeans became more torn.

Sequins on Penny's ensemble blended with the shine of the shards.

Blocked by the window's frame, the monitor made a closer attempt to fit perfectly into the hole. Anticipating the pain, they prepared for impact as the piece crashed into the building. The impact of it hitting their chest caused the air to be sucked out of their lungs instantly. Cuts formed into their backsides as they fell to the floor, becoming pinned against the secretary's counter.

Penny's vision blurred, and she noticed Ellie collapse beside her. Blood trickled down the side of her head, with the monitor resting on her lap. The glass once more lifted from the floor, taking on more solid forms like puzzle pieces coming together and settling back into the window. The cracks vanished and merged back into one piece as Penny watched the fog dissipate and the lone tree wink at her before fading away.

WENDY'S ARM STRAINED as she tried to pull on the door to the principal's office. Despite her frantic attempts, her hand remained still as the knob seared her palm. Andrea's hand struck the wooden surface as her shriek reverberated through the corridor.

"We need to go!" Zachariah said, pulling on Wendy's sweater.

Making their way into the lobby, they deftly maneuvered around the soda bottles strewn across the floor, like an untidy child's playroom. The sound of crunching chips filled the air as they walked into the open door of the gymnasium.

Darkness surrounded the four of them, except for the two spotlights that illuminated the clear backboards of the basketball hoops. Four red zeros glowed on the scoreboard, with six representing the home team and eight representing the away team.

The metal screeched as the bleachers extended from their resting place, transforming into their seating configuration. Their breaths shook as the frame shifted, stabilizing each row. The memory of Astrid gasping for air haunted Andrea, sending a shiver down her spine.

"What do we do now?" Wesley asked with searching eyes for an escape from the parameter.

Above the door near the stage, at the other end of the room, a flickering light appeared. A bit of metal became visible from the railing that started the guide to the stairs.

"Andrea, do you remember a way out from when we served detention?" Wendy asked.

"I don't think so," she answered.

"We don't have time to guess!" Wesley hissed, yanking on her arm. "Let's go!"

Their footsteps echoed from slapping against the wooden planks of the court. A loud cry ejected from the clock with a buzzer that scratched the insides of their ears with only a bit of aid from the cupping of their hands to drown it out.

Wendy's ankles were uneasy, stumbling down the stairs. The underpart of her arm became pressured with the firm grasp of Zachariah's hand, saving her from tripping on her foot. The sweat from her palms slicked the chipped paint on the handrail.

The revolting smell of decaying garbage overwhelmed Wendy and Andrea's nostrils, evoking painful memories. Milk cartons oozed their curdled spoils. Processed meat had a tang. Steam dampened their foreheads as the boiler emitted a soft, humming whistle. The arrangement of the totes on the rack remained unchanged.

"None of these doors are working!" Andrea screamed as she tried to yank one open from the other end.

Zachariah and Wesley were trying as well. One of the locked passages was so secure that even his strength couldn't break it open. They were solid as a rock.

"Where are we going to go?" Wesley asked, his shoulders slumping.

Wendy turned her gaze toward the far side of the shelves. Only a pair of black plastic bins now separate the place that used to be covered in trash bags. She ran to the door, pushing her body's weight onto it, causing the metal to screech. With a lack of traction, her toes slipped on the slick surface, resulting in her being dragged into the next room.

Dim candlelight accentuated shadows on the rusted metal slabs. Underneath the metal grate, the water was rushing with force. Above her, vacant cobwebs shimmered.

Their hearts stopped. In a state of confusion, they approached the table at the far end of the room. Andrea and Wesley embraced each other by locking arms, mirroring Zachariah's and Wendy's actions.

Traces of sand created patterns on the table. Wax pooled around the corners as circles enclosed curves and asterisks.

Andrea's tears fell as she gazed at the center, where she saw the school portrait of a familiar face. She longed to see that one smile again, a smile she deeply missed. A smile that could brighten a room and bring happiness to those who were feeling low.

Nora.

An assortment of objects surrounded her photograph. They expressed their confusion through raised eyebrows as they examined the lack of coherence in each one.

A seat belt buckle.

A jacket button.

A hot-pink scrunchie.

An earring.

Wendy's throat became tighter. Three small metal loops held an opaque red die that sparkled in the candlelight. The charm felt familiar, despite the time that had passed since she last saw it.

Malakai.

"This is how they were targeted," Wendy said, eyes narrowing.

"And maybe Nora was sent to them for her revenge."

Wesley observed the display of items. Guilt flushed his face when he realized his actions' responsibility, causing his community's demise. Touching the relics brought forth a flood of memories from each individual and their spirit. One staple held a small pile of papers on the other side. The content became blurred as water dripped from the leaking pipe above, smearing the words. Only the top corner with the name was legible.

Wesley Strain.

His chin quivered, trying to stand up straight with his shoulders back as he faced the consequences of his fate. He sniffled a bit of loose mucus back inside his nose.

"I don't understand," said Andrea, confused. "These items belonged to people that wronged my sister. Astrid died, and nothing of hers is on the table."

BANG!

Sparks bounced off the metal slabs, falling onto the floor. Losing a second of hearing, their ears emitted a screech. Their bodies shook as they covered their faces. Flesh fragments landed on Andrea's cheek, while blood dripped from her face. She could taste a hint of iron from a gummy piece near her mouth's edge.

Wendy's jaw hit the floor as she struggled to breathe, while Wesley's body gave way. An opening had formed in his right eye socket, with smoke wisping through. The grate collected the flowing blood, which was then washed away by the next wave of water. The soaking fibers of his jacket's collar are now adorned with growing shades of red.

"I told that dickwad to do his own homework!" a voice said from behind the three.

They turned back to the door. The cloak's black fabric provided a stark contrast to the silver pistol. Candy apple red lipstick stood out on her porcelain-white skin, accentuating a small smirk. Black gloves removed the thick, black spectacles away from her eyes, throwing them to the floor as she shook her hair away from the hood and lens, breaking next to Wesley's fractured skull and persona.

Ms. Woods.

Chapter 30

One and a half years ago, it was the same old school with the same students. The same drama flooded the hallways. Mr. Turlington was gawking at a different batch of athletes on his track team, scoping out others to take their place after graduation. Brooms were used to sweep away the remaining dust in the classroom which was left behind by the previous teacher who quit unexpectedly following her big lottery win. When she packed her bags and relocated her husband and child to a warmer place, she left all her belongings behind with no concern of taking them with her. A place where every day wasn't full of monotony in the small town and harsh winters that were depressing.

The doors swung open from the office. Ms. Woods's arms trembled as she hauled her belongings in the thin cardboard box. Without mentors, facing the chatter of children as a teacher was anxiety-inducing for her.

"Thank you for giving me the chance to work here," she said graciously, dodging two students' shoulders, nudging her as one chased another.

"Thank you for coming in on such short notice," Principal Stuart said, his whiskers twitching. "This will be a great experience for you being straight out of college."

"I'm just happy that I get a chance. I heard that many of my classmates have struggled to find promising work after graduation."

"Great to have you on board."

The corner of his eye caught the cock of an elbow; the burly build of two athletes laughed with their biceps bigger than the underclassman's face. Veronica chuckled while passing by Tanner, her eyes fixed on Bryce, examining his entire body. He flaunted his testosterone and eagerly sought a new victim to intimidate.

"Aren't you going to do something about those two?" Ms. Woods asked, appalled by the sadness in the prey's embarrassed face.

Principal Stuart studied the two athletes. Leaning against the wall, he scraped his penny loafer on the tile. A sigh of disappointment warmed Ms. Woods's arm.

"I'm kind of stuck. If I punish them, then their parents will have my ass."

"Seriously?" she said with disgust. "Who cares? Everybody should be treated as equals."

Paper airplanes flew in front of them the further they went from the office doors. Fresh carbonation hissed as soda bottles were opened by thirsty students.

"I know you're new to teaching, but you'll learn quickly that we can't enforce the rules with fairness."

"Fairness?"

The poor boy winced in pain as he retreated toward the bathroom. He held his hand over his nose, blood flowing down his arms and staining his new shirt.

"Certain people run this town. And I've learned early in my tenure here that it's best to not rock the boat."

Ms. Woods was dumbstruck. She tried her best to contain her anger. The bottom of her box crunched with the clenching of her fist.

"Are you at least going to check on that poor kid?"

"I guess I should," her boss said, unenthusiastically, without motivation. "He probably started it, anyway."

The bell tolled once again; her nostrils flared. Tanner and Bryce were the only things in her sight, celebrating with a high-five while Bryce cleaned the speck of blood from his jeans. Destiny and Maxine met up with Ellie at their lockers, bracing themselves for Veronica, who turned her back on Tanner; her butt swished like a tiny pendulum to allow the others to pant like crazed dogs.

A student nudged her shoulder, tipping over her box. As they toppled to the floor, her college history books revealed highlighted paragraphs on their wide-open pages. The writing utensils rolled away from her feet, her stuffed brown owl pleading to be tucked back inside.

She bent to the floor, letting out an annoyed sigh. Her head collided with another body, their hair acting as a cushion. The marble floor briefly appeared blurry for a minute. A silhouette of two girls' faces merged into one.

Blemishes were oily, reflecting light like tiny stars. Her hair, as dark as the night sky, had a few flakes of dandruff near the tips. The presence of dried lavender paint on her earlobe made it look like a miniature plastic earring.

"These people can be such jerks!" said the girl, grabbing a handful of pencils just inches from the wheelchair ramp.

"I guess things don't change, even when you graduate," Ms. Woods said, rolling her eyes before resuming her cleanup.

"Well, I hope that's not the case. I need to get out of here."

"It gets better," the teacher clarified, organizing her papers. "It's just that the social politics stays the same."

With a chuckle, the girl dropped another handful of Ms. Woods's belongings into the box. As she held two small picture frames, she recognized her new teacher's parents, who stood with pride beside her daughter, looking resplendent in her perfectly donned cap and gown. The sun shone bright, illuminating their love.

"I hope that's not the case, and that colleges or jobs won't do the same thing as it is here."

"I guess you'll have to find out for yourself when you break out of here whenever that is for you."

A grin formed on her face, showcasing her two front teeth while she gazed at the cute expression of the stuffed animal.

"I painted one of these before. Owls are one of my favorite animals."

Ms. Woods's stomach turned. Putting the final items in her box, her shoulders relaxed a little more.

"Maybe I could see some of your paintings sometime? I've always been fascinated with art."

"That would be great!" the young one said, glowing eagerly.

The hallway fell silent as the last batch of students entered the classroom, ready to begin their day of education. Strutting across from the drinking fountain, Mr. Turlington positioned himself conveniently close to the restrooms.

"You should get to class. I don't think I have the authority to write excuse slips on my first day," Ms. Woods said quickly, snapping back into her professionalism.

"I guess you're right," she said, sighing. "I'll see you around, Miss..."

"Woods. Miss Woods."

"Nora. Nora Crispin."

Her hair flew behind her. The teacher caught a whiff of a subtle blend of Secret deodorant and body odor. Sensory overload subsided as the teacher took a deep inhale. Her first day as an educator was something that brought her bliss.

September 22nd

MONTHS PASSED BY. THE students in Ms. Woods's class gradually got used to the monotonous routine of listening to her lectures on world history. Her heart was filled by every war's beginning and end, as well as events that resulted in the creation and enforcement of laws in society, even if snores drowned out her authority. Even with gum bubbles popping, other students still inspired her. Astrid's engagement in her curriculum gave her purpose. Each stack of notes, made from torn notebook paper, served as strong validation. Penny's average efforts gave her hope that her work had driven people to apply themselves for the betterment when they walk across the stage to get the diploma from Principal Stuart. There was one paper that was similar to one of her own. Each fact was accompanied by impeccable citations and several fascinating aspects of each topic, provided by the student. Wendy's work eclipsed those who didn't show seriousness in her class.

With her experience as a former student, she can identify which kids should not be burdened with excessive academic pressure as it wouldn't benefit their future. Their dreams of going to college were not on their radar, which was okay. Others who made popularity their top priority were also a lost cause, but they still needed attention, nonetheless. Veronica and Wesley, who spent more time mocking their peers than doing their work, might have annoyed the teacher. She obliged to raise awareness, especially because colleagues like Mr. Turlington avoided taking responsibility and dismissed students who weren't favored by him.

Her class left after the last bell rang for another day. The markers collided with the metal slab, creating a clanking noise as they were placed at the bottom of the whiteboard. Decoded notes of the Civil War battles, depicted in orange and red scribbles, were presented on a linear timeline. The first batch of children briskly entered the hallway, relieved to venture outdoors and feel the chill breeze as the snow gradually disappeared. Greenery revealed itself from the thinning banks like crocuses. Ms. Woods collected her stack of tests and neatly stowed them in her messenger bag. She set aside her *Newsweek* magazine so she could easily access the materials for her upcoming freshman civics class discussion on current events.

The hallway emptied quickly, leaving a few students to follow. Astrid organized the scattered assignments, ensuring that everyone's work was completed so they could enjoy more social time. With his phone in hand, Mr. Turlington left his office and locked the door behind him. The screen before him displayed a live feed, where he saw soft laughter coming from a woman. There were two people at the end of the hallway, engrossed in a conversation. With laughter, the older sister nudged her sibling.

"Hi, Ms. Woods," said Wendy, passing by with her textbook cradled to her chest.

"Hi," she said, tucking back a blonde strand behind her ear.

Her heels clomped on the marble. One more locker slammed, and the bathroom door squeaked, releasing its rusty hinges.

"See you at home, sis," Andrea said, nudging her sister again.

"See ya," Nora said with a smile.

"How long are you going to be here? Mom won't be home until late. I was thinking we can order a pizza or something."

"I'm not sure how long I'm going to be here," her sister answered. "I have this piece that I want to finish."

"You've been saying that for weeks!" Andrea said sarcastically. "When will it end?"

"This is the first piece I want to showcase, and it's very special."

"What? A couple of unicorns?"

"No, dumbass!" Nora chuckled. "I wanted to do something meaningful to me. I have to go big for my debut."

"Don't kill yourself over it. I'm sure it'll be good," Andrea encouraged.

"Don't jinx it! I'll see you at home."

The sunlight reflected from Andrea's beaming smile. With her hair trailing behind, she caught up to Wendy on the other side, her shoulder bumping into Ellie's as they passed each other near the bathroom.

"Bye, Andrea," said their teacher as the teen passed by the principal's office, allowing Ms. Woods to carry on with Nora as she faced her again. "So, what is it you're working on?"

Dimples became more defined on Nora's face. Her skin glowed with pride.

"Let me show you."

Nora strolled down the nearby hallway, a narrow corridor that divided into two paths—one leading to the art classroom and the other to the wood shop. The art classroom was empty. Wet paint and staining from the previous class's projects gave the workstations an unpleasant smell. Water fell into the tote beneath a clothesline holding tie-dyed t-shirts drying in the air.

"I haven't seen so much creativity before," Ms. Woods said with admiration, taking in the vibrancy of color.

"You don't even know what your coworker has been doing?" Nora said playfully. "Mr. Brinke is an awesome teacher!"

"I'm sorry, I've been busting my butt with all of my work," her teacher said with a chuckle.

"I'm just messing with ya!"

They reached the back of the room. Nora's arm strained as she pulled on the enormous, military-colored tarp, which could have been concealing a bomb. Warm-colored specks emerged from the blank canvas. Waiting to be filled with shadows, two black silhouettes of humans were taking shape.

"This is great," Ms. Woods said. "What's it supposed to be?"

"I'm doing this for Andrea," Nora said with pride. "I wouldn't be here without her."

"Really? But you two are so different."

"We're different. But through all the chaos in my life, I know that I have her here for me whenever I need it. She's the first one I will come out to when I'm ready. I feel like this painting will be the start."

"Are those two people women?"

"Yes. I can't wait to showcase myself as an artist. So many people on the eLookBook app have been following me and are so excited to have a voice like theirs to represent them."

Ms. Woods smiled. When her bag hit the floor, her stomach fluttered rapidly. Her blood pulsed with joy, causing her knees to give way. The urge to let all the tears flood out became more of a challenge.

"You're very brave, Nora," she said with sincerity.

Nora's body jolted forward. Her hand held onto the corner of a table, holding herself back. In an unsuccessful effort, she charged at the teacher and clasped her hands around Ms. Woods's head, trying to bring her closer. The magnetic pull of their lips brought them closer for a passionate, lingering kiss. Hearts throb together like drums, growing faster with every quivering breath escaping their nostrils. Ms. Woods's hands crept down Nora's back, shaking before giving her a forceful shove.

"What just happened?" Ms. Woods asked, wiping away the moisture from her lips.

Fear and admiration intertwined as their eyes locked.

"I-I don't know," Nora said, startled. "I just felt like it was the right moment."

Ms. Woods was at a loss for words. She froze, not knowing what to do.

"I'm sorry."

"I'm your teacher."

"I know," Nora said solemnly, the reality sinking in. "I just couldn't hold myself back."

Ms. Woods's mind couldn't stop racing. The conflict between her moral code and the idea of a teacher befriending students troubled her. Her mind echoed with the words of her college professor's lecture, reminding her of the ethics class lesson. On top of that, the age gap brought terror to her.

"I should go."

Ms. Woods scurried to the door. With a single tear streaming down her cheek, her bag trailed behind her.

"Wait!"

Ms. Woods struggled to steady her breath, attempting to regain composure. The fear of losing her job and being ostracized in her first year of teaching suddenly took hold of her. The way her career unfolded wasn't what she had in mind.

"I won't tell if you don't," Nora recommended. "I'm not like these other girls that use information to their advantage."

Again, her teacher said nothing. Suppressing a nervous breakdown, she sniffled as tears threatened to escape from her nose. Could she trust her? She didn't have much of a choice; the bell had already rung.

"You've been one of the few people that have been there for me. Aside from my sister, you actually care about my well-being. It was very important for me to come out to you, so I know how serious this is to not tell anyone."

"But you're sixteen."

"I'll be seventeen in the summer. I'm so close to being legal. Then we would just need to get through my next two years, and we could go away together if something comes of this."

The stool next to Ms. Woods received her collapsing body. She cradled her face in her hands as she wept. This had become too burdensome for her to handle. The sheer number of ideas brought about a wide range of consequences.

"You're such a nice kid," she said, meek. "You've made my move here so great. Most of these kids haven't made it easy for me. They goof around to where some days get us nowhere. Principal Stuart wouldn't do anything about it, so I have to suck it up."

Nora offered a comforting smile and stroked her teacher's back.

"I'm so confused."

"Me too," Nora said, sitting next to her. "Let's be confused together."

They paused again. Their tears accumulated along the bottom part of their eyelids.

"Promise?" Ms. Woods asked, scared.

"Promise."

TWO ADDITIONAL MONTHS elapsed, during which they were cunning and made their way through six towns to avoid the small-town gossip. Nora told her mother she was staying at a friend's house. Ms. Crispin didn't have any doubts, excited about her daughter's social life. Contributing to the family's image was her mother's primary worry, and simply staying in her room or going to school didn't meet her expectations. Furthermore, she longed for her daughter to give up the art supplies out of concern for her future. She didn't believe that a future in art would offer financial security and a promising career.

This Saturday was a celebration that they wouldn't forget. They toasted in celebration after dining at a trendy restaurant known for its gourmet wood-fired pizza. The flickering, dull flames from the fireplace accentuated the delighted atmosphere of the establishment.

"You did it," Ms. Woods said, elated, with a wink in her eye. "You finally finished your painting!"

Nora's skin was glowing. Despite the dim overhead lighting, she couldn't hide her pride.

"And it looks so good!" Nora said the condensation of her glass slicked her fingers.

"I think so, too!"

A small teardrop welled up in the eye of the young artist, dripping onto the defined bags below.

"I worked so hard on this."

"I know you did."

"I hope people like it."

"But do you like it? That's the important part," Ms. Woods said softly, her eyes looking deep into Nora's.

"I do. It's just that I don't want people to think of all of my hard work as a joke," Nora said, apprehensive.

"They won't."

A waitress balanced a large saucer over her shoulder. Her feet stumbled onto a chair that was pulled out in front of her. Interrupting the instrumental music, the sound of wooden legs screeched on the floor.

"People in the community were really looking forward to this. I want to establish a name for myself."

"They'll love it," Ms. Woods said, grinning with encouragement.

"And I hope Andrea likes it."

"She will, too."

"I hope she knows that everything I do in my life is because I know she supports me."

"She'll get that loud and clear."

Nora's glasses fogged up from the steam from the pizza that the waitress placed in between them, which helped to dislodge the oil embedded in the scratches. They both paused their conversation to exchange their gratitude with the service worker.

"Here goes nothing."

Her fingers scrolled on the screen of her phone. Every word of her caption was scrutinized, searching for any mistakes. With great attention to detail, she edited the picture she had taken of the final product by tweaking the light exposure. Nora was ready to set this out in the world; this was the start of a new life for her.

"And send!"

A small clap from Ms. Woods sent her fork sliding toward the edge of the table. Her teeth winked a bit of light.

"I'm so proud of you!" Ms. Woods said, her hand reaching over to Nora's. "I'm so glad I took the chance on you."

Nora grinned with warmth. Her chair scooted closer to her date. Sweat formed on their foreheads as their body heat mixed with the steam from their dinner. They both took relieving breaths, knowing that the other patrons in the establishment were those like them. The sense of feeling invisible empowered them with no eyes gawking at them as they all minded their own business. Nobody knew them and it was refreshing.

"I'm happy you took a chance on me, too. And we'll take this slow to cover our tracks."

The glass door behind them opened, and a new customer joined the rest of the patrons, a gentle breeze tickling their necks. Hairs on their forearms stood up. The temperature changes brought liveliness to their celebration.

"And after I graduate in two years, we can move away together."

"Really?" Ms. Woods asked, her hand grabbing the slice of pizza.

"Why not?" Nora said, hopeful. "I don't see a reason we couldn't be together. Don't you?"

"I don't see why not," she said in agreement.

"And we can move out of that crappy town. We can go far away from those jerks!"

Her girlfriend used her teeth to trim off the stringy part of the melted cheese, resulting in the mozzarella strand reaching close to the top of her plate. A piece of pepperoni dropped onto her plate alongside a small ball of Italian sausage.

"Why couldn't we just stay where we're at?" she asked, covering her full mouth with her hand. "They're not that bad."

"Come on! Don't you see how horrible these people are? There's nothing here for us."

"There's my job," Ms. Woods said, concerned.

"You can find a new one," Nora pitched. "We can move to New York or someplace bigger. You can teach in a more open-minded school, and I can pursue my art. It would be a win-win for both of us."

A giant gulp expelled from Ms. Woods's throat. She took a deep breath to cool down the heat that burned the roof of her mouth. Her stomach became tighter, with her shoulders locking closer to her chest.

"I know you're scared, but you're one of the bravest people I know," Nora said, putting her hand over Ms. Woods's. "I told you we're in this life together."

"I know you did," she said back to her quietly.

"I love you and want the best for both of us."

MONDAY ROLLED AROUND. The bell rang after the second period. Ms. Woods collected the pop quizzes on the Great Depression for the sophomore students during their unit review. The dust bunnies under her desk reminded her of the tumbleweeds during the dust bowl. She gave a gentle nudge to a student who had snoozed at their desk. Startled, the child bumped into her, almost knocking over the stack.

She let out a deep sigh of exhaustion. Even though she took a break from work over the weekend to support her loved one, her late nights of grading papers felt like a never-ending journey. Her knee bumped the bottom of her desk, causing a lone textbook to fall to the floor. Neon yellow and pink lines sprawl across the pages, covering black text. Lines of gray created scribbles like chicken scratches.

Reminiscing in the text, memories of her days in college flooded her mind. This wasn't your typical book that she bought at the campus bookstore. She received this one as a gift during her sorority initiation night. The bony part of her wrist burned with a blemish pulsating from the healed skin. Soft, feminine voices whispered in her mind, using words that were not in proper English. The text grew brighter and lighter, emphasizing each word in succession. These words lacked historical significance.

These were incantations.

Laughter became ghoulish, huffing into the air. The trembling of her hands made the pages quiver in fear as the book's spine remained unsteady on her lap.

"That part of me is over."

Slams of metal continued to grow from the hallway, startling her. She wiped away the sticky grogginess from her face before heading out. Walking down the hallway, she sought relief for her parched throat at the drinking fountain. Giggles tuned out the voices in her head. The fluorescence shimmered like lightning bugs under the glow of cell phone lights. The students huddled together, drawn to a faint whimper of sorrow.

Clicks from cameras chimed in the closer she got to them. Ms. Woods focused on the screen, disregarding the eye strain caused by the small text. On the small screens, orange and red hues merged while two black blobs transformed into human shapes.

Nora's painting.

She took out her phone and logged into her eLookBook account. She paid no attention to the pop-up for the newest upgrade and kept scrolling down the main page. Looking at the painting by her partner, a sense of pride washed over her, resulting in a small smile. Looking at the phrases below, her eyes widened as she scrolled further, noticing their increasing number. Comments of opinions overshadowed the constructive feedback. The brutality increased with each one, from the brushstroke patterns to the color blending. The following two came from screen names that referenced ones in her community. The community in which she yearned to establish her brand. The first one discussed their disappointment in the painting, hoping for something more than anticipated. The next one was a comment about how it didn't belong and was pure trash. The people she turned to for support shut down her celebration of diversity.

"Nora," she whispered to herself, a tear forming in her eye, her heart breaking.

With each push, her arm grew more resistant to the students' attempts to move them. Wesley's loud laugh, reminiscent of a hyena, reverberated in her eardrums as Zachariah attempted to quiet him. As the girls played with their hair, bubbles popped and a faint grape scent filled the air. The middle individual wore a self-assured smirk, their raised eyebrow displaying a sense of triumph.

Veronica.

One girl with brunette hair distanced herself from her friend's circle in disgust. Feeling repulsed, she couldn't recognize her friends anymore as the queen bee recorded the shame.

"Everyone move!" Ms. Woods said, her breath more labored, "What's wrong with you?"

Peter wouldn't budge; he stood there solid as a statue. In a state of annoyance, Ms. Woods directed the young man into her classroom. He tripped over his own feet while laughing uncontrollably.

"What the hell is going on?" Ms. Woods said, her face flushed.

"Haven't you seen this crap?" he said, pointing at his screen. "What garbage!"

"It's not garbage!" she hissed, slapping the phone out of his hands, the case protecting the glass from breaking.

"What's wrong with you?"

The laughter died down, and she ran back into the hallway. As the last group of teenagers moved away, the hallway light illuminated a girl standing alone. Her hair was greasy, drenched in sweat and tears. Hiccups of air cut into her panic, wheezing; pink hues flushed on her face, eliminating the pastiness. She tripped over her crumpled flannel shirt, causing dried-up paint to chip off onto the floor.

"Nora!" she said to her, temples pulsating.

Her girlfriend got up from the corner, wobbling as she allowed the blood to rush back into her legs. Nora disregarded the teacher, shoving her aside while maneuvering through the crowd. Voices muttered comments that reflected her wall verbatim. Her support system was powerless against the chants.

What a joke!

Pathetic!

Kill yourself!

Ms. Woods chased after her, moving past Wendy, who moved closer to her locker. Seeing Andrea approaching, Penny positioned herself behind the door, out of sight, as Andrea stormed off in frustration.

An icy breeze chilled Ms. Woods's spine. The bright light blinded her. Her heart pounded fiercely, trying to catch her breath.

Nora stood in the lot, her head in her hands. Tears invaded the cracked pavement as they moistened the dry blacktop.

"Sis!" Nora said, sniffling.

"Don't sis me!" Andrea hissed, her lip curled.

"What?"

"What the hell is all of this crap I'm seeing on this app?"

"I know," she said, sobbing. "They're so mean. Why would they say something like that?"

"And what you've done to Mom."

"You know I wouldn't disrespect Mom. Everything I do is because I know that the two of you support and love me. You know that!"

Nora's shoulders sank. Her increasing depression caused her body to become tense. Her ankles were weakening, teetering her uneven body weight.

"Don't give me that. I thought we meant something to you!"

"You do!"

"And you painted two girls?"

"They were sisters guiding each other through the unknown. You saw it last week."

"I didn't think that this is what it was going to become! And now everyone at school thinks that you're some kind of weird lesbian."

"Who cares if she is?" Ms. Woods thought.

"What?" Nora said, her knees buckling.

The student body congregated outside, watching their confrontation from afar. Phones captured images and videos of their disagreement with laughter roaring quietly. Lights flashed along the corner of her eyes. The back of her eyes became full of pressure with a headache growing to the top of her head. Ms. Woods became speechless with nobody stepping forth to care, not even Principal Stewart who only shook his head looking through the glass door.

"Did you even weigh out the consequences of doing this?"

"Doing what? Expressing herself?" Ms. Woods thought again, in disbelief with Andrea not seeing her sister's perspective.

"Y-you told me I should pursue this more."

"I wasn't talking about making something that will give people the wrong idea."

Shades of gray darkened the surrounding sky. As the wind blew, Nora's neck recoiled, and the air turned chillier, causing shivers to run down her spine. Sweat on her scalp trickled closer to the tips of her hair from the drops of rain that became heavy.

"I thought you loved what I did."

"I do. Just not this or anything like this."

Nora's teeth chattered, shaking like a vintage clock with the hammer striking the twin bells. Goosebumps became sharp on her exposed skin from the wind that got colder. Her tongue was dry, rough like sandpaper as it pressed along the back of her teeth.

"Don't do this to her," Ms. Woods muttered to herself as she made her way from the others.

"I'm going to Wendy's tonight. You're on your own for dinner."

"Andrea! Don't do this to me!" Nora cried out in desperation before a slap of thunder cut her off. "I need you!"

Andrea disappeared among the crowd, going past Ms. Woods, who concealed herself behind the tree. Hopeless, she watched the young artist whimper away from her. Her hands were tied, as any action on her part would expose them. The school wouldn't do anything about the students' behavior, and she would be breaking the law if she were to explain why she cared so much about one student's well's well-being.

"Nora!"

DURING HER LAST CLASS for the day, she watched a documentary on the First World War. All her thoughts revolved around Nora's welfare. She found herself unable to speak in front of the kids, who were quick-witted. The noticeable absence of concern repulsed her. Her fingers scrolled through the comments on her wall. Every phrase made her blood boil.

Comments aimed to be constructive, yet driven by ego, belittled their work. While evaluating each critic's profile, she observed that they also had their own flaws in their work. As she read through their comments on other artists' work, she realized that they only criticized and never uplifted, always bringing others down.

By examining the profile pictures, she began figuring out who made the comments on her wall. Malakai Benson, Caroline Hershey, Jeff Willow, Bryce Martin, Tanner Stohl, Zachariah Dahm, and Wesley Strain all had a hand in Nora's sadness.

She excused herself from the class, nauseated, as she ran to the bathroom. The sound of her footsteps reverberated through the empty hallway, overshadowed by faint cries of sadness. In the bathroom stall, she tried to hold back tears and resist the urge to vomit. Her urge to text her to check in was present, but she didn't want to have anything come back to her; she had a career to watch for, and Nora knew that.

The door opened once again, followed by a belted chuckle. Four girls walked to the sink, their flip-flops clapping against their bare heels.

"What a loser!" said the girl with curls.

"Did you see the look on her face?" asked the one with black hair.

The faucet continued to run with sputtering water, blocking out another bout of laughter.

"Was there a reason to do this?" the one with long, brown hair asked. Her concern made the blonde snarl. "She wasn't hurting anyone."

"She needs to know her place," said the blonde. "People like her don't deserve to get what I worked so hard for."

"What the hell does that mean?" her friend asked. "She isn't taking anything away from you!"

"Yes, she was! If she gets what we have, we'll soon let people like that wheeze ball, Astrid, sit at the table!"

"Ellie, chill out!" said the curly-haired one, popping her lips after glazing another coat of gloss on them.

The door slammed behind her. A tiny rush of air thrust into the stall. Ms. Woods restrained herself from cracking her knuckles, her eyebrow arching. She struggled to maintain balance on the toilet, her thighs trembling while she held her legs up to avoid being seen.

"She better watch herself. If I can ruin that pathetic excuse for an artist with the swipe of my finger, I can do it for her, too."

The teacher's chest palpitated, straining with terror as she witnessed the start of the chaos. Nora's work was criticized, but not by a stranger who pretended to be helpful. It wasn't a family member, confused by her intentions. It was one of her classmates, the queen bee.

"Nobody messes with Veronica and gets away with it!" she said as she walked out of the bathroom, leaving Ms. Woods alone with her thoughts.

THE BELL RANG, AND she ran to her car. She hurried through the doors at a speed surpassing that of any students eager to exit the establishment. Passing by Andrea, she eyeballed the remorse as she sat on the stone bench, her eyes glazed as she watched the trees blowing in the breeze.

Throwing her bookbag in the backseat, she revved up her engine. The roaring pistons made the children stop running. Next to his truck, Ian was motionless as he watched the puff of exhaust sputter out of her tailpipe.

With no pedestrians in sight, she rushed through the town, breezing past several stop signs. As she walked by the library, she couldn't help but curl her lip in disdain at the librarian leisurely smoking against the wall. Resisting the temptation to accelerate, she witnessed Mrs. Hershey raising her phone for a selfie next to the most colorful bushel in the city hall patch.

The tires screeched as the bus navigated sharp turns, paying no attention to the groups of elementary school children disembarking to rush to the nearby park for the first time since the snowfall months ago. The front bumper was two inches from colliding into the back of another as she parked down the street from Nora's house, trying to not get caught.

She couldn't ignore the voices personifying the comments on the page as she ran down the sidewalk, accompanied by the chirping of birds.

Kill yourself!

A trickle of sweat ran down her back, dampening the bottom of her blouse. The tears darkened the robin egg blue shade as they dropped onto the pointed edge of her collar.

Running on the lawn, she heard her ankles crack as she avoided a sprinkler spraying water onto the parched grass. Jumping onto the cement stairs, she vigorously tried to turn the knob to the front door of Nora's house.

Locked.

"Nora, are you there?" she screamed, pelting her palm on the wood.

Nothing.

"Nora, it's me!"

Still nothing.

Sprinting to the backyard, she leaped off the stairs and evaded the tree branches that threatened to scratch her face. Saliva made her throat thicker when she saw three letters spray painted on the side of the house, black trickled down making the font eerie.

Pig.

Her foot lost its footing on a slippery leaf while she was scaling the white lattice in the back. As she ascended the roof's incline, her calves throbbed, and she squinted to shield her eyes from the harsh sunlight.

Inside, the window at the top was dark, with white canvases sitting all around, eager to be painted. The walls displayed posters of artwork that oozed inspiration, leaving no room for emptiness. Without any wrinkles or signs of use, Nora flawlessly made her purple plaid comforter. On the floor was a person sprawled out with her ankles twisted. She held her chest, eyes pleading out the window for assistance. The face was pale, and her lips were blue.

Nora.

"No," Ms. Woods said, her head leaning onto the glass.

The shingles digging through her pants made her knees itch before she collapsed. Guilt overwhelmed her as she questioned how else she could have supported her. Their future promises shattered, leaving behind unattainable dreams.

Her head became lighter, fuming with anger. Memories of the comments made her eyes blink rapidly. The accusations from Andrea and the carefree initiation from Veronica and her friends deeply wounded her.

Whispering chants surrounded her, causing her wrist to burn. This time, it wasn't the voices of the hate she witnessed. A voice emerged from her car's backseat. The book in her bag, filled with sketches of occult formations and enchantments, caught her attention.

No one was taking action after the death of a young girl who was trying to express herself. Her art didn't harm anyone; instead, some people chose to feel hurt because it diverted their attention. Those who hurt her couldn't bear the attention being solely on them instead of celebrating others.

Ms. Woods's fingertips glowed as she knew what she had to do. She would undertake the task if no one else could punish them. The magic she put to the side when she graduated from college was something she would have to do without her coven. She knew she would be the one to bring justice to the trolls. She would be the one to seek vengeance for Nora.

Chapter 31

The water heater's humming drowned out their fear. Andrea sought shelter with Wendy, while Zachariah shielded them both. Seeing the pistol pointed at his head, he positioned his hands in front of him, hoping to defend vital areas. The teacher's smirk transformed into a bright smile, revealing her gleaming teeth in the dim light.

"W-why?" Wendy whimpered, Zach's jacket sleeve almost covering her mouth.

They synchronized their movements like an amoeba in an attempt to exit through the door. Ms. Woods stood stoically, bracing her legs against the frame, her cloak draped over her feet.

"Did you know Nora spent a lot of time here?" Ms. Woods said somberly, looking around the space in reminiscence.

"No," Andrea said, confused.

"This was the one place she could escape to when the art classroom wasn't in use. It's so quiet down here. Nobody could clean up all the rubbish enough to want to use it for anything other than storing trash. This school really has a budgeting issue."

In the room's corner, cobwebs glistened while the silver gun gleamed. Wendy remembered how the space was before. They barely managed piles of trash. The custodial staff managed the bins holding old cafeteria leftovers more frequently, with just a faint smell of decaying food in the air.

"She didn't mind it. She didn't at all. Anywhere was better than being with her classmates."

"She mentioned none of this to me," Andrea said.

"Well, I guess that you two aren't as close as you thought."

Andrea let out a gigantic gulp down her throat. Overwhelmed by the possibility of being mistaken, her stomach churned with fear.

"Ever since I got to this school, it's always about the who's who of children. Some could get away with murder, while others get punished. That's not what I signed up for!"

A drifting cloud of steam brushed her hair, dampening her forehead. The heartbreak in her eyes was stressed by her eyebrow, perched at a severe angle.

"They killed her. They killed my poor Nora."

"We know they did this to Nora," Wendy said, her breath shaky. "This isn't the way to go about it."

"Yes, it is!" she hissed, shaking the gun at them. "Nobody did anything when word got out! Nobody shed a tear or even cared about her."

"Believe me, we cared," Zachariah said, causing his teacher's forehead to define its wrinkles.

"Sure, and Veronica and those two dipshits get a vigil dedicated to them while nobody did a thing for her. Veronica initiated everything, yet she was perceived as a helpless victim in need of saving."

"Everyone knows how rotten she is," Wendy agreed, her left eye twitching. "She was going to get hers when word got out."

"Not enough! She needed to be punished right away! She let Nora die away in her heartbreak, and she needed to feel it too."

"W-what did you do to her?" Andrea asked, her hand shaky as it clenched onto Wendy's wrist.

"See for yourself," Ms. Woods said with pleasure. "You two were the last ones to visit her. By the way, thank you for moving that heavy tote. Even when I slowly let her bleed out, she was still too much to carry."

With her eyes fixed on the students, she emitted a maniacal laugh and observed the lone tote across from her. Wendy's body quivered as she pieced it together, realizing the challenge of transporting a deceased body. The smell that surrounded them was a mix of her decay and the forgotten garbage.

"I loved every minute of her screaming with nobody to come to her rescue, just like Nora did. None of her desperate apologies could save her. Every slash of my knife in her skin brought joy to me. All fifty of them."

Zachariah used his arm to guide the two girls to a safer place. As another rush of water flushed down the pipe, their feet wobbled on the uneven grate beneath them.

"She may not have written those comments on her page, but she loaded the gun for everyone to take a shot at her. She and those spineless minions had to go, along with the ones that had to put others down to make their cause more important. Their deaths meant more to me, and I couldn't let Nora have her way with them."

They looked at the shrine once more. The ghoulish screams stung their minds, brought forth by each relic. Witnessing their demise left them feeling sick. Pleads for saving made them cringe.

"Golly, did I miss those days in college with my friends. Bringing justice with all the tricks I learned through the spell books willed to me. What was I thinking when I wanted to put that all behind me when I moved here?"

"Look, I know we deserve to be held accountable for what we did," Zachariah said, inching closer to her. His hand surrendered closer to her reach. "Let's just get those names and take them down together. The police will do the rest."

Ms. Woods chuckled; her lips squeezed together with tension. The gun dropped to her side, effortlessly blending into the surplus fabric of her cloak.

"Gimme the gun, and we can work together," Zachariah said, inching closer to her, his knees buckling.

Metal struck his head. One of his molars became loose when the pistol barrel hit his jaw. With an overwhelming explosion of iron, blood trickled down his throat, infusing his taste buds.

Witnessing Zachariah's descent to his knees, Wendy hurried to his side. Blood from his lip seeped into the cuff of her sweater. Small bits of ivory sprinkled onto the floor, bouncing off the grate with a tooth rolling to Ms. Woods's feet.

"Perfect, just what I need," she said as she picked up the tooth. "Another belonging from a person who hurt my girlfriend."

"Girlfriend?" Andrea asked, quivering in the corner without someone to shield her.

"We were going to run away together after she graduated," Ms. Woods said, her eyes reflective with tears accumulating at the bottom. "She wanted nothing more than to show you how great of a person she was. We were going to move to New York, and she would pursue her art. But you took that away!"

From the gun's barrel, a tiny drop of blood trickled down and landed on the floor, separate from the puddle near Zachariah.

"I'll turn myself in," Zachariah pleaded, his chin pink with wiped blood. "You don't have to do this."

"I have to, I must," she protested, the gun trembling. "I already made a mistake with Astrid. I won't let another innocent life get taken away. Not when I have control. I should've known better than to take one of Wesley's papers for sacrifice. That dumbass couldn't even put his name on the paper without wanting someone else to do it for him."

"Ms. Woods, I know my sister meant a lot to you," Andrea said, her back glued to the wall. "She meant a lot to me too—"

"Horse shit!" Ms. Woods screamed, waving the gun in her direction. "You didn't care about her. I saw the way you treated her that day. You were so blinded by what others thought of you that you forgot why she did her painting in the first place!"

Andrea's face contorted, making the bags under her eyes more pronounced. Her quivering jaw caused her skin to crease with each rapid movement. Her face glistened with a combination of tears and sweat.

"She did everything because she knew you loved and supported her, no matter what!"

"I did, I swear."

Tears fell quicker down her cheek; strands of hair became soaked with tips poking her cheeks.

"You and your mom didn't care! Otherwise, you would've found out more. Instead, you shut her out, caring only about how it would make you look!"

The confronting facts caused Andrea's knees to shake, losing strength. She fell to the floor with the cement numbing her legs. Tingles in her toes gave the impression of static.

"You are just as guilty as the ones who started it. I couldn't let Nora do away with you, as you were so quick with her. It was so much fun watching your mom choke on the bleach. And now I get to finish it with you, both of you."

Zachariah and Andrea's heads bowed closer to the floor. With each passing moment, their hope dwindled and their demise became certain. Guilt overwhelmed them, leaving them with no means to make amends for their actions.

Ms. Woods tossed the tooth from her hand. Jumping over Wendy, it glided through the air, making her heart stop as it approached the other side. Like a basketball on a backboard, the bone hit the wall with only two tiny bounces on the altar's surface's scrunchie.

"We can close this chapter in her revenge," Ms. Woods said with satisfaction. "Nora kills you, and I'll get to enjoy removing her sister. Then, I'll get to move on to the others. I'll get them all if it kills me. One thing for certain is that Nora Crispin will be remembered! For her talents and her love, dammit everything that made her so special!"

Wendy's arms trembled as she battled to control her breathing. She dashed over to her teacher, her shoulder wincing in pain, and tackled her in the stomach. The bullets deflected off the metal tiles in the hallway, liberating them from the confined room. With a firm grip, a gloved hand pulled her hair back. Her screams echoed in pain as she flailed her hands, unintentionally wedging the gun into a wall crack, offering protection to the rats' abode with the barrel resting on their entrance deep inside.

They engaged in a struggle, rolling down the hall toward the shelves. Andrea pulled Zachariah by the shoulder, helping him stand back up. Amid the brawl, Wendy struggled to breathe while trying to grab her attacker's hand. Wendy's consciousness faded as her hand fell to her side. With strength, Andrea seized a trash bag and pulled the cumbersome black plastic across the floor. Like a pendulum, she swung the bag with all her strength as it hit the side of her teacher's head.

Ms. Woods fell to the floor, stunned by the impact of garbage. Andrea nudged Wendy, who was completely unconscious. With each passing second, the lights flickered, surrendering to the chilling darkness that consumed the space. As the shadows expanded, a gentle giggle emerged and grew more pronounced at the far side.

Nora.

"Shit," Andrea said, the color in her face flushing away to pale. "Run, Zachariah!"

With each stumble, Zachariah's steps became more hesitant, his hand roughening as he tried to regain his balance. His thoughts replayed the two words that caused so much agony, intensifying with each repetition.

Kill yourself!

His calves strained as they lifted himself up each step. The handrail became loose, with the screws coming undone from the wall. Sweat blinded his eyes, causing him discomfort while trying to concentrate. Despite the crackling of his cartilage, his ankle twisted as he reached the top and backed into the gym. As he neared the basketball court, his lungs weighed him down and he grew anxious watching the shadow appear.

With a loud crash, the glass shattered above him and the backboard disintegrated into small fragments. The leather on his sleeve came apart, protecting his head against the falling shards. The wind hit him in the face as the hoop swung dangerously close. Backing away in fear, he slowly got closer to the sidelines. The wood quivered as the bleachers shook uncontrollably, as if they were freezing cold. The row nearest to him pushed closer, almost hitting him in the shins.

"Why can't we be friends?" asked the voice, carrying loudly from the other end of the court.

He caught his breath as he saw the shadow transforming into a human form. Its cloak matched the shape of the teacher. As each blemish reached Nora's mortal form, a glow from its nose expanded throughout its face.

The door slammed open in front of him. His heart stopped with a thrusting strain. Highlighted by the moonlight, Ellie and Penny, in a disheveled state, stood on the other side with messy hair forming nest-like structures, and their clothes adorned with glimmering glass shards, reminiscent of rhinestones. Blood-soaked slashes had dried up on parts of their arms.

"It's after me!" Zachariah stuttered, paralyzed in fear. "Nora is after me!"

After seeing a window break and transform, Ellie and Penny were not hesitant to consider any logical explanation for the idea of a ghostly girl pursuing them. With the cloaked figure approaching, their eyes widened as the tattered fabric billowed like curtains.

"We need to find another way out," said Ellie, looking at Penny, whose focus was sharper with ambition.

"Let's go!"

Chapter 32

Ellie's nails left deep marks on Zachariah's arm when he left his jacket behind in the gymnasium. Sodas and snacks started swirling, as if awakened by a lazy river's current. Bottles fizzed and erupted, spewing sugary fluid from their tops.

The sneakers lost traction on the wet floor, sliding as they sprinted into the hallway. Bits of splintered wood flew toward them as the gym door exploded off its hinges. White powder stung their eyes as the ceiling tiles fell in front of them. The locker doors flapped rapidly like gasping fish gills, colliding and spilling their contents. Their jeans brushed against the textbooks, causing papers to fall like snowflakes.

"Where do we go?" Penny asked, wheezing from the polluted air.

"Hell, if I know," said Ellie, dodging a slew of pencils that shot in front of her face like arrows.

The drinking fountain came loose from the wall, causing a powerful rush of water like a burst fire hydrant that dented the lockers opposite it. Their clothing fibers became heavy, and their sneakers added weight with each step through the expanding puddles.

"Be my friend!" said Nora's spirit as it joined them in the hallway.

The glass cover of the trophy cases exploded into tiny fragments, causing them to break down into pieces. Like champagne corks, the plastic human figures burst out of the cups. As a result of the fallen shelves, the team pictures creased and the frames broke.

"This way!" Penny recommended.

They sprinted through the adjacent corridor, gliding past an English classroom. Ellie exerted all her strength as she tugged on the chemistry lab door handle. Blazing flames burst from the Bunsen burners, resembling the breath of a dragon. Beakers shattered with the force, thrusting them to the door.

"Not here!" said Ellie, watching the pieces falling to the floor.

Nora met up with the trio after turning the corner. With an inhuman smile, her dimples rose to the temples of her head. She let out a laugh that sounded familiar, but then it turned into a low, demonic snort.

The girls, paralyzed in fear, felt a nudge from Zachariah. Wendy and Andrea's encounter was completely truthful; they weren't making anything up. The sudden change in appearance was unfamiliar to them after her passing. The corridor shrank, and the narrow tunnel hallway led them away from her. A fork in the path led them to the classroom on their right.

In their attempt to enter, they caused the neighboring bookcases to fall over near the light switch. Ellie secured the broomstick by inserting it into the looped handle next to the teacher's desk.

Specks of sawdust filled the air, creating a dense environment. Bright moonlight filtered through the windows above, highlighting the blades of the band saw.

"Oh, shit," Ellie said to herself, her eyes gazing at the plethora of equipment that shed danger.

Switches clicked; a tiny hum roared as the serrated edges of metal spun faster into a straight line. The machine growled as the battery powered the power drills.

The shelves sprang open, causing a chaotic scene with tiny screwdrivers and wrenches scattered everywhere. Zachariah's arm absorbed the impact of the pliers with his strong bicep. Waves of pain coursed through his arm, reaching all the way to his fingertips. Blocks of wood fell onto the band saw tables. The pieces inched closer to the blade as the power vibrated.

Pew!

A piece hit a blade, causing it to fly across the room. They made successive attempts to dodge every multiplying piece. Cans of wood stain toppled from the shelving behind her with the aid of the wood blocks. An object struck Ellie's leg, causing her to stagger. Screaming in pain, she tumbled onto the table, narrowly missing another object that flew toward her stomach.

"Ellie!" Penny screeched as she watched her get knocked back.

Her body flew into the closest table, hair covering her face. The coldness of the metal surface touched her cheek. The surface trembled, a switch flipped, and a spinning saw blade came alive, just inches from her. With the floor stained, her footing became precarious and her hand slippery from the blood oozing from her leg. She screamed helplessly as the blade moved closer; the reflection of the metal magnified the widening of her eyes.

Sliding across the classroom, Penny deftly avoided the pelting blocks. She yanked Ellie away by grabbing the back of her hair.

Ellie gasped for air, trying to shield away her panic. Zachariah reached out to grab her and Penny's hand. Their bodies slid across the room with the aid of the stain. Her tears mingled with the oily residue on her cheeks and fell onto her shoes.

Zachariah grimaced in agony when a piece of wood struck his shoulder, nearly dislocating it. His breath made him wince as it got into his open wounds. The sudden thrust of his gut made his stomach heave with a dry gasp. A deep gash formed as blood seeped through his shirt, staining the neckline.

With a powerful explosion, the door sent the shelves flying. Bits of rubble that resembled scrap shingles covered the floor, but Nora glided over them. A textbook flung across the room and hit Ellie in her head.

Ellie collapsed onto the floor. Her unconscious body lay surrounded by a puddle of flowing stain. Blood pooled from her lips, surrounding her chin.

"Let's get out of here!" said Penny, nudging Zachariah as guilt flooded over him.

The forceful push of the supply wall set the saw blades, sounding like a wind chime, in motion. Frisbee-like discs were launched at them, ricocheting off the walls like a game of Pong. A piercing pain shot through Penny's hand, causing her to scream. Blood spurted from her wrist, blinding her in shock.

Another shelf collapsed; screws sprinkled onto the floor like sundae toppings. The power tool dropped and released nails like bullets in their direction. Each shot nail left a dent in the metal cabinets. With no protection nearby, the two flinched, praying the nail gun would completely miss them. The metal pierced their muscles, coming close to the bone.

Their hands trembled, processing the pain that grew. While Penny got nails in both shoulders, Zachariah had two in his right thigh. Extracting the nail caused them to experience a sharp pain, making them throw up in discomfort. Penny's jaw dropped closer to the floor when she looked at Zachariah; moonlight reflected from the flat surface of the five nails scattered over his arm.

The windows exploded with fragments of glass cutting up their faces. Penny hid her face, hoping to defend herself from the familiar substance. As her shoes' soles became slicker, she slid toward the wall that was close by. Her fingers grasped the shelf's edges, leading to a dance with the towering wooden structure. As she grasped it tighter, textbooks tumbled down and caused her to collapse. The shelf wobbled precariously before yielding to gravity, resulting in the furniture tumbling onto her.

"Penny!" Zachariah yelped, trying to lift the pieces of wood piled on her.

Her hand trembled, shaky with fear and pain. With her bun undone, her hair cascaded over her face. Her hairline had a four-inch gash, resulting in blood trickling over her eyes.

"G-go!" she said, raspy.

Drifting away from consciousness, her face crumpled onto the floor, her gaze fixed on the broken window. Zachariah's face was wet with tears as he released her fingers.

"Ready to play?" Nora asked as the power in the band saws dissipated.

Silence filled the room, interrupted only by his terrified breath stirring the air. The view of Ellie and Penny lying helpless made his heart stop. He pushed through the pain in his leg as he limped toward the door, carefully stepping over its debris.

He sprinted down the hallway, leaping over the soaked rubble that turned as dense as papier mâché. Despite his diminishing physical power, he found that every door he attempted to open had become insurmountable. With haste, he swiftly crossed the lobby, wishing that the back door had erupted like the wood shop, granting him a stroke of luck for his escape.

It didn't.

Lockers clattered once more, colliding in the distance. With his throat closing up, he instinctively ran toward the locker room.

Light flickered from above as he stumbled down the stairs. His path was clear as blood marked his every step. The scent of body odor permeated the area as jock straps dangled from a few locker doors.

Hurrying to the back, he collided with the showers and fell onto the white-tiled floor. He collapsed in one stall as he stepped over the tiled entryway.

Consumed by guilt, he realized the pain he caused Ellie, Penny, and others was horrible. Although Wesley coerced him, he bore an equal share of guilt for the blood spilled. His lip trembled, a tangible manifestation of the pain he had inflicted and the pain that was catching up to him.

Metal screeched with shower handles turning. The sprinklers above him erupted, drenching everything in the water. Shampoo and body wash bottles emptied onto the floor, creating a slick surface covered in growing suds. Sparks sputtered from the tips of fraying wires as an overhead light fixture fell to the ground. The water surged up by one inch, flooding the surrounding area. The only thing preventing the water from pooling into his stall and endangering him with electricity was the three-inch tiled entrance.

Nora's laughter echoed as her shadow danced next to the benches, aligned with the lockers. Her eyes were black, empty like holes in the ground. Reaching down, she cleaned the bloody bristles of her paintbrush in the pool.

"What you did to me was a dirty thing. I think you need to clean up your act."

Chapter 33

Using her sleeve, Ms. Woods wiped the sweat from her face. Like a forming tumbleweed, her hair was in disarray. Andrea scanned her surroundings, her chest rising and falling rapidly, searching for an escape route. The teacher's teeth stood out as she smiled, her lips thin and grinning.

As she backed into the dark hallway, her Chuck Taylors' shoelaces became loose, the plastic tip on her strings crunching beneath her soles. She opened a neighboring door and ran up the gradual slope to reach a garage door at the top. As she opened the hatch, her shoulder clicked, and she crawled underneath it while it stopped halfway to the ceiling.

Trash bins rolled away from her when she knocked into them. Her damp fingers squished the food crumbs from the drain as she crawled under the half-open hatch. Mildew spiked the air as she met with the gigantic sink protected by the dishwasher's wall.

The door slammed, echoing into the kitchen with Ms. Woods sauntering behind her. Andrea backed away, pulling the speed racks one by one to block her path. If she could find any method to delay her, it would afford her valuable moments to consider a means of getting away.

Lights flickered above her; the gas line clicked with the stove, growing a tiny flame underneath the circular grate. The ovens buzzed like an engine, swiftly heating the area.

The spray hose shook uncontrollably, causing Andrea to gasp as water splashed all over her, mixing with the layer of sweat on her body. Her scream pierced the air as the racks moved to the adjacent walls, creating a pathway for her teacher.

Rushing into the cafeteria, she was met with tall windows that provided visibility and tables with polished surfaces reflecting light. Hoping for an exit, she checked each door she encountered, expecting it to open behind her, but was repeatedly let down.

Every door was locked.

"Shit!" she hissed with panicked disappointment.

The door slammed, screeching in the silence.

"Don't make this difficult like it was for your sister," Ms. Woods said as she stood at the other end.

"I didn't mean to break her heart," Andrea said, wailing with desperation. "She knows I love her."

Ms. Woods chuckled; the tip of her gloved hand fiddled with the blade, digging under her fingernail casually with disdain.

"I've waited the entire year to figure out how I'm going to avenge Nora's death," she said, passing by one row of tables at a time. "You left her to bleed out, drowning in her loneliness."

Andrea's attempt to take a generous gulp was hindered by her dry mouth. The strain of her tear ducts being overworked made her eyes feel scratchy.

"I'll kill you slowly, just like how she died."

The knife cut Andrea's arm, leaving a mark on her skin. Her injury resulted in a rapid outpouring of blood, which trickled from the gash. Bodily fluid splattered onto the floor, making the teal and aqua tiles dirty.

"Please, don't do this!" Andrea pleaded, grabbing her wound with her hand to clot the flow.

Swipe!

Her shoulder blade and clavicle were being marked by yet another gash. Her pale skin showed for a moment before blood darkened it closer to her neck.

The slow blood loss made Andrea's stomach feel queasy and her head lighter. Her knee was restless, scrambling to come up with a quick solution. Preparing for another strike, Ms. Woods raised her knife once more. Andrea wasted no time and immediately tackled her attacker, sending her crashing to the ground and the knife slipping out of her fingers. Andrea's reach for the knife ended in agony as it fell just out of their range.

Ms. Woods's fist pelted against her student's face. She found renewed strength when she tasted blood on her tongue. Her love for Nora pushed her to persevere, even in the face of the truth. Ms. Woods would never comprehend the memories of their childhood adventures and supportive conversations during their teenage years. She acknowledged her mistake but was determined not to let others misinterpret her intentions. With a powerful blow, her fist sent Ms. Woods flying.

And another.

And another.

Andrea's knuckles split open tiny cracks with blood, unknown if it was hers or Ms. Woods. While a puddle formed around Ms. Woods's head, she wiped away her tears and regulated her breath. The skin around her nose revealed cartilage that had shifted, resulting in a disfiguration with flared nostrils toward her eyes.

Andrea got back to her feet, inching closer to her teacher. The lowering of adrenaline made her lip quiver, making her realize the harm she had caused in her rage. Unbeknownst to her, she had been carrying anger within her for the entire year, until it finally overtook her.

Ms. Woods's eyes opened, spooking Andrea as she fell back. With a scream that originated from deep within, the murderer caused the earth to quake. With their hinges working, the tables emitted a shrieking noise from their foldable creases. The glass shattered behind Andrea as the windows broke into small pieces, cutting her face and embedding a pair into the back of her neck.

Andrea let out a cry of pain as she reached behind to evaluate the injury. The realization hit her like a wave, causing bile to expel from her mouth and seep deep into her skin.

The tables' wheels screeched, shoving themselves into Andrea. The attached stools rotated their plastic discs as one levitated from the force. She sprinted back to the kitchen, only to be pursued by the furniture with an intense burst of force.

Flames engulfed the stove tops, coating the entire pan as scalding water burst forth. The heat was too intense for her skin, causing it to dry and stretch.

The utensils rattled against the walls as they struggled against the magnetic strip holding them in place. A collection of knives whizzed past her, and one grazed a sliver of her hair. Pans above the center prep station rattled along the overhead rack. The drawers swung open, causing tools to spill out and ladles to hit her knee. Waves of pain shook her bravery with the carving fork lodged into her thigh. Every time she tried to pull it out, the flesh wrapped around the prongs made her hands shake.

The door swung open, and Ms. Woods crept closer to her.

"Don't worry. I can trick the others into thinking you're alive when I'm done with you. You'll join my collection of spirits alongside Ian and Mr. Turlington."

"You killed them too?"

"Silly girl!" Ms. Woods said with a huff. "Ian died last year. He was my practice pet when I found out that nobody cared about him either, no matter how much of a shit he was. And Mr. Turlington was just a victim of his own drinking. He should've died more horribly than what he got. I suppose taking too many pills was the only option."

"You're sick!" Andrea said in disgust, her hand trembling as she tried to grip the wooden handle of the fork.

"No, everyone deserved to go! And when this is all over, all those that hurt my Nora would have become just a mere memory, slowly fading away with time until the next batch of rotten students repeats the trolling to another innocent classmate with lots of potential."

"You will fade as well. You're not going to get away with this."

Ignoring her pain, she pulled the fork from her leg. Andrea rushed toward Ms. Woods, walking as if the stabbing had not affected her. Her teeth clenched, grinding against each other with force. Andrea felt Ms. Woods's hand clutch her arm, the fingers pressing into her open wound. With a tiny clink, the utensil hit the floor and landed on the tile. Andrea held onto Ms. Woods's face; the moisture of her breath slicked onto her palm with the pain from her nose.

A boot thumped Andrea in the stomach, compacting her innards. The force flung her onto the table. As her energy dwindled, her limbs buckled, and she slumped onto the metal slab upon the impact of the back of her head. Bits of glass broke off, with the ends digging deeper into her back. Watching the blood trickle from the table and drain away filled Ms. Woods with excitement, causing her to laugh.

"This is what I like," Ms. Woods said as she paced around the table. "Finally, you're doing what was expected. If this were an assignment, you would get an A."

Andrea quivered as the lack of blood made her weaker. The sensation of numbness and tingling extended to the ends of her fingers, close to the nails. Pots moved over her head, reflecting her despair shining back at her. The warmth of the oven made the bottom of her shoes sizzle.

Ms. Woods grabbed another knife by her feet and raised it. Her hands were too weak to resist as the pointed edge made her twitch in response.

"But now, you get an F for being a sister!"

A jolting wave of pain surged through Andrea as the heat scorched her heel. The table was shoved into Ms. Woods by Andrea's legs kicking off the oven. Her teacher fell back, knocking her into the stove. Splashes of water burned Andrea's head as the pot teetered on the edge. The liquid caused Ms. Woods to struggle to find her footing on the slick floor. When she bumped her shoulder into it, she tipped the pot over, causing everything inside to fall down.

Steam surrounded Andrea's feet, similar to the effect of dry ice, as she left the table. Her spine shuddered at the screams of agony and the sight of quivering boots. Surrounded by water, Ms. Woods shook violently as she was observed.

Bubbles emerged on her exposed skin, while blemishes appeared on her cheeks and forehead. Ignoring the discomfort in her legs and the equipment's movement, Andrea hurried toward the garage door. Before descending the slope, she glanced at her teacher and saw Ms. Woods's hand reaching up for help. As her student pushed down on the handle to close it, the last attempt for help vanished.

"Class dismissed."

Chapter 34

The more Andrea went down the incline, the lower her adrenaline dropped. Waves of pain shot through her throbbing head as the wounds on her body started stinging again. With each step, she left a trail of blood behind, the small droplets on the floor clotting in the warm air.

The memory of the harm she inflicted on her sister before her death made tears cascade down her face. She should've been there for her unconditionally, but she wasn't. Instead of swallowing her pride and comforting Nora, she let her personal feelings get in the way.

Andrea attempted to revive the lifeless body by nudging them with her hands. No matter how many times her friend tried to make amends, she was never able to receive forgiveness for the pain she had caused. Her grief was too intense to let Wendy in; it was too strong to let anyone in.

"Wake up, Wendy," she said to the body, shaking her frantically.

Wendy didn't move. On the cement floor, her head rolled loosely while her hair fell across her face.

"Please, don't leave me," she pleaded, observing her uncharacteristically pale skin, highlighting the tint of blue on her lips.

Still nothing.

Getting up from the floor, Andrea's knees grew weak as they held her up. With a lightheaded feeling, she leaned against the wall pipes to steady herself and find her way out. She clung to her chest; her heart strained with palpitations, tensing up with each second of regret.

It should've been me.

She made it to the door. Blood and sweat had made the handle slippery, making it hard to pull open. Over her head, a single fluorescent light blazed, temporarily blinding her. The ends of her hair, once greasy and dirty, began to dry and clump together.

The door wouldn't move.

Each inhale forced her lungs to expand rapidly, depleting her energy even more. Panic and despair overwhelmed her while she was trapped in the basement. The doors should have opened when Ms. Woods died, as all of her enchantments would have been undone.

The pull behind her intensified, causing her scalp to sting. When she hit the floor, her limbs became loose, and she suffered several cracked bones in her back. The light flickered and blurred as she struggled to recover from hitting her head on the pavement.

A lone shadow stood over her, blocking the light. Pink hues covered its face as the expanding bubbles on her cheeks released a draining fluid. Bruises transformed into shadows, darkening like burnt firewood. Horrified by the grotesque face of Ms. Woods, Andrea felt her warm breath seep down onto her. Lukewarm water dripped from the bottom of her cloak, becoming cooler.

Blood trickled down Ms. Woods's chin as she bit down hard to bear the pain of the water. She mounted her student, absorbing the panicked gasps that immobilized her. The wet fibers of her glove coiled around Andrea's neck as a fraction of her skin brushed against hers through a rip in the seam of her middle finger.

"I got you now!"

STEAM FILLED THE DELICATE sheets, creating brief gusts of clouds in the locker room. The spigots of the sprinklers kept releasing water, refusing to quit anytime soon. Amidst the lockers, the sleeves of a lone sweater floated, driven by the pull of the drain's suction that obstructed the bodice.

From the floor, the water level increased by about two and a half inches. The collapse of a pipe made the water tremble, creating a creeping wave pattern on the tiled wall and floor.

Zachariah tried to climb over the privacy barrier to buy himself time. The weight of his weary and weakened body made his arm shake in strain. With each movement of his muscles, the nails embedded in his arm caused excruciating waves of pain, rendering him paralyzed.

Little sparks sprinkled into the pool outside his shower, reflecting blood that puddled on the floor. His bodily fluids made the soles of his shoes slippery, causing his soul to slide. Each time he failed, Nora's laughter frustrated him while she sat on the bench, playfully dipping her cloak in the water.

Another inch became filled with belongings floating like a shipwreck's rubble. The jockstrap's crotch floated past him, spinning because of the elastic's weight. Toilet paper rolls doubled in size from absorbing the moisture at its highest capacity. The bases of the lockers were littered with empty soap bottles, giving the impression of a foamy lake where suds took on different shapes like clouds.

No matter how much moisture surrounded him, Zachariah's mouth became dry. His throat scratched with every fearful gulp. His bile surged up his windpipe, threatening to expel from his body. He collapsed onto the floor, his blood pooling around him, while only fragments of his clothing remained unsoiled. Sweat and tears left a salty taste on his chapped lips.

"It's almost time!" said Nora eagerly, her body floating over the water, hovering closer to him.

"P-please don't do this," Zachariah begged, a nail chipped as he clawed one tile.

"That's what I said when you all laughed at me. All you did was watch me suffer."

"I'm going to turn myself in. I want to make this right!"

Nora let out a light chuckle, gradually descending into a terrible fit of anger. She tilted her translucent head back, finding amusement in his plea.

"Watching you suffer will be just the thing to make this right!" she hissed, flying over him.

The skin on her face slowly melted away, transforming her once familiar visage into something horrifying. The temporomandibular joint ligaments revealed themselves, enhancing her cheekbone definition. Her hollow eye sockets decayed, causing her eyeballs to shrivel into small marbles as black goo dripped down like tears.

Zachariah screamed, cowering into the fetal position. The level of water matched the barrier as tiny droplets teasingly made their way onto the shower floor. Nora's decayed teeth formed a smile that reached the empty spaces where her ears used to be. Anticipating the end of his life, he recoiled as the electrical current coursed through him, memories flashing before his eyes. His cowardice was confirmed by regrets of not standing up for what's right and defending against hate. Knowing he wouldn't have a second shot at it, his chin shook. The moment he conformed to his classmates' expectations became his defining one, overshadowing any other chances he had to do what was right. Worst of all, he couldn't make it up to Wendy, whom he cast off to the side to be someone he's not.

Nora's scream pierced his ears as the lights flickered on and off. The drain couldn't handle it, causing the puddle to overflow and touch the hem of his jeans. He clung on to the handlebars to brace himself for the electricity to end it all. The transition of light made his pupils strain, making the strobing effect even more unbearable.

The lights turned off, along with the water pressure from the pipes. The power of the emergency lights increased, causing them to reflect off the pool. Clothing floated away allowed water to drain downward. The wires of the damaged fixtures dangled, no longer releasing sparks onto the floor.

Zachariah's breathing relaxed while he observed the drain gulping down the puddle originating from his shower. Once again, the tiled barrier increased in height, while the water levels subsided near the floor. Leaning out of his shower, he glanced at the two stalls next to him, straining his neck as he spun. The wounds in his arms stung once again as they braced his weight to stretch out further, looking for the one thing out of place: the one person who was taunting him but just vanished, leaving him alone and sopping wet in his sorrow.

ANDREA'S LUNGS EXPELLED the air, while the cartilage in her neck emitted a crinkle. With each twist of her wrist, her punches grew weaker, causing her fingers to give way and fall to the floor. She gazed into the bloodshot eyes of Ms. Woods, which resembled a floating inner tube in dark pink puddles. Her eyebrows had little patches of hair that were visible on her swollen pores.

"Please, no," Andrea whispered, choking on the last bit of saliva.

"I need to do this!" Ms. Woods grumbled with blood sprinkling on Andrea's face.

The room became lighter, blurrier. The pipes camouflaged against the wall's darkness, while the water heater roared to life with the pilot light. The teacher's figure transformed into a mere shadow, making it difficult to discern her identity.

Lights flickered again, startling Ms. Woods. She loosened her hold on the teenager's neck. With a sense of relief, the student wriggled and coughed generously, allowing air to circulate through her body once more.

"What's happening?" Ms. Woods asked herself, her heart racing as the lights became more dim.

She looked beside her. One area in the room remained dry amidst the moisture. The shape of a figure with four limbs splayed out resembled a crime scene tape outline.

"It's time for justice for Nora!" said a voice across from her, echoing in the tiny confinements of the room.

With a bone fragment twinkling in her fingers, Wendy stood beside Ms. Woods's shrine. Zachariah's tooth pressed against her skin as she steadied it with her thumb. With blood dried up on the tip, she held a metallic object in her other hand.

Her gun.

The shrine trembled as Wendy laid the weapon upon it, causing a whisper to grow around them. Shattered glass chimed onto the floor as the light at the end of the hallway exploded with a pop. And then another, and another.

Behind them, the door exploded as a shadow entered. With only its tattered edges touching the surface, her cloak's hem barely contacted the floor. Nora's face glowed white, illuminated by the light above. Her smile was playful, eager to be in the company of her lover.

"Nora, please don't do this," Ms. Woods begged as she cowered against the wall, her arms spreading like a snow angel.

The corridor reverberated with Nora's laughter. Black liquid began dripping from her decaying teeth, splashing near Andrea.

"We can be together now, just like I wanted."

The glass shuddered, quivering as if an earthquake had agitated it. The dust separated from the specks as they dropped off the floating pieces above the ground. When the bits floated closer to her, she noticed little twinkles of luminescence reflecting on their surface.

"No!" she screamed, flinching with her arm shielding her face.

One by one, the glass thrusted across the space. With a flinch of pain, Ms. Woods felt the first shard penetrating her forearm, causing a sharp, two-inch ache. A smaller object pierced her upper thighs while another larger one stabbed into her stomach. The pierce of each stab caused blood to trickle to her feet. The most important item spun through the air like a ninja star, gathering steam to create a haze before getting tucked between her breasts.

Prior to blood pouring from her mouth like a faucet, the teacher choked, trembling as she looked at Wendy in despair. Seeking respite from the suffering, she reached out to her favorite student. She hit the ground, overwhelmed by the child's cold dismissal, as the sizeable chunk pushed further into her. Her arms were immobile as the last pint of blood drained from her body. As her grip loosened, a small charm slipped from her hand. Into the blood, a small brown owl charm tumbled. The last bit of her identity became one with who she was on the inside as she reunited with the love of her life and the one she fought for.

Chapter 35

Seeing Andrea on the floor, Wendy ran over to her, noticing her lack of energy. Her complexion regained color, and her freckles became more pronounced. Wendy observed a bruise on Andrea's neck that matched her own.

"Are you all right?" she asked Andrea, whose pupils adjusted to the light.

"I hope so," Andrea joked, the veins on her neck pulsating as she hoisted herself.

Andrea saw the pool of blood and dark substance around her. A shiver ran down her spine as she stumbled upon her teacher's lifeless body, surrounded by glimmering shards of glass.

"You did it," she said to Wendy; her elation was unreadable through the pain.

"I guess I did," Wendy replied, rubbing Andrea's arm. "But who won here? Nora is gone, along with many others."

With the departure of a tiny shadow, Nora's face started to look more like her usual self. As the translucent glow disappeared, her complexion returned to its original mortal shade. As she vanished, there was a forgiving twinkle in her eyes.

"I love you, Nora!" Andrea said, letting out the only tear her body would allow.

Wendy helped Andrea back on her feet. The weight of her shoulder bared the unsteady balance; her grip was slippery from the blood glossing her body.

"I truly am sorry for all of this. I'll say it a million more times if I have to," Wendy said, looking into Andrea's slightly bloodshot eyes. "I should've been there for you."

A faint chuckle escaped Andrea's lips as she smirked. Her lightheadedness was causing her vacant gaze to fade.

"Well, I think you made it up to me for saving my life," she responded with a weak wink.

The two giggled. The sound of their laughter filled the empty basement, only to be overshadowed by the loud roar of the generator.

A subtle radiance emanated from the intact lights, illuminating their side of the basement. They looked at each other once again. Andrea observed Wendy with envy, realizing that she had suffered far less damage compared to her own disheveled state, with only a few spots not soaked in blood.

"Let's get out of here," Wendy said, wrapping her arm around Andrea.

"Wait!"

Andrea moved with a limp as she distanced herself from her friend, grasping onto the nearby wall. Struggling against her fatigue, she could only rely on her left foot because of the pain in her right.

Inside the small room, she held onto the door frame. The image of her sister amidst the collection of ancient objects caught her attention. The flame on the candles was feeble, struggling to keep the remaining wick burning above the melted wax. She wasted no time and toppled the shrine, causing all the pieces to scatter. Holding her brother's cherished keychain, Wendy pressed it against her heart, quietly apologizing for his premature passing. Water flooded the picture of Nora under the grate from another wave of water, flushing away her image and her baggage.

WHILE HEADING TOWARD the exit, a door unexpectedly opened in the hallway. The hinges creaked in the silence. The sneakers' crease held squished water, leaving a trail of puddles behind. The sight of Wendy next to Andrea left Zachariah speechless. Tears streamed down his face as he cautiously approached her, fearing it was all in his mind.

His cold, wet body caused Wendy's sweater to become completely drenched. As Zachariah collapsed into her arms, her skin brought him comfort, soothing his trembling. Their reunion was surreal; the entire night was something out of a dream.

"I'm so happy to see you!" he said, weeping into her shoulder.

"Me too," Wendy said, squeezing him tight, his heartbeat drumming against her chest.

Their heads moved apart, and they locked eyes with each other. Zachariah noticed the bruise on her neck when he saw the moonlight reflecting on her tears.

"You look like hell," she said to him, touching the nails on his arm that caused him to wince in pain.

"I feel like hell," he said with a faint chuckle.

Embracing once more, they found solace in each other's arms, feeling secure. Through the grime on her face, Andrea's smile beamed brightly.

"I'm sorry for everything I've done to you," Zachariah said, his voice raspy. "I took you for granted all for some recognition. All I kept thinking about when I was close to death was how much I've wronged the people in my life, mostly you."

Wendy smirked, acknowledging his guilt. In order to combat the cold caused by the water runoff on her sweater, she crossed her arms over her chest. A wave of soreness engulfed her biceps, caused by the lack of oxygen, which did nothing to relieve her tension.

"I hope you can forgive me when this is all over. Maybe we can start over, and you'll get to know the real me?"

She gazed into the sorrow in his eyes. His immense fear was revealed by the visible pulsation of the vein on his temple that she could see. With her hand extended, she gripped the blood-stained surface.

"I'd like that," she said warmly, her tight grin relaxing as she reached inside her pocket. "Plus you still owe me for doing your homework for you."

He expelled a sigh of relief, ignoring the pain in his hand as he clenched onto hers. Waves of admiration coursed through him as her pulse reverberated, warming his chilled skin. His fingers felt the chain moving into his palm. The little corgi winked at him in its natural color before being covered in a red, bloody film. His smile grew, and his redemption has been validated.

"Let's go."

As Andrea's knees trembled, the two clasped their arms around her. They walked over to the door and were greeted by flashing lights. Like a disco ball, the cobweb of shattered glass sparkled with blue and red lights that dimmed as they opened the door.

Officers raced inside, with one going after each teenager. Wrapped in blankets, Andrea and Zachariah dried themselves off and prepared for the chilly night. They found solace in the cold air, which was a welcome change from the torment they had endured indoors.

Inhaling the air rejuvenated them, providing relief from their ordeal. The way they embraced it made it seem like they hadn't left their homes in months. Police vehicles and ambulance trucks swarmed the parking lot, causing Wendy's body to surge with adrenaline.

"Are you all right?" asked the officer to Wendy, whose eyes were closed from another relaxing breath like she stepped into a hot shower for the first time.

"I am," she said with a cough. "How did you guys know about us? We had no service to call for help."

Upon retrieving it from her pocket, she shifted her attention to the screen on her phone. Her screen bombarded her with notifications while she observed the bars returning to their usual state.

"Someone called from the woodshop," said the officer. "She and her friend were able to reach us."

"Penny," she said frantically. "Is she okay?"

Two stretchers rolled out the front doors. The sight of a single rhinestone shining under the streetlamp brought her a sense of relief. Wendy rushed across the lot to reach her friend. Sadness clouded her eyes as she gazed upon their condition. Patches of blood splattered all over their torn clothing, affecting almost every seam.

Wendy extended her hand to Penny, who felt as cold as the night sky. Penny's fingers received a gentle pinch, bringing her relief as the fog lifted on her oxygen mask, allowing her to express a thankful smile.

"You tough little bitch!" she said to Penny, letting her go as the paramedic lifted the stretcher into the vehicle, catching a glimpse of Ellie lifting her hand to give off a labored wave.

The ambulance doors closed just as the loud sirens pierced her ears. Flashing lights illuminated the sidewalk as crowds gathered, curious to know what happened that night. In the darkness, camera lights shimmered like fireflies, eager to capture and preserve every moment.

She approached the other ambulance and witnessed Andrea being placed inside. When she sat in the chair, the flickering fluorescent light was a familiar sight above their heads.

"I'm coming with you," Wendy said as she stepped inside.

"We're coming with you," said Zachariah, who appeared from the other side to join them.

The door closed to secure their safety. They grew accustomed to the motion of their transportation, causing their stomachs to churn. Andrea lay peacefully amidst the tubes that hung from IV bags, steadily infusing fluids into her.

"I just wanted to let you know I told the officers about Nora," he said as his hand touched Andrea's. "I confessed to my part in her death."

Andrea took off the oxygen mask and smiled gratefully. Wendy snuggled along the wall to get comfortable; her heart fluttered with relief as she noticed the change in Zachariah and him taking responsibility. Since her initial infatuation, the person she had always dreamed he would be revived her spirit.

I guess people can change.

Wendy checked her phone and saw a multitude of missed calls and text messages from her parents. Her palm trembled as eLookBook streamed live recordings from her classmates.

She could see the ambulance from various camera's perspectives. Looking through snapshots of herself, she relived the joyous news of Penny and Ellie being alive and remembered her reaction. Her memory appeared to be in a time-lapse state.

The final picture showed a close-up of Zachariah by the curb outside the high school when he went to talk with the police. Filled with remorse, he rested his head in his hands while the officer diligently made extensive notes. A single picture contained a confession with the power of a thousand words. It wasn't his admission's truth that caused her spine to tremble, but what was beneath it. With every refresh, the smiley face emoji shined brighter, and the number grew, unveiling the name of the most recent person who reacted the photo. Her heart raced just as fast as the ambulance's engine when the most recent name appeared. As fast as the change in personality for maintaining an image. The air was sucked from her lungs like the grip clenched by a gloved hand.

Nora Crispin liked this.

Acknowledgements

There are too many people to thank who made this book possible. I must thank my husband for being there for me during this process. Without his support, Troll wouldn't have become what it is. I also have to thank my family for allowing me to express myself creatively through my work.

This book was conceptualized and drafted at the height of Covid. The isolation has made me create the bonds that has gotten me through the start of my writing career. Aside from my family, struggling through the pandemic has created bonds that I cherish greatly.

Last, I want to thank my readers for allowing me to be in your lives as you read my work. I appreciate all of you horror lovers!

About the Author
Brady Phoenix

BRADY PHOENIX IS A self-published author. With a love for 1980s and 1990s slasher movies, his goal is to add diversity to the horror genre through his work. When he is not writing, he enjoys long nature walks, hanging out with his husband and two cats, along with reading and supporting the self-publishing and horror community.

Facebook- @Brady Phoenix
Instagram- @AuthorBradyPhoenix
X- @BradyPhoenix
TikTok- @AuthorBradyPhoenix

Also by Brady Phoenix

Cardinal Rules
Nun Taken
Troll